AXIS SALLY

Other Books by Robert Livingston

The Sailor and the Teacher

Travels with Ernie

Leaping into the Sky

Blue Jackets

Fleet

Harlem on the Western Front

W.T. Stead and the Conspiracy of 1910 to Save the World

AXIS SALLY

ROBERT LIVINGSTON

AXIS SALLY

iUniverse books may be ordered through booksellers or by contacting:

iUniverse
1663 Liberty Drive
Bloomington, IN 47403
www.iuniverse.com
844-349-9409

Because of the dynamic nature of the Internet, any web addresses or links contained in this book may have changed since publication and may no longer be valid. The views expressed in this work are solely those of the author and do not necessarily reflect the views of the publisher, and the publisher hereby disclaims any responsibility for them.

Any people depicted in stock imagery provided by Getty Images are models, and such images are being used for illustrative purposes only.
Certain stock imagery © Getty Images.

ISBN: 978-1-6632-1936-7 (sc)
ISBN: 978-1-6632-1937-4 (e)

Print information available on the last page.

iUniverse rev. date: 03/12/2021

CONTENTS

DEDICATION

To my good friends upon whom I have foisted my writing…

A FEW WORDS

Most people have a bit of curiosity running through their veins and are fascinated by the 'what if's" of history. Of course, the "what might have happened possibilities" are never answered easily or fully. They do, however, tease and provoke. They can cause heated debate. This is especially true if we relished a different outcome. If President Kennedy had survived his bullet wounds? If the "9-11" attack had been averted? If we had responded sooner to the "climate change crisis?" No matter. It is always a challenge to joust with history and to parry with the actual events, knowing full well that in the end what eventually happened will always have the last word.

Two years ago, I researched and wrote about a young American woman, Iva Toguri, who found herself stranded in wartime Japan after the Pearl Harbor attack. I attempted to retrace her life and to understand how she became a traitor, the infamous *"Tokyo Rose,* who broadcasted over Radio Tokyo. In doing so, I tried to envision a plausible reinterpretation of her effect on American citizens in the post-war period in light of new information. I injected into this controversy Robert Samuels, my alter ego, and a reporter working for the *San Francisco Chronicle*, who was on a quest to determine whether or not Iva was indeed a traitor. The "twists of history" carried him along to determine what really happened so many years ago.

In the process of researching Toguri's story, I came across the name of Mildred Elizabeth Gillars, who was also convicted of treason for her radio broadcasts on behalf of Nazi Germany during World War II. At the time of her trial she was better known as *"Axis Sally,"* and for some, "the Bitch of Berlin." I decided to investigate and write a sequel. Once more, Samuels' quest was to determine if the guilty verdict reached by the jury was correct. And was it still possible for Gillars to find redemption in a world steadfastly critical of her traitorous broadcasts on behalf of the Nazi regime? Samuels pursues this challenge. In doing so, he uncovers a story as unbelievable as that of Tokyo Rose.

One additional word; Mildred Gillars was employed by the German National Radio Service, which was known as the Reichsradio or Reichsrundfunk. For the purposes of this story, I refer to these German names as simply *"Radio Berlin."* Finally, certain dramatic liberties were taken, of course, to enhance the impact of the story, while, hopefully, I remaining faithful to what actually took place.

I trust you will enjoy the story.

Robert Livingston
Northridge, California
2012

CHAPTER 1

THE DEDICATION

<u>San Francisco – A Few Years Ago</u>

The storm was gone now.

No longer did ponderous, grayish dreadnoughts move in battle formation, clashing above the city, firing mighty broadsides across the night sky. Nor were there crescendos of ear-splitting thunder and flashes of jagged shafts of lightning reminding those below that mere mortals are but pliable clay in the hands of fickle gods who, if they choose, would toy with their lives. Such was the world of those who would challenge their fate.

The storm left the city drenched after three days of heavy rain, and, for some, a city now cleansed of its sins. A bright sun hovered lazily above the Bay Area, a brilliant, flaming celestial ball bringing warmth and comfort to those who lived and worked among the towering skyscrapers of Market Street or in the uniquely charming communities that etched the San Francisco landscape from the lower Mission to the beach-fronting Sunset District. The air was crystal clear, charmed by a gentle Pacific breeze that ruffled ship flags in the Marina and leafy branches in Golden Gate Park before lapping at carefree children at play in the Richmond. The great bridges, touched by the same soft winds, gleamed in the bright sunshine, one a metallic gray connecting the touristy Embarcadero to Oakland's busy, blue-collar port; the other, suspended high above the Straits of the Golden Gate, a string of orange and reddish cables that united the Presidio with Marin County and the entire Northern California coast.

The very same breeze gave *Bagdad by the Bay* an air of expectancy. It was as if the city, built on seven hills, were holding its collective breath awaiting one more fling of the dice by the vagaries of time and history. Such was this day.

The Celebration

In the lower Fillmore District the crowd was already gathering. Over 500 students were seated on portable plastic chairs just beyond the infield between second and third base. This kept them off the still damp grass of the baseball field. Overtaxed custodians had worked through the night setting up the chairs, which were cashiered from schools around the city. Another hundred or more parents and community folk, a few standing but most seating patiently, awaited the morning's events on still more chairs procured at the last possible moment. On a metal riser erected for the celebration, located approximately where the pitcher's mound was found, the day's dignitaries, all dressed stylishly, were seated, less than patiently, waiting for the cue to start the celebration. All but three elected officials that is…

The Mayor, compulsive by nature, was constantly walking about the riser pressing the flesh of all within the reach of his lanky arms and passionate handshake. The man was always in motion, unwavering in his excessive need to campaign regardless of time or place. Politics was his life, and most agreed he was good at it. Somehow he found a tenable ethical balance between a "little-off-the-books" kickbacks, or what some referred to as rather innocent corruption, while at the time conducting the people's business in an efficient, if not in a generally cost-effective manner. At least that was what his supporters claimed.

His face, as always, was nicely tanned, this time from a recent business trek to Acapulco on the city's dime to drum up trade with the locals.

Nearby was the Superintendent of Schools who was, as was his way, sitting ramrod straight with one ear cocked to the ground to catch the latest rumor, whisper, or gossip about the schools, and any comments concerning the superb job he believed he was doing. If you weren't sure about this last point, one had to only ask him. Though a shy man, he was not opposed to tooting his own horn. He was scrupulously honest. No dollar was wasted. No scandal attended his administration. He was also a cautious man who weighed each decision with the preciseness of a fine watch.

Adjacent to the Superintendent was the school board President, a devotee of pomade by the pound. His hair was, as always, slicked back, smooth and shapeless, a sort of miniature runway waiting for planes that never quite arrived. For some, his hairstyle suggested the way he ran the Board, smoothly without a hair out of place. Today, however, as he looked out at the assembled folks, he had a satisfied look to his countenance, which hinted at pride and accomplishment for which he was willing to take full credit.

For these three, all products of personal ambitions and the periodic need to stand for reelection, it was nice to see such a large turnout and, hopefully, the media to cover the day's events. Though they would never state it publicly, one thought ran through their collective mentality: so many people, so many possible votes come election time.

Also on the riser was an older man in a wheel chair. Unlike the others, he was unelected. He was a guest of honor, a former Marine with lifeless legs, which were covered by a lovely quilt fashioned in patriotic colors and festooned with a large American eagle. He wore a light sports jacket, tan in color, and beneath the quilt brown slacks clung to his waist before draping downward, only to be tied in a bunch. Sitting on his immediate right was a tall, handsome young man with strong, deeply blue eyes, who kept a vigilant, but compassionate watch on his wheel chair-bound charge. Where others wore tweed sports coats and stripped suits just off the Brooks Brothers racks, he donned a CAL jacket emphasizing his temporary role in life as an EVENTS STAFF employee of the university.

Sitting somewhat nervously on the immediate left was a rather attractive woman approaching the outer limits of middle age. She was dressed professionally, which meant modestly for an assembly of students and parents: a dark, wool dress, fashionable black boots, and a short coat, again black in color. She was the new principal of the school hosting the day's celebration. In her lap, which she glanced at frequently, she held a 3 X 5 card with her prepared words carefully written down. What she had to say was important. She was prepared to do a good job. She needed to do a good job.

For these people, all part of an incessant struggle during the past year to build and name a new school, it was rewarding to finally have this day.

Gazing at all this was the electronic eye of the *KRON* television camera as well as other stations. They were here to mark and record the culmination of a remarkable story and the beginning of a school venture emphasizing pluralism and idealism in public education. Through the magic of television news there was a wonderful human-interest story here. The print folks were present too with their notebooks and off-brand ballpoints. Tomorrow's *Chronicle* and *Examiner* would banner the story, and, along with appropriate editorials and commentaries, retell the dramatic events leading to this day. It was a good day to be in the news business. It was nice to have a story with a happy ending for once. Even jaded reporters enjoyed a respite from the daily carnage afflicting the city and providing testimony to tragic human events. For once, assuming the city enjoyed a crime-free day, the old adage, "if it bleed, it leads," might take a day off. But that, of course, was a mighty big assumption.

Lingering in the crowd toward the back and eschewing sitting down was a couple best described as in the twilight zone between middle age and senior status, between membership in the auto club and newly minted Medicare enrollees. They looked like a couple who had spent years together by dress (conservative) and demeanor (quiet alertness), and in the way they frequently finished each other's sentences. And, of course, it was true. Forty or more years of marriage does have that effect. By standing they could see all, and what was about to take place was important to them. They didn't want to miss out on any of it.

"Robert, when will they begin?"

"Patience, my dear Lynn. Remember, this is a city function. Time stands still until…"

Just at that moment, the Mayor went to the podium and asked all in attendance to join him in the *Pledge of Allegiance,* which the students knew by heart, and the parents tried to remember. Following this, the Mayor said a few appropriate words ending with, "What a great occasion this is for our city." Polite applause greeted his few words.

Next the Board President added words of welcome including an oft-quoted line during the next few days: "We believe in this experiment. Students fully participated in naming our new school and its five major buildings. It paves the way to a better future for all our community." Even politer applause greeted his utterance.

The Superintendent reaffirmed what had been said earlier, remarking that "the road has been hard and difficult, but here we are at last." He then said, "At this time I would like to introduce your new principal, Miss Rachel Samuels." The applause was sharper and longer. Of course, it was difficult to discern for whom the clapped hands were clapping for, the Superintendent or the new principal.

"Robert, our moment. Our daughter…"

"No, Lynn. Her moment…"

The principal, still somewhat anxious, checked her note cards one last time and then, after placing them aside, spoke in a surprisingly calm manner, even to herself.

"My name is Miss Samuels and, just as you are the first class in this school, I am the first principal. I take great pride in this dedication ceremony. It is an honor to say that today School Site 1776 will officially opens its door to 521 students as Freedom High School."

In response to this the new student body rose and applauded, whistled, hooted, and yelled for a full minute. The students, it appeared, needed to stretch their legs. A moment later the new principal continued.

"This incoming class represents the diversity and pluralistic makeup of San Francisco, as do the buildings in which students will pursue academic achievement and a high standard of ethical behavior. History walks with you in these buildings. For those majoring in literature, Building A, now named after Martin Luther King, invites you to harness the magic of language, and to soar, as did Reverend King, in creating a better world based on merit, not one's racial or ethnic background. For the mathematics and computer-focused students, Building B is named for Cesar Chavez and offers you a home in which to advance your studies just as he tried to advance the hopes of migrant workers toiling in our agricultural fields."

"Robert, she's so eloquent."
"She is, isn't she?"

"Building C, bedecked with microscopes and telescopes, awaits those who would peer deeply into the hidden world of the atom, while others stretch their imagination to explore the heavens above. Fittingly, the world of science will honor in name and action Dr. Sun Yat-Sen, who studied medicine and sought to create a modern China free of foreign domination. The baseball field where we sit today and the almost completed gymnasium will recognize a native citizen, Joe DiMaggio, who swung for distant fences in the pursuit of excellence in athletics. For our future teams we will always seek the same effort."

"She's coming to the last building."
"At last, Lynn…"

"And for those of you prepping for a future legal career or a place in government to do the work of the people, we offer you Building D, which proudly reminds us of the price of liberty and the meaning of freedom within our starry understanding of active citizenship. The name of Iva Toguri will honor and adorn this hall."

"She did it, Robert."
"Almost."

"I would be remiss if I did not introduce one other person, Mr. Michael Simms, the man known to many of you as the *Warrior*."

Michael Simms and Tokyo Rose

Slowly Michael Simms propelled himself across the riser toward the principal. Unbelievably, the attending students and others were hushed. Not a sound was heard except for the scraping of the wheel chair. The principal handed him a microphone. Without any preamble, he began.

"Many years ago I dropped out of high school during my senior year. I was not yet eighteen. I lied about my age and enlisted in the Marine Corps. I was young and immortal and I wanted to avenge Pearl Harbor. In 1943 I waded through blood-streaked coral waters at a hellish place called Tarawa. Bullets cut me down before I ever reached the beach and only the bravery and skill of a medic saved my life. I came home with lifeless legs and spent months in a VA hospital. I was eighteen years old, and my life, I thought, was over. Truly, I wished I had died in the Pacific. I was angry. I withdrew into myself. I rejected the affection and assistance of others. Self-pity devoured me."

Michael Simms hesitated. His voice cracked, even as his chest heaved. His whole body, mind, and soul, it seemed, strained to continue, but continue he did.

"Last year I heard that Iva Toguri, whom I remembered as the traitor, Tokyo Rose, might have this school named after her. I could not bear this. I tried to stop this from happening, sometimes not too wisely, or legally. Eventually, as new information about Mrs. Toguri emerged due to the research of a reporter for the *Chronicle*, Mr. Robert Samuels, I was forced to reassess my view. It was slowly apparent to me that Mrs. Toguri did not broadcast propaganda during World War II, that she was not a traitor, that she should not have been imprisoned, that a pardon was rightfully forthcoming, and, that I was wrong. Yet, until I met her at a board meeting last year, I still harbored painful memories and a cold heart. What she said to me has been recorded and, if you will bear with me, I will quote her, for what she said changed my life."

Mr. Simms, we have each suffered incalculable loss. You, rifle in hand, lost your legs defending America on a lonely beach. I lost my family and freedom defending our country behind a microphone at Radio Tokyo. Each of us was transformed by Pearl Harbor. For you, the attack required a call to duty. At the opposite end of the world, I was stranded in the heart of the enemy where I, too, answered the call to the extent I could. You challenged the foe from outside. I did so from the inside. And each of us paid a high price for our willingness to defend America.

"Her words," Michael Simms reminded the students in particular, "were almost poetic in nature. They were certainly, for me, a painful reminder of a mystical bond that existed between us, between a once youthful woman and an under-aged Marine. She went on to say:

You answered America's call during a desperate time against a foe who seemed truly alien to you, and it is understandable that my name and face could only remind you of the past. Simms, an Irish name, and Toguri, obviously Japanese, two names, two cultures, two languages, yet each connected by their undying love of this country, and again, we each paid so dearly for this love. If I could, I would give you back your legs. If you could, you would, I believe, give back to me my dead infant son and my estranged husband, and my family that was so unfairly forced into a relocation camp during the war. And not to mention the eight years I spent in jail on the basis of perjured testimony.

But we cannot undo the past. We are bound together, I think, by a human tragedy. Michael Simms, I ask you to forgive me for the transgressions you attribute to me. I want you to remember me as a person who made mistakes but never uttered a word against our country. I remained loyal to America during the war.

"As Mrs. Toguri spoke, I knew she was right. I could feel her pain, yet my own suffering still hardened me against her words until she said with heartfelt conviction:"

Michael Simms, you can either sit in a room, as you do now and feel sorry for yourself, or you can go outside and look ahead. I have always tried to look ahead. I have tried to forget the past. I believe in what I did. I tried to sabotage the enemy's propaganda. I have no regrets for doing that. You did what you could do. You should have no regrets. I don't hate anyone for what happened. You shouldn't hate anyone either. It's time for us to make peace.

"Mrs. Toguri was right. It was time to stop hating. It's time for all of us, to stop hating. It was time to make peace with our demons. And this I have tried to do. And I remind you, the new students, as you walk through the building named after her, remember a woman, now recently pardoned by President Ford, as a person who was never a traitor. She was a tiger who never changed her stripes. She was always loyal to our country."

With that, Michael Simms stopped. Seconds passed... Then the quiet was broken by long minutes of uninterrupted applause as those in the crowd, many with tearful eyes, all captured by the humanity of the moment, broke out in a sustained rendition of *God Bless America*. Finally, as the song's last words drifted away, an emotionally spent gathering returned to its seats to hear the principal's final words.

"You should know that the Board of Education has offered Mr. Simms a job at Freedom High. He will work in the library. You should also note that your student council has adopted a motto for our school recalling Mr. Simms' last words before the Board a year ago to this day: *'It's time to move on.'*"

Again, there was applause, spirited and heartfelt.

"I ask you to stand now and applaud not just your new school, but those who will walk with you while you attend Freedom High, those who in the past contributed so much in the progressive march of humanity. Upon their shoulders you will seek your education always sheltered by the trials and tribulations of their day, even as you deal with future challenges in your own lives, challenges which begin in thirty minutes when instruction commences."

And, as the principal had requested, applause rang once more. The audience, young and old alike, stood, applauded, and again whistled and howled, and generally voiced and gestured their delight at the dedication of the new school. It was a moment to be remembered.

In time, the dignitaries departed and the parents returned to home or work, and, with quiet, but labored efficiency, the custodians folded and collected the portable chairs for transport, while others picked up assorted items from the still damp grass. The baseball diamond would be left pristine.

Two people did, however, linger.

"Robert, this was a day never to be forgotten."
"I couldn't have said it better, Lynn."
"Our Rachel was wonderful."
"Spoken like a proud parent."
"Too bad Rachel has to work today. It would be nice to go out."
"She is the principal, Lynn."
"Duty calls?"
"Right."

The Mysterious Woman

Even as they spoke, endearingly and happily about their daughter, fate squeezed into their lives, changing forever the day's "opening day" celebration.

An older woman approached them. She was in her late-60's or more, though those things are difficult to judge. She wore a long, dark brown coat that totally encased her, leaving only her black, rather modest and prudent low-heeled shoes showing. Unlike many women today, she wore both patent leather gloves and a black hat resembling a cup cake for the lack of a better image. Her sensible wardrobe was fit for a cold day. She walked straight toward the obviously happy parents, her eyes intently focused on them.

"Mr. Samuels? Mr. Robert Samuels?"
"Do I know you?"
"The reporter for the *Chronicle*, are you not?"

Robert Samuels really didn't want to admit to his professional calling. Today of all days he just wanted to be a happy dad enjoying his daughter's grand moment, and free of a news deadline. He just wanted to have lunch with his wife at the *Golden Valley*, a local Chinese restaurant they often frequented. He didn't want any complications.

Still, he had been a Boy Scout. It was difficult for him to lie, even to lightly fabricate. And he was also, if the moment called for it, capable of being gallant. That he had a nose for a story was a reality he quietly bore with a mixture of joy and dread. That said, he had to acknowledge the woman

"Yes, I work for the paper," he said.

"Heaving a sigh of relief, the woman said, "Thank God, I wasn't sure I would find you in this crowd today."

Aware of her husband's discomfort and with her stomach churning for heated egg rolls, Lynn said, "Perhaps Robert might speak with you later. Would tomorrow be okay?"

"Yes. I'll be in the city for another day, perhaps longer."

"Well then," Samuels said.

"But, if I could speak with you beforehand, I would be most grateful."

"I'm afraid…"

"Today, now, please."

"You don't understand. My wife and I…"

"Mr. Samuels, I'm an old woman and I've traveled a long way to see you. I need to speak with you. I must speak with you."

"A long way, you say?"

"Ohio."

Lynn caught it first. A certain frantic edge to the woman's voice, a quiet desperation bubbling just below the surface, welling up from some deep reservoir of despair and sadness. This she could not ignore. Nor could she let her husband do so.

"Robert, perhaps you should speak with the lady."

"What about our lunch date?"

"I'll take the car and pick up enough for dinner. You know how Rachel loves prawns and those spicy sauces. You stay."

"Carless."

"Live life on the edge, dear. Grab a Yellow Cab, or better yet squeeze onto a Muni."

"You're all heart."

A slightly modest peck on the cheek, and Lynn was off leaving Samuels with his mid-west visitor.

"I don't think I know you. You're…?"

"Mrs. Edna Mae Herrick."

"Doesn't ring a bell."

"My maiden name was Edna Mae Gillars."

"Gillars? No. I don't recognize the name."

"Mr. Samuels, I'm sure you have. You must have come across the name during your research about Iva Toguri."

Gillars… Mental files were opening and shutting at rapid speed as Samuels' mind searched for the illusive name. True, he had heard it before. But he really hadn't wanted to admit to that, fearful that one thing would lead to another. But where had he heard the name? And in what context had he heard it? She had mentioned Iva. Why? Accused traitor. Turncoat. Propagandist. Broadcaster for the enemy… Tokyo Rose… The name given her by sailors and Marines in the Pacific… Tokyo Rose, an American female broadcasting on Radio Tokyo, lacing the air waves with hit music, news from the home front, and, when available, letters from POW's to friends and family. Intertwined with all this was the propaganda, the effort of the enemy to weaken the will and morale of Allied soldiers to fight on in an unforgiving war of island-hopping slaughter. Tokyo Rose and the other woman, a counterpart in so many ways, a mirror image.

"You're recalling the name, Mr. Samuels?

"You have a sister?"

"A half-sister."

"Mildred Elizabeth?"

"Yes."

"What do you want, Mrs. Herrick? Samuels asked in a voice perhaps too harsh.

And so she told him.

Samuels' response was summed up in less than eloquent terms. Indeed, his voice resonated with disbelief and deep seated anger so unlike his usual calm and reserved demeanor:

"You're kidding, aren't you?"

CHAPTER 2
THE REQUEST

<u>Later</u>

As always, the Chinese food from the Golden Valley was great. True to her word, Lynn picked up dinner for the family, large, juicy prawns for Rachel, pork fried rice for Samuels, and lemon chicken for herself, three wonderful entrees which, of course, would be shared, as would the egg rolls. For the ladies, there was white rice; for Samuels, there was brown rice in recognition of his recent diagnosis, which determined he was a Type 2 diabetic. No more sugar. Hello brown rice. Goodbye greasy stuff, at least after tonight. Green tea and hot war won ton soup whet everyone's appetite. After a full day of emotional excitement, Rachel and her mother dove headlong into their food with relish. If the chopsticks had flown any faster, fires would have been ignited. Not true though for Samuels. He just picked at his food, barely touching any of it. This did not go unnoticed.

"Dad, you've hardly touched your food," Rachel commented quietly. "Not feeling well, dear?" Lynn asked.

Samuels heard his family, but he didn't respond. He was "zoning." That's what the kids called it when, not for any apparent reason, he seemed to merely drift away, barely acknowledging their presence. The same thing happened at work. One minute he was thoroughly involved in a heated conversation in the newsroom, the next moment he was somewhere else though the body remained in place. Over the years he had come to understand it as a kind of defense mechanism that permitted him to escape for a few seconds into another reality, a shelter of sort, a place where he could think, a place where he found perspective. It was a kind of metaphysical projection over which he did not always have complete control. And that was tough for a guy who believed in free will almost as an absolute.

"Robert, did you hear me?"
"He's doing it again, mom."

Indeed Samuels was. He was looking out the large glass window of their Kronquist Court home. The window faced eastward, and, since the home was located in the Diamond Heights area, just above Market Street, he could view the grand street lit up at night all the way to the Ferry Building and the Bay Bridge and beyond to Oakland and the campanile on the Cal Berkeley campus. It was quite a view, and, almost for Samuels anyway, hypnotic. At moments like this, he was more bird than man, or so he felt, soaring above the absurd vanities of the human condition, and, to the extent he could, oblivious to the frailties of their actions that were too often the focus of his own news reporting.

"Robert!"
"The house is on fire, dad!"
"What?"
"Do we have your attention, dear?"
"Was I?"
"Tuned us out completely, Dad."
"I did?"
"You seemed so preoccupied," Lynn said. "Then you were gone."
"You just kept stirring your brown rice and looking out the window," Rachel added. "Something on your mind?"

Of course, something was on his mind, or more to the point, in his mind. If only that woman hadn't shown up out of nowhere.

"Fess up, dear. You haven't been yourself since you returned home after meeting that lady."

"What lady?" Rachel asked.

"The lady from Ohio, Rachel," Lynn quickly said.

"Ohio! Did she come for the dedication?"

"I don't think so, at least not solely for that. Am I right, Robert?"

"On the nail."

"Well, dad, don't keep us in suspense. What did she want?"

"A miracle."

In many families the word "miracle" would have been met with skepticism at the very least, and incredulity at worst, along with facial grimacing and rough attempts at levity at someone's expense. Here the word, however, was accepted, at least in a literary sense, as common coin of the realm. It was because of Samuels' many books, *Miracle at Pusan, The Miracle of the Fifth Chaplain*, and his newest book just out, *The Miracle of the Tarnished Rose*.

"Okay," Rachel said. "You can handle that."

"Perhaps not this time."

"What kind of miracle are we talking about, Robert?"

"Resurrecting the dead."

"Well, at least it's not something too difficult, Dad."

"Her half-sister," Samuels volunteered.

"Robert, I think you should start from the beginning."

"My egg roll is cold."

"Don't change the subject. I'll reheat it. You talk."

"The lady I met was Edna Mae Herrick Her half-sister is Mildred Elizabeth Gillars."

The Request – Earlier in the Day

"Mr. Samuels, I assure you, I'm not kidding. I traveled a long way to make this request at considerable cost, I might add. I am not a daft old lady."

"Mrs. Herrick, what you ask is not possible."

"I've read your books, Mr. Samuels. You do perform miracles."

"Only with words, if at that."

"You did it for Iva Toguri."

"Tokyo Rose?"

"Yes."

"She was innocent. In this case…"

"What?"

"Your sister was guilty."

"Axis Sally?"

"That's what she was called, guilty by name and action."

"But they said Tokyo Rose was guilty, too. That didn't stop you. You still tried to help Iva Toguri. Won't you even try?"

"You want me to prove your sister wasn't guilty of treason?'

"Of course."

"You want me to help win her a pardon?"

"That would follow."

"And you want the unfinished Drama Building at Freedom High to be named after her."

"That sums it up. Imagine it. Two women on different sides of the world, each stranded in a foreign country, each forced to survive in an alien land, each hounded by the secret police, and each forced to broadcast, one from Radio Tokyo, the other from Radio Berlin. Both were apprehended by the military police after the war. Both were accused of treason. Both were found guilty in government-sponsored political trials, and both were sentenced to prison, only to be eventually pardoned."

"Innocence may not apply to each."

"You can determine that."

"I can't."

"You won't."

"I mean I can't. The business with Tokyo Rose took a lot out of me. It was an emotional experience. I took a lot of heat from Iva Toguri's detractors, including the *Warrior*, Mr. Simms, before he saw the light. I'm not ready for another crusade. I just want to disappear for awhile."

"From what I know of you, you're not the kind of person who folds his tent and slips quietly into the night. Not when there's a story scampering about. What is the real problem, Mr. Samuels?"

"You insist?"

"I do."

"I'm Jewish."

"Robert! You told her that? A desperate old lady asks for your assistance and you told her a lie."

"I didn't lie. I exaggerated, perhaps."

"Dad, come on. You usually devour the pork fried rice, and you've been known to mix milk and meat, and to enjoy a bacon burger."

"And when was the last time you went to the synagogue, Robert, any synagogue?"

"Depends on who just got married or died."

"That's what I mean, dear."

"I did have a circumcision."

"Lots of men have one, even Gentiles, Dad."

"I had a bar mitzvah. Gentiles don't do that."

"And after that, dear, you retired your skull cap."

"I support Israel."

"So?"

"I take off for the high holidays."

"Half the world does. Instant weekend conversion."

"Thanks, Rachel."

"Well, what happened? What did she say, Robert?"

Objectivity

"You're Jewish?"

"That puts me in a difficult position, Mrs. Herrick. Surely, you can see that. How could I be objective? And, more to the point, why should I even care?"

"Because of what Mildred said?"

"Yes. Because of what she broadcasted to the entire world."

"You've already made up your mind?"

"I know this. Three things: first, the jury was right in finding her guilty, as was the Appeal Court in its decision to uphold the verdict of the lower court. Second, your sister hurt a lot of people, particularly families of POW's captured by the Germans after D-Day. Third, she was anti-Semitic."

"I can't disagree with you, Mr. Samuels."

"Yet?"

"Yet, I want you to help her."

"You persist."

"She's my sister. There are, I think, extenuating circumstances, which should be considered."

"Mrs. Herrick…"

"You're a fair man, Mr. Samuels. I believe that. I'll make a deal with you."

"Please, Mrs. Herrick."

"Meet with me tomorrow for three hours. At the Fremont Hotel where I'm staying… Let me tell you about my sister. Then, if you still feel the same way, we'll each go our own way."

"Three hours, that's all?"

"I'll pay for lunch and drinks. What do you have to lose?"

"If I still feel the way I do?"

"You get a peck on the cheek, and I return to Ohio."

"Before I agree to meet, a question."

"I think I know what you're going to ask."

"Does your sister know what you're doing?"

"No."

"Would she support what you're doing?"

"That's two questions. And the answer is no again."

"Would she agree to meet with me if I get involved?"

"Probably not, and that's three questions."

"You're on your own hook?"

"I am."

"Why?"

"I told you before. She's my sister."

"What did you decide, dad?"

"I'll have some lemon chicken."

"Dad!"

"And some tea, preferably hot."

"Enjoying yourself, Robert?"

"Immensely."

"Want to sleep in the garage tonight?"

"I agreed to meet her."

CHAPTER 3

THE MEETING

<u>The Next Day</u>

The Fremont Hotel was a second tier hotel, an older spot for out-of-towners who were on a budget, yet didn't want to go Motel 6 or Super 8. They wanted something more than the basics: bed, shower, television, coffee maker, and packaged shampoo. The Fremont provided the little extra. An actual bar of perfumed soap, up-graded coffee with choices such as French cream or hazelnut, both regular and decaf. The refrigerator bar was fully stocked, and, though the diminutive bottles of Four Roses or Wild Turkey, or a cola were not inexpensive, the cost of a soft drink or something more substantial wasn't prohibitive. The beds were queen size and comfortable with fluffy pillows and a towel-designed creature on them every evening along with two chocolate mints. The room maids were courteous and punctual, as was room service for a late hour sandwich. The lobby had comfortable couches and padded chairs, and quiet music floating throughout. Copies of the daily newspapers were around on well-polished cherry-wood tables, the *Examiner*, a Hearst paper decidedly to the right, and, of course, the more liberal edition of the *Chronicle*. Copies of *Fortune Magazine* and *Forbes* were also scattered around in neat little bundles of economic wisdom, or so the publishers claimed. And, of course, there was *USA Today*, the traveler's newspaper. The lobby was a friendly place where guests chatted, while sipping a white wine from, as would be expected, Napa Valley, before entering the dining room for a noon meal.

All in all, the Fremont was a perfect hotel for, as in this case, a mid-westerner who desired comfort, but not an immense bill. As such, it was perfect for Edna Mae Herrick, who met Robert Samuels as he stepped through the front door.

"Mr. Samuels, very punctual."
"I learned long ago to never keep a lady waiting."
"No matter her age."
"Especially when she's buying lunch."
"Well then…"

Entering the dining room, they were escorted by a stiff-collared young lad, most probably a college student earning tuition money, to their table, which was close to a window providing them with an excellent view of people scurrying by outside. Once seated, they quickly scanned the menu before ordering wine and entrees. Edna Mae chose a chicken salad with a side of honey mustard dressing. Samuels opted for the club sandwich. Livingston white zinfandel wine accompanied their meal at Samuels urging.

"You like that brand, Mr. Samuels?"
"The name intrigues me."

Samuels noticed that Edna Mae's cupcake hat was elsewhere today. Her long black coat was also nowhere to be seen. Her long hair, now free of safety pins and a severe Victorian bun style, reached down to her shoulders. Her hair, he noticed, was so very blond as to be almost be white. A bit of silver tint added to its attractive luster. Without her neck to ankle coat encompassing her, Samuels could see that his host had a slim, athletic form cloaked in a simple black woolen dress. Her appearance, all in all, was appropriate for a former professional dancer. For a woman of her age, she was, Samuels admitted, doing just fine.

She had a healthy, wholesome look that seemed partial to folks from the Buckeye state.

Once their wine arrived, along with their lunch, Edna Mae surprised Samuels with her toast.

"I trust this will be the beginning of a long relationship, Louie."

"Casablanca," Samuels replied with a smile. "Last scene as Rick and Louie head for a free French outpost."

"And our first scene, Mr. Samuels."

Glass clicked, and Edna Mae got right down to business, even as she attacked her chicken salad with zest.

"Mr. Samuels, what do you know about my sister?"

"Probably, very little. I do know she was found guilty of making propaganda broadcasts for Radio Berlin in Nazi Germany during the war."

"Beyond that?"

"She was born Mildred Elizabeth Sisk in Portland, Maine in 1900. After her mother divorced and remarried, she assumed the name of her stepfather, who, I believe, was a dentist. She became Mildred Gillars. She went to public school in Conneaut, Ohio and later enrolled at Ohio Wesleyan University in Delaware before transferring to a school in New York. Hunter College, I think."

"You've done your homework."

"Just basic stuff I picked up while researching Toguri's past and the involvement of other Americans in propaganda broadcasts."

"You know my sister never graduated from Ohio Wesleyan?"

"She had been pursuing a degree in dramatic arts but dropped before her senior year."

"Transferred to Hunter to focus on acting."

"Where Koischwitz entered her life."

"You surprise me, Mr. Samuels. You know about him?"

"Max Otto Koischwitz, a German born professor of philosophy who taught at Hunter and enjoyed the company, and affection, of young women, possibly including Mildred."

"Koischwitz, how I detest that name, that man. All that went wrong started with him. If Mildred had never met him things would have been different."

"As I recalled, he renounced his American citizenship and returned to Germany just before the invasion of Poland, August 1939. Once back, he became an official in the Nazi radio service."

"Where Mildred eventually found herself just before the war."

"In Berlin?"

"Sadly, yes, where she stayed even though our mother went to Europe to bring her home. She feared for my sister."

"Your sister declined the offer?"

"Koischwitz had a hold on her. He convinced her to remain and to work for Radio Berlin, to make broadcasts for Hitler's Reich while they lived together."

"She appears to have been easily persuaded," Samuels replied.

"Not as easily as you might think."

"They were lovers. Was that it?"

"That was only one aspect of their relationship."

"You know more?"

"I do."

"Willing to share?"

"Later."

They ate the reminder of their meal in silence, each considering what had been said and what still had to be said. Their interlude was interrupted by their waiter who took their dessert orders, a large brownie with whipped cream on it for Edna Mae and hot apple pie for Samuels.

"No ice cream, Mr. Samuels?" Edna Mae asked.

"Got to watch the sugar intake."

"Type 1?" she questioned.

"Two."

"Me, too."

"And you're eating a brownie? With whipped cream?"

"Sinful, isn't it? But at my age a little sinfulness at lunch is okay, don't you think so?"

"Well, we do have something in common, it would seem, beside your sister."

Of course, the brownie and apple pie soon arrived, cheerfully carried by their waiter, who wanted to make a good impression before the diners were finished and the bill was presented, and a tip was given. Gratuities permitted collegians to survive. The young man was no fool.

Nazi Radio Propaganda

"Her propaganda program, Mrs. Herrick, was known as *Home Sweet Home*, Samuels stated in a matter-of-fact manner. It aired daily and was heard all over Europe, North Africa, and the United States. Mildred referred to herself as *Midge at the Mike*, though the GIs dubbed her *Axis Sally*."

"You have done your research, Mr. Samuels."

"Barely scratched the surface. The propaganda included taunting and teasing allied soldiers, and their wives and girlfriends, their sweethearts back home."

"For what purpose?"

"To break down GI morale and resolve."

"Unfortunately, true."

"And not very successfully. The GIs were more amused than horrified by the broadcasts, but they did enjoy the pop American music she played. Of course, that was before D-Day. After that, her propaganda intensified and focused on POW's and wounded soldiers. This did not endear her to anyone. The GI's had other names for her after that."

"I've noticed you have stayed away from two subjects, Mr. Samuels. You haven't said a word about President Roosevelt and Mildred's anti-Semitic statements."

"That was in deference to you."

"I appreciate your kindness, but let's get it out. Then we can move on."

"I did come across one statement from a broadcast she made in May 1943. It was in a transcript used in trial by the prosecution."

I love America, but I do not love Roosevelt and all his kike boyfriends who have thrown us into this awful turmoil.

"In one full sweep, she pulled together politics, anti-Semitism, and homosexuality. That was a mistake on her part. That quote did not play well with the jury in 1949. Though hated by some, FDR was loved by more, and, following the death camp disclosures… Well, you understand."

"As you say, it didn't play well, Mr. Samuels.

Arrest and Trial

"After Germany's defeat, she was arrested by the American military police in Berlin, detained for a year in Frankfurt, and then returned to the United States where she was incarcerated in Washington D.C. before finally being charged with ten counts of treason."

"You know, Mr. Samuels, that Mildred was not permitted to see an attorney while locked away in Frankfurt. She wasn't even charged with a crime at that time."

"I didn't know that."

"And at her trial, did you know that 10 counts were brought against her, but she was only found guilty on the basis of one, count number 10."

"Again, no."

"What do you know, Mr. Samuels?"

"The trial lasted six hectic weeks. In the end, she was found guilty and sentenced to prison for 10 to 30 years, and a $10,000 fine was imposed. I believe she was paroled after 10 years and is now living in the Midwest."

"And what do you know about her parole?"

"Only that it was granted."

"A question: did you know that my sister waived her first opportunity for a parole? She preferred to remain in jail than to life outside of the prison walls. She had no prospects. She had no place to live. She had no job. No income, and she was 58-years old. I might add, she didn't want to face ridicule as a traitor. Two years later, she did, however, apply for and receive a parole. It was 1960. She had been in one jail or another since late 1946."

"I will, of course, check your facts."

"I certainly expect you to so. There is so much more for you to know."

"And the 'more' will convince me to help you."

"That is my hope."

"You asked for two hours. One is gone."

"Then I suggest we walk over to Union Square. It's such a beautiful day. Let's continue our talk there. I just need to get my coat. Dropping three twenties on the table, she continued, "and please take care of the bill and the young man."

"And what will we talk about?"

"Mildred, of course, and how Axis Sally, the most hated face of Nazi Germany's propaganda, became, after imprisonment, a teacher in a Roman Catholic elementary school for girls in Columbus, Ohio."

CHAPTER 4
THE UNCONVINCED

Union Square

Robert Samuels was surprised. Despite her age, Edna Mae was more than keeping up with him as they walked at a brisk pace down Geary Street from her hotel. Or was it he was trying to keep up with her? She maneuvered around on-coming pedestrians and scampered across busy intersections much like one of those twisting, darting halfbacks from football-crazy Ohio State University. And she did so while maintaining a running conversation and wearing heels.

"What a perfectly glorious day, Mr. Samuels."

"That it is. A perfect day to visit the 'square.'"

"I must admit, I know nothing about it beyond the tourist brochures."

"It's really a plaza several blocks long and wide and bordered by some of San Francisco's most famous streets, Geary, Powell, Post, and Stockton. Within this enclave is the theater district, very upscale department stores, out-of-the-way boutiques, art galleries, and, as you might expect, trinket shops for the less than discriminating tourists."

"That is, if I may so, a mouthful."

"Union Square requires more than a morsel."

"It's name... How did it come by it?"

"It all goes back to the city's first mayor, John Geary, who in 1860 named the plaza in honor of the pro-Union rallies occurring before Fort Sumter."

"You could work for the Chamber of Commerce."

"A reporter comes across all kinds of trivia. For example," Samuels said as he pointed ahead of them, "do you see that tall monument?"

"One could hardly miss it."

"It was built in 1903 and stands 97 feet high. It was built right in the center of the plaza. It commemorates Admiral George Dewey's victory at the battle of Manila Bay during the Spanish-American War."

"Somewhat similar, I think, to the statues we have in Columbus for our namesake."

"Probably fitting, since both seaman opened up new worlds."

"A bit philosophical, aren't you?"

"A reporter's lament."

"What's on top of the monument?" Edna Mae asked as they crossed Post Street and entered the plaza.

"Glad you asked. That's 'Victory,' modeled after the likeness of a local heiress, Alma de Bretteville Spreckels. Her hubby made a ton of money in the sugar-refining business. You probably used his product at one time or another."

"Sweet."

"Well put, Edna. Two other facts you might want to know in case you end up on a senior quiz show."

"Senior, I haven't that many years on you, Mr. Samuels."

"True enough. I repent. The monument also remembers William McKinley, who had been only recently assassinated before the pillar was commissioned."

"I guess that's one way to get your legacy in stone."

Try as he might to maintain some bonding distance from Edna Mae, Samuels did enjoy her quick wit and refreshing candor.

"And below us is the world's first underground parking garage built back in 1939."

"Imagine that. The first. I now feel armed for the senior quiz show after all that."

"Remember, we share the winnings."

Samuels had to admit it. He was coming to like Edna Mae. True, she had disrupted his life a bit asking him to do something he really didn't want to do. But she hadn't pushed. That would come soon, he expected. Edna Mae, he figured, was a cagy one. He'd have to watch himself. He directed her toward a vacant bench from which they could view the entire plaza. Everywhere, people were at tables or on benches, some reading, others feeding the unofficial ambassadors of the city, the gray-whitish colored seagulls, and a few folks were wrapped up in a life and death game of chess. On the Geary side of the plaza, one fellow carried a sign warning of the impending end of the world and enjoining all to accept Jesus.

Secretly, Samuels hoped it wouldn't happen until he had heard Edna Mae out.

The Little Sisters of the Poor

"You said your sister was now teaching elementary school children."

"Yes, back in Columbus. When she was released from prison in 1966, a stipulation of her parole was that she would have a job and a place to live. The Little Sisters of the Poor Child Jesus provided for these requirements. The sisters were members of Our Lady of Bethlehem Convent, which was founded in 1956 in Columbus."

"I've never heard of them."

"Their history begins in 1844 in Aachen, when Clara Fey and other women founded a congregation for the support and education of poor, orphaned, and destitute children, especially girls. The girls were clothed, fed, and taught the necessary skills of their day, training as domestics, modeling of wax figures for statues, and church embroidery. Of course, it was hoped that many of them would consider marrying the church."

"Becoming sisters?"

"Exactly. Their efforts were successful. They established convents and schools throughout Europe, and in more recent times they expanded to the New World."

"With the Papacy's permission, I assume?"

"Generally speaking, yes, but not always with the civilian authorities, where political and religious currents sometimes collided."

"And these good sisters took in Mildred?"

"Oh, they did more than that, Mr. Samuels."

Samuels studied Edna Mae. She had that look on her face. The look one has when a trap is about to be sprung.

"You're tempted not to ask, Mr. Samuels?"

"Yes."

"During the war, many sisters of the Poor Child Jesus were imprisoned in Germany and elsewhere in Nazi-controlled Europe. Many of them died in the concentration camps. But the sisters never lost their faith in a compassionate and loving God. After the war, they collected themselves, and what was left of their order and went about their work in war-torn countries. And, as you already know, they made the decision to migrate to the United States. Wherever they established a convent, they also founded an elementary school, which was especially for the poor. At heart they were educators. They tried to provide a superior education in a safe, well-structured Christian environment focused on love and nurturing. For them, this was the quiet path of righteousness in a world of excessive poverty and pain."

"And the point of all this, Edna Mae?"

"When the sisters in Columbus heard about Mildred's need for a job and home, they responded. They provided both. They didn't turn her away, even thought they had good cause. After all, many of their colleagues had died at the hands of the very government that Mildred broadcasted for during the war. The Nazi regime had enslaved them, tortured them, and slaughtered them. Yet, and this is the point, Mr. Samuels, they were able to transcend their own pain in order to save a soul."

Crash! Bang! Samuels could hear the trap doors slamming shut. Edna Mae had indeed snared him. Without ever saying it directly, she had posed the salient question. Would he, a Jew, find it in his heart, as had the Sisters, to help a woman who had worked for the Reich, while his people were carted off at gun point in crowded, suffocating railroad cars, starved to death in overcrowded camps, used for slave labor, and in the end gassed or shot all in the name of racial purity? He might, he thought, come to that conclusion. But not just yet… He would thrash around for a time first much like a trout on the fly hook. Eventually, he might be hauled in but it would only be after a spirited struggle more with his conscience than Edna Mae's wily trap.

"These sisters sound like good people."

"They kept Mildred on the payroll for seven years. She started at $30 a month and worked her way up to $100. During those years, she also worked first with elementary school children, and later with high school girls at a school run by the convent, where she taught English, German, and French, plus piano, drama, and choral music. She was a real renaissance woman. Sister Mary Assumpta, her principal, often remarked that Mildred had a 'good influence on the girls (and) that she expanded and developed their taste for art and literature.' Now that's quite an endorsement for the most infamous employee of the school."

"Which gets me back to a point I raised earlier. What's the point of all this, Edna Mae?"

"I think you know, but I'll spell it out for you. If the sisters could find a way in their heart to assist Mildred, might you, a Jew, not find a way in your mind to at least investigate her past, especially her trial and appeal before judging her out of hand? Hear me clearly. I'm not asking you to condone what she did. Certainly, I don't sanction what happened. In many respects what she said was deplorable. I'm only asking that you first take an objective view of the history involved and reach what conclusions you will."

Edna Mae was good. Very good. Samuels had to admit it. Still, he resisted. Like the trout on the line, he wasn't yet ready for the frying pan.

"Even if my conclusions fall short of your hopes?"

"I believe I will prevail."

"But if you don't?"

"I will have tried. I will have remained true to my sister."

"Edna Mae, something is missing here. How did the sisters come to know about Mildred? Surely, someone had to bring her to their attention?"

Father Thomas Kerrigan

"Your instincts are good, Mr. Samuels. The answer is Father Thomas Kerrigan.

Samuels nodded and waited. Sometimes it was best to just be quiet. Edna Mae would fill the void. Of that he was sure.

"Father Kerrigan was born in West Virginia in 1922. In 1948, he was ordained. Over the following years, he had many assignments, including serving as the chaplain at the Federal Reformatory at Alderson, West Virginia, where, of course, both my sister and Iva Toguri were sentenced. It was there that he met America's two most despised women traitors, the faces of Nazi Germany and Imperial Japan. With Iva, Father Kerrigan found an individual who had made an imperfect peace with the past but was striving to be positive and forward-looking. And, of course, it didn't hurt that evidence was mounting that would eventually lead to a pardon. In short, Iva knew she was innocent of the charges brought against her, that perjury had indicted her, that, and most importantly, she had conspired to undermine with others the very propaganda broadcasts she was forced to make at sword point. With Mildred, it was a different situation in many ways. When the priest first met her, he found an embittered woman who never tried to undermine the broadcasts she made, even if they were made at gunpoint. She had conspired with the devil and paid the price for this dance with evil. Nevertheless, the good priest decided to give his time to her. She had a soul worth saving."

"He certainly sounds like a man of God."

"He was. He befriended, Mildred, and slowly, over many months, she accepted the Catholic liturgy. Apparently, she found some small measure of solace in the deep meaning of Catholic rituals. Though she had been raised as an Episcopalian, she converted to Roman Catholicism. She was baptized and confirmed in the church in 1961."

"She must have had very intimate chats with Father Kerrigan."

"She did."

"And those chats must have included confession, expunging your sins in order to purify yourself for initiation into the church."

"That was the case."

"But what did she confessed to?"

"Of that, we can only speculate."

"But it was enough."

"For the church, yes. Mildred received the sacrament of the Holy Eucharist and entered the body of the church. I think she found in the mythic images and rites of the Catholic Church a reality somehow paralleling her own life, where, as she believed, destiny was always at work. No matter, the church offered her peace. Mildred was once quoted, saying as did Saint Augustine, 'you would not have found me if I had not been seeking you first.' She was very fond of that quote. I just don't know who was really doing the seeking."

Samuels knew it was over. He was lost. More to the point, he had lost. If Father Kerrigan and the Sisters of the Poor Child Jesus could show compassion for Gillars, where did that leave him? Sure he was a Jew, a weak-kneed agnostic, a continuously born-again skeptic who could not accept the notion of a personal God. As a reporter, he was at best at secular humanist adrift in a wilderness of human depravity and enduring love, each competing with one another, good versus evil in an age-old struggle with savagery and rationality at each other's throats. And that was why he was lost. He could not wage war on savagery without accepting Edna Mae's challenge.

"The conversion changed her life?"

35

Alderson Federal Prison

"Completely. A 1950 early evaluation of Mildred at Alderson Prison stated, if I can remember the words correctly, that:

She had a superior manner, was abrupt with the receiving officers and rude to the two girls admitted with her. She objected loudly to being committed under the name of Sisk (which she hated) rather than Gillars. She was alert and observant but very uncooperative. At first she was annoyed at everything, carried a chip on her shoulders, could not be reasoned with, felt persecuted, and expected bad treatment. She smoked alone, retired to her room to read during all spare hours rather than join the group, and at the table seldom said much. She appeared to be daydreaming. In some ways, she was most pleasant and interesting but, at times, was selfish, greedy, grasping, and asked for favors or disregarded regulations to suit her convenience. When annoyed, she always felt bad and retired to her room sometimes requiring insistence to get her to meals.

"Mildred sounds like she was a handful."

"She was always that. But sometimes it was not completely her fault. At Alderson the gossip mill caused her fellow inmates to be aloof and condescending toward her."

"Why was that?"

"Rumors were spread that my silent, silver-haired sister had made lamp shades out the skins of our soldiers, that she was the *Bitch of Buchenwald,* which, of course, she wasn't. It took awhile for those rumors to be discarded."

"Her attitude improved over time?"

"Very much so. But it was the music, I think."

"Music?"

"In 1957 she began to direct the prison Protestant choir, and soon was asked to assemble the music for the Catholic Mass. She did so in the absence of a civilian music teacher. She was enthusiastic about the work. She not only coached the singers, but she strived to teach the choir members the meaning of the lyrics. Her dedication to the music proved contagious for many. This was noted in a progress report concerning her behavior that year.

She (Mildred) makes a real effort to show the choir members the meaning of music in worship and the necessity for it being well done... Although she has some difficulty with the Latin, she studies diligently and tries very hard to have the members of the Catholic Choir pronounce it correctly. She also interprets to the best of her ability, so that they may appreciate the meanings involved.

"Is this when she began her religious conversation?"

"I think so. She needed to find some spiritual peace, some fulfillment and meaning in her life. This, I believe, all this led to a determination to serve God, and music and Catholicism were the vehicles for this striving."

"Father Kerrigan came into the picture at this time?"

"Yes."

"He was involved in her parole proceeding?"

"Again, yes. But before I explain how, first a little history."

Samuels could feel it again. Edna Mae was setting him up again. She was about to entrap him once more in the emotions of Mildred Elizabeth Gillars. And try as he might, he found himself resisting less, and on some level even welcoming the entanglement.

Changing American Opinion

"In January, 1956, Iva Toguri was released from Alderson. She was granted her parole and moved quietly back to Chicago where she reentered the family business hoping, of course, to leave behind her the legacy of Tokyo Rose. But that was not entirely possible, as you know from your research. Immigration authorities hounded her and tried every way to have her deported. The Justice Department was determined to send her back to Japan where she had committed her treachery. For Toguri that would have meant she was forsaken in America, and probably unwanted in Japan. Only the strenuous work of her legal team stopped the deathly wheels of injustice from crushing her. As her own parole proceeding approached, Mildred realized this would probably be her fate too. But she would have no legal team to protect her. She would be alone again. How would she survive?"

"If I remember correctly, Samuels said, by the late 50's American public opinion had changed. It was moving slowly toward a degree of tolerance where former collaborators were involved. It wasn't forgiveness exactly. Rather, just a willingness to let people get on with their lives. The horrors of the war were drifting into the past. The new horror of a hot war with the Soviet Union in the atomic age had taken precedence."

"Exactly, but not necessarily for Mildred. In 1959, she waived in March of that year her first opportunity to apply for parole. She was 58 at that time, and time, and imprisonment had added years to her. She was without question fearful of reentering the outside world. She was afraid she would be penniless and homeless. Again, a question that had haunted her throughout her life shadowed her. How would she survive? Perhaps more to the point, would she survive? Who would help her? Would she be arrested once more on some technicality? Might she be deported? Would the Germany Federal Republic even accept her? She didn't want to face all that. She was considering not applying for parole. However, with the support and encouragement of Father Kerrigan, she did so. Her application was denied."

"This is when the cavalry rode in?"

Sister Mary Assumpta

"In the form of Father Kerrigan who now knew how the system worked. He was a quick learner. The savvy priest enlisted the assistance of the sisters from the Our Lady of Bethlehem convent to develop a release plan for Mildred. Sister Mary Assumpta, who had witnessed my sister take her first communion, became the main ringleader. Two things were necessary: first, Mildred needed a place to live. Second, she needed a job. The convent agreed to provide room and board, plus one dollar per day, the thirty dollars per month we noted earlier. She would do general work, which came to mean teaching music and other subjects to girls in the convent school."

"Mildred agreed?"

"First, she had to agree to one other provision the sisters demanded. Mildred would strictly have to adhere to it. No reporters or cameramen would be permitted on the convent grounds when she arrived to take her teaching post. The sisters were adamant about this. Her past, the Catholic Church, and the sisters would not be exploited by unwanted and unwarranted publicity. Mildred was more than happy to comply."

"On January 12, 1961, the Parole board approved her release. Axis Sally was now a free woman, right Edna Mae?"

"I'm impressed Mr. Samuels."

"I'm not totally deficient in what happened, especially on the cold, rainy Monday morning in July when the doors of Alderson opened and she departed the prison. I seem to remember details. But don't ask me what I had for breakfast yesterday."

"You know about the reporters?"

"They were waiting. Sadly, like vultures, over twenty of them, all wanting a glimpse of the traitor. She had entered Alderson as a 48-year old. She was now 60. They expected to see an old lady appear, not the rouged lips, tight, black, very attractive dress, and arrogant manner of the woman convicted of treachery over a decade earlier. They expected to see an old lady, one old enough to be a grandmother, exit Alderson. They were in for a surprise."

"I know. I was there to meet my sister. Her teaching assignment wouldn't begin until the fall. Until then, she would live with me in Ashtabula, Ohio, along with my new husband. We arrived at the gate in our late model De Soto and waited for her expected arrival at 6 a.m. She was late. At 6:30 she arrived in a large, black Department of Justice sedan. Exiting the car, she burst through the prison gates, and into my arms. We were finally reunited. It was apparent that she had aged in prison, but she still had a sense of the dramatic, and, like an aging movie star, she posed for photographs. She was back in the limelight, and she was no grandmotherly lady, her age not withstanding. She still had a presence. You either have it, or you don't. She did. I had to admit she did not show her 60-years once the actress in her took over. For a brief moment she enjoyed the attention. Whatever she was feeling inside, she kept to herself. Her earlier stage life acquitted her well. Of course, it couldn't last."

"The questionable interview, I suspect?"

"Once more, Mr. Samuels, I'm very impressed."

"I came across her interview while researching Tokyo Rose. The interview stuck with me. Your sister was, to say the least, totally unapologetic about her actions during the war."

When I did the broadcasting, I thought I was doing the right thing. Would I do it again? Certainly, given the same knowledge and the same circumstances. I was a professional broadcaster in Germany when the United States entered the war. It was my job. Besides I was very much in love with a German and hoped to marry him. At the time I felt I could love the United States and still serve the Berlin Broadcasting Corporation. Admittedly, I would not have made the broadcasts if I had known about the crimes of the Nazi state.

Unanswered Questions

There it was, thought Samuels, the back door to the trap. The way out. But would he take it? That was the question. If Mildred Gillars was unrepentant, why should he, at the urging of Edna Mae, seek to vindicate the Nazi broadcaster? If Mildred would do it all over again, how could he seek redemption for her? And this business about not knowing anything about the crimes of the Nazi state, that was difficult to accept. Had she really not known? Or had she deceived herself as to the nature of the concentration camps? Was she not aware of the "final solution," or at the very least, the disappearance of Jews from Berlin? Yes, there was a back door, and Samuels could take it. He could simply tell Ida Mae the weight of evidence was too great against her sister.

There were too many questions unanswered by Mildred, which, when added up, suggested either purposeful deception on her part, or a delusional personality that manipulated reality in order to justify her survival in the land of Brown Shirts. Which was it? Without question, he favored the former but was unsure about the latter. And he had to admit it. He was curious. He really did want to know the truth of the matter. Given this, he wouldn't exit the trap. For a time he would be compliant, neither outwardly resisting Edna Mae's offer or overtly accepting her overtures.

"Mr. Samuels... Mr. Samuels!"
"No need to shout, Ida Mae. My hearing is okay."
"Perhaps, but you certainly seemed lost in your thoughts."
"Not lost. Just weighing the possibilities."
"As to whether or not to accept my entreaty?"
"Entreaty, good word. Not many folks use it these days."
"And you're begging the question."
"I'm close to a decision, but I'm still unconvinced I should take up her cause."
"Perhaps all you need is a little push in the right direction?"
"Which, I suspect, you are about to provide, dear lady."

Edna Mae looked intensely at Robert Samuels before the hint of a smile emerged.

"My last volley, Mr. Samuels. It was one thing for my sister to be convicted for her actions. But it was quite another thing for her conviction to be the result of other broadcasts by the another Axis Sally."

CHAPTER 5

THE IMPOSTOR

The Saint Francis

The drinks arrived almost immediately. For Edna Mae, a whiskey sour, for Robert Samuels, a gin and tonic. They were sitting in the Blue Room of the St. Francis Hotel enjoying a quiet afternoon respite after their walk to Union Square. The hotel offered them a secluded spot where they could continue talking. The room was large with ornate chandeliers hanging from the ceiling, which spread sparkling light and brought into relief the traditional wallpaper bearing caricatures of sailing ships and lighthouses, all reminders of the hotel's harbor past. Sturdy mahogany tables and stuffed and very accommodating chairs and couches provided for comfortable seating. Nary a spot was vacant. In one corner of the room was a beautiful grand piano, highly polished and obviously well-tuned. A fine fellow in a tight tuxedo was working the ivories. His partner, also in a black tux, sauntered around the piano with one hand holding the microphone while his other hand curled around a long cord much in the manner of Frank Sinatra. He was singing an "oldie."

> *I don't want you*
> *But I hate to lose you*
> *You got me in between the devil and the deep blue sea.*

"Drinks were a good idea, Mr. Samuels."

"After hearing about a second Axis Sally, I needed one."

"You weren't just romancing an old lady?"

"I plead the fifth," Samuels said with a big smile. "Whatever I might say would certainly incriminate me, if not with you, certainly with my wife."

"Have no fear, sir; I'm no longer in the business of seducing reporters."

"Really?"

> *I forgive you*
> *Cuz I can't forget you.*
> *You've got me in between the devil and the deep blue sea.*

"This is a lovely hotel, Mr. Samuels."

"Dates back to just before the 1906 earthquake. And it has a past."

"Which you will now share with me."

"It was built as an investment by the trustees of the estate of Charles Crocker who was one of the 'Big Four' railroad magnates in California. They were responsible for building the western terminus of the transcontinental railroad. The investment was for Crocker's two young children, Templeton Crocker and Jenny Crocker. Originally, the name of the hotel was slated to be The Crocker Hotel. Other voices prevailed and it took the name of one of the earliest hotels of the Gold Rush, the St. Francis."

"That's a lot to remember for the senior quiz show."

"You'll do just fine, Edna Mae."

"You think so, do you?"

> *I want to cross you off my list*
> *But when you come knocking at my door*
> *Fate seems to give my heart a twist*
> *And I come running back for more.*

"Tell me about the second Axis Sally."

The Other Axis Sally

"You've been to New York? Rockefeller Center?"

"Of course."

"Did you ever stop for a bite at Zucca's Italian Garden?"

"Never heard of it."

"It was a popular Rockefeller Center restaurant in the 1930's and '40's. The owner's motto was 'the quality of our food is always higher than the price.' Kind of catchy, don't you think?"

"And how does this relate to a second Axis Sally?"

"Patience, Mr. Samuels."

Edna Mae reached into her purse and retrieved a postcard, one, that was apparently old by the wrinkled look of it.

"Know any restaurants with their own postcards? Just look at this."

Samuels checked out the postcard. Though the colors were faded, he could still make out the fine details of the restaurant: rows of tables with lace cloth on them, along with fine China and crystal glassware. The place looked inviting, a nice stop for a mid-day meal or supper under the lights. Turning the postcard over, Samuels saw that indeed it carried the return address of Zucca's Italian Garden, 116-118-120 West Fifth Street, New York City.

> *I should hate you,*
> *But I guess I love you,*
> *You've got me in between the devil and the deep blue sea.*

"Okay, Edna Mae, what gives?"

"The owner had a daughter, Rita Louis Zucca."

"Fine."

"Her father sent her to Italy to a convent school in Florence between 1925 and 1930. She returned to New York and worked in her father's restaurant. In 1938, she returned to Italy where she worked as a typist for three years."

"You are dragging this out, Edna Mae."

"In 1941, she renounced her American citizenship. She became an Italian citizen. Now why, Mr. Samuels, would she want to do that?"

"She didn't like Joe DiMaggio?"

"Wrong. The family held property in Raveno and in Turin. She became an Italian citizen in order to save the properties from expropriation."

"I don't understand."

"In June of 1940, Benito Mussolini signed an order confiscating all lands owned by foreigners in Italy. By renouncing her American citizenship, she could maintain control of the properties for the Zucca family. She did this by informing the American Vice Counsel in Rome. This legal change was finalized when she signed a statement renouncing her American citizenship."

"Okay, she's no longer a Yankee. So what?"

> *I want to cross you off my list,*
> *But when you come knocking at my door,*
> *Fate seem to give my heart a twist,*
> *And I come running back for more.*

"Two things; first, she met and fell in love with an Italian soldier, a handsome fellow by the name of Siro Mariottini. They planned to marry after the war. That would never happen. A British bullet took care of that. Second, Rita lost her job and after a year of unemployment finally found a position. She was hired as a radio announcer for the FIAR (Radio Roma) in 1943."

"The plot thickens, Edna Mae."

"FIAR, which was under government control, wanted to start a new program that would focus on British and American soldiers in North Africa. In particular, Tunisia."

"Propaganda?"

"Yes. As fate would have it, she was hooked up with a German broadcaster, Doctor Charles Goedel. It appears that he gave her the radio name *Sally* and together they created a program — *Jerry's Front*

Calling. It was also known as *The Sally and Phil Show.* In designing the show, they copied, almost to the letter, the format Mildred was already using at Radio Berlin in her show, *Home Sweet Home.*"

"Why reinvent the wheel?"

"Indeed. For instance, the longhand scripts written by Goedel were severely critical of President Roosevelt and US and British intelligence. In Berlin, another PhD did the same for Mildred. His name was Max Otto Koischwitz. We spoke of him earlier. Rita, as did Mildred, read out the names of captured Allied soldiers, discussed the American and British home fronts, and told stories about wives and girlfriends seeing other men. Of course, the emphasis here was to foster homesickness and, if possible, break morale. Anything to impede the Allied advance… The Italian military even provided secret intelligence information to Rita, which, once aired, left Allied soldiers wondering how this woman could know so much about their battle plans. At times that could be frightening. Still, the programs, one emanating from Rome, the other from Berlin, were immensely popular. Two sexy female voices from mysterious women that soldiers could only fantasize about. Both women played popular music, mainly jazz and swing. Each radio station had its own band. Rita's band was called *Jerry's Swinging Tigers* as compared to Mildred's guys, *The Smiling Through Trio.*

"Edna Mae, how do you know all this?"

> *I should hate you*
> *But I guess I love you*
> *You've got me in between the devil and the deep blue sea.*

"I've been busy for almost a decade, researching my sister's trial, the evidence presented, and the decisions of the Court of Appeals. It didn't hurt that Columbus is also the home of Ohio State University with its exhaustive library and excellent professors of history. One professor in particular, William Woodrow Wilson, aided me. He had researched a book entitled *Radio Wars.* It was most helpful."

"Perhaps I should read it."

"It's my hope you will. Professor Wilson included quotes from Rita's broadcasts, which you would find interesting. I've written a few down."

Edna Mae dove into her oversized purse and, after some shuffling of contents, withdrew an obviously well used notebook. Thumbing through it, she finally looked up at Samuels.

"Here we are. Now, don't forget, Rita's broadcasts were scripted by her mentor, but the real power behind the words was the German Embassy in Rome that controlled what was broadcasted. And at Radio Rome, she was strongly supervised by serious men from the intelligence agency. This was also true of Mildred in Berlin. In each case there was no ad-libbing. Spontaneity was out. Conformity was in. Any deviation would lead to punishment from the mild the loss of a food ration card to threats about jail or even the concentration camps."

"You bring this up because?"

"Because it's difficult to know what the two women actually believed. The scripts tell one story. Ever present threats reinforced the propaganda aired. But what did they really believe? That's the question. For example, Rita said, speaking to the wonderful boys of the 504th Parachute Regiment:

We know where and when you are jumping and you will be wiped out.' And on another occasion: 'Hi boys… *how are you tonight? A lousy night it sure is… Axis Sally is talking to you, you poor, silly dumb lambs, well on your way to be slaughtered.*

"That's what she said. That's what was recorded. But was that what she really believed?

"I assume you're suggesting that the same question can be asked of Berlin's Axis Sally."

"That's the point, isn't it?"

> *You've got me in between*
> *The devil and the deep,*
> *The devil and the deep blue sea.*

"I assume Mildred eventually found out about her southern counterpart?"

"She did. She was incensed. She threatened to quit Radio Berlin if the other Axis Sally wasn't retired. But, of course, her threat was meaningless. She was well paid. She had a nice apartment. Her food rations were generous. And she was a celebrity of sorts. If she quit, assuming that she would be permitted to quit, she would find herself on the streets of war-torn Berlin, out of work, no income, and without friends in high places. How would she survive? As such, then, she only had empty threats. But that begs the real problems for her."

"Which was?"

"You will recall, Mildred always felt she could love the United States and still work for Radio Berlin as long as she avoided broadcasting overt propaganda. To some extent, she felt she had some control over what she said. But she had no control over her Italian neighbor. She feared, that in the absence of a German victory, she would be in an untenable position after the war. She feared that she would be blamed for what another Axis Sally broadcasted. At her trial, she said:

I felt that I could be held responsible for any confusion after the end of the war as to what I said. It could cause me a great deal of trouble.

What did Mildred really believe? That's what Edna Mae was getting at. Another trap, Samuels thought. Stir questions. Create doubt. Suggest possibilities. Get me wondering. Edna Mae was turning entrapment into an art form. And she was getting to him. What did Mildred Elizabeth Gillars actually believe? Was she really the Berlin Bitch as some described her? Or was she something else? Samuels wanted to know.

I forgive you
Cuz I can't forget you
You've got me between the devil and the deep blue sea.

"Musing again, Mr. Samuels?"

"Reflecting."

"Considering what I've told you?"

"Reviewing."

"Thoughtfully?"

"Yes."

"And?"

"I'm considering."

"Good. I won't ask which way. And by the way, how do you like the music we've been listening to?"

"Now that you ask…"

"Between the Devil and the Deep Blue Sea?"

"You know it?"

"Sure. Cab Calloway recorded it in 1931. Been a hit since."

"You know, Mr. Samuels, when Rita would sign off each night, she would say, 'and with a sweet kiss from *Sally*.' She would also play her signature song."

"Let me guess… *Between the Devil and Deep Blue Sea.*"

"You do have a quick mind."

> *I want to cross you off my list,*
> *But when you come knocking at my door,*
> *Fate seems to give my heart a twist,*
> *And I come running back for more.*

"Edna Mae, when we first arrived in the hotel, you excused yourself to go to the powder room."

"Ladies have been known to do that."

"You were gone for some time."

"At my age, lots of powdering."

"When I saw you again, you were by the piano."

"So?"

"You asked them to play a special song."

"I did?"

"You are devious."

"I'm fighting for my sister."

"And with me, I suspect. Let me relieve any concerns. You're winning."

For the first time, a wide, generously happy smile covered Edna Mae's face. Her eyes sparkled, literally jumping out at him in an embrace of joy and relief. She extended her arm and gripped his hands with surprising strength. And then a single tear drifted down her cheek, a solitary tear carrying with it the pain of a loving sister adrift in the currents of history.

"You will try?"

"I will."

"I can't thank you enough."

"There are conditions."

"Of course."

"I don't guarantee a favorable outcome."

"I understand."

"I will need time to research the issues, especially Mildred's appeal."

"Certainly."

"I will need my editor's okay at the *Chronicle*."

"Trouble there?"

"Hopefully, no. As I progress, I file my stories as I did with Iva Toguri. Our readers will, I trust, be interested, and *Chronicle* sales may even increase, and that's good. We're a business. News is the vehicle by which we sell advertising."

"Axis Sally might increase circulation."

"Yes. And one more thing."

"You took your time, Mr. Samuels."

"I will need to speak with your sister. Will that be possible?"

"It won't be easy."

"It is necessary."

Samuels escorted the lady from Ohio back to her hotel, where they shared a final thought.

"Mr. Samuels, what changed your mind?"
"I like Cab Calloway."

With that, Robert Samuels gave Edna Mae a slight kiss on her cheek and departed singing, *"But I guess I love you. You've got me between the devil and the deep blue sea."*

CHAPTER 6

THE HUNT

Mrs. Samuels' Questions

"You certainly seemed to have enjoyed your dinner, Robert. Stirring your food around appears passé. Generous second helpings are your thing now? Should I adjust our food budget?"

"I'm hungry tonight; plus we ate very late, Lynn."

"That's because you locked yourself away for three hours in your study. As I recall, it was, Hi, baby. Hold off on dinner. See you at 10 o'clock.' And with that you disappeared."

"I had to check on a few things."

"Not even a kiss. Just 'Hi, baby.'"

"I thought our pre-dinner smooching was okay."

"Who uses a word like smooching? Only my husband."

"Admit it. Our smooching, by any other name, still meant great kisses, dear wife."

Great? You are a bit full of yourself tonight, aren't you?"

"Me? Never!"

"You and yes. I know the signs."

"Signs?"

"Second helpings."

"Sherlock, you win. I am a gluttonous cad."

"Gastronomical cad, you mean."

"I hope you can still stomach me, Lynn."

At that, they both started laughing, even as Samuels devoured the Irish stew, buttery biscuits, and luscious green peas seasoned just right."

"I still know the signs, Robert. Something has put you into a better mood, mister. Care to share?"

"After hot apple pie, a large slice."

"Pie, yes, sliver size, Sir."

"Heartless woman."

Samuels finished his meal. Lynn cleaned up. And together they retired to the living room, where Samuels grabbed his wide-lined notebook now crammed with his crimped, almost illegible handwriting. Lynn mixed two *Chapin and Gore* blended whiskies with ginger ale over a little ice, and they toasted.

"Toast to what I'm about to hear, Robert."

"And to what I'm about to share, Lynn."

Glasses clinked.

"I had a good meeting with Edna Mae."

"That I figured out on my own."

"I'm going to help her."

"Does that include her sister, Mildred?"

"I'll follow the facts. I'll see where they lead."

"Edna Mae agreed?"

"Yes."

"I'm glad. You've done a good thing."

"Time will tell."

Samuels just nodded and glanced at his rumpled notebook on the table before him.

"I had something on my mind when I came home."

"No kidding."

"After leaving Edna Mae, one thought kept pestering me. A question really."

"Which was?"

"How did the military police catch both women? I knew I had notes relating to this question. It took me an hour to find my notes."

"Both women?"

"Mildred and Rita, one American, the other Italian, and each a Sally."

"Of course. But who is Rita?"

Samuels explained.

"Two women with the same tagline. How curious. Who would have thought?"

Samuels interrupted.

"My files were a mess."

"Filing isn't one of your skills."

"Another two hours to read and reread them."

"And?"

"I'm busting to tell you."

"Don't bust. Talk."

Turning to his notebook, he opened it to a paper-clipped page, and began speaking as if he were filing a story for the *Chronicle*.

Finding the Second Axis Sally

"The invasion of North Africa in 1943 and the later fall of Sicily meant that Italy would be defeated before Germany. It also meant that the Roman Axis Sally would be caught first once Italy was invaded by the Allied troops. This was indeed the case. But Rita Louisa Zucca proved to be an elusive prey. As the American forces in Italy trudged up the merciless Italian landscape against determined German resistance, Rita (as I will refer to Rita Louisa Zucca) and her radio gang fled northward for Florence, where they tried to continue broadcasting from the Hotel Excelsior. Due to the rapid advancement of Patton's tanks, they exited the city two days later and headed for Milan, even further to the north. They resumed broadcasting on June 17, 1944 and continued their program for another two months. Incessant American air attacks forced them to move again, this time to a tiny slice of Italy's north known as Mussolini's Social Republic. The *Repubblica Sociale Italiana*. It was really a puppet state under German military control."

Samuels paused to catch his breath, or simply to provide a dramatic moment before moving on.

"I never heard of it."

"Not a common topic in our history books, Lynn."

"Mussolini went from controlling all of Italy to a slice, as you say."

"He lost more than that. Recall, he wanted to recreate a new Roman Empire in, of course, his own image. He referred to the Mediterranean as *Mare Nostrum*, our sea, and considered all that bordered it fair game for his vision of a Fascist empire. Defeats in Greece, North Africa, and the British naval victories in the Mediterranean, ended that dream. And with the invasion of Italy, his empire ambitions turned into a nightmare."

"I remember somewhere, Robert, that his government turned against him, or did I just make this up?"

"Good memory... On July 24, 1943 the Italian government, really the Fascist Grand Council that was the supreme constitutional authority of Italy, revolted against Il Duce. He was dismissed out of hand. Mussolini was stripped of power. Later that day, he was arrested. Within a short time, he was transported to a hotel high in the mountains of Abruzzi. This lavish hotel, once used by the rich and powerful, was his new home, where he was to live under house arrest. It was thought to be impregnable to any rescue attempt by his hard core followers."

"Which means, I'm assuming, he was rescued?"

Samuels could only smile. Lynn was a quick study. Not much got by her.

"Right out of Hollywood. German commandoes flew into the area in gliders and surprised Mussolini's guards. He was whisked away to Munich, and then, following a deal with Hitler, was brought back to Italy. While in Germany, he had agreed to Hitler's suggestion. He would return to Italy and control a small section in the north under German protection. What else could he do? Hitler was calling the shots. His empire was now reduced to a mere sliver of Italy. His historic pizza was down to a single slice. Anyway, he ruled his fragmentary empire with his mistress, Claretta Pietacci."

"Sounds like a Hollywood script."

"With a bitter ending. Eventually, both the American army and Italian partisans closed in on his dwindling realm. He was caught with his mistress by partisans when trying to escape into Germany. The partisans shot them on April 28, 1945. Later, their bodies were hung, head downward, in the Piaza Loreto in Milan. A few months later, Hitler would share a bullet with his mistress, and the Fascist combo was kaput."

"Ugly. Let's get back to Rita."

"Intrigued?"

"Completely."

The Liberty Station and Confusion

"Rita's show became part of *Liberty Station*, a German military propaganda unit. Rita was treated like a celebrity and broadcasted from a castle near Como. It was a live show, which suggested Germans were still enjoying a rich lifestyle, notwithstanding the ravages of war. There was laughter and the clinking of wine glasses, and good food all around. The whole point was to encourage the dog-faced GI to go home. Of course, that didn't happen. Troops got used to hearing the enchanting, sexy voice of a mysterious Italian babe. Naturally, they didn't know she was well along in her pregnancy, compliments of a boyfriend who loved her and then went off to war to die. The baby would be born on December 15, 1944.

"Life and death."

"War, it seems, sanctions both. As to Rita, she made her final show on April 25, 1945."

"Then, Robert, she took off."

"But not like a bat out of hell. With her baby, she boarded a train to Milan. She was met at the station by a relative. He took her to the family home in Turin. She resided there until her capture."

"Seems straight forward. Flee, hide, get caught, have a trial, and go to jail. Right, dear?"

"Wrong. Her capture led to confusion. The American press and the military police made a foolish announcement. They said Rita was Axis Sally, and that it was her voice GI's heard at Anzio and on the road to Rome. At that time, military intelligence had no conception that there were two women, each calling herself Axis Sally. The Army's newspaper, the *Stars and Stripes*, got into the picture with a picture of Rita before a radio with her baby cradled beside her. The picture ended up in the *New York Times* (January 1945). That did it, of course. The mystique of Axis Sally was gone. She looked like any ordinary mom. A million GI fantasies imploded."

"I wonder how Mildred Gillars felt about all this, Robert?"

"She didn't know about it. But we can speculate based on her later reaction. She was ticked. An impostor had stolen her celebrity spot and then destroyed her celebrity status. Mildred, a former dancer, actress, singer and extremely attractive in her own right, was competing with what some called a 'cross-eyed, bow-legged' woman broadcaster. It was too much for Mildred. She had great legs. She had stage presence. She was a star. And, because of what Rita broadcasted, Mildred herself might be blamed."

"Still, Rita did go to jail, didn't she?"

"Well, yes and no."

"Great, Robert, that cleared everything up."

"How about a refill?"

"And you'll clarify?"

"Absolutely."

Reprieve

"First, the Zucca family hired a New York lawyer, Max Spekle, to defend Rita. Her father, Constantine, wasn't about to let his daughter be tried for treason. There was, he thought, an important legal issue to be considered. Rita's lawyer would bring this issue before the Justice Department. The old man was smart. He knew the public wanted a pound of flesh from Rita for tormenting and teasing American soldiers. He found a way to make sure that didn't happen. She would never be tried for treason. Indeed, she couldn't be tried for treason in an American court. How could that be? Very simply Rita had protected herself without knowing it. When she renounced her American citizenship and became an Italian citizen, she put herself beyond the reach of American justice. Treason, as defined by our Constitution, only applies to American citizens. Rita had legally renounced her American citizenship. The legal documents substantiated her attorney's claim. She was beyond the writ of American law. With that in mind, the Justice Department closed the case against Rita."

"She got away with it."

"Not exactly, Lynn. On September 30, 1945, an Italian court found her guilty of collaboration, and she was sentenced to four years and five months in an Italian jail."

"Good."

"She only served nine months."

"Bad."

"The Italian government declared a general amnesty for collaborators in early 1946 and that, as they say, was the game."

"But I don't understand. Why didn't Mildred take this position to avoid a trial and prison sentence?"

"She couldn't."

"Because?"

"She never renounced her American citizenship. She always insisted she was an American citizen, just one who was working for a foreign radio station during the war. She was adamant that she loved America."

"Ironic, isn't it?"

"Looking back, yes."

"What happened to Rita?"

"I'm still researching that question," Samuels said with a big yawn.

"Tired dear?"

"The pillow is looking very attractive to this old guy."

"Continue at breakfast?"

"Sounds good to me."

"One Axis Sally at a time is enough for me, Robert."

"Me, too. How about a smooch and then bed?"

"Is that like a big kiss, mister?"

"Come here."

"Oops."

"Oops? What does oops mean?"

"I just remembered. A package came for you earlier today via UPS."

"There was a return address."

"Yes. Mailed a week ago."

"So?"

"It came from an Edna Mae Herrick of Columbus, Ohio. The package was marked LEGAL DOCUMENTS AND COURT TRANSCIPTS – HANDLE WITH CARE."

"Edna Mae," Samuels thought before breaking into a glowing smile, "you are something."

CHAPTER 7
THE FUGITIVE

<u>The UPS Package – The Next Morning</u>

"What's this?"

The sight Lynn Samuels was taking in almost blew her mind. Sitting at the kitchen table was her husband in an old rumbled white robe, which he had picked up on a cruise long ago to the Panama Canal. She could see he was still wearing his favorite pajamas with the blue and gold colors of CAL and cute little Bears scattered throughout the material running after footballs and basketballs. She assumed he was wearing his ancient slippers that knew him so well they could, she once thought, actually put themselves on. It was apparent he hadn't even stirred his hair, which resembled a dried out rumpled mop with hairs flying in every different direction. All in all, he made the term disheveled look good. But it didn't seem to matter to him this early morning. He was gazing intently at what appeared to be a batch of legal documents. So engrossed was he that she wasn't even sure he heard her. Looking further, she saw that the entire table was covered with multi-colored folders and all kinds of printed material. There was hardly room for his half-eaten bagel and cup of decaf coffee.

"Robert."

"You're up, Lynn."

"It is 7:00 a.m."

"Really?"

"How long have you been out here?"

"Since about 4 o'clock. Couldn't sleep."

"What's all this?"

"Remember the UPS package?"

"From Edna Mae."

"Yes. I've been looking at the contents. These are all documents related to Mildred Gillars' arrest, trial, and appeal. Edna Mae has been collecting stuff for years. She would have made great investigative reporter. Really fascinating stuff here."

"You've been reading this for three hours?"

"Yea."

"Unbelievable."

That was her husband, thought Lynn. Once his newspaper nose smelled a story, that was it. Goodbye, Robert."

"Grab a cup of coffee. *Mr. Coffee* is hooked up and perking."

"Thanks."

"Grab a bagel. I left one for you in the toaster."

"You certainly know how to treat a girl."

"And come and sit with me. I want to read something to you."

"Very romantic of you."

"I'll let that pass."

After draining *Mr. Coffee* and reheating a tired egg bagel, Lynn Samuels sat down.

"Okay, read."

"Preface first. Edna Mae included a letter with all these documents, and a book called *Radio Wars* by some Ohio State history professor."

"So?"

"She sent all of this a week before we met."

"Meaning?"

"Think about it, Lynn. She knew, it seems, that I would bite and become interested in her sister's case."

"And take it on."

"She gambled."

"For high stakes. What's in the letter, dear husband?"

"Much I was unaware of, that's what."

The Letter

Samuels hunted around for a moment before uncovering the folded letter in question from beneath an uneven stack of imposing *Xerox* printouts. He carefully unfolded the letter and began to read in a voice resonating with equal measures of disbelief and unresolved curiosity.

Dear Mr. Robert Samuels,

I trust the legal documents and book got to you in good shape. You will find them very helpful in researching my sister's case. Her name is Mildred Elizabeth Gillars. You will recognize her by another name, Axis Sally, the woman accused of treason against our country.

I believe these documents, taken as a whole, will provide you with a perspective you do not have at the moment about her and what she did during the Second World War. These documents will help you, I believe, in reaching more balanced conclusions with respect to Mildred's actions as a broadcaster for Radio Berlin and the trial and jail sentence she was forced to endure. Regardless, I am satisfied that you are the best person to pursue the goal of redeeming her in the eyes of her fellow citizens.

By the time this documents reach you, we will have talked at length, and you will know what I hope to accomplish concerning this matter. If all this sounds a little mysterious, I beg you to go along with an old lady's eccentric wishes. I assure you I am quite sane. All will be made clear shortly. I do apologize for any presumptuousness on my part in pulling you into this affair before we've even met in person. Frankly, I've nowhere else to turn.

"She signed off, Edna Mae Herrick, Ashtabula, Ohio. What do you think of that, Lynn?"

"I think Edna Mae put her bet on the right horse. At least for a time, I am very pleased that she will be the other woman in your life. But only for a short time, Robert... Catch my drift? Now I think we should get back to Axis Sally's arrest. The Berlin Axis Sally, that is."

"Right. Now where did I place my notebook?"

Samuels push piles of papers in every direction. He upended stacks of documents. All to no avail.

"What could I have done with my notebook?"
"Stand up, Robert."
"What?"
"Stand up. Don't argue with me."

Robert Samuels stood up as directed to reveal his notebook on the kitchen chair.

"How did you know?"
"I know you, my absent-minded Robert. You always sit on papers you don't want to lose. Now tell me everything."

Finding Axis Sally

Since the Roman Axis Sally, Rita, had been able to evade the Justice Department at first, American authorities redoubled their efforts to find her German counterpart. The prosecutorial mood to hammer the yet unfound Mildred was strong. Someone was going to have to pay for the vicious and treasonous statements made over the air, whether in Rome or Berlin. Only in this way could justice be applied. The most listened to female broadcaster of the war, the *Mistress of Ceremonies* on Radio Berlin who had tried to demoralize America's fighting men would not escape the long arm of Washington. What did it matter that American soldiers and flyers couldn't get enough of her sexy voice, pop music, and unabashed efforts at propaganda? What did it matter that American fliers listened to her on their bomb runs over Germany, only tuning her out to maintain radio silence when forced to? What did it matter that servicemen felt, paradoxically, less homesick by listening to this wicked woman? She would be caught, and she would pay.

To this end, the CIC (the Army Counter-Intelligence Corps} dispatched Hans Wintzen, a Special Agent, to search for the woman who would replace Rita Zucca as the poster face of Axis Sally in the minds of millions of Americans. He was an excellent choice. He was a born sleuth, a Sherlock Holmes from the new world. And the game was afoot. He was determined to bring this female Moriarty to justice. But where was she? Post-war Germany was a mess. Millions were on the move across the country attempting to reunite with their families. Returning soldiers were everywhere, displaced and disgruntled. Hunger stalked the streets. Housing was almost non-existent compared to pre-war Germany. War damage was everywhere. The black market flourished. Bureaucratic confusion within the new German police department compounded all efforts to locate anyone. And, of course, no one knew exactly who she was or what she looked like. It was like looking for the fabled pin in the ubiquitous haystack. Wintzen, good as he was, needed a break.

He got one right out of the *"wild blue yonder."*

"Our guys?"

"Yes. A B-17 pilot, Raymond Kurtz, came forward with the key to locating Mildred Gillars. He had been a POW after being shot down and captured. While in a prison camp, Mildred visited. He was told she was from Radio Berlin and had a show called *Midge at the Mike*. To some degree he recalled what she looked like. He was also told she had an alias, *Barbara Mome*. On the assumption that Mildred might still be using this alias, Wintzen had posters plastered all over occupied sectors of Berlin. He was hoping for another break. This was in August 1945. He wanted to catch her before Christmas. She would be a nice present for Uncle Sam.

"The CIC really didn't know who Axis Sally was or what she really looked like?"

"Correct, Lynn. Her broadcasts had been recorded each day throughout the war by the Federal Communication Commission in Silver Hill, Maryland, but no one had a name, or photograph. And remember, she never coined the name Axis Sally. She picked it up from the GI's who dubbed her with it. And Rita got it from her. Before that, Mildred always referred to herself as *Midge*. And another thing, No American POW witnessed her making broadcasts. And, at least at that time, no Radio Berlin employee had pointed the finger in her direction."

"So tell me. What happened?"

The Big Break

"The CIC got a tip on March 4, 1946 that Barbara Mome had been seen in the British sector. Wintzen, always a rationale thinker, reasoned that that this person was a fugitive from the law. Therefore, she had no identification papers to receive a rations book. She could only buy food on the black market. From that, he surmised, she would need cash. But how would she get the money? That would be a problem for anyone on the run. The banks were closed. Again, he reasoned, this Barbara

Mome had to be using her own money and anything else she had of value. She had to be selling property. But where what would she sell and to whom? He determined to check antique stores. This was one way of getting hard currency. Kind of like a pawn shop today, Property would be left on consignment. But which antique store? He made the decision to keep these shops in Berlin under constant supervision.

Weeks later, another tip came his way. A former neighbor stated that a "Barbara" had left some personal effects in a basement storeroom adjacent to her former apartment at 7 Bonnerstrasse. The building superintendent was questioned intently. What could the poor man do? The CIC, American military police, and German authorities were all over him. He revealed that an American woman had asked for her possessions to be stored away in a safe place once she had left her apartment for the last time. She left and this was done. Guided by the superintendent, the storeroom was searched. Mildred's cache was discovered. And what a discovery!"

"Don't keep me in suspense, Robert. What did they find?"

"You won't believe it."

"I'd like the opportunity to decide that."

"They found seven acetate records containing full programs that featured the voice of Axis Sally. If used in a future court trial, this would be damning evidence against Mildred. They also found an expired US passport. And it showed her real name, Mildred Elizabeth Gillars. It also contained a photograph. Now the search was really on."

"Go on."

"Wanted posters with Mildred's picture were plastered all over the British, French, and American sectors. The picture was not flattering. Rather than looking like every GI's dream girl, she looked more like a schoolmarm. The glamour was gone. The fantasies burst. The search picked up steam. A twenty-four-hour surveillance was established at places where Barbara Nome (really Mildred) was known to visit. German police helped in the stakeout. Tips came in suggesting she had been seen at various restaurant and beauty shops, and other businesses in the Kurfurstendamm section of Berlin. The information coming in was slowly narrowing down the area where she might be. What was needed was one more really good tip."

"You're stalling, Robert."

"For dramatic tension."

"I'm tense. Want me to be dramatic?"

"Okay."

"A small table was found by government agents in a antique shop. It belonged to Mildred. It was a small shop, almost hidden from view on a side street. Under pressure, the storeowner gave the name of the person who brought in the table. That person was soon interrogated and, under extreme pressure, he admitted selling the item for Mildred. He also gave her present address."

"The circle was closing, Robert."

"Right. Mildred had been a fugitive for over eleven months. Always on the run, she had eluded the Germany police and the CIC. But her luck had come to an end. It was now known that she was living in a rented room in the British sector. On March 15, 1946, Mildred returned home late at night, only to find an American soldier in her living room. He was holding a loaded revolver. He was pointing it at her. A moment later, Special Agent Robert Abeles said, "Miss Gillars, you are under arrest.""

Mildred's only response after the initial shock of arrest was to take one photograph from the room as she was escorted out. It was a photo of Max Otto Koischwitz, her former teacher at Hunter College in New York, and her supervisor at Radio Berlin. She was permitted to take the photograph. It would be many years before she would be a free woman again.

Wintzen had finally caught his fugitive, though a little late for Christmas.

"That's one heck of a story."

"It didn't take long before Mildred realized she was in real trouble. Partially, she brought the house down own herself when she told reporters at a hastily arranged press conference, 'my conscience is clear, and I don't have anything to hide. Everything I did, I did of my own free will. Later, in response to what she had said, another reporter told her, "Well, I just would like to tell you, Sally, that we are all looking forward to your hanging and it is going to be some field day in Washington."

Hanging and death were shadows that followed her from this point on. Unlike Rita, she didn't have a father to hire her an attorney, nor did she have a child to soften attitudes. She was alone, an American citizen who had committed treason by broadcasting for Radio Berlin. From this point on, it would be Gillars vs. the United States Government."

"Unfair odds."

"She was her own worst enemy."

"Why do you say that, Robert?"

Mildred's Defense Strategy

"She refused to follow Rita's strategy, which was to state that her collaboration with the Nazis was not political, that she was not a Fascist, that she was not a Nazi. Rather, Rita claimed that a need to survive drove her to Radio Rome. On the other hand, Mildred contended that, though she wasn't a Nazi or committed Fascist, she was correct in criticizing the now martyred Roosevelt for bringing America into the war on the side of Great Britain. And she further implied that dead American soldiers had sacrificed their lives for nothing. By defeating Germany, they had ensured a Communist victory in Europe. She then added that industrialists, bankers, and Jews were the real beneficiaries of the war. She couldn't have said more to firmly plant American public opinion against her. Unlike Rita, she wouldn't be permitted to just disappear into history."

"But Mildred couldn't have known what Rita was doing."

"Right, Lynn. Each woman followed her own star."

"Mildred never should have propagandized."

"No question about that."

"No good could come of it."

"Not completely, Lynn."

Lynn looked at her husband. He had that look on his face. The one that hinted, "I know something., Lynn." She hated it when he did that.

"Okay. Spill it."

Ham Operators

"Private First Class Richard E. Kells isn't a name most people would recognize beyond his own family and circle of friends. He was just an ordinary guy who was captured by the Germans. He was taken to a nearby command post for interrogation. While there, he was given a postcard and told to fill it out with a message for his family. This he did. He spent the next five months as a POW, eventually joining thousands of POW's from all over Europe at Luckenwalde, just south of Berlin. A circus tent had been erected to house the POW's. On April 22, 1945, the Russians liberated the camp. A few days later, he was turned over to American authorities, who sent him to *Camp Lucky Strike*, the departure point for Americans going home from the port of Le Havre, France. Once back in America, he hitchhiked from Springfield, Massachusetts to his hometown of Greenfield.

It was there that he discovered something amazing. Unknown to him, the information on his postcard had been read and then broadcasted from Radio Berlin. The broadcaster was Mildred Gillars. The information was sent over the airwaves and ham operators from Canada and the United States picked up the message and his home address. These unknown ham operators then sent letters and telegrams to Kellis' mother explaining that her son was okay. She received over a dozen messages. Some of them might break your heart.

"We heard last Friday night about him (Kells). Hope you hear direct from your boy soon."

Another family wrote, "We have a son in the war and we have had no personal message from him except his capture notice, and so we know how eagerly you must be waiting for any news, however meager, of your loved one."

One ham operator wrote, "This makes the 3312 POW messages of various types that I have relayed in recent months."

"See what I mean, Lynn."

"Such beautiful messages from complete strangers."

"That's the irony, isn't it? If Axis Sally hadn't broadcasted the names, serial numbers, and hometowns of captured Americans, along with their short messages, thousands of American families wouldn't have known about their sons."

"Strange how things turn out."

"What are you getting at, Robert?"

"After Gillars was brought to the United States and placed on trial, some American ham operators and POW families actually solicited support for her, for Axis Sally, on the basis of what they called *humanitarian work*, providing information about their loved ones. Of course, it was to no avail. She would eventually be convicted of treason."

"How do you know all this, Robert?"

"Good memory and I'm a reporter."

"My husband who couldn't find his own notebook?"

"Selective memory."

"Well, Mr. Reporter, what are you going to do now?"

"I need to place a long distance call to Ashtabula, Ohio."

"What are you going to tell Edna Mae?"

"I'm going to bring her up to speed and then quote from one of the ham operators…"

"I hope this news make the days brighter."'

CHAPTER 8
THE CHALLENGE

Professor Jonas Morgan

"You've worked it all out, Robert?"

"In theory, yes Lynn. In practice, who knows?"

Robert Samuels and his wife, Lynn, were in heavy traffic as they, slug-like, crawled down 19th Avenue toward San Francisco State to keep an early morning appointment with Professor Jonas Morgan, who was the head of the Journalism Department at the college. Fortunately, they had left early, always one of Samuels' better habits. Better to be five minutes early than one minute late was his cardinal principle unless, of course, housework was involved. In that case, he had all the time in the world.

"A lot has been accomplished in one week."

"Couldn't have done it without you, Lynn."

"I know."

Lynn Samuels had been a great help once her husband informed Edna Mae of his decision and what his plans entailed. It all began with a simple declaration on her part.

"Robert, I want to assist you with this project."

"Good meals and a ready drink. What more could I ask for?"

"You miss my point. I want to get out of the house, so to speak, this time. I want to be an active part of the research. I want to be involved from the get-go. What do you think? And before you answer, remember that my minor at CAL was history to go along with my major in English. That's a good combo, isn't it?"

"Something more than just editing my stuff?"

"And correcting your imprecise spelling."

"That's harsh. I'm usually within a couple of letters."

"Just not the right ones. So what do you think?"

"This is really important to you?"

"Extremely. I've taken a liking to Edna Mae and her cause. Maybe it's the woman thing, one lady battling the world, trying to set things straight for her sister. It just feels right for me to be in on this."

"This women's thing won't get in the way of objectivity?"

"As you always say, the facts will determine everything."

After many years of marriage, Samuels knew when to bend. It was obvious Lynn wanted in. She wanted to be part of the research, the daily grind to decipher the facts, and the mental footwork of figuring out what it all meant. One other factor, of course, helped him to accommodate Lynn. He really did need another hand. The project was too much for his small research team.

"Consider yourself on the team."

"You've got something juicy for me to pick at?"

"Two women."

"Tell me more."

"One you already know. Iva Toguri... You'll need to visit her in Chicago. I've all ready arranged with her for your trip."

"You what?"

"I was going to ask you."

"You set this up before our little talk?"

"Guilty, I'm afraid."

"Presumptuous of you!"

"I needed your assistance."

"Okay, I'm delighted. Now why Iva?"

"She spent time at Alderson Prison with Mildred Gillars."

"I'm aware of that. Mildred's name came up when Iva discussed how racial prejudice influenced the public toward the two convicted traitors."

"Iva didn't tell me everything. There's more. She'll speak to you in person, not on the phone, not by mail."

"I'm on it. Now what about the other woman?"

"Jane Anderson."

"Never heard of her."

"She has something in common with Mildred."

"Oh."

"As an American, she also broadcasted from Radio Berlin during the war."

"Another impostor?"

"You'll find out, won't you."

Slowly, the traffic thinned out, and San Francisco State loomed ahead. Samuels knew the school well. Thanks to Dr. Jonas Morgan, he was a part-time instructor at the college. Indeed, prompted by Morgan, who wanted journalism students actively working in the field, not laboring behind a textbook and windy lectures, Samuels had tapped his first class to assist in researching Iva Toguri's story. He was doing so again with two star students, Rita Howard and Ron Siegel. After parking and placing their *Faculty Permit to Park* sticker in the windshield, they headed up to see the professor.

"I need to warn you, Lynn."

"Too late. I already married you."

"About Morgan."

"He flirts?"

"He's all Navy, even though retired."

"Okay."

"He speaks Navy."

"That's a new language?"

"You'll see."

They entered the Journalism Building and soon found themselves in the Department Chair's office.

"My God, it's good to see you again matey! Ah, and this must be the skipper," Morgan said with a hearty smile, as he wrapped a large arm around Lynn's waist and escorted her to a comfortable looking leather chair, while letting Samuels navigate for himself.

"Professor Morgan, I've heard so much about you."

"Jonas, please, and don't believe any scuttlebutt coming from the riff-raft I must put up with. Pirates, all of them, all plundering fame and fortune around me at my expense… Skulduggery everywhere I look. I don't know why I put up with it. It's a good thing I have my own Scapa Flow, this office, to protect myself from these privateers. Isn't that right, Robert?"

"You're under constant attack from these bootjacks, the bean counters who sap your department of funds and pillage your efforts to turn young recruits into crackerjack reporters. They botch your efforts. Scurvy is too good for them."

"Aye, Robert, you're a good shipmate."

Lynn could hardly believe her ears. So this is what Robert meant by Navy talk. She felt as if she had entered the world of Long John Silver. And looking around Professor Morgan's office only reinforced that view. Everywhere there were reminders of America's nautical past: photographs of sailing ships, modern warships, and crew pictures. A collection of swords, shining brilliantly, covered one entire wall along with 19th-century pistols, all affixed to pieces of old wood. On another wall were ships flags meaningless to Lynn, but important to Morgan. In the midst of all this were countless file cabinets, neatly labeled, and bookcases, on each shelf with books in their very precise place. But it was Morgan's desk that really caught Lynn's attention. It was made of heavy dark wood and highly polished. Rather than being rectangular in shape, as one might expect, it was shaped like a ship's bow. Seen from above, it looked like a triangle with Morgan, the obvious Captain, sitting at the base. The desk was barren of everything except for a clock with a miniature anchor attached to it and one file folder.

Lynn found herself thinking that the office was shipshape and ready for action. She almost expected Black Beard's men to come rushing in, brandishing swords, and with knives drawn. Another thought quickly emerged and tugged at her. Who is this man I married? A former sailor, yes, but a devotee of "seadogs?"

"Do you two always talk this way?" Lynn asked with a slight smile.
"We walk the deck together, dear lady, bow to stern."
"Port to starboard," Samuels added.
"Guns always manned," Morgan said. "Manned and ready for the brigands. You never know when they'll appear on the horizon prepared to run a cutlass through you, or leave you marooned on some forsaken desolate island."
"Battle flags hoisted, Lynn."
"Cutting through the waves, full speed ahead," Morgan announced.
"Until we're in a safe harbor," Samuels suggested.
"Aye, Robert."

Lynn started to laugh. She couldn't help herself. Two older men, each Navy, still happily sailing the high seas.

"There must be a reason why we're here, right Robert? Please share it with your loving wife before there's mutiny in the ranks."
"The skipper grows impatient, Robert."
"I guess we should get to it. We don't want a mutiny on our hands."

Wartime Propaganda

Professor Morgan retrieved a folder on his desk, saying as he did, "Cannon fodder for our discussion."

"You compiled what I need?"

"Absolutely. You came to the right man. I was in Naval Intelligence during the war. And no jokes about that NI being an oxymoron, my lovely woman. I know about propaganda."

"Which is why we're here, Lynn. We can't reach conclusions about Mildred Gillars' alleged treacherous broadcasts until we have a working definition of propaganda. Jonas is an expert in this field."

"Robert is quite right. Not only did I track it during the war, I also created it for our side. It's a necessity of war. Got to get the folks to support the war effort. Let's begin with this. All combatants engaged in propaganda during the war, which was fought with guns and constant radio bulletins, bombers in the air and posters on the ground encouraging morale and greater production. If submarines prowled under the sea, newspaper censorship was everywhere on terra firma keeping evil ideas submerged, and appropriate views afloat."

"What American, then, do we look to, Samuels asked, for an understanding of propaganda and its uses?"

"Not an American, a German. In fact, the German, Adolf Hitler."

"Hitler," Lynn found herself, almost shouting.

Opening up his folder, Morgan said, "He was the expert. Believe me, the rest of us were mere students playing catch up. Permit me to read what he wrote in his best seller, *Mein Kampf.*"

Propaganda must always address itself to the broad masses of the people. All propaganda must be presented in a popular form and must fix its intellectual level so as not to be above the heads of the least intellectual of those to whom it is directed. The art of propaganda consists precisely in being able to awaken the imagination of the public through an appeal to their feelings, in finding the appropriate psychological form that will arrest the attention and appeal to the hearts of the national masses. The broad masses of the people are not made up of diplomats or professors of public jurisprudence nor simply of people who are able to form reasoned judgment in given cases, but a vacillating crowd of human children who are constantly wavering between one idea and another.

Propaganda must not investigate the truth objectively... It must present only that aspect of the truth, which is favorable to its own side. The receptive powers of the masses are very restricted, and their understanding is feeble. On the other hand, they quickly forget. Such being the case, al effective propaganda must be confined to a few bare essentials and those must be expressed as far as possible in stereotyped formulas. These slogans should be persistently repeated until the very last individual has come to grasp the idea that has been put forward."

"That's it, all you need to know about propaganda. Hitler nailed it. Propaganda in its simplest form is a message the government wants you to believe, either something good about your country, or something bad about the other guy."

"Certainly, Americans are not like that," Lynn said. "Masses to be led."

"My lovely lady, if only that were true."

"Little difference between the mustached one and Madison Avenue advertising", Samuels commented, "or for that matter, the way presidential elections are run."

"The process is the same. Only the message differs," Jonas added, "though the goals are the same. Win or sell, it all amounts to the same thing. Get your message out. Trample the other guy's message."

"Jonas can be a little cynical, Lynn, when it comes to this topic," Samuels said, turning to Lynn. "He knows how the game is played."

"As do you, my fine newspaperman."

"Jonas and I walk the same planks, Lynn."

"I can't believe you two. You really think Americans are influenced by propaganda? That they are unthinking? That they can be seduced by words?"

"Unfortunately, yes," Jonas said. But permit me to add a point, really a little history."

The Radio – Instrument of Power

"In the 1930's technology provided an instrument by which Nazi Germany, using Hitler's propaganda strategy, would prove instrumental in convincing an entire people to rush headlong into a tragedy of incalculable destruction. The technology was the radio. Dr. Joseph Goebbels, who was the head of Germany's Ministry of Public Enlightenment and Propaganda, was a master "spin-doctor." He once said, "I consider radio to be the most crucial instrument for influencing the masses." He also claimed that radio was the "eighth great power." With that in mind, Germany embarked on a plan under the Nazi Regime to provide over 70% of the German population with radios by the time Hitler invaded Poland. The radios were in addition to loudspeakers in public places and workplaces. The regime's message was delivered 24/7, and you couldn't get away from it. But that's not the end of it. Goebbels provided funds to radio manufacturers, and required them to build cheaper receivers, so that the radios couldn't pick up non-German broadcasts, especially those emanating from Britain or the United States. Beyond that, the government enacted a law to stop people from listening to non-German broadcasts. If caught doing so, they could be executed.

"The background to all this involved the Reichs-Rundfunk-Gesellschaft (RRG), which, loosely translated, means the *State Broadcasting Company*. This was the national network of German regional public broadcasting companies on the air from 1925 until 1945. RRG broadcasts were receivable in all parts of the country and, once Hitler took power, were used exclusively for Nazi propaganda. The RRG broadcasted from the Haus des Rundfunks in Berlin, the world's first self-contained broadcasting center. One department of the

RRG was the Deutschlandsender broadcast that aired live programs and news long-wave from powerful transmitters. Eventually, the RRG grew to 17 departments with over 2,000 employees. The RRG also divided the world up into zones for broadcasting purposes. One was called the USA Zone. High-powered transmitters covered all of Europe, and an immense 100 kilowatt transmitter was built to reach the US and South America. German shortwave radio reached most of the world around the clock in twelve different languages.

"It was, of course, necessary to have well-qualified and competent broadcasters. In time, one employee of RRG, or what others simply called Radio Berlin, would, by fate, chance, or choice, become an employee for the USA Zone. That person was Mildred Elizabeth Gillars." "It's almost like radio made Nazi Germany," Lynn said.

"The message airing made the regime," Jonas responded. "And the fact that people were predisposed to accept the message, especially anti-Semitic statements. And, of course, extreme censorship of books, newspapers, and radio conditioned a population to believe the message."

"The radio was important in the US, too," Samuels interjected. "FDR was our first radio President. Remember his 'fireside chats?' With his charming aristocratic voice and preeminent optimism that resonated in his talks, he communicated with Americans as if he were sitting in their living rooms. By use of the radio, he rallied the public in the struggle to combat the Great Depression, and later in the war against the Axis Powers."

"He was a Navy man through and through," Morgan quipped. "He took hold of the rudder of government and steered a steady course through shark-infested waters of ultra-conservative resistance to the New Deal. And when war came, his hands were always on the compass taking us in the right direction."

"It was good to have him on the bridge," Samuels added.

"I'm glad that can't happen in America," Lynn interrupted this love fest for President Roosevelt, "controlling people for evil ends."

""Beautiful lady," Jonas rejoined, "don't be so sure. During both world wars, along with other belligerents, America waged her own propaganda war. I should know. I helped to prepare some of the campaigns. Let me explain."

Poster Propaganda

"In 1942, President Roosevelt created the Office of War Information (OWI), my employer for a short time. This agency was involved in the dissemination of war information and propaganda, and all to often, it was difficult to discern a distinction between the two. The OWI used many tools to communicate to the American people including Hollywood movie studios, radio stations, and the print press. Curiously, the United States used posters more than any other type of propaganda. Over 300,000 different designs were printed during the war, or more than all the other nations at war. A number of themes were emphasized by these posters, including conservation, production, secrecy, and efforts to boast morale. Mostly, the posters were placed in post offices, railroad and bus stations, schools, restaurants, and retail stores. To a great extent, the American posters were mostly positive in their messages. They focused on patriotism, duty, and tradition, and less on fueling hatred for other people, though, of course, there was some of that. Scenes showing war casualties and/or battlefield images were in the minority. Unlike Germany and Japan, US posters were not designed by the government, but by artists who received no compensation for their work. The government simply held competitions for artists to submit their designs. The government, however, made the final choices.

An interesting sidelight was that private companies developed advertising campaigns, which supported the war while keeping their product names before the public. This was true even if the companies had no products to sell because of the conversion to wartime production. The OWI and the War Advertising Board supervised such efforts. For example, car manufacturers such as GM and Ford that retooled for war making tanks, trucks, and planes took out ads showing their efforts. Two companies in particular connected their products in some way with the war effort. Coca-Cola depicted its soda being drunk by defense workers and members of the armed forces. Lucky Strike suggested the change from green to white in its packaging of cigarettes. This saved bronze needed for the war effort. Its sales skyrocketed."

"I never knew posters played such a role," Lynn said as Jonas was catching his breath."

"Permit me to show three examples, nice lady."

Jonas brought out a long cardboard tube. He withdrew from the tube a batch of long rolled paper held together by two tight rubber bands. After removing the bands, he unrolled the paper to show a host of American war posters, circa 1940's.

"One of my little habits, innocent enough, I think, collecting posters. Here let's look at this."

The poster shown illustrated a battle torn American flag at half-mast flowing in the winds of history. Above the flag was a short quote from President Lincoln's speech at Gettysburg: *"We here highly resolve that these dead shall not have died in vain."* Beneath the flag were a few words, all recognizable to Americans: *"December 7th."* A second poster encouraged the sale of war bonds. With planes above Uncle Sam and soldiers below, the message was clear: help pay for the war. A third poster connected children to the conflict through the use of comic books. In this case the comic book was the *4 Favorites*, and they are shown supporting an animated war bond that was knocking over Hitler, Mussolini, and the Japanese Emperor.

"These are just a few examples," Jonas said.
"But good ones," Samuels piped in with relish.
"Jonas, where's the one for the girls?"
"Yes. Forgive me for overlooking it. Such remiss. I should be thrown into the brig. Where is it? I'm sure I have it. Ah, here..."

Jonas rolled out perhaps the most famous poster of the war. It showed a young woman in blue work clothes with her sleeves rolled up and one muscular arm bent. Holding her hair down and in place was a red and white bandana. The caption was: *"We Can Do It."* The poster was created by the Westinghouse Company to celebrate and encourage its large group of female employees. The young woman pictured was Geraldine Doyle. She was 17-years old. The poster was closely related with the mythology of *"Rosie the Riveter,"* who built tanks, ships, and guns on the assembly line throughout the country.

"That's my gal," Lynn said with obvious pride.

"As well she should be," Jonas chimed in with enthusiasm.

"Only 17?" Samuels stated. "Quite a lady."

"You know a little about propaganda now, but not, I'm afraid, your main problem concerning Mildred Gillars," Jonas reminded Samuels and his wife.

"What that?" Lynn questioned.

"Disproving she was guilty of treachery by broadcasting on Radio Berlin. That's the juggernaut you fend with, my girl. Not an easy thing to do. And not just because of the verdict already rendered. You're dealing with the legal nature of treason itself."

"I don't understand," Lynn responded.

"Permit me to illuminate. Though I'm not a constitutional scholar, I do have a few pebbles of jurisprudence wisdom."

Defining Treason

"Our Constitution delineates both a definition of treason and the four elements composing such an action. The definition is simple enough:

Treason against the United States shall consist only in levying War against them, or, in adhering to their Enemies, giving them aid and comfort.

"The first element of the crime is that the treasonable act must be *overt*. The second element states that *two witnesses* must give testimony to the act. The third element must show an *understandable intent* to betray the United States. To a large measure these first three elements are objective. For example, if you sabotage a shipyard or torture American POW's, that is overt. Broadcasting enemy propaganda falls under this heading too. Two witnesses... What could be more objective unless, of course, perjury is involved as it was in Tokyo Rose's case? Intent is usually related to the first element, the overt act.

"The problem is element four, *"giving aid and comfort to the enemy."* The Supreme Court has reasoned as follows:

The "very minimum function that an overt act must perform in a treason prosecution is that it shows sufficient action by the accused in its setting, to sustain a finding that the accused actually gave aid and comfort to the enemy."

"So what does that mean? The first three elements are not distinct and separated from the context in which they take place. Alone, one element might not be sufficient to prove treason. But together, again within the context of the time and place in which they occurred, a case for treason can be built. And this is what the Justice Department did concerning Axis Sally. *"Aid and comfort"* were built on this concept. The Court precedent for this was *Cramer v. United States (1950).*

"Admiral, I'm at a loss. What's this case about?"

"Thanks for the promotion, Mrs. Samuels, but I'm a mere officer in 'this man's Navy. As to the case, I will right your ship.

"Anthony Cramer was a German-born naturalized citizen, a mechanic if I remember correctly. He knew two other Germans, Werner Thiel and Edward Kerling. Apparently, they were in the country to sabotage war industries, or any target of value to the American military. Their mission was a failure. They were arrested and Cramer, because of his association with them, was also indicted and convicted. The penalty: 45 years in prison and a fine of $10.000. Judge Henry W. Goddard didn't fool around. Cramer appealed to the Court of Appeals, but his conviction was upheld. He then appealed to the US Supreme Court where the case was decided on November 8, 1945."

"And?"

"The Court, dear lady, decided 5-4 to overturn the jury verdict."

"Why?"

"Good woman, right to the main question, which Justice Robert Jackson dealt with: 'the constitution is clear in its definition of treason. It is limited to the waging of war, or giving material assistance to an enemy. For the majority, the government failed to demonstrate that this was the case. Indeed, the prosecution could only show an association and not that Cramer had provided 'aid and comfort.' Association was insufficient to convict Creamer for treason."

"How is this related to Axis Sally?"

"The government would have to show more than an association. If it could then treasonable behavior might be shown. It's all in Article III of the Constitution"

"Your challenge is to somehow find a way to undo the jury's decision that "aid and comfort" to Nazi Germany were provided by Axis Sally. It won't be easy. Mitigating circumstances have an outside chance, but I wouldn't bet on it. The jury sifted through a great deal of evidence. and the US Court of Appeals upheld their decision. Perhaps, if you could find something new.

"Robert, can we do that?"

"We can try? But as Jonas pointed out…"

"It won't be easy."

"Right."

"Permit me to add another point which I've hesitated to bring up. Forgive the imagery, but you two are headed into formidable headwinds. Those of us in the Navy remember all too vividly the deaths wrought by the German U-boats in the unforgiving North Atlantic. I, for one, am not sympathetic toward the Nazi Regime or Axis Sally, whom I believe did commit treason. As you delve into this story and articles are published in the *Chronicle,* there will be a response from those who suffered at the hands of the Nazis. They will not be delighted in your efforts. My second point is this. Mildred Gillars will again become a public figure. For some, she will always be an infamous figure. Does she really want this negative celebrity status so many years later? Tread carefully here Robert and Lynn. This is a short plank for all of you. These are deep waters."

"What do you think, Robert?"

"Much to consider."

Samuels and his wife were returning home with a great deal on their minds. The traffic was light, but not their conversation.

"I think I need to speak with Mildred Gillars."

"When?"

"After the team has researched for at least two months, and we have something to work with. Then, on that basis, we'll decide to forge ahead or just drop the whole enterprise. If it's a go, we'll contact Mildred for her blessings."

"If she doesn't want us to continue?"

"We'll stop."

"It's a good team you've put together, dear husband."

"Pirates all."

"Dear God, don't start that business again."

"Two former students, each bored to death at their part time jobs, and each within a semester of their graduate degrees. Sea worthy mates, all."

"That's our team?"

"Well, there's you and I, too, Lynn."

"How short is that plank Jonas was alluding to?"

"One misstep and we're with Davy Jones."

CHAPTER 9
THE UNHAPPY SKEPTIC

<u>The Upset Reporter – The Next Day</u>

"Damn it! Damn it to all hell!"

Lynn Samuels heard the words. But had they really come from Robert's office? And on his day off...

"Damn woman."

Assuming that Robert wasn't referring to her, Lynn dropped her basket of laundry by the washer/dryer combo in the basement of their home and eased toward the half-closed door to Robert's bunker, which is how she described his hideout. Like many homes in San Francisco, first the cement basement is built, or what folks call a garage in other parts of the country. Then comes the residence part of home, usually one story with two to four bedrooms. In their case, since they had a two-bedroom bungalow, room space was always at a premium, especially when you have two kids. Because of that, they had built two rooms in the basement, which provided a room for Samuels and one for their son, Matt. For Matt, of course, that was great. He didn't have to share space with the *Chevy*, gardening tools, cardboard boxes containing precious items, which hadn't been perused in years, bikes, athletic equipment, and one large container with the most indispensible item in Western Civilization, rolls of stacked toilet paper just in case the country went to hell, and a shortage resulted. Samuels was a bit paranoid about this. Next to that toilet paper was a small carton, always at least half full. It contained an emergency supply of *Chapin and Gore* blended whiskey. And finally, there was the washer/dryer combo, newly bought from Sears, which condemned the clothesline and pin to near obscurity.

"Damn woman!"

There is was again, an agitated voice.

Lynn peeked into her husband's office. He was standing in the middle of the room, still wearing his rag-tag pajamas with grinning CAL bears adorning his night garb, and now, apparently, his day clothes at 11 o'clock in the morning. But she really couldn't blame him. It was his day off, sort of. It was Friday and he was taking a work/sick leave day off from the *Chronicle*. It was a deal he had worked out with his editor. In order to research Axis Sally, he needed time away from the presses. He would take Fridays to give him a three-day period to work on Mildred Gillars' story. Of course, he still had to get his regular weekly stuff in on time.

Very much like Professor Morgan's office, Robert's room was ship shape, everything in its place, neat and tidy. What was it with these Navy guys? Facing the enemy in mortal combat was no problem, but an unkempt room threw them into a tizzy. Nerves of steel with guns going bang was okay. A book out of place, and it was Pearl Harbor. Maybe, thought Lynn, it was their steady diet of beans and coffee that caused this behavior. It certainly wasn't her cooking.

The only exception to this was the temporary mess that hounded Samuels when he was researching, or when he was sitting on something important.

"Damn, damn, damn…"

Lynn knocked on the door and went in saying, "Well, Robert, with all the *dam's* I'm hearing, either you're the new director of the TVA or the devil has taken up residence in your den. Which, my dear, is it?"

"I should be so lucky."

"The Tennessee Valley Authority?"

"The long-tailed one."

"Really? The Devil's in this room, my God? Want to share?"

"No."

"Playing hard to get, are we? Come on. The laundry can wait. The Devil sounds so much more fun than a box of *Tide*."

Samuels paced around the room before answering. Truthfully, he did want to unload what was bugging him, but, at the same time, he didn't want to warp Lynn's day. On the other hand, she was entitled to know what the damn problem was, wasn't she?

"Have a seat."

"That bad."

"Worse."

"Give."

Lynn sat down on a hard wooden chair, the only type Robert permitted in his lair, while he took the other one after first grabbing two *Diet Cokes* from his portable mini-refrigerator. The man was all heart.

The Jewish Question

"Well, Robert? You've plied me with drink. Now what's going on?"

"In a nutshell, I've been going over one of Mildred's statements during her trial, and things just don't make sense."

"What…"

"She said, she had no idea about the oppression of Jews while she was at Radio Berlin, including the death houses in the concentration camps."

"Many Germans said that, Robert."

"She wasn't just any German, even if by proxy. She was an expatriate and a witness to history. She was living in the Third Reich-world from 1934 through the Russian takeover of Berlin in1945. She worked for a guy, Max Otto Koischitz, at Radio Berlin. He had an in with the 'big boys,' especially the one and only Dr. Joseph Goebbels, a sociopath with a doctorate in death, and in charge of propaganda as you know. Max Otto was also her lover, and her former professor when she attended Hunter College in New York. They lived together in Berlin unless his wife was in town. Mildred worked at the hub of Nazi propaganda. She had to hear things. She lived in Berlin. How could she have not noticed what was going on?"

"She's lying, you think?"

"Or in some deep water denial, Lynn."

"Either way, what?"

"Either way, it makes it difficult to take her side in all this."

"You're not quitting on Edna Mae?"

"Of course not. Edna Mae sent this stuff to me. It's just difficult to go all out for her sister, especially after what I've been researching this week."

"That's why the damns?"

"Yes."

"Well, tell me all. Make me an unhappy skeptic, too."

"Let's start in 1935."

"In 1935, prodded by Hitler, the government passed the *Nuremberg Laws,* which essentially stated that (1) no Jew could be a German citizen as ordinarily understood; (2) Jews couldn't vote; (3) Jews couldn't participate in political activities; and (4) Jews couldn't hold political office. This was the beginning of a process of exclusion and isolation, which ultimately would lead to the *final solution,* what today we call *genocide,* a word that had to be created to define the premeditated attempt to exterminate entire nations and races. It was a modern form of barbarism, a nation-state using science and technology to kill civilians, Jews in particular, on an assembly-line basis. The techniques used to build a million V.W.'s were harnessed to exterminate perhaps as many as 12,000,000 people, men, woman, and children in gas ovens, torture chambers, and mass graves. This barbarism forced almost 7,000,000 people into forced labor camps. This was a reversion by a civilized people to some dark past on an unheard of scale. The 20th Century descended into a new Dark Ages. This barbarism was what we later called *'crimes against humanity.'*

"The Nuremberg Laws and all that followed came right out of Hitler's autobiography, *Mein Kampf (My Battle)* which he wrote while in jail for trying to stage a *putsch* in Munich in 1923 when he tried to take over the local government. In this book he laid out his views of history, including these points: first, history is made by great races, and the greatest race is the Aryan, whose most perfect exemplification is the German people; second, mixed nations always deteriorate due to contact with inferior peoples such as Poles, Slavs, and, above all, Jews; third, Jews were the archenemy, the worst criminals of all time. Contamination from Jews had to be stopped. Fourth, democracy was decadent. Hitler had only contempt for the average man casting a vote. Fifth, after the Jew, the real menace in the world was International Communism. He would, if he had the political power, do something about the Jews and Moscow; sixth, a great leader was necessary for a people to realize their destiny. For Germany to realize her place in the sun."

"Barbarism… What a perfectly appropriate term to describe what happened, Robert."

"Which gets us back to Mildred. She had to have seen the effect of these laws. How could she not have? In many of her broadcasts she alluded to Hitler's ideas, even if the script was written by her boyfriend, Max Otto."

"Enlighten me."

"Angry that America had entered the war against the Axis Powers, she said, and I quote:

Well, you seem to think you have a grudge against Germany? You prefer perhaps the Jews? You'd like to crony around with them. You prefer Communism. You prefer Bolshevism. Well … that's no America for me, I must say, and I'd rather die for Germany than live for one hundred years on milk and honey in the Jewish America of today.

"She said that?"

"Recorded by the FCC by their listening station in Maryland. Every single word she ever broadcasted. And entered as evidence at her trial."

"Did she believe it, what she said?"

"She read it, Lynn."

"But did she believe it, Robert?"

"On balance, yes. She certainly saw Germany as the ideal nation. In the same broadcast, she said:

Well, if you folks want to fight, to aid and abet the decline of the West, well you are certainly taking the right action. Germany has a vision. Germany has culture. Germany has supplied all of Europe with culture.

"See what I mean."

"Pretty brazen."

"She went on…

What have you (the US) done for posterity? Can you answer me? Here are the three things for which you people are known all over the world — money, jazz, and Hollywood. Compare your contributions with Germany…

"I like Hollywood.," Lynn quickly responded. I like jazz, and a few bucks in the bank isn't all that bad."

"That's because you're uncivilized, pro-Red, not to be trusted liberal thinker with musical tastes gone astray, my darling."

"That bad?"

"I'm afraid so."

"Well, it's better than uncouth."

"There's a certain irony in what she said," Samuels commented.

"I love irony, especially if it pricks the other person."

"She's critical of Hollywood, yet she spent her early years seeking stardom on the legitimate stage and would have jumped at the chance to be a silver screen celebrity. All her life, at least until she became the highest paid employee of Radio Berlin, she suffered from an impoverished life, always dependent on others for her next meal or rent money. And here she is knocking cash. Finally, she played jazz on her program. She knew the GI's liked it."

"Once more, Robert, do you think she believed everything she said?"

"Most of it, I think so."

"Because of Max Otto, as you refer to Mr. K?"

"Mr. K. I like that. He was her mentor, wasn't he?"

"In more than one way, it would seem."

"True enough."

"If she had refused to read the scripts?"

"According to the trial transcript, you cooperated in the Third Reich or things happened."

"So she read out of fear for her life?"

"She intimated that."

"Does that absolve her?"

"Now that is a good question."

"Meaning?"

"I don't have a final answer yet."

"Any other happy news?"

German Blood

"Also in 1935, Germany implemented the Law for the *Protection of German Blood and German Honor*. It forbade intermarriage and/or sexual relationships between Jews and Aryans. This was followed by the *Reich Citizenship Law*, which changed the definition of German citizenship. This law established 'German or kindred blood,' as the only factor determining citizenship. The term 'Jew' was defined in law as anyone descended from Jewish grandparents. Jew. The definition even included, as a Jew, the offspring of a mixed Gentile-Jewish marriage. In short, the new definition was attempting to eliminate Jewish blood in Germany. Soon it would lead to just eliminating the bearer of that blood. Before that, however, would come the removal of Jewish children from the public schools and the unfair expropriation of Jewish businesses and property to loyal Nazis."

"Jesus," Lynn said.

"Neither JC nor Moses was around to help. Even if they had been, they weren't dealing with a Pharaoh. The dregs of the gutter were in power with a chip on their shoulders. In 1938 they got a chance to vent their anger.

"Kristallnacht?" Lynn asked.

"Yes. Very good, Let's began with a footnote to history, a young man named *Herschel Grynszpan.*"

"What follows is a sad commentary, not only because of what the Nazis did, but also because of the world's muted reaction.

"On October 18, 1938, the Reich ordered over 12,000 Polish-born Jews to be deported to the East. Approximately 4,000 deportees were reluctantly accepted by the Polish government and permitted to enter the country. The remaining deportees remained at the German-Polish border without a country. All the Polish Jews had been stripped of their passports, property and money before being herded to the border in crowded trains. As they got onto the trains, non-Jews screamed at them, *'Jews get out! Out to Palestine.'*

"Two Jews exiled to Poland were Sendel and Rivka Grnszpan. Herschel Grnszpan, their son, heard of their stateless" situation. He decided to do something about it. On November 7, 1938, he quietly walked into the German Embassy in Paris and asked to speak to an official. Ernst von Rath, a junior official, came out to speak to him. Crying, "You're a filthy boche," Herschel shot him five times in he stomach. He then waited for the arrival of the French police. On his person, he carried a postcard on which he had written:

My dear parents, I could not do otherwise, may God forgive me, the heart bleeds when I hear of your tragedy and that of the 12,000 Jews. I must protest so that the whole world hears my protest, and that I will do. Forgive me.

"He was right to some degree. The world would hardly remember the single death of one German civil servant. But it would really remember what followed.

"There's more irony here, Lynn. "In her trial, Mildred would claim she was also a *stateless' person* after her passport was taken from her in 1941. Had she wanted to return to the US that would have been impossible because she lacked said passport. Parenthetically, she was then in the same position as the Polish-Jews. She was stuck, she concluded in Germany. The Polish-born Jews were stuck at the border. And, of course, this was also the problem of Iva Toguri at that time. Also lacking a passport, she was stuck in Japan."

"You're right. How ironic that the absence of a document could determine so much."

"I ask my question again. How could Mildred be unaware of the mass exile of Polish Jews and what took place next? Sure, it's possible, but it's very improbable."

"I think you're right, Robert."

Kristallnacht

"Following the assassination by Herschel Grnszpan, Joseph Goebbels, the Propaganda Minister, reminded the German people by radio that the killing took place on the fifteenth anniversary of the *Beer Hall Putsch of 1923*, when Hitler attempted to take over the Munich government. This day was known in Nazi mythology as the *Day of the Movement*, the most important day on the Nazi calendar. What he said next to revenge the killing was a cue to the German people that would unleash the dogs of prejudice. He said, 'It would not be surprising if the German people were so outraged by the assassination by a Jew that they took the law into their own hands and attacked Jewish businesses, community centers, and synagogues. Such spontaneous outbursts would not be openly organized by the Nazi Party.'"

"On November 9th and 10th, a coordinated attack occurred throughout Germany, and even in parts of Austria. The German police looked on without intervening as the streets were covered with broken glass from the windows of Jewish stores, buildings, and places of worship. The anger of the German people was in the streets. It was the worst pogrom in Jewish history. It was also called *Kristallnacht,* the *Night of Broken Glass.* More than 90 Jews were killed in the attacks, and in excess of 30,000 were arrested and sent to concentration camps. Jewish homes, hospitals, and schools were ransacked as buildings were destroyed with sledgehammers. At least 1,000 synagogues were burned in addition to as many as 7,000 businesses being burned to the ground. Goebbels had been quite accurate in his prediction.

"From this point on, the road to the concentration camps was open. Social inhibitions had been thrown away. Now a holocaust loomed."

"How could they do it, Robert?"

"Hitler, and many who came before him, had planted the seeds of prejudice and then they harvested that fruit. We recall it bitterly the 'scapegoat concept.' It had been around in Europe for a long time. Hitler in particular applied it to the armistice of 1918. He claimed Germany had never been defeated, the homeland never invaded. Rather, Germany had been 'stabbed in the back' by pacifists, communists, and Jews. Defeat had not come on the battlefield, but in the backrooms of Versailles."

"Still, why should this lead to such anger against Jews years later?"

"Other mythologies abounded. Jews were Christ-killers. In banking, they promoted usury and cared only for profits. They were an inferior people, who refused to be assimilated. They were condemned for their aloofness. It was charged that all Jews were wealthy, and, at the same time, stingy, greedy, and devious in addition to wanting to take over Germany."

"A bitter harvest to use your metaphor, Robert."

"It's an illness, this germ called prejudice. And it can strike anywhere, even here. Our feelings about minorities, the native-Americans, blacks, Hispanics, and Asians are replete with prejudicial ideas. And even those groups hold outlandish views of others. This disease has always been with us. We have no form of inoculation except for education, and even that recedes when emotions are stirred."

"Did Mildred comment on any of this during her broadcasts? Something so awful was too big to cover up. She had to know."

"She knew. Every shocked foreign journalist worth his salt filed blistering criticisms of what had taken place. One quote from a *New York Times* reporter comes to mind:"

No foreign propagandist bent upon blackening Germany before the world could outdo the tale of burnings and beatings, of blackguardly assaults on defenseless and innocent people, which disgraced that country yesterday.

"She knew, Lynn."

"Privately, do you think she agreed with what happened?"

"The excesses, hopefully not. At least she hinted at this during her trial. For the rest, we'll really never know for sure."

"Heart of heart, what's your view, Robert?"

"She was anti-Semitic."

"Proof?"

"One of her broadcasts... In 1943, she alluded to the Great Depression when she discussed her bitter and near starvation days in New York City when she still yearned to be an actress. She told her listeners that in a 'weathered shanty you will never find a Jew. No sir, the Jews are all in the marble palaces along Park Avenue and Fifth Avenue...' Enough proof?"

"Obviously, she never knew your father. He was at least one out-of-work Jew with his family almost living on the streets. No penthouse for him."

"And no money in the bank. So much for stereotypes?"

"It's a good thing FDR came along."

"Dad joined the CCC, got one dollar per day, and the family survived. For Mildred, I guess we were an exception to her prejudice."

"Thankfully."

Samuels got up again and began pacing around his room as if he were again on the bridge of the *USS Ward*, fearfully peering westward for incoming suicide plans. Finally he stopped and slapped a balled-fist into his other hand. Whack. Then he blurted out, Damn! Damn! Damn!"

Isn't this where I came in," Lynn asked. "So what's under your skin?"

"Three birds and a boat, and a question."

"Good. Nothing important, then?"

"Here's the question, Lynn. Though Mildred, by my reckoning, was anti-Jewish and expressed those views in her Radio Berlin broadcasts, does that make her guilty of treason? Especially, if other people, American citizens all, were saying the same thing at the time."

"Well, does it, my unhappy skeptic?"

CHAPTER 10
THE UNWANTED

The Late Lunch

"Well, that's more like it, Robert."

Lynn Samuels was in her kitchen preparing a late lunch or, if you wish, an early dinner. Either way, she was scouring around the kitchen, apron flying, as she prepared the meal, ladling ham-bone soup from a large pot, tossing the salad makings into the heavens, and extricating from the double oven stove newly baked bread. She conducted this three-ring gourmet circus, while still finding time to comment on her husband's clothes.

"I see you've discarded the CAL bears for more fashionable clothes; well-worn Levis, a tired white tee-shirt, and your favorite barely held together sandals. All in all you look like a beachcomber who should be walking along a Cuban beach, checking out the senoritas and drinking a cold one."

"Cuba, you say. Actually, we might just go there today."

"Dr. Castro will let us in?"

"No problem there. The question is whether the State Department will let us out."

"I know you, Robert. You choose your words carefully. Something's up."

"Never could fool you, Lynn."

"Just remember that. Now about some food?"

They ate their meal with gusto. The morning discussion concerning Nazi persecution of Jews had taken a toll on them. Strangely, they found themselves ravished. It was if they wanted to eat for two people, as if they were somehow compensating for the starving victims in the camps. They ate in silence, sharing only knowing eye contact. But that was enough. Volumes were spoken. How could all this happen? Was Mildred truly unaware of the tragedy? Was she really an anti-Semite? And, on larger scale, why didn't the world stop it? Too many questions...

"Great meal, Lynn."

"You pour the coffee. I'll clear the table and then let's get back to this painful discussion. Deal?"

"We need to clean some things up besides the dishware."

After a few minutes, with chores done, they sat down again with coffee cups and another of Samuels' folders, which he placed on the kitchen table. He withdrew from it an old photograph of a ship.

Defending Prejudice - The St. Louis

"At her trial, Lynn, Mildred's defense argued that she shouldn't be found guilty of treason for broadcasting opinions which many other Americans shared, and in some cases, even more adamantly. Continuing with this line of reasoning the defense claimed that her right to 'freedom of speech' was violated by the Justice Department in a prejudicial manner. Moreover, the defense maintained that our own government, by its failure to severely condemn the Nazi atrocities, actually sanctioned them indirectly. In other words, culpability crossed the Atlantic."

"Did her defense have any supporting evidence?"

"Sadly, yes."

"It might begin with this. This is a photo of the *SS St. Louis*, just another German leisure cruise ship that sailed the trans-Atlantic route from Hamburg to Halifax, Nova Scotia, and New York, and often to the West Indies."

"Where was this photograph taken?"

"Havana, June 1939."

"What makes this ship so important, Robert?"

"The *St. Louis* sailed from Hamburg to Cuba on May 13, 1939. She carried 930 Jewish refugees, mostly German, who were seeking asylum from Nazi persecutions. Upon arrival in Havana, the Cuban government refused the passengers entry."

"Why?"

"Money. The Cubans wanted $500 visa fee from each passenger, including children. Of course, the refugees couldn't pay. Gustav Schroder, the Captain, attempted to negotiate with the Cubans. It was fruitless. He steamed out of Cuban waters and headed toward Florida, where events became murky."

"Meaning?"

"Taking the Captain's account at face value, American authorities refused permission to dock and even fired a warning shot to keep his ship away from Florida shores. Others say the Coast Guard was not ordered to turn away the ship. Accepting this as factual, the problem was this: the State Department and Immigration services had made no provisions for the entry of the refugees who lacked passports, tourist visas, or even a return address."

"Passports again."

"The Captain next tried to make port in Nova Scotia. He was denied entry by Canadian authorities, many of whom, as in the US, were hostile to Jewish immigration. He even considered beaching the ship at Halifax. Eventually, he had to sail eastward, back to Europe. The *SS St. Louis* docked at Antwerp, Belgium on June 17, 1939. Though unwanted in the New World, the refugees were scattered to different

European countries, France, Belgium, England, and the Netherlands. Of the original 936 passengers, 709 survived the war."

"I can't believe our government refused entry. Why would it do this?"

"Good question with a disheartening answer."

"On the surface, the State Department was enforcing the national origins quota system which restricted the number of people allowed to enter from a given country. According to some, an unfeeling, even prejudiced State Department used the laws on the books to keep out Jews. America in 1939 was at odds with itself concerning the Jewish immigration. On the one hand, over 250,000 refugees of every background were admitted between 1933 and 1945. This was more than any other Western nation. But given the size of the US, more refugees should have been taken. On the other hand, attempts to liberalize immigration laws ran into a series of obstacles.

"The StateDepartment was riddled with anti-Semitics, who resisted all attempts to change the law. The Assistant Secretary of State, Breckenridge Long, was an avowed anti-Semite and an admirer of Benito Mussolini. He was in charge of refugee matters and used his position to stymie increased immigration. He also used his power to limit information related to what was happening in Germany. There was widespread indifference to change in America, especially in the southern and western states. This attitude bordered on open hostility in parts of the country. In 1939, a Gallup poll found that only 29% of the population approved of a bill before Congress to rescue 20,000 children. Other factors also played into all this. Many people feared that refugees would compete for scarce jobs. The depression still lingered, and the coming war economy was still more than a year away from Pearl Harbor. The country was also obsessed about security and was afraid Nazi spies might enter as refugees. It was not a good time to be a Jewish refugee.

"The upshot of all this was that the German government concluded that Americans approved of what was happening, or at least were indifferent to the fate of Jews. The Nazi regime convinced itself that Jew-haters abounded in the US, not just Berlin. They could point to the American Legion and the Daughters of the American Revolution, two groups that railed against the notion of admitting more helpless Jews into the country. Goebbels in particular could also point out the anti-Jew comments made on American radio and in the country's newspapers. For him, anti-Semitism was virulent and international. Germany was just taking the lead in dealing with the "unwanted.""

"Where was I when all this was happening, Robert?"

"We were both getting on with our youthful lives, dating, school, working."

"I feel so guilty."

"Don't. It won't change anything."

"I need to think about that."

"Think about this, too. Mildred broadcasted a lot of things, and went to jail for saying what she did. But in many respects, she was merely voicing what other Americans were already thinking. But they didn't go to jail."

"But she spoke on Radio Berlin during the war."

"Still espousing what many believed in the US."

"You're defending her now?"

"Trying to find some perspective. She doesn't make it easy."

"Okay, I've got that. We've covered the ship. Now, what about the three birds? My curiosity is aroused."

"Why not? Three birds... One was a priest. Another was a mechanic, big time. The final one was a pilot. Interested?"

"Even more so."

Father Coughlin

"Father Charles Edward Coughlin was a complex character, a Catholic priest with his own radio show and network during the 1930's with a mass weekly audience of over 30,000,000 people. That was almost a third of the nation. He received on the average almost 80,000 letters per week. He was phenomenally popular. Though originally an FDR supporter, he quickly became a harsh critic of the President for being too friendly to bankers, especially Jewish bankers. He used his radio program to broadcast anti-Semitic commentary and to support some of Hitler and Mussolini's political and social policies. He considered these leaders an antidote to Soviet Bolshevism.

"He blamed the depression on 'an international conspiracy of Jewish bankers.' On November 27, 1938, he claimed that Jewish bankers were behind the Russian Revolution. 'There can be no doubt,' he said, 'that the Russian Revolution was launched and fomented by distinctively Jewish influence.' He claimed that 'Marxist atheism in Europe was a Jewish plot against America.' Referring to Kristallnacht, he said two weeks after the incident, 'Jewish persecutions only followed after Christians were first persecuted.' When the American government pressured to end his show, demonstrators rallied to his support, many saying, 'Send Jews back where they came from in leaky boats!' Some even said, 'Wait until Hitler comes here.'

"Clearly, he catered to nativist sentiment among Americans. This 'Radio Priest,' as he was called, envisioned Wall Street and Communism as the 'twin faces of a secular Satan.' At the heart of both evils, he implicated the Jew.

"Father Coughlin was extremely popular in New York City, and certainly when Mildred was seeking, mainly unsuccessfully, work in the 'Big Apple.' His published newspaper, called *Social Justice,* was read by thousands in the city and influenced many. It's more than possible that Mildred heard about him and his ideas. Certainly, what she later broadcasted paralleled his thinking. In a May 1943 broadcast she said without apology:

I am not on the side of Roosevelt and his Jewish friends. I've been brought up to be a 100 percent American girl: conscious of everything American, conscious of her friends, conscious of her enemies. And the enemies are precisely those people who are fighting against Germany today. I'm so convinced that it's the truth and I'm sure the truth will win.

In the same vein she broadcasted:

After visiting an American POW camp, I altered and edited to twist one young man's words around until they rang with a Berlin tone. The young solider said that only recently did he understand that American films and newspapers were wrong about Germans, that it was nothing more than "Jewish propaganda." In the same broadcast, I questioned American women, asking them, "Why are we shedding our good young blood for this 'kike's war,' for this British war." In the same vein, a month later she said on her show — Home Sweet Home — "While you're over in North Africa fighting for Franklin D. Roosevelt and all his Jewish cohorts, I do hope that way back in your hometown nobody will be making eyes at (your) honey." Mixing sex, love, and politics made for good propaganda.

"Two peas in a pod," Lynn said.

"Indeed. But only one pea ended up in jail. The good priest's radio license was challenged by the FCC and church authorities threatened to defrock him if he didn't break from his show. He did so and remained a parish priest. No jail time for essentially the same ideas."

"You're back to defending Mildred again, Robert."

"Not the words. Only the treatment, and I've still got lots of questions."

"Tell me about the next bird."

Henry Ford

"It's hard to believe that Henry Ford, the industrial genius who built the model T and perfected the mass production of motorcars, was an anti-Semite. But he was. Between 1900 and 1918, he became increasing anti almost everything, immigrant, labor, liquor, and Jew. He 1919 he purchased the *Dearborn Independent* and installed writers and editors to get his views across to readers.

"He asserted that there was a Jewish conspiracy to control the world. He harshly blamed Jewish financiers for fomenting World War I so that they could profit from supplying both sides. He even accused Jewish automobile dealers of conspiring to undermine the Ford Company's sales policies. He hired investigators to prove that Jewish bankers wanted control of the world's finance. He contended that Jewish organizations promoted radical movements. He editorialized that Jews manipulated diplomacy to cause wars in which Christians died to enrich Jews. He pointed out that President Wilson secretly took orders from Justice William Brandeis. He believed that a Jewish member of the Federal Reserve Board had thwarted Ford's plan to purchase nitrite mines from the Federal Government.

"There was literally no end to his provocative charges. He claimed that the national debt was a Jewish inspired plot to enslave Americans. He defined Jews as an 'international nation,' which had an unfair advantage in business over Christians who relied on individualism to get ahead. And, of course, this came from a man who tried to create an auto monopoly and hired thugs to breakup attempts to unionize his plants. He even described Jewish aid to oppressed Jews overseas as part of the conspiracy.

"His downfall as a famous and wealthy bigot began with the publishing of the *Protocols of the Elders of Zion*. A Russian émigré, Paquita de Shishmareff brought the papers to him. She convinced Ford that the papers were legitimate. Actually, they were a forgery that had been created by the Czar's secret service at the turn of the century. The purpose of the forgery was to document a Jewish conspiracy to overthrow European governments. The protocols were a series of lectures by a Jewish elder outlining this "blueprint" for world domination. Ford's newspaper printed the protocols over a period of weeks, which only increased anti-Jewish feelings in the US. After all, if the greatest capitalist in the country believed it… Eventually, Ford learned that the protocols were fake. He claimed that he was 'mortified' to learn the Protocols were forged. He then said he was 'fully aware of the virtues of the Jewish people, and offered them 'future friendship and good will.' All of this occurred at a time when Jewish leaders were calling for a boycott of Ford motorcars, and Ford sales were slumping to an upstart, General Motors."

"I loved my old Ford," Lynn said after Samuels stopped to reshuffle some papers. "Had I known…"

"Though he was prejudiced, he built a fine car. Can't take that away from him."

"But the accusations, Robert."

"Any worse than what Mildred said? Listen to this. 'And I say, damn Roosevelt, damn Churchill, and damn all of their Jews who have made this war possible.' She also spoke bitterly of wounded American POW's, saying they were perishing, 'losing their lives. At best coming home crippled, useless for the rest of their lives. And for whom, she asked? For Franklin D. Roosevelt and Churchill, and their Jewish cohorts.'

"Taking her side again, aren't you?"

"Trying to look at all sides."

"But she said those things. Every word was recorded."

"And Ford's every word was published."

"But only Mildred went to jail, right, Robert?"

"Right. For broadcasting… For providing an opinion… For reading scripted copy… Yes, she broadcasted. But a lot of Germans, including dyed in the wool Nazis with blood on their hands, never went to prison. That's what bugs me. What she said was wrong. But was prison right?"

"Ugh. Let's get to the third bird.

Charles Lindberg

"They called him the *Lone Eagle*. Others liked to describe him as "Lucky Lindy," or just plain "Slim." Regardless, Charles Lindberg was in the 1930's America's most famous aviator, author, inventor, explorer, and social activist. It all began for him May 20ᵗʰ and 21ˢᵗ 1927 when he took off from Roosevelt Field in New York State and flew 3,000 statute miles to Le Bourget Field in Paris, France. In doing so, he won the Orteig Prize for the first solo flight across the Atlantic in his single-engine plane, the *Spirit of St. Louis*. Since he was still in the military, he was awarded the Medal of Honor for his historic exploit. He was 25 years old and the darling of the nation. By the late 1930's he was also the guiding light of the American First organization that wanted to keep the country out of a new war in Europe. It was at this time that he flew into new, uncharted skies.

"In a 1939 edition of the *Reader's Digest*, he wrote:

We can have peace and security only as long as we band together to preserve that most precious possession, our inheritance of European stock, only so long as we guard ourselves against attack by foreign enemies and dilution by foreign races.

"No one questioned the need to be prepared against an attack. But many asked, 'What did he mean by the dilution of American by foreign races?' For many, Lindberg meant Eastern Europeans in general and Jews in particular."

"Following the *Night of Broken Glass*, he wrote:

I do not understand these riots on the part of Germany. It seems so contrary to their sense of order and intelligence. They undoubtedly have a Jewish problem but why is it necessary to handle it so unreasonably.

"He never, however, expounded on what the Jewish problem was or how it could be handled in a more reasonable manner. About Jews, he wrote in his diary:

We *must limit to a reasonable amount the Jewish influence. Whenever the Jewish percentage of the population becomes too high, a reaction seems to occur. It is too bad because a few Jews of the right type are, I believe, an asset to any country.*

"When conducting his anti-war meetings, he pointed out that the three most important groups promoting war were the British, FDR's administration, and the Jews. Continuing, he said:

Instead of agitating for war, Jews in the country should be opposing it in every way, for they will be the first to feel its consequences. Their greatest danger in the country lies in their large ownership and influence in our motion pictures, our press, our radio, and our government.

"Once again, he left open what the actual danger was, and what were the possible consequences."

"He really flew off base," Lynn said. "He almost sounds like a fascist. God, to think he was one of my heroes."

"His flight was heroic. And after Pearl Harbor, he gave invaluable service to the country. He had strong views, but he wasn't a Nazi. Nevertheless, he remained popular for many people, regardless of what he said. And, of course, many people concurred with his views. He was provocative. And he never went to jail. Compare what he said to Mildred's pearls of wisdom.

Mildred's Prejudice

The Jews are in this war, have got us into this war — for an ideal, not for the love of humanity, but for money. They had no feeble concern for America... No, the Jews are sending our men over to Europe to fight so that their moneybags will get filled.

"Continuing, she broadcasted on another occasion:

My dear listeners in America... you're having some difficulty now with your rationing. You've got your ration books already; well, you've getting them rather late. In the meantime, all of the Jews, they have confiscated the lovely things, which you have in in America like your Heinz 57 Varieties and such things. So between the Black Market and the Jews you have a much worse time than the people in Germany. I've told you before it's my firm conviction that, in reality, this is no war between Germany and America, in that sense of the word, but a war between the Jews and the Gentiles.

"That's the kind of stuff that get's you an appointment with the Justice Department, Lynn."

"I can't believe she believed her own drivel."

"Whether she did or didn't, she said the words."

"So where do we stand on her, Robert?"

"The case for her is straightforward, or at least from her perspective. One, she didn't write the scripts. Two, she couldn't deviate from the scripts. Three, she was supervised while broadcasting. Four, she feared for her safety if she didn't conform. Five, she really thought she was helping America by keeping the country out of the war."

"The other case?"

"She really was pro-Germany insofar as her war against Britain and the Soviet Union. She was anti-Jew, perhaps before she ever came to Germany. She was excessively opposed to FDR. She bought the Nazi line about both, either intellectually or emotionally.

"When you add it all up, Robert?"

"I get tendencies, possibilities, not unassailable conclusions."

"Meaning?"

"Meaning, you're off to Chicago to interview Tokyo Rose and I'm meeting tomorrow with Rita Howard who will be flying in from New Jersey."

"Oh. Another woman in your life?"

"Actually, two more."

"Robert, at your age," Lynn said playfully.

"No need to worry, my lovely lady, not with Rita telling me about the *Rebel Girl.*"

CHAPTER 11

THE REBEL GIRL

<u>Rita</u>

"Rita, over here. It's me. Over here."

Robert Samuels was at SFX at 9:00 A.M. to pick up a former journalism student at San Francisco State, and now an intern at the *Chronicle.* As always, the airport reminded him of the newsroom, that is, organized chaos with people surging in every different way. But there she was, Rita Howard, wheeling her suitcase and headed directly toward him with a big smile on her face. She was on loan to him for special assignments, which meant she was assisting him in researching Mildred Elizabeth Gillars. She was the right person for the job. She was a tough eastern kid from Pittsburgh, who had attended the city's university before moving westward for a warmer climate and a graduate degree in journalism. Samuels often compared her to a bulldog. She was short in stature and, perhaps because of this, she had learned to push hard with her studies, or, if necessary, to bang through a crowd. Of course, when it came to going after a story, he was also apt to describe her as "fullback in skirts." She would dig her teeth into a story and hang on for dear life.

"Mr. Samuels, thanks for meeting me."
"My pleasure. How was the flight from Washington?"

"Hunting through the archives at the National Library was a joy. The midnight flight from D.C. with a stopover in Dallas was a chore."

"That's our *Chronicle.* Spare no expense. Book the cheapest flight possible. Hungry?"

"Famished."

"How about a burger, then back to the paper. I can hardly wait to hear what you learned."

"Mels Drive-In on Geary?"

"Where else? Best burgers in town."

Two hours later they were sitting in Samuels' small office at the *Chronicle,* where they hoped to speak privately. Unlike his office at home, Samuels' office appeared to have been the target of a whirlwind. Everything was scattered everywhere with one exception. The space around his old Underwood was immaculate, clear of all human travail, yet posed for the next incessant chapter in the human drama that snuggled up to Robert Samuels. Rita was just getting out the first of three large notebooks, when the first interruption occurred. Irish Mike, Samuels' oldest buddy at the paper, popped in saying, "Mr. P, AA on his way down and he's on the war path."

The early warning system was working. AA was Abraham Adams, the editor and chief tormentor of all good reporters. "The story... Where's the story? We go to print in 30-minutes!" His belabored mantra...

"Morning, Miss Howard. Nice to see you again. I'm out of here, Mr. P., where it's safer."

"Mr. P? Rita asked.

"Win a Pulitzer and they'll call you Mr. P around here."

A moment later, AA burst into the office. He resembled a squat fire hydrant in wing-tipped shoes looking for a fire. Chomping on an illegal Cuban cigar, he said, "Where's the first installment on Axis Sally?"

"Almost written."

"I hate the word almost."

"Tomorrow."

"You wouldn't kid the man who signs your pay voucher?"

"Me?"

"You, Mr. P."

"Never."

"What do you think, Miss...?"

"Howard. I..."

"Intern, aren't you?"

"Yes."

"Don't pick up any bad habits from this guy."

"I'll try not..."

"Good. Tomorrow, Mr. P."

As AA left, Gloria Gorham entered with a flourish. Known as GG, she was the gossip column writer for the paper. Juicy stories were the grist of her typewriter. Always dressed to kill, she sometimes did so with her inside stories. She considered the jugular the prerequisite target for a gossip gal.

"Rita, this is GG."

"Kid knows me, Mr. P. Anything salacious I can use? You know, how many lovers did dear Axis Sally have?"

"We're still hunting that one down."

"And?"

"Enough to fill up a few columns."

"Mr. P, you're a dear."

"Now, if you're done..."

"Stick with him, kid. You'll learn a few tricks."

Zip. And out GG went, her spirits raised considerably. Clandestine love affairs always had that effect on her.

"This place is worse than Central Station, Rita."

"I think the next train just pulled in."

The door to the office quietly open and a well-tailored gentleman proffered his hand to Samuels, while nodding to Rita.

"OP," Samuels said, "say hi to Rita Howard."
"Oliver Pine, and I think we've met. You're the new intern?"
"Right on both scores."
"Nice to see you again, both of you. Mr. P, anything for my financial and legal column?"
"Still researching."
"That's the stuff. Get to the bottom of it. That's what I always say. And with Axis Sally's trial, there's a rich vein to mine. Don't you think so?"
"Prospecting? You bet."
"You'll keep me in mind, won't you?"
"Buddies always."
"Then, good. Bye all."

OP left, and Samuels quickly hurried to the door, hung an "OUT TO LUNCH" sign, pulled the door's shade and locked it.
"People know we're here."
"True, Rita, but they think I'm interviewing someone important. We don't bug when the sign is up. Unwritten law."
"Okay, one other thing. Does everyone have initials around here?"
"Once you've been around long enough, yes."
"Why?"
"Tradition."
"Fiddler on the Roof?"
"That's what reporters are, Rita, fiddlers on the roof of life, clinging precariously to a few shingles as we try to comprehend that small space between illusion and reality and always hoping to avoid slipping off our perch."
"You're a poet, Mr. Samuels."

"Nope. Just an old reporter who probably has seen too much of this world. Now, what about the *Rebel Girl?*"

"You were right, Mr. Samuels. Hidden away in the recesses of the National Library was lots of information, which a couple of industrious librarians helped me to dig out, lots of primary stuff on Elizabeth Gurley Flynn. That was the easy part."

"And the other part?"

"Difficult. Nothing in the stacks… Nothing in the computer… Nothing!"

"I get the picture."

"Then I got lucky.

"Alas."

"Another librarian, Ms. Helen Camp, who works in the legal section, sought me out. I guess she heard about what I was looking for and whom I was working for, mainly you. She liked your new book on Iva."

"And?"

"We hit it off. As I recall, it went something like this."

"That's right, Ms. Camp. That's why Mr. Samuels sent me eastward. Did Flynn have any conversations with Axis Sally when they were each incarcerated in Alderson Prison?"

"No question about it. All three were housed in the same cottage."

"Three?"

"Flynn, '55 through '57… Axis Sally, '49 though '61… And Tokyo Rose, '50 through '56… They overlapped in the '56 – '57 years."

"Really?"

"The fickleness of history, Miss Howard. It's always with us. Imagine two convicted traitors and the head of the American Communist Party all sharing bread at the invitation of the Justice Department, Miss Howard."

"I wonder… Did Flynn and Mildred converse? And, if so, about what and do we have any record of their conversation?"

"Lots of questions. Exactly, what are you looking for?"

"Anything that will help us to understand why Mildred Gillars became the face of Radio Berlin."

"And you think she might have shared this intimacy with Flynn?"

"Samuels hopes so."

"His instincts are good."

"And?"

"Perhaps. If I appear guarded in my response…"

"You do."

"The problem, Rita… May I call you Rita?"

"Of course."

"And call me Helen. The problem is that I'm researching a book myself on Flynn's life, while you're seeking information about Mildred. We're not at cross purposes, but we need to make a deal."

"Which would be?"

"We share. Will Mr. Samuels go for that?"

"He really doesn't have a choice, does he?"

"Was I wrong to make a deal, Mr. Samuels?"

"You were pragmatic. We'll share. Just call me next time before you commit."

"I was afraid I would lose her."

"Been there myself. Now, what did our two jailed ladies talk about?"

"Rita, some background first on Flynn before we get to what Mr. Samuels wants. Believe me, it will help. But one point."

"There's always one point, Helen."

"We can't talk in the library when I'm on duty. Let's meet at my apartment this evening. I live in Georgetown. Here's the address. After dinner and drinks, we'll talk. Just grab a cab."

"Okay, Rita," Samuels said. What's this leading up to?"
"Music, Mr. Samuels."

"As instructed, I hailed a Yellow Cab outside the Ramada Inn that evening and joined Helen for dinner. Her Georgetown brownstone was on the first floor, a lovely place just crammed with books, mostly biographies and history, and a complete set of law books. I guess that having lots of books comes with being a librarian. Perhaps that happens too, when you're single and a bit of a spinster. Just pop psychology on my part. Dinner, as it turned out, was imported BBQ ribs and wedged fries from the local deli, and really good. A little upstate New York wine added to the moment. As we were eating dessert, delightful mint and chip ice cream, Helen turned to *Elizabeth Gurley Flynn*."

"A little music okay with you, Rita?"
"Sure."
"This is a little something by *Joe Hill*," she said as she placed an old record in an equally old phonograph. "Ever hear of him?"
"I'm afraid not."
"He was an American labor activist, song writer, and member of the *Wobblies*, the International Workers of the World in the early 1900's. The IWW was the first major union to take on the excessive abuses of American capitalism. It did so at a time when corporations and business was unrestrained in the exploitation of workers. Hill was a union organizer. He was a fighter, and, as might be expected, the 'captains of industry' of his day attacked him without mercy. In his mid-thirties, he was falsely accused of murdering a former policeman and his son in Salt Lake City. In what is now considered a rigged trial, Hill

was found guilty of the murders. While in jail awaiting his execution, he had a repeated visitor. You can guess who it was, Elizabeth Gurley Flynn. They were close friends and he wrote a song about her in 1911, a few years before he died. It was called *The Rebel Girl* to honor Flynn and her work, which mirrored his own. I like to play it when I'm thinking about her. Not loudly… Just background lyrics… Okay?"

"Sure."

There are women of many descriptions,
In this queer world, as everyone knows,
Some are living in beautiful mansions,
And are wearing the finest of clothes.

"First, at the age of 16, Flynn was expelled from high school in the Bronx for making a speech at the Harlem Socialist Club, about 1906. The speech was entitled, *What Socialism Will Do For Women*. That's what happens when your parents are Socialists and union organizers. It rubs off on you, I guess. Fifty-eight years later, now Chairperson of the American Communist Party, she died in Moscow while visiting the Soviet Union. She was given a State funeral, which over 20,000 people attended. Between those events, she lived, as you can imagine, a most interesting life.

"By 1910, she joined the IWW, the International Workers of the World, the fledging new union that strove to assist the working man. She was a union organizer and she believed the IWW 'blazed a trail like a great a comet across the American labor scene.' Her work took her around the nation. She helped organize the garment workers in Minersville, Pennsylvania, and the silk weavers in Patterson, New Jersey. The same was true with the hotel and restaurant worker in New York City, as well as the miners in Minnesota's Mesabi Iron Range or the textile workers in Lowell, Massachusetts.

"Flynn's view of labor was expressed in her description of the silk weaving industry, and, of course, by implication to other industries. She said:

The silk workers, for instance, may make beautiful things, fine shimmering silk. When it is hung up in the window of Macy's or Wanamaker's it looks beautiful. But the silk worker never gets a chance to use a single yard of it. They make a beautiful thing in the shop and then they come home to poverty, misery, and hardship.

Flynn questioned the fairness in all this, and called for economic justice.

There are blue-blooded queens and princesses,
Who have charms made of diamonds and pearls;
But the only and thoroughbred lady
Is the Rebel Girl.

"She was a feminist before the term was in vogue. She fought the oppression of women and children. She criticized male chauvinism wherever it was found, including unions. She was a strong supporter of birth control, and the suffrage movement, child-care centers and excellent education for women. Because of her fierce struggle to defend her right to organize workers, she was arrested and tried twenty times but never convicted of criminal activity.

"An articulate speaker and writer, she was always a defender of free speech. She opposed Attorney-General A. Mitchell Palmer and his assistant, J. Edgar Hoover after World War I and their total disregard for constitutional rights, particularly, free speech and assembly. She totally opposed the federal government and the 'Red Scare.' In the same vein she fought for seven years, along with others, to keep Nicola Sacco and Bartolemeo Vanzetti, two accused anarchists, from being executed. And, as you might expect, she was a founding member of the ACLU.

"In 1936 she joined the Communist Party. For her, Socialism was the wave of the future. In a May Day speech, she said, 'I believe in a socialist America. What a May Day that will be to celebrate. Hail to it.' She was not afraid to criticize Stalin's brand of Marxism. Unlike some, she believed Socialism could be achieved peacefully in the United States through public participation in elections and by running for public office. She not only preached, she practiced her own oratory. In 1942, she ran for Congress to represent the Bronx. She lost, but she did get 50,000 votes."

That's the Rebel Girl, That's the Rebel Girl
To the working class she's a precious pearl.
She brings courage, pride and joy
To the fighting Rebel Boy.

"With Pearl Harbor, she became fully supportive of the war effort, even campaigning for the aristocratic capitalist from Hyde Park, FDR. She favored the draft for women and urged Americans to buy war bonds and savings stamps. She advocated equal economic opportunities for women and minorities in the new war industries. Specifically, she wanted equal pay for all. To this end, she tried to enforce the Fair Employment Protection Act to help African-American women in particular, who she thought were the most discriminated and exploited group in America. She fought the Ford Motor Company because it would not even accept applications from black women until militant demonstrations forced a change in policy.

"During this period, she got caught up in the Great Sedition Trial of 1944 when the government sought to imprison those who were not sufficiently anti-Communist and/or supportive of President Roosevelt. The vehicle for the charges was the Smith Act, which was enacted in 1940. Proposed by Representative Howard W. Smith of Virginia, it was a product of America's prewar anxiety of Nazis and fascists. Two provisions were at the heart of the act. First, it was prison time for anyone attempting to undermine the morale of the armed forces. The second provision applied to those advocating the violent overthrow of the government. For the record Flynn never did these things.

"Flynn argued against the act and was almost jailed because of it. Curiously, the lead attorney for those indicted in 1944 was an unknown public defender named James J. Laughlin. After the war, as fate would have it, he would be appointed by the court to defend Mildred Elizabeth Gillars."

We've had girls before, but we need some more
In the Industrial Workers of the World,
For it's great to fight for freedom
With a Rebel Girl.

"Following the war, she lobbied against the worst afflictions of the McCarthy period. Eventually, she was caught up in the government's infamous anti-Communist witch-hunt, when she and other leaders of the party were accused of advocating the overthrow of the U.S. Government by force and violence. On January 21, 1951, she was accused of violating the Smith Act, and after a seven month trial, was sentenced to Alderson Federal Prison in West Virginia. She would remain in prison from January '55 to May '57.

Yes, her hands may be harden'd from labor
And her dress may not be very fine;

But a heart in her bosom is beating
That is true to her class and her kind.

"Wow," Rita said, perhaps a little too loudly. "Helen, I have to ask. Do you think the Rebel Girl was in love with Joe Hill?"

"That's your question?"

"I'm a romantic."

"Fondness, yes. Beyond that… I don't know."

"Hill was executed?"

"Firing squad, Rita. His last word was 'fire.' An amusing choice of words, don't you think?"

"History can be so juicy at times, Helen."

"And painful. Let's continue tomorrow. It's my day off. What about meeting at the Smithsonian?"

"We can talk about Flynn and Mildred?"

"Perhaps we should, if possible, let them speak for themselves."

And the grafters in terror are trembling
When her spite and defiance she'll hurl,
For the only and thoroughbred lady
Is the Rebel Girl.

"Rita, you met with Ms. Camp the next day, I take it?"

"Nothing could have kept me away, Mr. Samuels."

"Well, before you tell me more, here's a little something I came across myself about Joe Hill, a little song he wrote entitled *The Preacher and the Slave.* I think you'll like it."

Long-haired preachers come out every night,
Try to tell you what's wrong and what's right;

But when asked how 'bout something to eat
They will answer with voices so sweet.

You will eat, bye and bye,
In the glorious land above the sky,
Work and pray, live on hay,
You'll get pie in the sky when you die.

"That's Joe Hill," Rita said, "defender of the defenseless."

"Nicely put, Rita. Poor bastard, he never had a chance in court. There was no direct evidence that he had committed the murders, but enough pieces of evidence to persuade a jury to find him guilty. His case was known throughout the world. Over 10,000 letters were sent to the governor to protest his conviction and sentence. The day he was killed by a firing squad, machine guns were set up at the prison gate to warn off protesters. Damn waste of a man."

"You always surprise me, Mr. Samuels. You're a fan of Joe Hill?"

"I liked his music and his politics. Now tell me about your trip to the Smithsonian."

CHAPTER 12

THE UNWRITTEN BOOK

The Net Day and The Hidden Files

"You found your way, Rita."

"Helen, only by the grace of God and the Yellow Cab Company."

The two women were standing outside of the Smithsonian Institute on what promised to be a perfectly beautiful day in the nation's capital. Already long lines of tourists were waiting for the doors to swing open. And why not, you might ask? Thanks to the generosity of James Smithson, a British scientist, the largest museum complex in the world existed in the New World. Bestowing 104,960 gold sovereigns or almost $500,000 in US dollars in 1835 can do that sort of thing, particularly if the US Congress acts on a great deal. It did at the behest of President John Quincy Adams. For Rita, it was fascinating to watch people from all over the world, who lived their lives wholly in the present moment, yet were perfectly happy to shell out good money to get a glimpse of the past.

"God, the line extends around the street," Rita said anxiously. "It will be hours before we get into the museum."

"More like minutes. Follow me."

Helen pushed through the waiting lines and brought Rita to a side entrance, where she slipped a magnetic identification card into a slot. A moment later, the door opened to reveal a slender, rather tall balding man around forty, who heartily welcomed them with a big smile before quickly closing the door behind them.

"Helen, so good to see you again. And this must be your new friend, Rita, whom I've heard about."

"John Smith, curator of the Smithsonian's underground vaults, say hello to an aspiring journalist from the *San Francisco Chronicle*."

"Delighted. You work for that fellow Samuels who wrote about Tokyo Rose, right?"

"Yes, I helped him with his research."

"And now you're on the track of the Rebel Girl?"

"Precisely."

"Well Helen has brought you to the right place. Just follow me."

The curator turned and moved quickly down a long hall, turned left, and continued through a maze of corridors and past a myriad of uninviting doors. As she followed, Rita thought how comfortable *Converse* tennis shoes would be compared to her two-inch heels she was wearing. And given this wandering through the bowels of the Smithsonian, it might have been appropriate to bring along a bag of breadcrumbs.

Being Rita, of course, she had to ask Helen how she knew Smith as they scurried along behind the curator.

"We were once an item."

"Once?"

"He was married. I was newly divorced and things never quite got squared away between us."

"I'm sorry."

"Don't be. We've remained good friends. He loves the past, and I'm passionate about digging into it. We make for a good platonic combination just short of a clandestine rendezvous when his wife was away. John couldn't give up his family and I didn't want to break one up. So there you have it. Really not too complicated. Anyway, I owe John a debt of gratitude concerning Flynn, which he will surely explain."

"Here we are ladies. My hidden lair."

"A den of in iniquity," Rita popped up unabashedly and then quickly wondered why she had been so foolish."

"Oh, worse than that, Rita. In this room are secrets of the heart."

The Hidden Room

Smith unlocked the door and the three of them entered. The room, a perfect square, 12 X 12 feet, was laced with metal shelves containing cardboard cartons, each labeled in dark, three inch black print. In the middle of the room was a small metal table with a single lit reading lamp. There was also one unopened cardboard box. Three metal chairs, all looking very uncomfortable, were braced against the table. Talk about an austere place. Latin monks and inky-fingered scribes would have been right at home in this quasi-dungeon rewriting the *Bible* in colorful script according to the latest canon. It wasn't that the room was foreboding. Rather, it just wasn't up to *Home and Garden's* minimum standard of comfort.

"Please be seated, ladies," Smith said directly, "I have a story to tell."

"See, I told you, Rita," Helen said under her breath.

"You already know, Rita, that Elizabeth Gurley Flynn was at Alderson Prison at the same time as Iva Toguri and Mildred Gillars. Since this was the major Federal reformatory for women at the time, whether by a conspiracy of historical events, or judicial verdicts and tough sentences, the three ladies found themselves in Cottage 7 where they bunked and lived together for two years. Gurley, I like to refer to her as Gurley, was the oldest, almost 65. Iva was the youngest, age 33, and Mildred sandwiched herself between them. She was 49. Each woman had been found guilty of something nasty, either treason or, as in the case, of Gurley, advocating the violent overthrow of the government. Two of the ladies, by the way, are still kicking and both live in the Midwest. Mildred is 77 and resides in Ohio. Iva is 61 and lives in Chicago. As for Gurley, she died in 1964 and is buried in the Chicago area."

"At the Waldheim Cemetery," Helen contributed. As requested in her will, she's buried next to the martyrs of the Haymarket Strike."

"As you say, Helen."

"Three lives wrapped up in a few words, a few dates," Rita commented.

"Only a preface," Smith retorted. "Gurley was like a fish out of water when she was assigned to Alderson. She was, by the standards of the day, an old lady, arthritic and overweight, with high blood pressure, but, of course, a threat to America. She had a hard time with the constant banging of metal doors, the loud music enjoyed by more adolescent personalities, and just the cultural spread between the young and the old. Still, she used her time to read over 200 books, including poetry, plays, psychology, and the classics. And she wrote and wrote even though prison officials censored her writing, and at other times, made it difficult for her to have writing paper."

"John, tell Rita what Gurley was writing."

"Of course. I was just getting to that. She was writing a history of her stay in Alderson. Published a few years after her release, it was entitled, *The Alderson Story: My Life as a Political Prisoner.*"

"And the other book, John…"

"We now know she was working on a second book, which was going to focus on the irrepressible currents of history that brought her to West Virginia to share a cottage with two despised women, Axis Sally and Tokyo Rose."

"She even had a name for it, Rita," Helen added. "*Rebel Girls*. How about those apples?"

"How far along did she get?" Rita asked.

"John?"

"Two years ago, and quite by accident, I discovered two cartons of Gurley's papers from Alderson. Somehow, and don't ask me how, they found their way into my catacombs. I realized at once what I had on my hands: notes, telegrams, diaries, clippings, invitations, pamphlets, articles, speech, and poems, all reflecting on Gurley's life. There were even a few galley proofs of her pre-jail time books. I called the only person I knew who had an interest in Gurley."

"Helen," Rita said. "Who else?"

"For almost two years I've been fussing through these two cartons trying to make sense out of a puzzle that would do justice to Egyptian hieroglyphics. I had, I thought, all the pieces. I just didn't know how to make sense out of all these fragments of her life. And I wanted too. I wanted to finish her unfinished, unwritten book. I wanted to ghost write *Rebel Girls*."

"Things looked quite dark for Helen," John recounted. "And then?"

"John found it," Helen said triumphantly.

"Found what?" Rita questioned impatiently.

The Lost Notebook

"The *Rosetta Stone* to Gurley's papers," John said quietly. "The key to unlocking the puzzle."

I know about that rock Rita reminded herself. What was it? World History at State with Dr. Wall; yes, that was it. He had brightened the class with his charming lecture on, as he put it, an ancient manuscript, the Enigma code-breaker of its day that opened up Egyptian religion, literature, her civilization, the *Gift of the Nile*. My professor said it was a stele inscribed with a decree issued at Memphis in 196 BC by King Ptolemy V. The decree was in three scripts, each saying essentially the same thing. It was like discovering the code to the past. Hieroglyphs would no longer remain inscrutable. Was that what Smith was talking about? Had Helen really unlocked Gurley's secrets?

"I discovered a battered old notebook in which Gurley had tried to compare and contrast the three 'rebels' with a kind of shorthand. I immediately turned it over to Helen. She has been working with that shorthand for at least six months. Like the Rosetta Stone, it opened up not only Gurley's past, but insights into Iva and Mildred."

"What things, especially, Mr. Smith?"

"Fluttering of the heart, Rita. You know, what made them tick? Why they did what they did? Any regrets? One point though, at times it seemed that the focus of Gurley's interest was in the contrast between herself and Mildred, and less so with Iva."

"Do you have a theory about this?"

"Helen?"

"I think it has something to do with their politics. After all, one was a socialist, the other a Nazi broadcaster. Gurley supported the Allied effort, and was especially concerned about the survival of Red Russia, not Stalin per se, but Marxism and the Soviet Union. Mildred wanted Germany to prove victorious and for the Bolsheviks to lose. For each, Japan and Iva were a kind of sideshow. Does that make any sense, Rita?"

"Yes, I think so. But tell me, why didn't Gurley finish her book?"

"Her busy life, I think," Helen answered. After her release, she finished her Alderson expose and then was off to Copenhagen for the fiftieth anniversary celebration of International Women's Day. After Denmark, she traveled through Eastern Europe visiting the various socialist countries, including celebrating May Day in Moscow. All this took time. In addition, she was elevated to the post of Party Chair in the American Communist Party. She just kept not getting to the 'rebels." In August 1964, she traveled again to the Soviet Union. Within a month, her already poor health turned worse. She had stomach and intestinal inflammation that was aggravated by a blood clot to her lungs. On September 5, 1964 she died. She had run out of time."

"How sad."

"No Rita, how great. Gurley lived her life the way she wanted. No compromise, no equivocating, and no backward looks and regrets. She lived her life as a free woman. What could be better?"

"I see what you mean. "You're going to let me look at the stone, Helen?"

"Of course, Rita. That's why we're here. But keep in mind it stays here in this room. You can take notes, even quote, but no alluding to the source until my book is published later this year. Mr. Samuels will understand. Just say you met the 'deep-throat of the Nile.' If you wish, refer to me as Horus. Okay?"

"Okay!"

"One last thing. Ordinarily John wouldn't give access to a journalist, since, and don't take this personally, you're not a recognized scholar doing academic research. But he's made an exception in your case."

"Because of you?"

"Appealing thought, but no."

"It's for Mr. Samuels, a sort of belated gift," John said.

"I don't understand."

"Rita, my father was in the Marines, the 1st Marine Division. He was stationed in South Korea in 1950. He was a Colonel in charge of training the ROK troops. In his book, *Miracle at Pusan*, Mr. Samuels quoted my dad about the historic American and Republic of Korea stand against the overwhelming North Korean offense. And now inconceivably, you came along, Rita. I figured I owed Mr. Samuels one."

"Hard to believe," Helen said, "but here we all are brought together by..."

"Coincidence?" Smith asked.

"Or perhaps the 'ghosts of the rebel girls.'" Rita said. "I wonder..."

CHAPTER 13
THE REBEL GIRLS

<u>Searching</u>

John Smith had excused himself a few hours earlier, leaving Rita and Helen in his lair. Helen had busied herself with the contents of the now opened cardboard box and Rita had pored herself into Gurley's trove with an abandon she would not have thought possible. Except for one visit to the restroom and water fountain just across the hall from their self-imposed star-chamber, each woman remained glued to the task before her, the uncomfortable metal chairs notwithstanding. They had things on their mind.

They read…

<u>September 10, 1955 – The Flynn Papers</u>

What you will read represents the true and accurate rendition of my conversations with Iva Toguri and Mildred Elizabeth Gillars, which took place over a number of days at the Alderson Prison in West Virginia. While I, Elizabeth Gurley Flynn, have tried to be objective in what follows, this has not always been possible, as my own views, biases if you wish, percolated to the surface and influenced my conclusions. The reader, I am afraid, will have to bring a degree of skepticism and perspective to this work.

It would be too much to say that we began our conversations as friends. At most, we were hesitant jail buddies thrown together by forces beyond us. Truth be told, I felt a compelling anger toward Mildred. After all, she had been the mouthpiece of the Nazis, whereas I was a tried and true Communist for whom the fascists were my mortal enemy. It took a great deal of effort to quiet my feelings. I suspect the same was true for Mildred. Moscow was her sworn enemy. Perhaps it was curiosity that got the best of us. We wanted to know something of the other. As for Iva, she really was the neutral factor. Her interest was simple. She wanted the Emperor to lose. She wanted the US to win. Europe was another matter for others to decide.

Survivors

Without question, I reminded the other women when we began our chats that the three of us shared one common trait beyond being prisoners of the Justice Department and guests of West Virginia. We were all survivors. We all found a way to live through the war. This would be our first theme for discussions. Survival! How had we done it? Iva quickly agreed and pointed out immediately what she had experienced.

"I was alone in Japan after Pearl Harbor, a Japanese-American gal who spoke almost no Japanese and liked a cheeseburger and fries, not a steady diet of fish and rice. The culture and traditions were not completely unknown to me, but they might as well have been. I was really a fish out of water."

"And what were you doing in Nippon?" Mildred piped in quickly. "Seems like a strange place to be just before the war."

"Taking care of my sick aunt at my mother's request."

"Plausible?" Mildred questioned rather than declared.

"That's just the way it was, Mildred. After Pearl Harbor, the Japanese secret police wouldn't permit me to join other Western internees, nor would they give me a food rations book. I had to find work on my own, which meant giving piano lessons, translating materials, and later working for Radio Tokyo. But always, hovering in the background, were the police, watching my every step, always suspicious of my actions, seemingly ready to pounce the first chance they had. Just getting through each day was a major effort."

"You should try the Gestapo on for size," Mildred said. Damn psychopaths, all of them. Those bastards enjoyed hurting people. They came out of the gutter. Torturing people was in their blood. Keeping people in fear was their trademark. Like you, I was also trapped after Pearl Harbor. I couldn't get out of Germany. I needed a food ration book and to keep my job at Radio Berlin. Any step out of line was always met with the threat of the concentration camp. And that meant death."

"It appears, ladies, I had an easier time of it after December 7th. It's true the FBI and local police kept tabs on me. They couldn't help themselves. I was a professed Socialist and a member of the American Communist Party. But what could they really do? Russia was our ally after Pearl Harbor. But there was intimidation and scrutiny of my activities, tapping of the phones, opening my mail, and always a Justice Department official reminding me of my patriotic duty. My survival had little to do with a job or my next meal. It was all about politics and keeping my nose clean until the war was over. So I guess I was lucky. I was in the land I loved, even if it sometimes mistreated me. But I wouldn't give in to threats. I believed in what I was doing; that is, working on behalf of the exploited worker. By comparison, you ladies were aliens in fascist, dictatorial countries."

"I believed in America," Iva countered. "I believed my country would win the war. I really did believe in the democratic system and the American experiment. I saw myself... I saw my family as proof of this promise, even when my own government turned on me. I never lost faith,"

"In some ways I envy the two of you," Mildred said. "I loved America and hated the Soviets, but that was about it. Everything else revolved around one question. How could I survive? How could I avoid the Gestapo rapping on my door? Pretty basic stuff, isn't it? "I remember one incident," Mildred added, "which almost did me in over the most trivial of things."

I was an enemy national without papers in Nazi Germany. It was in 1942, late in the year at a train station where I realized how precarious my situation was in this land of fear. I was making a phone call from a booth. Something silly had happened. I had left my food ration coupons in a nearby coffee shop. I was calling the shop when a large crowd gathered around the telephone booth. They were yelling, "She's an American. You can tell by her accent." Suddenly, a very strong man ripped open the door to the booth and grabbed me. And then he said the most dreadful words I ever expected to hear. "I'm from the Gestapo, come with me." I tried to explain that I worked for Radio Berlin. I showed him my identification card. He simply brushed it aside. And then he arrested me. That doubled the situation. I, almost in a panic, pointed out to the man, that if I didn't go to work, such an action could be considered sabotage for neglecting to do my job. I asked him to call the station and speak to my manager, Schmidt-Hansen. This he finally did and then we both went to the station, where he finally released me with an off-hand apology: "Well, ten times out of eleven you're wrong, but the eleventh time you're right." The incident reminded me of my complete dependence on my job at Radio Berlin, and the good will of people there if I were to avoid future harassment and arrest.

"Survival was dependent on papers," Iva said, especially a passport. Unfortunately, I didn't have one. I had left America so quickly in early 1941 that all the State Department would provide was a *Note of Identification.* Just before Pearl Harbor, the American Embassy in Tokyo refused to issue a passport to me, fearful that I might be a spy, a 'third columnist.' I was stuck. Because I was of Japanese ancestry and without a passport, I was denied, as I said earlier, internee status. At the end of the war, of course, no passport was needed to return to the US. I was arrested in Japan and returned home under with a military police escort."

"Passport… I hate the term Mildred said once Iva finished. The loss of this document can condemn you to near death. I remember…"

I went to the US consulate in Berlin in the spring of 1941 to renew my passport. It is not true that I was summoned by the vice counsel, a man named Vaughn. I don't know how that rumor began. While meeting with his secretary, I did mention I worked for Radio Berlin. I explained I didn't see anything wrong with my professional work. I was asked to return the next day, which I did. This time Vaughn was there to meet me. He seemed very agitated. He "snatched" the passport from my hand and then locked it in a desk drawer. I was given a receipt for the passport and asked to leave. Without papers, I was stateless. I think he did so because I refused to be repatriated to America with war looming. And before you ask, I am aware of another theory put forth by those who wanted to demean me to explain Vaughn's action. At its heart, this view found me guilty of criticizing President Roosevelt. The claim was I had mixed anti-Semitism and homosexuality when I linked the President to his kike boyfriends. That was not my intention. I was only pointing out that the White House and American Jews were intimately connected by politics and money and both wanted America in the war. Of course, as I often wondered, when did it become a crime for an American to insult the President? As you know, surviving in Germany without papers was difficult. The shadow of the Gestapo was always in the background. As in the case of Iva, I wouldn't

need a passport after the war. Escorted by military police and the FBI, I was given a free ride home courtesy of the Justice Department.

"I must admit, Iva and Mildred, that my passport problems were, by comparison, less complicated and certainly not as potentially dangerous. The State Department merely made it difficult to travel to the Soviet Union in the late'50's due to the politically repressive oratory of Senator Joseph McCarthy of Wisconsin and the general right-wing attack on American civil liberties, particularly free speech. During my eventual nine-month trial for "advocating the violent overthrow of the American government," which I never did, I was given a quasi-passport, newly minted for me alone. Essentially, the judge said I could avoid prison time if I voluntarily agreed to deportation to the Soviet Union. Naturally, I rejected the judge's kind offer. And I'm glad I did. Otherwise, I would have missed meeting the two of you."

SEPTEMBER 28, 1955

By our third meeting, we were letting our hair down somewhat. Mildred was still wary of me and I of her, while Iva, apparently oblivious to our belligerency, smiled and sailed blissfully between our warring ships. This meeting touched on the question of patriotism. That is, our feelings about the United States following Pearl Harbor. All of us knew, of course, that our views, to some extent, were a matter of record. We also knew there were nuances which, hidden from the public's purview, provided a fuller understanding of our behavior. As was becoming our pattern, Iva spoke first to this question of loyalty.

Iva's Story

"I was born on July 4, 1916 — Independence Day. Given that start, how could I be an unpatriotic American? And then there was my immigrant father. He wanted his children to be Americanized. We had to speak English at home, not Japanese. We ate American food, unless it was a special holiday. We celebrated American traditions and holidays, not those of the homeland. I was a Nisei, a second generation, American-born child. I was a citizen according to the 'Fourteenth Amendment.' I was a Girl Scout. I had a crush on Jimmy Stewart, my favorite actor. I listened to radio shows. My favorites were the *Shadow* and *Little Orphan Annie.* I went to Compton High School and attended UCLA, where I earned a degree in Zoology. I intended to become a doctor. I was even, if you'll believe it, a registered Republican. I voted for Wendell Wilkie in 1940, not Roosevelt. I couldn't have been more American. And naturally, the Justice Department considered all this irrelevant to the charges against me. Maybe next time I'll vote Democratic.

"I despaired when I heard about Pearl Harbor. I was living with my aunt in Tokyo. Immediately, I was a 'suspect' in the eyes of our neighbors, possibly a spy. And because of my initial angry comments about the 'sneak attack,' I was labeled a turncoat. I wasn't a real Japanese. The authorities wanted me to renounce my American citizenship. I refused to do so. Paradoxically, if I had, I couldn't have been tried for treason. Of course, being young and foolish, I openly voiced my pro-American views. The Kempeital, the secret police, made life miserable for me, always threatening me with imprisonment. This became especially true during the 'Doolittle Raid over Tokyo.' I could see the American insignias on the low-flying planes. I hooped and hollered during the attack. Not a wise thing to do.

"Eventually, I got a job with Radio Tokyo translating radio scripts and related materials. That brought me into contact with POW's, who were forced to broadcast propaganda to Allied troops in the Pacific. Soon I was smuggling morsels of food and what medicines I could to these men. Had I been caught, I would have been executed. Because the Japanese authorities wanted a woman broadcaster, the radio-POW's requested me. I agreed on the condition I would not be engaged in propaganda. I did agree, however, to undermine the propaganda value of the broadcasts right under the noses of our Japanese supervisors, who had little understanding of the English language, our pop culture, or American idiosyncrasies as related to our syntax. I was with Radio Tokyo for over two years. At no time, however, was I unpatriotic. I wanted America to win the war. I believe my actions demonstrated my love for my country, even though a latter judge, jury, and Justice Department took another view of my loyalty.

Mildred's Story

"No question about it," Mildred commented. Pearl Harbor changed my life, too. I was working in the studio at Radio Berlin when the news came in about the attack. I freely admit. I was stunned at the news. Who wouldn't be? I broke down in front of my colleagues. I became hysterical and lost all discretion. I denounced both Japan and Germany, though I don't remember the actual words. Some said I screamed, '… sons of bitches. The dirty, yellow, slant-eyed bastards! Goddamn Hitler. He's behind this. I know he is.' My colleagues tried to stop me. I remember that. They were grabbing me even as I continued to rant. I know I yelled, 'How many deutsche marks did you pay the Japs to bomb Pearl Harbor?'"

"Dangerous words, Mildred," Gurley quickly added.

"You have no idea."

"Of course, I was committing an offense that could have resulted in my immediate arrest, and deportation to a concentration camp. My whole situation had changed drastically. No longer was I from a neutral country. America was now a belligerent. I was now an enemy national. But in the moment of my anger, I wasn't thinking about those things. I wasn't really thinking about the Stars and Stripes and Francis Scott Key. I wasn't thinking about the tragedy of lives lost and ships sunk. No, my mind, that part that was thinking rationally, was appalled by what all this meant. Now the US would enter the war against Germany and, if successful, defeat the Nazi Regime. But that would only mean a Russian victory in Europe and the advance of Communism westward. I hated the Japs for this. For me, that was the real tragedy of December 7th.

"I couldn't choke back the words. I was told to go home and not to report to work the next day. When I did return, the manager of Radio Berlin, Johannes Schmidt-Hansen disciplined me about my remarks about Germany's ally. I was told I would be dismissed from my job and possibly be deported to a prison camp unless I signed an 'oath of allegiance' to the German Reich. Such an oath would not make me a German citizen, nor would it end my American citizenship. Given the situation, I felt I had no other choice but to sign an oath. On December 9th, one day before Hitler declared war on the US, I returned to work with a signed oath. What else could I do?"

"Mildred, there's a story that Goebbels himself threatened you with piano wire or the firing squad if you didn't sign the oath. Any truth to that?"

"None, Iva. I don't know how that story came about. Certainly, he knew what I had said. Informants were everywhere. And I'm sure he contacted Schmidt-Hansen, who never did anything without an okay from above. As to piano wire, had I been sent to a prison camp, who really knows what would have happened? They used a lot of piano wire in those days."

"A couple of follow up questions… You always argued that you could broadcast without hurting America, right?"

"Of course."

"That you loved America throughout the war?"

"Naturally."

"But that you hated Roosevelt for bringing America into the war?"

"I did hate him, Iva."

"That you hadn't abandoned America?"

"I didn't. America abandoned me by taking away my passport."

"And you acted this way because?"

"To save my job, to save my life. What real choice did I have? Unlike you, Iva, the authorities were not prepared to let me starve to death on the streets. In my case, the Gestapo would not have been so compassionate. Do you understand? I wanted to live."

"And the propaganda broadcasts you made following Pearl Harbor?"

"Gurley, again, the scripts were written by someone else."

"You could have followed Iva's tack. Right?"

"Wrong. The Germans were too smart for that game. At Radio Berlin, there was no plot to undermine the broadcasts. In my shoes, I don't think Iva would have either, or you Gurley. The luger was always pointed at my head."

"Mildred has a point," Iva said.

"Still, she might have done something."

"Don't try to make a heroine out of me. I wasn't that brave. It was easy for you, Gurley, to be strong, safe in America where the worst thing that happened was food rationing, a 'meatless Tuesday,' oleomargarine, no nylons. Not bombs falling all around you, not starvation in the streets, not the Russian armies marching toward Berlin, not piano wire. If you wish, call my views self-serving. So what? We all rationalize. Otherwise, how could we really accept our own thoughts and actions? I did what I had to do. Didn't you? A critic of Roosevelt before Pearl Harbor, a supporter after, not much consistency there. But, I'm sure, Gurley, that you've rationalized things, too."

Gurley's Story

"What can I say? Mildred, you have me there. From the look on Iva's face, she had reached the same conclusion. All of us had to justify our actions. It was the glue that kept us going. I had been a critic of Roosevelt's military buildup prior to the Japanese attack. I was against the draft. I was opposed to the "destroyer deal." I felt he was leading us toward war. Once again, we would be aiding the British. The Irish in me rebelled at the thought. But World War I also hung on my mind. We were doing the same thing all over again. Getting embroiled. As a Socialist, I saw the vices of the Nazi Regime and the sins of fascism. I didn't want a powerful Germany attacking Russia and destroying the revolution. As to Stalin, I could have done without him. He was just a Czar in a new uniform. Of course, I was out of step with most Americans, who saw both Berlin and Moscow as threats.

"After Pearl Harbor and Hitler's declaration of war on the US, I came out four-square for America. I remember writing:

We cannot live complacently in a world where homes are destroyed, children starved, women raped, religion violently suppressed, democracy stamped out, minority group's exterminated, human dignity degraded. There can be no peace and happiness for all people until Nazi-fascism is destroyed.

"In acknowledging this, I was at odds with Mildred. She, of course, wanted Russia defeated. I didn't. So be it. As to being a Communist and I quote my own words, Remember in Germany and all fascist countries, the Communists were outlawed but so were all people's parties, the unions, and the women's organizations. All democratic rights and institutions disappeared. One thing you can say about the fascists, they didn't discriminate. The Nazis ran an equal opportunity prison. It all got down to this after Pearl Harbor: our security, our honor, our self-respect, and our humanity were all at risk. All of this demanded that we win this just war. There can never be compromise with savagery and slavery.

"The difference between Mildred and me was that I could come out publically against Hitler and Tojo, and Il Duce. She couldn't. Certainly, not after she signed the "oath of allegiance." What did Mildred really believe? That was the question. Her one outburst suggested a reservoir of locked up anti-Nazi feelings, which for one moment, were given free rein. Did she really want the US to lose the war? Or was it that she simply wanted Germany to win the conflict? Either way, she wanted Russia to lose. Definitely, she would have been happier with America on the sidelines.

OCTOBER 5, 1955

Girls being girls, even if our ages balked at that terminology, our sixth meeting was about love, our romances, the men in our lives, the bearded, charming creatures who brought us joy and pain, adventure and troubles, the men who stood by us, and sometimes hastily left the scene. It was obvious that both Iva and Mildred were reluctant to take the lead with this topic so I was forced to do so. This patch of our lives was not, as time proved, easy for us to share.

Gurley

"I was very much in love with Carlos. He was tall and darkly handsome with a challenging fierceness to his words and actions. In so many ways, he was my exact counterweight. I had flaming red hair and what some called alabaster skin. He was Italian. He had dark skin. We shared politics and the fight to uplift the workingman. Already we were sounding the distant chords of our fight:

Work is the right of all, regardless of sex, color, creed, or language. A lack of clarity on this creates discord in families and the shop, indifference in unions, and insecurity among women workers. Just as discrimination causes the deepest resentment among Negroes...

"In time, we also shared a common bed. Our affair continued for 10-years. We lived with my mother and sister in a cold-water railroad apartment in the South Bronx. And then it all ended. Carlos was a notorious womanizer. Perhaps I could have lived with that, but he was also open about it. That was too much. In 1922, he fathered a son with my sister, who was eight years younger. That finally ended our relationship and not on a happy note. A pity, though; I really loved him. One final point: I never remarried. I needed to be independent. I needed to be free. I needed to do my work. By this time in my life, I saw marriage as an anchor. A domestic life and a large family had no attraction for me. I wanted to speak and write. I wanted to travel and meet people. I wanted to organize for the IWW. I saw no reason why I, as a woman, should give up my work for marriage. I was a Socialist. I was involved in the campaign for suffrage. I wanted the vote, not the altar."

"What about Joe Hill?"

"Iva, I liked Joe. But he was headed in another direction. I'll always wonder, not regret, what might have been. In some ways, with his music, you know, Joe gave me more love than most men."

"Than you're ahead of me," Mildred said. "Way ahead."

"Want to talk about it?"

"Not really, Gurley. Iva?"

"Sure. Why not?"

Iva

"I had the usual teenage crushes on the cute boy in class or the movie star who captured my heart. Nothing really serious at UCLA, a few dates. My studies came first, and helping my parents with the family business.

"About 1943, I met Felipe d'Aquino, a Portuguese national who was living in Tokyo, and who was working at Radio Tokyo. We really hit it off. We shared the same pro-American sentiments. When I was almost destitute, he provided me with financial assistance and helped me to keep my spirits up, no strings attached. He was there for me when I was in the hospital with pellagra and beriberi, and malnutrition. The hospital costs were beyond me. He helped. Eventually, I moved from my work at a news agency to Radio Tokyo where we were reunited. In 1944 we were married. We had a brief period of happiness. The next year I lost our only baby soon after he was born, and just shortly before the war ended. All too soon we were separated. American military authorities placed me under arrest. I was placed in a Tokyo jail with other war criminals prior to my return to the US to stand trial for treason. The FBI wouldn't permit Felipe to come with me. Later he was allowed to testify on my behalf and then was quickly returned to Japan. I'd been told that after I'm released, if and when that occurs, I might visit him in Japan, but I could never return to America. What kind of harsh justice is that? Felipe was told he would be arrested if he tried to return to the United States to see me. I'm afraid I'll never see him again."

"I'm sorry, Iva."
"Me, too, kid," Mildred added. "The deck was stacked against you."
"Against you, too?"
"You think so, Gurley? Decide for yourself."

Mildred's Many Loves

"I didn't have much luck with men. Maybe it all started with my biological father, Vincent Sisk, a Canadian, who married my mother Mary (Mae) Hewitson in 1900, the same year I was born. My father worked hard as a blacksmith. He was big and strong, always good qualities unless you're using them to beat your wife, which he did regularly, especially when he was drunk. He drank a lot and also used opium. Being physical with his wife happened once too often. My mother finally divorced him, arguing 'cruel and abusive treatment' in court. She was awarded full custody of me. My father never beat me, but I was always fearful that he would. He was a constant companion who even followed me in my dreams."

"Jesus," Gurley said with a mixture of compassion and anger.

"What happened then?" Iva asked.

"My mother remarried."

"My mother met a dentist, a railroad dentist by the name of Dr. Bruce Gillars. On the face of it, he was completely different from my biological father. He was a graduate of the Philadelphia College of Dentistry. No question, that he was a hard worker, very professional. My mother married him in 1908. About a year later, my half-sister was born, Edna Mae Gillars. Dr. Gillars never formally adopted me. I, however, took his name. Sisk was a dirty word as far as I was concerned.

"What's a railroad dentist?" Eva asked.

"Most of his patients were railroad workers, both those building them, and those who maintained them. As they moved, so did all of us. It was a bit rootless for our family until we finally settled in Conneaut, Ohio. That was his base of operations. From there, he traveled around the state to pull teeth and earn a living."

"Sounds like he was a big improvement," Iva commented.

"In many ways, yes."

"And in other ways?"

"Let's put it this way, Gurley. He was an alcoholic. He didn't beat our mother. He just drank too much. It ruined his health. And it led to other things."

"Such as?" Iva asked.

"Such as my mother putting me in a Roman Catholic convent school before we moved to Ohio to get me away from home."

"Meaning?"

"Let's just say I was 'hurt' by him, and by the strict way he treated me during my high school years when it came to dating. I couldn't wait to get away from home. I came to despise my stepfather. As you can see, I was batting two for two, at least with father-images."

"I guess I'm the lucky one," Iva said. My father always supported me. I always knew he loved me. He always stood behind me. He almost went broke paying for my defense. He's an honorable man. He loves this country, even after our family was forced into a relocation camp. When I leave this place, I'll work in the family store. I can't wait for that day."

"You are the lucky one, Iva," Mildred said. "I never seemed to get a break where love was involved."

"Perhaps it all began at Ohio Wesleyan University which I first attended in 1918. There I met Calvin Gladding (Kelly) Elliott, a handsome young man, who was known as the Bohemian of the class. He was what they called a 'free spirit.' He was also the first boy on campus to grow a beard. Because I was a bit of a rebel myself, he fell for me and my long hair, shoulder-length when most coeds wore their hair in a bun. We were inseparable on campus and, of course, our studies suffered, but not our romance. He gave me his fraternity pin as a token of his affection and proposed marriage. I accepted his overture. A couple of years later I broke off the engagement and then dropped out of Wesleyan in my senior year. I thought those were good decisions at the time. Looking back, I knew I wanted to be loved, but after watching my mother's two marriages, I just wasn't ready for Kelly. I was beginning to think that marriage was a great way to destroy love. And I wanted to follow a career in the theater.

"I came under the influence of Professor Charles M. Newcomb. He headed the Wesleyan drama department and encouraged me to leave the school and attend the Chronicle House in Cleveland, a for-profit school for aspiring actors. I felt I was ready for this and followed him to

Cleveland, where he took a new job, minus his family. This was about 1922. My mother, of course, was against this whole business. But what could she do? Off I went with the newest man in my life. Over the next few years we drifted apart. In the late 20's I was posing regularly for the sculptor Mario Korbel in New York. I was 28-years old and still trying to break into the legitimate theater. Posing helped pay the bills. Korbel was most kind to me. He paid my way to Paris where I hoped to find work as a dancer or model. I crossed the Atlantic, and he soon followed. Paris was beautiful, the sun, poetry, good wine, and art. And, of course, Korbel… Naturally, we went our separate paths in time. Somewhere in this period I met Bernard Metz, who worked for the British government. We hit it off. When he was transferred from Paris to Algiers in 1932, I followed along. He was the man in my life at the time, but again things didn't work out. He was moving up the diplomatic ladder and I wasn't on any of the rungs. I kept our past relationship to myself once I began work at Radio Berlin. You see, Bernard was not only British. He was also a Jew."

"Mildred, you should have come home after all that," Gurley said in obvious distress for the younger woman. "There was nothing for you in Berlin."

"My mother said the same thing, you know. She traveled to Europe just before Poland was invaded. But I couldn't leave."

"I don't understand. What was left for you?"

"A last chance at love."

"I met Dr. Paul Karlson, a physicist and chemist, who was born in Estonia. He had emigrated to Germany where he became a citizen. By 1941, I was seriously involved with him. He wanted to marry me. And I wanted to marry him. The problem was he would not leave Germany. If I did, I would do so alone. A little unsure of my own feelings, I shared my problem with Erwin Christiani, a friend at the station. He gave me the only advice possible. If I were sure Karlson would marry me, I should stay." He was kind, pointing out with discretion that at the age of 41, my marital opportunities were diminishing. And so I stayed for love, not for political views, not because I endorsed the Nazis, not out of any conviction for fascism. As the final ships out of Germany left for England and America, I remained behind. As it turned out, all for naught."

"What happened?" Iva eagerly asked.

"I was told he was conscripted and sent to the Eastern Front. He left without marrying me."

"What happened to him, Mildred?"

"Gurley, I was never told. I guess he didn't survive the war."

"How awful," Iva said.

"My life in spades."

"But you did meet another man?"

"I did, Gurley."

"Care to tell us about Dr. Max Otto Koischwitz?"

"You know about him."

"I followed your trial."

"Not today, Gurley. Perhaps, not ever."

"A final love?"

"Yes."

Rita put down the manuscript and gave a giant sigh, distracting Helen from her intense studies.

"Done?" Helen asked.

"I think so."

"Did you find what you were looking for?"

"Oh, yes, and more than I expected."

"Good."

Unexpectedly, the door opened and Smith popped in, saying, "Anyone for lunch? The Smithsonian is treating, which means the best hot dog in the Washington Mall."

"Rita?"

"Sure, Helen, with sweet mustard and chili beans on the side. And a diet soft drink to balance off my diet."

"Good. I just felt my stomach flip over at the mere mention of a Hebrew National."

"Thanks for your assistance."

"Well, you did a great job, Rita. You've earned your internship pay."

"Starvation wages! But at least Samuels will be happy. Your Rosetta Stone really helped fill out Mildred's story."

"I'm sure there's more," Helen said.

"That's what Samuels always says. There's always more."

Edna Mae's Questions

Even as Rita and her Smithsonian buddies headed for their hot dog lunch, far away in Ohio, Edna Mae found herself engrossed in one of the three scrapbooks she kept about her sister. Over the years she had collected every letter, newspaper or magazine article that came her way. Along with any photographs, she had carefully pasted everything dealing with Mildred's life onto the stark, black pages. Always a detail person, she had added identifying words, and here and there longer commentary.

Now, as she again turned to the scrapbooks, the same old questions refocused to challenge her sisterly support for Mildred. What did you really believe, Mildred? Did you buy the Nazi line? Why did you dislike Jews? Was stardom so important to you? Did money mean that much?

And then other questions would emerge. Do you realize what pain you brought to this family? How much you hurt mother. She worried so much about you during the war years. No letters. Nothing. And then the accusations that you were a traitor, and that you had conspired against your own country. That took years off her life. And how much you hurt me... Did you ever consider that? The looks people gave me.

Guilt by association with a turncoat sister, that's what people said. The jobs I lost when people found out who I was. It wasn't fair. It wasn't right. Why couldn't you just fall in love and settle down? Why were you always the rebel, the non-conformist, the free spirit?"

And then the tears would come. You're my sister. I can't abandon you. I won't forsake you.

Alderson Federal Prison For Women

Axis Sally Prison Photo

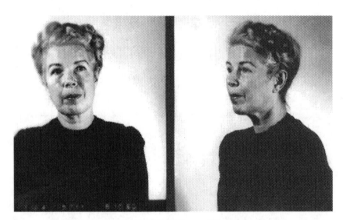

Gillars arrives in the U.S. Greeted by Newsmen

Axis Sally returns to the United States   Axis Sally

Gillars in the German Prison Cell   Gillars returns home escorted
by Katherine Samaha

Mildred Gillars Interviewed by the ARMY

Tokyo Rose in prison

Released from prison

Mildred Gillars

Youthful Axis Sally

CHAPTER 14
THE UNHOLY TRIO

Samuels' New Chair

Robert Samuels sat back in his new, highly padded, very comfortable office chair. He had a happy look of satisfaction on his face. Brown in color, his favorite hue, and tufted attractively, the chair provided a solid wall of fine leather that in turn gave his bad back the therapeutic resistance it needed. He had requisitioned it two months ago, and now it was finally here courtesy of his editor, who, bless his frugal heart and conniving soul, had approved the purchase with one predictable request: "Keep the Axis Sally stories coming. One per week... No let up... Our readers are into it."

And they were... After the first two installments, letters to the editor were piling up as readers became fascinated with the Ohio girl who broadcasted propaganda from Berlin. There was very little old-fashioned pro and con stuff on the topic. People just wanted to know more. At least to this point, the public wasn't taking sides. And that was okay with Samuels, especially after the year-old struggle concerning Tokyo Rose. He liked writing. He disliked being a target for people's frustrations and anger, and the nasty letters with dire warnings.

Now, as he sat back in the comfort of his new chair, he thought about the fine work Rita had done. The young lady was good. Her notes were complete. Her conclusions were well thought out. Her suggestions were appropriate. She was one heck of an intern. He was fortunate to have her services.

For the first time, he as if he were finally getting a real handle on Axis Sally. Out loud and only to the four walls, he had said a moment ago, "I'm getting closer to you, Mildred." To himself, he knew what was happening. He was beginning to understand what made Mildred Gillars tick, not fully, not completely, but enough. Her scent was in his journalistic nose. He was going to track her down. His thoughts now turned to his phone call to Edna Mae made earlier in the day before his new chair arrived.

"Edna Mae."

"Mr. Samuels."

"I thought we should chat for a moment."

"How thoughtful of you."

"You read the first two articles in the series?"

"Yes. Thank you for sending me advanced copies."

"And?"

"Well written, Mr. Samuels. Very objective, very fair to Mildred."

"Good. Does your sister know what's going on?"

"Mildred does. I gave her copies."

"Did she blow a fuse?"

"Interestingly, no. In fact, and I hope I'm not reading too much into her response, she actually seemed to enjoy a little late notoriety. Oh, she never came right out and said it, but I could see she was pleased."

"A last chance at senior stardom?"

"She always enjoyed being a celebrity."

"Perhaps this is the edge we need to convince her to meet with me. Did the subject come up, Edna Mae?"

"No. It never came up. My fault really… I figured it made no sense in rocking the chair too soon. Know what I mean?"

"At some point, I will have to meet with her. You know that."

"I do."

"Then we understand each other?"

"We do."

"Take care of yourself, Edna Mae. I'll ring back in a couple of weeks."

"I'll look forward to your next call, Mr. Samuels."

Edna Mae, you're a good sister, Samuels thought to himself after hanging up. You've always stood by Mildred. Pushing through a small stack of 3 X 5 cards, he came across what he was looking for, an old quote by Edna Mae from the time of Mildred's trial. Samuels had found it most revealing:

I believe if my sister did anything, which was treasonable to her country, she did it unwillingly. If she is in trouble, I want to be by her side.

What more could any sibling want, Samuels reflected? Even though Edna Mae and her family had suffered because of what her sister did, she still stood by her. That took real love and conviction. After all, Edna Mae had lost her job when Mildred was arrested in March 1946 as word spread like a prairie wild fire that Axis Sally had a sister. Unfairly or not, her affiliation with Mildred was the sole reason for her termination. One sister was in jail. The other was out of work. Edna Mae had been stained by her sister's wartime activities and haunted by the immediate post-war reaction to Axis Sally's arrest. Regretfully, the media seemed to attack the entire family, not just Mildred. It did so in a mean and coarse manner.

The shame of the whole affair landed right on anyone connected to Mildred. Edna Mae and Mildred's mother would be the first final casualty. Her mother died in 1947 heartbroken that she had been unable to bring Mildred home from Europe years ago. Still Edna Mae wouldn't back off. She would also be there for her sister's moral support whether Mildred desired it or not, Edna was going to be there. She, Samuels knew, would always be there. That was Edna Mae.

Still musing, thinking, and considering, Samuels' zoning moment was abruptly interrupted by a repetitive knocking on his office's half-closed door. Standing there was a very tall, good-looking young man with a broad smile on his face, Ron Siegel, another former student. As always, he was wearing his San Francisco State EVENT STAFF jacket, denoting both his school of choice and current job of need. Looking at him, Samuels recalled their very first meeting in the college's parking lot well over a year ago.

"Sticker, Sir!"
"Sticker?"
"Faculty sticker, Sir. I don't see one on your windshield."
"You're right. No sticker, no laundry."
"Sir, we've been trained to avoid ethnic or racial slurs. Please show your sticker or remove your vehicle now."

"Here it is. Are we okay now?"
"You're good, Sir. Sorry for the inconvenience."

"Ron, good to see you're still protecting State's parking lot from the forces of evil lurking on the faculty."

"With diligence and working here at the *Chronicle* as an intern."

"And with the research topics I gave you?"

"Equal determination."

"Good, have a seat and tell me all."

"First, thanks for the job and the pay. It really helped. Just one semester to go."

"My pleasure and the *Chronicle's* money put to good use. Now…"

"New chair, Mr. Samuels?" Ron asked, completely off topic.

"Yes. Like it?"

"Plush."

"You can't sit on it, Ron."

"Territorial imperative, Mr. Samuels?"

"Squatter's rights."

"After all the work I've done for you?"

"You almost gave me a ticket, Mr. FBI."

"I did save your car from being broken into. Doesn't that count for something?"

"Yes, your present and precarious job with the paper. Now J. Edgar, what did you learn?"

"You asked me to check on the three American broadcasters. I did. I refer to them as the 'Unholy Trio.'"

"Catchy, Ron."

"All traitors, all scum, all deserving of their fate in my opinion."

"It seems you've clearly made up your mind, Ron?"

"Completely."

"Good, Ron. We are, would you believe it, in total agreement? Scum is too nice a word for these guys. Still, let's hear what you found out."

Radio Berlin Traitors

"To begin with, each man, William Joyce, Frederick W. Kaltenbach, and Robert H. Best, all worked at Radio Berlin during the war along side of Axis Sally."

"And from that you reached certain conclusions, I assume."

"Five. First, they were, as they described themselves, all professional colleagues. They interacted with each other, which meant they shared ideologies and perspectives they held in common. Second, they completely bought the Nazi line and the Hitler 'hero worship.' Third, they commented on and influenced each other's show, either directly or indirectly. Fourthly, they had a profound dislike, even hatred of

Churchill and Roosevelt, and all of them were violently anti-Semitic. Fifth, their avowed propaganda goals revolved around three things: one, keep the US, if possible, out of the war; two, break down American troop morale if the US entered the war; three, justify all comments by the need to stop Soviet bolshevism from spreading across. Europe."

"They influenced Mildred?"

"Yes. Axis Sally to one degree or another, found herself drawn into their web of distorted beliefs in order to maintain her own show in competition for scarce Reich marks and the finite celebrity status available at Radio Berlin. In short, to remain a star, she had to out dazzle the others. And in many respects she did."

"Of the trio, whom do you want to start with?"

"His Lordship."

"The British press called *William Joyce, Lord Haw-Haw*, even though he was an Irish-American born in Brooklyn, New York, April 24, 1906. He got his moniker after going to work for Radio Berlin in 1939. In response to Joyce's propaganda broadcasts, Jonah Barrington, a British reporter for the *Daily Express*, tagged him with the name, Lord Haw-Haw. The nickname was originally been applied to James Brudenell, the 19th-century British general who led the infamous Charge of the Light Brigade. The London reporter pointed out sarcastically, "He (Joyce) speaks the English of the 'haw-haw, dammit-get-out-of-my-way' variety." The name stuck, especially as Joyce's fame and popularity grew in response to his show, *Germany Calling*. He was so popular with English listeners that he was introduced on the air as William Joyce, otherwise known as 'Lord Haw-Haw.'"

"Curious thing about his British listeners. Very few of them agreed with Joyce's views, especially when he asked the British people to surrender. Few liked his jabbing, jeering, sarcastic, and menacing tone, which flavored his ranting and radio rages. So, you might ask, why did they listen to his spiel? The answer was, of course, censorship. What

Brits were permitted to read and listen to was severely censored by the government, and with good reason, particularly in the first days of the war. There was very little good news. In Europe, the Nazis were on a roll, as were the Japanese in the vast Pacific. But there was still a desire by civilian listeners to hear what the other side was saying, since information during wartime was so restricted. For a time it was only possible to get more information than the BBC was providing by listening to Radio Berlin. Strictly speaking, it wasn't against the law to tune in Joyce, though many did so on the QT. At the height of his popularity and influence in 1940, Joyce had an estimated 5 million regular listeners and as many as 18 million occasional listeners throughout the United Kingdom. Sometimes it was the BBC itself that contributed to his fame by reporting fictitious military successes that were later recanted after Radio Berlin broadcasted the truth of confirmed British losses. The British wanted to hear details that their own government was holding back. This was especially true concerning Dunkirk. As Joyce reported:

As you listened to the British radio a week ago did you get the impression that there was going to be any withdrawal at all? Until defeat turned into rout —absolute — the whole world was being told hour after hour by the BBC that the situation was well in hand. We have long recognized that the British people have been deceived.

"Strangely, as the war went on, and better news was forthcoming, the BBC loosened up with the censorship. Then it was the German turn to covertly tune in Radio London, which in Nazi Germany was against the law. Things were now reversed. It was the German people who wanted to find out what was really happening.

"Joyce's anti-Semitism was well known, even before he left England in 1939 to seek out his destiny in Berlin. His view was adequately summed up when he said:

International finance is controlled by great Jewish moneylenders and Communism is being propagated by Jewish agitators who are at one fundamentally with the powerful capitalists of their race in desiring an international world order, which would, of course, give universal sovereignty to the only international race in existence.

"Many concluded that Joyce's anti-Semitism began in 1924 when he was attacked at a Conservative Party meeting in London. A young man cut his face with a razor slash that ran across his right cheek. It left a permanent scar from his earlobe to the corner of his mouth. Joyce considered the attacker a 'Jewish communist.' Though already influenced by fascist thinking, this incident had a marked bearing on his political outlook.

"In the 1930's, Joyce led marches through Jewish neighborhoods in London after he joined the BUF, the *British Union of Fascists* led by the influential Oswald Mosley. The marches, very much like his verbal attacks on Jews, were intended to be provocative, to stir up anti-Jewish passions, to cause riots, and to bring violence into the city's streets. In response to these demonstrations of fascist sentiment, the British government tried to check the 60,000 strong BUF-membership by passing the Public Order Act in 1936. It was an effort to rein in Britain's equivalent of the "Brown Shirts" in Berlin. The act banned marches in the London area and elsewhere and made it an offence to wear political uniforms and to use threatening and abusive words.

"Still, Joyce spoke out. His oratory was described as such:

Thin, pale, intense, he had not been speaking many minutes before we were electrified by this man's voice, so terrifying in its dynamic force, so vituperative, so vitriolic.

"Joyce also attacked Winston Churchill, Britain's Prime Minister. He asked, who is this man who is supposed to frighten Adolf Hitler? His answer was less than complimentary:

He (Churchill) was the providential leader who was going to lead Britain to victory. Look at him today, unclean and miserable figure that he is, and contrast his contemptible appearance with the bright hopes his propagandists aroused in the minds of people foolish enough to believe that this darling of Jewish finance could really set the might of National Socialist Germany at naught.

"Fortunately, Joyce was wrong about Churchill," Samuels said, interrupting Ron's running report. "Churchill proved to be quite an Imperial lion, who had the last roar. One thing though, Ron…"

"Yes?"

""Why did Joyce flee England in 1939? I never understood that."

"M15."

"Of course, that explains everything," Samuels said with a blank look on his face.

"A friend and fascist-leaning government worker in the British spy unit warned Joyce that the British government was considering interning fascist leaders if the country went to war. This was just after Hitler took over Czechoslovakia and just prior to the invasion of Poland. War was coming. Everyone knew that. The British didn't want 'fifth columnists' in their midst. Thus, the desire to intern fascists in Britain. One step ahead of the authorities, Joyce and his wife left for Germany on August 20, 1939. A few months later, he was working for the German Radio Corporation as an English language broadcaster. Though born in America, and having migrated with his family, first to Ireland and then to England, he now was in his third home, and for this, he would eventually pay the full price."

"His arrest after the war?"

"He was arrested on May 28, 1945 when he made a foolish mistake. He spoke English to two British officers, who immediately recognized the voice of Lord Haw Haw. He tried to deny the accusation and was shot in the hand on the spot. The story goes like this. He was reaching into his pocket to get a false identity paper, which had been supplied to him by the Nazis. The officers thought he was retrieving a weapon.

"His big mouth finally did him in," Samuels said with distain. "Too bad it couldn't have happened a decade earlier."

"Once in British hands there was a problem, however, His trial began at the Old Bailey on September 17, 1945 under cloudy legal circumstances. It was determined that he was an American citizen. Could a citizen of the US be tried for treason against Britain? And once in Germany, he had become an official citizen of that country. The legal entanglements were becoming quite complex. In the case of Rita Zucco the answer had been no. In the case of Mildred Gillars, citizenship had not been an impediment to government prosecutors. The British decided to charge Joyce with high treason and found the hateful figure guilty on a legal technicality. He held a British passport during the early stages of the war. He had committed treason, it was argued, by broadcasting for Germany between September 1939 and July 1940, or before he became officially a German citizen. On January 3, 1946, he was hanged for treason."

"The gallows was almost too good for the bastard," Samuels said, totally lacking in any compassion. "If there's a hell for his strain of fascist, I trust he's enjoying the fires of his transient fame."

"Mr. Samuels, let's stop. You're really worked up. You need a break. We can continue later. What about a Reuben across the street? Great deli there."

"Worked up? You bet. I guess so. I'm not much of a Jew, but that rat rankled me. Lunch, you say? You buying, Ron?"

"It's on the *Chronicle's* dime, I hope."

"As well it should be."

CHAPTER 15

THE BEST MAN

Sandwich Talk

"What a sandwich," Samuels said with obvious joy. "No cheeseburger will ever replace a Reuben."

Robert Samuels and Ron Siegel were walking along Market Street, just a few blocks from the *Chronicle* located at Mission and 5th. They were in no real hurry to get back to the paper. It was a beautiful day in San Francisco. The sun was a bright ball in the sky, the temperature hovered around 77 degrees, and a light breeze shuffled through the city ruffling flags and short skirts with equal dexterity. Tourists and locals mingled on Market, all concerned with their own lives and the important things they still had to do today, even as trolley cars and buses jostled with cabs and visitors on the busy street, carrying within them shoppers and workers, twin sinews of any great city.

"My mother used to call the Reuben a deli stew between two slices of bread, Mr. Samuels."

"Ron, she was far off. It is a sort of stew with layers of corned beef, Swiss cheese, sauerkraut, and Russian dressing on rye bread."

"And grilled."

"Not a Reuben unless it's grilled."

"Whoever came up with it was one smart cookie."

"The award should go to Arnold Reuben, at least according to his daughter, a lovely lady named Patricia B. Taylor."

"And how would you know this, Ron?"

"I'm a bit of a food historian. Keeps me going when I'm not handing out parking tickets to the faculty."

"Surely, we wouldn't want to interfere with that," Samuels replied, his voice coated in equally heavy layers of sarcasm and levity. Tell me more."

"The legend is that the first Reuben was made in 1914. According the story, Charlie Chaplin's leading lady ran into the restaurant yelling, 'Reuben, make me a big sandwich, a combination of whatever you have. I'm so hungry I could eat a brick.' Reuben, as others remembered, cut two thick slices of rye bread and stacked slices of Virginia ham, roast turkey, imported Swiss cheese between the bread slices. He then topped it all off with coleslaw and lots of his own special Russian dressing. After one enormous bite, the actress pronounced the sandwich a hit, saying, "Mr. Reuben, that's the best sandwich I ever tasted in my life. You ought to call it an *Annette Seelos Special."* He thought about that for less than a minute before replying, "Like hell I will, I'll call it a Reuben Special."

"No sauerkraut and corned beef?"

"A later edition, Mr. Samuels."

"I suppose you know who concocted the first cheeseburger?"

"Well, as a matter of fact, Lionel Sternberger is reputed to have invented the iconic burger in the mid'1920's when he was 16-years old. He was working at the *Rite Spot*, a sandwich shop in Pasadena owned by his father. The teen was working as a fry cook when he accidentally dropped a slab of cheese on a sizzling hamburger, and that, as they say, led eventually to the *Big Mac.*"

"Enough, Ron. I'm convinced."

"Sternberger," Ron said with a big smile, "what name could be more perfect for this triumph of American civilization?" By the way, are you interested in knowing how the French fry got its name?"

"No."

Thirty minutes later, Samuels and Siegel were back at the *Chronicle* discussing Robert H. Best, the second of the *Unholy Trio*. Seated very comfortably in his new leather chair, Samuels waited as Ron, sitting very uncomfortably on his hard, wooden chair, shuffled his notes.

Robert H. Best

"Any time, Ron."

"Robert H. Best and Mildred Gillars didn't get along. It was her job to introduce his commentaries at Radio Berlin, what we would call crude diatribes against the Roosevelt Administration and Jews. He was so off the wall that even she was given pause. It wasn't that his anti-Semitic ravings that troubled her. Rather, it was the vehemence and blistering passion that bothered her. It was, many have surmised, the torrent of irrationality, laced with anger that accompanied his propaganda that jolted even the Gestapo bosses at the radio station. Something was not quite right with Best. Beyond that, he had the temerity to criticize Mildred's commentaries. He was always making suggestions as to how she could improve her Jew-baiting skills. According to what I've been able to determine, he wanted her to use the term 'kike' more often in order to 'dress up' up her radio show. Interestingly, if it can be believed, she refused to do this, at least to the extent he wanted. One gets the feeling that Mildred wasn't really that upset with the term 'kike.' What got to her was the insolence of Best, a former newspaper correspondent, questioning the quality of her work. Who was this man to chide her? At the time, she was earning 3,000 Reich Marks per month, more than any other broadcaster. She was living comfortably in wartime Germany. She had generous rations for butter and cheese and the means by which to purchase anything she needed on the black market. She had made it. How dare he to presume to tell her anything.

"Not a match made in heaven, Ron."

"Best, it appears, did not like her using American magazines and newspapers to assist her in preparing her broadcasts. Her boss and lover, Max Otto Koischwitz, used his influence to get her the materials she wanted, even though she was not a high member of the Nazi Party. She wanted the materials in order, or so she said, to avoid being influenced by German propaganda. She wanted to know what was going on in the States, unfiltered except for American censorship. Of course, it was for this reason that Best wanted access to the foreign press denied."

"Tough lady."

"Tough enough. She despised his holier-than-thou image at work. Whereas she played popular music, he refused to have any form of light entertainment on his show because it might detract from the important things he had to say. He displayed an indifferent attitude toward his pay, yet counted every Mark as he was comparing his salary to others. Mildred made no pretense about money. She liked it. She wanted it. Money meant survival. Money meant status, if there were enough of it. Money meant success, something she always coveted and never took for granted. She had spent too many years failing to fulfill her dreams to make it big on Broadway. As for Best, she considered him a phony. After all, for a man who described himself as totally pro-Nazi, he carefully avoided membership in the party, refused to carry a state identification card, and always acknowledged allegiance to the US."

"Is this the pot calling the kettle black?"

"If so, she didn't like the kettle. She pushed Max Otto to remove Best from a shared program, *Home Sweet Home*. This he did. At the least, Best and Mildred were bitter rivals from that point on."

"In your notes Ron, you mentioned the 'exchange incident,' but no real details."

Ron stood up, flexed his youthful limbs and muscles, and stretched to the high heavens before seating himself and answering.

"Any chance of getting a second leather chair?" he asked. "Sitting on this old wooden chair is like the bleachers at my high school. Rough on you know what…"

"It keeps visitors from getting too comfortable. They tend to leave sooner than they expected."

"You are devious, Mr. Samuels."

"Pragmatic. There are only so many hours in a reporter's day. I don't like to waste any of them with idle chat. So now that you're comfortable again, *'Onward Christian Soldier.'*"

"I'm Jewish. Like you."

"Okay. How about *'Onward Jewish Warrior?'*"

"Doesn't have the same ring."

"I agree. Now what about *'onward'* to the exchange incident?"

"After Pearl Harbor, Best and other Americans, including reporters, diplomats, and business people found in Vienna, were taken into custody by the Gestapo and placed in jail before being relocated in an internment camp in Bad Nauheim, Germany. As a group, they were designated 'exchangeable Americans.' That is, at some point, they would be exchanged for German nationals already held by American authorities. At the camp there were 145 internees, who ate dumplings and sauerbraten ad nauseum. During the winter of 1941, they almost froze to death. And, of course, the Gestapo provided daily lessons in bullying, something they were very good at with captives. Understandably, all the internees looked forward to the exchange. Who needed sauerbraten for the duration of the war? Best, however, surprised everyone at the camp. He decided to remain in Germany, and so informed Leland M. Morris, another internee in the camp and the Charge d'Affaires at the US. Embassy. He also notified German authorities of this request.

"According to the Germans, Best wanted to remain in Germany to record events and to tell the story of the war from the Reich's point-of-view in order for Americans to understand what was actually going on. In short, he wanted to interpret the German mind to his fellow countrymen. With such grandiose thinking, he wanted to act as a sort of mediator between Hitler and America after Germany won the war. He also pointed out to German officials he could best do this by working for Radio Berlin. Another reason he stayed, many thought, was Erna Maurer, a 41-year old admirer of Hitler, who later married

Best. In time Best was interviewed by Werner Plack, a member of the Radio Division of the Foreign Office, to determine his fitness for broadcasting. Plack found Best's fanatically charged views about Jews and the Bolshevist menace to be more than appropriate. He was hired and was soon hosting a show called, *'Mr. Guess Who.'* He referred to the show as BBB (*Best's Berlin Broadcasts*).

"He certainly thought a lot of himself."

"He was an ugly man, Mr. Samuels. In October 1942, he pretended he was running for Congress and asked Americans citizens to vote for him. Can you imagine that? He described himself as a protest candidate, stating that he would do his 'best to bring about peace before America had fallen into a state of complete chaos and Jewish slavery.' A year later he told his audience he would run for President in 1944 and pledged, as Roosevelt's successor, to 'recall US arms from Europe and to liquidate one Jewish gangster for every American lost in combat.' He even had a name for his new American political party, *Christocracy.* And he had a new name for an old foe, *Jewdocracy.* There was no limit to his ravings. He ranted against 'funny Frankie as the dupe of the American Jewish interest. He inveighed against the Semitic takeover of Masonic lodges in the United States.'

"Grandiose hardly describes this guy."

"There was no limit to his commentary. Even after he was caught following the defeat of Germany, he said, 'Not only is the Department of Justice powerless to arrest me but no executioner could be found in America so low as to kill a man who had dedicated his life to saving America from the Jews.'"

"He was certainly impressed with himself."

"You should hear his take on Mussolini."

"Somehow I feel I'm about too."

"After Hitler rescued Mussolini from his mountain, Best was able to get an exclusive interview with Haupsturmfuhrer SS Otto Skorzeny who led the raid. Rather than talking about Mussolini's overthrow and the surrender of Italy to the Allies by Marshall Pietro Badoglio's provisional government, Best beamed quite a different story to the US."

Eisenhower had a whole airborne division poised and ready for a dramatic occupation of Rome. The General lost his nerve when he learned from the traitor Badoglio that some Germans had arrived from the sky. The Jews and Jewdocrats behind the Allies were arranging a "cheap publicity stunt." Mussolini was to go to Palermo on September 14, to Gibraltar on the 15th and then on to New York City on the 16th. Pressmen were to cover a tour of a shackled Mussolini led by a Jewish Rabbi.

"As I said, he was very impressed with himself, Ron."

"To the very end. Even after he was sent to jail in the United States, Best continued to live in a world of illusionary hopes, which, I believed, helped him to justify his life. After the US Circuit Court upheld his conviction as a traitor on July 7, 1950, Best, still not resigned to his fate, wrote to President Truman.

As one who has been battling against Soviet Communism unremittingly for almost thirty years, I beg herewith to offer my services in any desired capacity to you as our Chief Executive… And now that the Korean actions of the Comintern has awakened you to at least partial appreciation of the fact that the Soviet Union has been a war-to-the-death enemy; may you never again "backslide" into the errors of understanding such friends as Stalin.

"Truman, I should add, Mr. Samuels, never responded to Best's request."

"Harry knew the backside of a donkey when he saw one. Still, this guy had balls. He just kept coming."

"The other side of the coin is quite different. He was an adequate correspondent. No question about that. He worked for the *Chicago*

Tribune. His critics, who were numerous, took a different stance. According to them, he never achieved the fame and celebrity status he sought before the war. In this, he was very much like Mildred. He was bogged down with a miserable salary and little advancement on the horizon. He was a discouraged man, an expatriate with very few friends, and, to a large degree, dependent on others in the German/Austrian society of his day. He wanted to be a great man, just as Mildred wanted to be a great actress. Each wanted the acclaim accorded greatness. Neither achieved it prior to World War II. Each found an imperfect substitute. They each thought, as they stated repeatedly, it was possible to broadcast for the Nazi Regime and still, as an American citizens, remain loyal to their US roots, though they constantly attacked the President and hammered at a distinct minority within the country. Again, as with Best, Mildred shared many of these self-imposed afflictions and questionable achievements."

"Anything in his background, Ron, to suggest what Best became?"

"At first glance, no. He was a Southerner. He was born in Sumter, South Carolina, on April 16, 1896. His father, Albert H. Best, was an itinerant Methodist preacher. The son was always a good student. In 1922 he graduated from Columbia University's School of Journalism. He also received a Pulitzer Traveling Scholarship, which he used to travel to Europe, Vienna in particular. It was there that he found work as a foreign freelance news correspondent for the United Press in 1923. During the next few years he wrote articles for the *New York Times*, *Time*, and *Newsweek Magazines*. He was what was called a freelance writer or *'stringer.'* To this point, or so it appears, he had Jewish friends and gave no indication of the latent anti-Semitism smoldering beneath the surface. What turned him into a devotee of fascism and Jew-baiting has never been fully explained."

"In the end it really doesn't matter, does it?"

"Not according to Judge Ford, who officiated at his trial. The Judge didn't buy the defense's argument that Best was a fanatic, a crusader, doing what he thought was best for his country as any other person. The Judge summed up the matter as such: 'A fanatic can do as much harm to his country as any other person. He (Best) knew what he was doing. When a man intends to betray his country, his motive is immaterial.'"

"The Judge's words, Mr. Samuels, would, of course, apply to Mildred equally well. Whatever her intentions and motivations, the result was treason."

"Wasn't there a foul up when Best was flown home to stand trial?"

"For a guy who didn't know about the Reuben's origins, you really surprise me, Mr. Samuels."

"How's that?"

"Almost no one knows about Best's crazy flight back to the US. Yet, here you are asking about it."

"Wartime trivia, Ron. It's a curse. So make me happy. Fill in the gaps in my knowledge."

"It really is a funny story."

"Hard to believe anything could be funny where this guy was concerned."

"Hear me out, Mr. Samuels.

"According to a provision in our treason laws, persons accused of treason while abroad must be tried in the district where they first reenter the United States. That sounds simple enough. In Best's case, the plane returning him to America landed at Westover Field, Chicopee, Massachusetts, because of inclement weather. At least that's what the pilot said. The plane, however, was supposed to fly up the Potomac River and land in Washington D.C. So, you ask, how did it get to Boston? The pilot chose not to stick to the original flight plan. He deliberately flew to Boston, the weather notwithstanding. Why, you ask again? He had a girlfriend in Boston and wanted to see her. So what's the problem?

"The treason provision noted created a legal nightmare for the Justice Department. It was a real snafu. Best had to be indicted again in Boston. Witnesses who had testified before one grand jury, now had to be brought back from Germany to do it again before a newly empaneled Grand Jury. The FBI investigative unit dealing with the case, had to move from D.C. to Boston. What appeared to be a simple mistake or a problem with the weather ultimately cost the federal government over $100,000. As for the pilot, he got to see his girlfriend at the government's expense. As for Best, he spent three hours in the airport lounge enjoying a good meal. I don't know if he had a Reuben. Probably not, sounds too Jewish. It was, however, probably the best three hours he'd have in America.

"The upshot of this humorous story concerned our Axis Sally. The FBI was determined there would be no snafu when Axis Sally returned to America. To make this happen the FBI developed a full-proof plan. Once Mildred was in the air, a telephone call was placed to Washington, where prosecutors immediately sought a warrant for her arrest. The route of the plane was predetermined with refueling stops in the Azores and Bermuda. This time the plane would fly up the Potomac and land in Washington D.C. at Bolling Field. There would be no foul up. Then she would be turned over to the FBI and arraigned by a US Commissioner.

Other precautions wee also taken. John M. Kelly of the FBI was assigned to Mildred's case. The Justice Department told Kelly, to be extraordinarily careful in how she was handled. This was to be the case no matter how notorious her reputation. Kelly understood the power of public opinion. He didn't want the government accused of mistreating a defenseless older woman. There was to be no mistreatment. She was to be given food and necessary medical treatment prior to her arraignment.

It was also determined beforehand that the pilot had no romantic inclinations on the East Coast.

"Ron, bring it full circle. What happened at his trial?"

"Besides the fact that Best chose to defend himself, not much. He lost big time. He was convicted of 12 counts of treason on April 16, 1948, and was sentenced to life imprisonment, first at the federal prison in Danbury, Connecticut, and later at the federal medical center for prisoners in Springfield, Missouri. He appealed his case to the US Supreme Court, which refused a hearing. The verdict stood. He had given 'aid and comfort to the enemy.' Three years later, in August 1951, he suffered a brain hemorrhage. A year later he died on December 16, 1952 and was buried in Spartanburg, South Carolina five days later. The best man had come home to his native state."

"Jesus, I'm glad it's the unholy trio," Samuels exclaimed. "Only one more to go. It's tough dealing with these anti-Semites."

"Makes it difficult to look at Axis Sally objectively when these characters were her professional colleagues."

"Very difficult, Ron."

"But?"

"We'll try. Who's up next?"

"Lord Hee Haw."

"Joyce? We already dealt with him."

"Lord Haw Haw? We did."

"So?"

"Lord Hee Haw was his brother in words."

CHAPTER 16
THE OTHER LORD

A Quiet Breakfast – The Next Day

"Great breakfast, Rachel."

"Thanks, Dad."

Robert Samuels was sitting in his kitchen finishing up a scrumptious breakfast prepared by his daughter, Rachel. He was not alone in his assessment of the meal. With him were Ron Siegel and Rita Jackson, both of whom chimed in with their own appreciation.

"Best scrambled eggs I've had in years," Ron said as he pulled the last of his toast across his plate, gathering in every last vestige of Mother Hen's offering. "And those great country potatoes… Wow! So tasty…"

Not to be outdone by Ron, Rita nudged in her two cents and more, saying, "Those homemade hot biscuits were outstanding. You must give me the recipe."

"Well, everyone," Rachel responded, "I gratefully accept your praise. As for the biscuits, Rita, I have a confession. I just follow the directions *Betty Crocker* lays out for me."

It was a quiet Saturday morning in the City by the Golden Gate. A day for sleeping in late, enjoying a lazy morning meal, perhaps mowing the grass, certainly washing the car, and eventually watching a game on TV followed by a BBQ with good friends and family, and, of course, well cooked New York steaks, braised corn covered in butter with a touch of garlic, and Boston-baked beans heated to perfection. Just an untypical weekend day in San Francisco, at least weather-wise…

Unfortunately, Samuels' planned day was less than typical unless, of course, one were a reporter sniffing out an unsightly and uninspiring page in American history concerned with deplorable rascals who committed treason in wartime. If that werethe case, the Samuels' home was most typical of a small group determined to hunt down the country's Nazi past, at least as it flowed through the shortwave air currents during WWII.

"Rachel, again, thanks for the breakfast. You more than filled in for your mother. And Rita and Ron, thanks for coming over. We have two days, I hope, to complete, our review of Mildred's colleagues and to get a handle on why she joined them in a clubhouse of hatred for Jews and distorted view of National Socialism practiced by Hitler's sewer thugs."

"I think that lays out the situation quite objectively," Rachel said as she whisked plates away from the table. "One wouldn't want to let personal feelings enter into this enterprise."

"Indeed, not," Ron quickly remarked, "unless the bastards were just that, pardon my French."

"Your French is okay, Ron," Rita added, "but these Nazi creeps were anything but. The world is better off without them."

"Rachel, it looks like we'll need you to keep us straight. I'm afraid we're a bit partisan at this point."

"Dad, you want me to play the Devil's advocate?"

"When you feel it's warranted, yes."

Rachel finished clearing the table and very quickly notebooks and ballpoint pens and pencils replaced dishes and serving platters.

"Okay, let's get to it," Samuels said. "Ron, you're up."

Before Ron could speak, Rachel yelled from the kitchen, "Ron, don't let my dad push you too hard. Just give him another ticket. It's good for his soul."

"I was considering one for the blasted bleacher-type wooden seat he's been making me sit on in his office for two days."

"Is there a ticket for that?" Rita asked with a smirk that was anything but innocent.

"Bleachers aside, it would be nice," Samuels interjected, "to get started before the Fourth Reich emerges from the ashes of the Third."

"Impatient, aren't you?" Rita asked.

"He's always that way when he's waiting for a phone call from my mother. He's been that way for thirty years."

"Thirty-one to be exact, Rachel."

"That's a lot of impatience," Rita added with a slight laugh as she noticed Samuels' usually cool demeanor evaporating.

"Children, perhaps we could forgo the levity at my expense and move on."

"Now we're dependents on his IRS return," Rita joked. "I do hope he'll share the refund."

"Consider it a status thing, Ron, Rita," Samuels said in a lowered voice through clenched teeth.

"I think we've pushed the old guy enough," Rita said. "What do you think, Rachel? He's your dad."

"Rita is right. We should get down to business. Ron, I'm told you know the history of food. Right?"

"Rachel!" Samuels stormed.

"Some menu items, yes," Ron said.

"What about French fries?"

"My specialty."

"Is this really necessary, Rachel?"

"Relax, Dad. Ron is going to provide us with thought for food.'"

"The beloved French fry refers to thin strips of deep-fried potatoes. We call them fries in the US. In England and Australia they are referred to as chips. The origin of the fry is difficult to determine. One version is that American soldiers in Belgium during WWI called them French fries. Another version goes back to Thomas Jefferson who had 'potatoes served in the French manner' at the White House. Another possible explanation…

"Cease and desist, Ron."

"Dad, are you pulling rank?"

"I am."

"Right," Ron said, caving into the inevitable. "Let's put things in perspective for a moment. We've asked the question, 'Why did Mildred become a traitor?' Let's look at the possibilities. What did Mildred and the others have in common?"

What is a traitor?

"In the immediate postwar years, historians and psychologists have tried to answer this question. The eminent writer, William L. Shirer described the traitors as 'being no different than other human derelicts who were drawn to Nazism as 'a flame attracts a moth.' He considered all of them to be rootless individuals for the most part and incapable of integrating into normal society. Rootless meaning migrating souls roaming outside of the USA and the country's depression-ridden society in the 1930's. Since Shirer knew most of the people who eventually worked for Radio Berlin, before they did so, his words carry weight. He considered them 'renegades,' and possibly mentally unbalanced, and certainly calloused given their personal racist attitudes and immense devotion they gave to Adolf Hitler For Shirer, these people couldn't discriminate between reality and hallucination, especially when it came to justifying their tirades on air.

"Another view focuses on the historical context in which these people lived, or perhaps better said, what these people saw in Germany before the war. This view suggests that circumstances influence behavior. For Joyce, Best, and Mildred, and Frederick W. Kaltenbach, my main topic today, they saw a Germany that had endured the human slaughter of the First World War and the humiliation of the Versailles Treaty, and in particular the clause placing "war guilt" on the German people. In the aftermath of the war, they saw rioting in the streets and revolution in the air. Anarchy, they believed, was overtaking the country they loved. Wherever they looked, they saw the impact of hyperinflation that destroyed the middle class and political instability, and then the unemployment crisis brought on by the Great Depression. And on the horizon, there was always the specter of Bolshevism. These were the conditions that influenced their thinking. These conditions, for these traitors, demanded a scapegoat to explain the cause of these traumas. They also demanded a personality to vanquish these problems, a romanticized warrior on a white horse to save them.

"In the Jew, they found the scapegoat. In Hitler, they found their salvation. In National Socialism they found a fascist vehicle by which Germany's demons might vanquished once and for all. Frederick Kaltenbach summed up the situation in 1936 on Radio Berlin as follows:

There was unemployment everywhere and in the industrial areas everyone of them (workers) were Communists, while Jews were living in luxury. Then Hitler came to power and gave the German people a new lease on life.

"There it is again," Rita said, "the Jews and Communists were at fault for Germany's failings."

"For Kaltenbach, Ron said, "this was the case. He believed in the motto, *'Better Hitler than Stalin.'* He saw the leaders of the Soviet Union as bloodstained criminals who were seeking to overthrow the West. In holding this view, he wasn't all that different than many Americans and British citizens at the time. Wasn't it Churchill who wanted to strangle Bolshevism in the crib in 1918? A major difference was that Winnie didn't assign Jewish authorship to Soviet intentions."

"Didn't Hitler resolve many of Germany's problems?" Rachel asked.

"Kaltenbach alluded to this when he wrote that criticism of Hitler was unfair, unjust, and without merit. He claimed that American propaganda slanted the news negatively, that such rhetoric was motivated by American jealousy of Germany's renaissance during the 1930's. He stated flatly that Roosevelt 'knew he could not tackle the social ills the way Americans thought he could and should, and the only way was to blame Hitler and his (Roosevelt's) failure and to detract public criticism by focusing attention on an imaginary threat from the other side of the ocean.' That in a nutshell was his view, one shared by Mildred, Best, and Joyce."

"He failed to mention," Samuels said, 'that Hitler put Germany on an immediate war footing after taking power.' Putting 2,000,000 plus young men in uniforms certainly gave unemployment a swift kick."

"And hiring others to build tanks, guns, and ships didn't add to the unemployment rolls," Rita added.

"Still," Samuels said, "there was an attachment to Germany that transcended any rational, objective analysis of the Third Reich."

"Which is what we're trying to avoid here," Rachel pointed out.

"The American journalist Joseph C. Harsch, who wrote for the *Christian Science Monitor*, claimed that Kaltenbach was the most effective radio traitor because...

He sincerely believed in Nazism — that he had had a conversion to Nazism — much like Paul to Christianity — that could not be understood on the basis of logic and rationality alone. Like many Germans and the radio traitors, he was attracted to the mysticism of Nazism — to a fabric of flesh and blood beyond thought and analysis — to the Teutonic gods of old wrapped up in an adoring citizenry, which paid homage to the Fuhrer.

"Hard to understand that," Rita said. How could Mildred buy into all that?"

"Perhaps she didn't, at least not altogether. We may never know for sure."

"But enough," Samuels said.

"There were," continued Ron, examples of Nazi adoration that challenge us all. For example, Compiegne."

"Sounds like a French wine."

"If so, Rachel, it was the wine of history. On June 22, 1940, following the French defeat, the victorious Third Reich gathered at the exact spot where years earlier German generals and civilian officials had signed the armistice ending the First World War in a small railroad car. Now after the fall of Paris and Dunkirk that same railroad car was returned to Compiegne for the surrender proceedings. And Kaltenbach was there to write about the event. William Shirer was there, too, reporting for American papers. He watched as Wilhelm Keitel read the instrument of France's humiliation. He noted that Kaltenbach seemed in a trance. He gazed longingly at his Fuehrer as other men might toward their God. There was reverence in his gaze. At that moment, if not sooner, he was without question a 'born Nazi.' Given that, Shirer wrote, 'it was not a surprise that Kaltenbach remained in Germany after Pearl Harbor, as did most of his colleagues.' To one degree or another, Mildred was caught up in this euphoria. For all the traitors fascism, that is, Hitler, promised to end the social, economic, and political lethargy that, as they put it, characterized the 'feeble and plodding liberal democracies.'"

Getting up from her chair, Rachel said, "I need some strong coffee. Any takers?"

All hands went up and Rachel proceeded to the kitchen to grind the Columbian beans her dad always used. It was evident that everyone needed a break. Analyzing Nazi thought was exhausting and depressing. It was very opportune, then, that Samuels' wife called at this moment. Samuels answered and spoke for a few minutes before ending the call as he had done for 31-years, saying, "I love you, too." Rachel returned with the coffee soon after, pointing out that the decaf was for the "old guy," and the high octane was for the kids.

"Old guy! Who's an old guy, Rachel?"

"What did mom say?"

"What you would expect. Did you put out the garbage? Did you feed the cat? Did you stick to your diet? You know, the usual…"

"She didn't mention Iva?"

"In passing, yes."

"Well?"

"She's had two constructive meetings with Mrs. Toguri. They're getting along famously in the 'Windy City.'"

"And?"

"They're talking about Iva's conversations with Mildred at Alderson."

"Pulling teeth is easier than this. Anything new?"

"Lots."

"Well?"

"Leave it at this. She's learning a lot about the *Vision of Invasion* program Mildred starred in."

"So?"

"Recall that eight indictments were brought against Mildred. Seven of them were thrown out. Not guilty. But the eighth did her in and it concerned the *Vision of Invasion* program. That's why this information is important."

"Good for Mom."

"Ron, let's continue."

"We were talking about why ordinary Americans went to work for Radio Berlin. Part of the answer may rest in the programs themselves. That is, what did the broadcasts hope to really achieve? And, if achieved, was this a reflection of the belief systems of the traitors? In my view, the answer is yes. Intent and belief were knitted from the same fabric of ideological zeal and political conviction that Germany's Nazi government represented the wave of the future. And they saw themselves as radio soldiers to bring about this future. The presidential election of 1940 and the resulting debate over the Lend-Lease Act of the same year suggested this.

"Initially, Nazi propagandists sought to split Americans from their leaders and to push labor against management, Blacks against whites, and Gentiles against Jews. Clear attempts were made to enflame

American isolationist passions against interventionists, all the while enhancing the image of Nazi Germany. Later, of course, the focus would shift to breaking down Allied morale to fight, and in the last years of the war, when all was lost, to criticize the West for permitting the Asiatic hordes of Stalin to destroy European civilization. But in the beginning…

"This effort focused on the 1940 election. Kaltenbach and others wanted to prevent Roosevelt's re-election to an unprecedented third term of office, an event the Nazis knew would ensure continued support for Britain. When their efforts failed, the propaganda shifted the emphasis to attack the efforts of the president and the interventionists to aid Britain. This was especially true of the Lend-Lease Act debated in March 1941. Kaltenbach was furious the United States would now lend (provide) Britain with weapons to fight Berlin. There would be no demand for cash on the barrelhead by Washington.

"Kaltenbach voiced the anger and frustration of the traitors once the bill was passed. Now that Roosevelt has signed the Lend-Lease Bill he said:

I suppose the Germans should be bowing before the new lords of the universe, George VI and Emperor Roosevelt I. The Germans have been too busy dropping their iron pellets on Englishmen to worry about the "Union Now" boys in Washington. There is no doubt, however, that Bill 1776 cancels out the year 1776. Compared with the patriots of 1941 Benedict Arnold was a mere piker. All he did was to betray a fort to the Redcoats. The "Union Now" boys have betrayed a whole country. As to Churchill's role in the bill's passage, he wrote, "It's all bunko cooked up by that liar Winston Churchill, First Lord of the Sea Bottom.

"You're not being overly harsh?" Rachel asked Ron.

"I think not. Again, the writer and historian, William L. Shirer, who knew most of these traitors, said of them:"

Most of the Nazi hierarchy consisted of derelicts from the First War, who could not find a place in the Germany of the Republic. Nazism offered them, as it offered our American traitors, a chance to become somebody. It offered them a career and it offered them something ready-made on which to vent their hates.

"These same people," Ron continued, "also bestowed on their anointed savior an uncommon devotion for lifting them out of the gutter, which had been their lives before the mustached one resurrected them."

"Ron, just the facts," Rachel said, perhaps a bit too heatedly.

"Facts! You want facts? Okay. In 1940, Kaltenbach, the *'other Lord,'* wrote this of his favorite Bavarian wallpaper hanger:"

The American people should not be astonished at the enormous popularity enjoyed by Hitler in Germany. Hitler gives life and time for his people: his selflessness has earned him popularity. Christmas holidays given up to be with his soldiers at the front... Where did Chamberlain or Daladier spend Christmas? Hitler was the first soldier of the Reich among soldiers, not the Commander-in-Chief.

"The 'other Lord?' What did you mean by that?" Rita asked.

"Kaltenbach's show, *'Letters to Iowa,'* was beamed to the American Mid-West in particular to build on the isolationist sentiment of the region. Usually, he opened his program by speaking to his friends in Dubuque and by addressing an old friend, Harry, whom he had grown up with. Whatever he aired, there were always two messages for Iowans. 'Don't let the British drag America into this thing, Harry,' referring to the widening war in Europe. 'And don't pull Britain's chestnuts out of the fire again.'"

"Kaltenbrach's program was also heard in England, where he was soon nicknamed *'Lord Hee-Haw'* to distinguish him from his colleague, William Joyce, who had already been dubbed *'Lord Haw-Haw.'* Kaltenbach relished the distinction and enjoyed immense popularity in the US for a few years. The latest research indicates that as many as 300,000 Americans listened to Kaltenbach and others on a regular basis. Until Germany declared war on the US, the German Library of Information in New York mailed out 75,000 free bilingual program guides each week to known listeners. It's hard to believe today but even American newspapers carried program schedules. On an annual basis, 1938 – 1941, the Nazi short-wave system received over 50,000 letters. Kaltenbach, of course, encouraged letter writing via airmail, where, as he said, 'British snoopers can't get at them.' To say the least, he was quite popular. And most of all, he loved turning the Hee-Haw bit on the British with his lively banter."

England is fighting for freedom of the seas — Hee-Haw. England is fighting for the rights of small nations, including India and Ireland — Hee-Haw. English methods, including the hunger blockade and incitement of Russia against Germany are humane — Hee-Haw. England thought Germans would revolt — Hee-Haw. Churchill thought he could tackle submarines and magnetic mines — Hee-Haw. England thinks she can starave Germany and hang up her washing on the Siegfried Line — Hee-Haw.

"How does a Hawkeye end up in Berlin?" Rita asked.

"Ron, take a breather," Samuels said, "I can help you with Rita's question. I know a little about the guy."

"Frederick Kaltenbach was born in Dubuque, Iowa on March 29, 1895. His father was a butcher, Presbyterian in background, who had emigrated from Germany four years earlier. From all accounts, the boy was a good student and had a normal childhood. He was described as a 'studious, introspective' high school student. In 1919, he entered Iowa State Teachers College (now the University of Northern Iowa). After graduation, he worked seven years as a farm appraiser before obtaining a teaching position at Dubuque Senior High as a history teacher. At the age of 36, he was still single and living a rather simple life. He lived at the local YMCA, took French lessons at night, and earned an M.A. in history from the University of Chicago. Outwardly, he appeared to be a model citizen, who worked hard and stayed out of trouble. Then fate intervened.

"Kaltenbach received a scholarship from the University of Berlin to work on a Ph.D. He was granted a two-year leave of absence from teaching to pursue his studies in Germany. It was 1933. Little is known about those two-years beyond this. He witnessed firsthand the changes wrought by the Nazis, which lifted, it seemed to him, Germany out of the Great Depression. He returned to America a changed man and got into trouble almost immediately with the school board.

"In 1935, he formed a student group named the Militant Order of Spartan Knights. Since the "Knights" were the school mascot, everything seemed innocent enough at the beginning. In time many parents saw the group as something akin to the Nazi Hitler Youth movement. The group held secret meetings with initiation rituals, dressed in brown military-style uniforms and carried menacing walking sticks during weekend hikes. One thing led to another, including physical fights with parents, until the school board disbanded the group and terminated Kaltenbach's teaching contract in late 1936.

"At this point, Kaltenbach returned to Germany to continue his studies, and to work part-time as a free-lance writer and translator. He also did short stints of radio work at the Nazi Ministry of Propaganda. By 1939, he was close to completing his studies. Then he met and married Dorothea Peters, a German woman from a well-known military family with influence within the Nazi Party. With her strong assistance, he gained a favorable position with Radio Berlin.

"After Germany attacked Poland, the State Department contacted all Americans living in Germany to encourage them to leave before they were stranded abroad. He refused, as did most of his broadcasting colleagues. During questioning, he reaffirmed his loyalty to the US, and, at the same time, declared his deepest sympathy for the German people. When asked about his present work at Radio Berlin, he said what others would consider contradictory views. 'I have tried to further relations between the land of my father, Germany, and my native land, America. I love them both.'

"He was also asked about a monograph he wrote just before the war entitled *Self-Determination*. In it, he turned one of Woodrow Wilson's cherished Fourteen Points on its head to justify Germany's aggression into the Rhineland and Austria (the Anschluss or annexation), and later the dismemberment of Czechoslovakia, when Germany troops marched into the Sudetenland. He argued that the controversial territorial settlements imposed by the Treaty of Versailles ripped Germans in Austria and Czechoslovakia from their homeland, and that nationality was a 'state of mind,' not something that could be arbitrarily created by diplomacy. As he put it, 'blood was thicker than water, and those who lightly choose to disregard this do so at their peril.' He was advocating an ultranationalist view based on Wilson's view that ethnic and national groups have a right to self-determination. What the West would call aggression, he interpreted as "adjustments," and warned that Germany, with regards to Poland and the loss of East Prussia lands to that country, would 'take over the Polish Corridor and the Free City of Danzig whenever she wanted to. And this, of course, what later happened.'"

"Dad, how can you know all this?"

"I had a chance to check Ron's notes earlier."

"Don't let him fool you, Rachel," Ron added. "He checks and researches each topic before handing it off to us. He's far more astute, knowledgeable, than his innocent demeanor would suggest."

"Ron has me there. I do cook the books a bit."

"But did Kaltenbach have a point?" Rita asked. "I mean it's true, isn't it, that Germany lost territory to the French and others at Versailles?"

"No debating that," Samuels remarked. "The problem was how to adjudicate the problem. Hitler chose the point of a sword, not the negotiator's fountain pen."

"What happened to Kaltenbach?" Rachel asked. "Did he survive the war?"

"The war, yes. Afterwards, no... Ron, your turn."

"On May 15, 1945, US Army CIC officers went to Kaltenbach's residence in Berlin to place him under arrest. Russian agents beat them to him by a few minutes. He was taken into Soviet custody. The Russians denied, at first, that they held him. American investigators traced him to two camps but the Russians would not acknowledge his presence. His wife, who was now working for the US Army as a translator, kept the pressure on but to no avail. She feared ill health and brutal treatment would kill her husband while he was in Russian hands. Finally, in June 1946, the Russians finally admitted having Kaltenbach and promised to release him in a few weeks. When this didn't happen, a Red Army major general finally informed the US Army that Kaltenbach had died of natural causes in October 1945. No camp records or death certificate was provided, nor was the location of his body disclosed. Unable to produce a live Kaltenbach, the Justice Department closed his case and dismissed the indictment of treason against him in 1948. He had escaped a trial and imprisonment in the US. Of course, that was not Mildred's fate, all because, as you will recall, she walked out the back door of Radio Berlin as the Russians entered the front door.

"I wonder how he really felt about his actions?" Rachel asked. "I wish he were here to speak for himself. I always feel like we're speculating."

"Not completely," Ron said quickly. "Kaltenbach did write in his own hand a telling statement in 1944 that, to some degree, may have reflected the views of Mildred and the others:"

To have deserted the German people would have been an act of treason against my conscience. Thus on December 8ᵗʰ, 1941, I was suddenly confronted with the choice of committing a possible act of treason against my native America, or of deserting the German people in their hour of need. If I had taken the easy way out, I could have ceased my broadcasting activities with the excuse that as an American I should not be expected any longer to plead the cause of a country with which America was at war. It was not easy to turn my back, perhaps forever, on my friends in the United States, never to see the land of my birth again. I made then my choice, and I have never regretted that choice for an instant. Not even now.

"In and around that time, he also pointed out," Ron continued, "that he refused to make apologies for doing my (his) allotted bit to help the German people to a better future." He went on to say:

I am not an enemy of the American people, but I shall remain an implacable enemy of those forces in America who wish to deny Germany her rightful place in the European sun.

"I don't like what he did," Rachel said earnestly, "but I do admire his frankness."

"I can't go that far," Rita declared. "What he did was to support his romantic notions of a suffering Germany regaining a place on the world stage. But to support the Reich meant, indirectly or not, to sanctions the Gestapo horrors. A better future for Germans should not have been predicated on the slaughter of innocent millions."

"I must agree with Rita," Ron said. Kaltenbach conveniently looked the other way when it came to the abuses of the Third Reich. Honesty is fine as far as it goes. But where was his empathy for the dead and dying? Where were the tears for those who perished in the concentration camps? Where was his condemnation for bombing London and other great cities?"

"Dad, we're back to you, I guess. What's your take?"

"Wrong question, Rachel. What you want to know is what Mildred really thought?"

"You're begging the question."

"I am."

"Why?"

"To avoid…"

"What?"

"Tainting your views, and all of you. We still have a ways to go before we must decide questions of legal and moral culpability in Mildred's case. After all, Rachel, you did chastise me earlier for a kind of historical harshness. Perhaps we should all keep that in mind."

"You're not taking a position?"

"I am. The one to which I just alluded to my youthful friends."

"This business with Kaltenbach," Rita said, "was right out of Hollywood."

"No," Samuels said, "it was right out of Iowa."

CHAPTER 17
THE DEADLY DUO

<u>The Following Day</u>

"Well, Rita?"

"I just need a moment, Mr. Samuels."

Robert Samuels, his daughter, Rachel, Ron Siegel, and Rita Howrd were gathered in his living room the to continue their self-imposed challenge to more fully understand the world of Radio Berlin and Mildred Gillars' role as Axis Sally, for Rita's topic for today was the *"Deadly Duo."*

"Okay, I'm ready," announced Rita. "Dropping your briefcase is never a good idea, especially when you're dealing with two subjects and your notes get all mixed up."

"We're a compassionate group," Ron said. "Not a problem."

"Ditto," Rachel added.

"To begin… During World War II, four American women were charged with treason. You already know about Tokyo Rose (Iva) and Mildred (Axis Sally), both of whom were convicted of collaboration with enemy regimes. Two other women, Jane Anderson and Constance Drexel, were also indicted, but they never stood trial, and consequently, they never went to prison. In their cases, the indictments were dropped by the Justice Department. This, of course, presents us with a question, one raised by Mildred's attorney at her trial. Why was she indicted for and convicted of treason, while the others weren't, though all broadcasted from Radio Berlin?"

"You've nailed the key question, Rita," Samuels quickly commented. "A question of consistency and judicial equity exists here."

"Isn't a traitor a traitor, Dad?" Rachel asked.

"Apparently, not always."

"Because we're dealing with two personalities, I'll limited myself to those points, which most shed light on their behavior. Otherwise, we'd be here all night. My written notes, Mr. Samuels, will provide additional supporting information."

"Good strategy. Go for it."

Jane Anderson

"Let's begin with Jane Anderson, who eventually was known as 'Lady Haw-Haw' by the Brits. She was born into an unusual Southern family in Atlanta, January 6, 1893. Her mother, Ellen Luckie Anderson, came from a wealthy, pioneer family in the city's development, sufficient to have a street named after them, Luckie Street. Jane's father, Robert M. Anderson, who was known as 'Red,' was once the sheriff of Yuma, Arizona and an associated of Buffalo Bill Cody besides being the chief of police for General George W. Goethels during the construction of the Panama Canal. He was known to have a revolver with twenty-eight notches, one each for each criminal he had killed, not including Mexicans. At the age of 78, he added another notch. He had a mistress half his age.

Jane's schooling included Piedmont College in Georgia, where she was a good, but not outstanding student. She did make friends, one of whom was Meiling Soong, whom we know by another name today, Madame Chiang Kai-shek. She also attended Kidd-Key College in

Sherman, Texas, where she received high grades in French, music, and English literature. After college, she went to New York City to make her mark as a writer. This didn't happen. But she did meet and marry a world-famous musicologist, Deems Taylor. Unfortunately, the marriage quickly soured and she headed for London, trying again to be a writer, this time for newspapers.

She went to work for the *Daily Mail* and quickly proved she had a bit of her father in her. She was the first reporter to fly across the English Channel in a plane and to do a loop-the-loop over Hyde Park in London. She showed a fine hand in writing about her flying experiences."

I was up in some new world, where blue immensity had substance, where men in machines of their own making set themselves in defiance of all laws of space, and time, and proportion... I am the first woman to make a flight across London in one of his Majesty's war machines.

"After a German Zeppelin raid over London killed scores of people, she raced to see the wounded and dying crew of an airship, which had been shot down. She disguised herself as a nurse to get through the military cordon. She got her story. Again, she displayed a certain moxie.

"During the Great War, she interviewed soldiers on each side, braving the lice-infested bunkers and deadly trenches, which afflicted the French and Germans alike in order to get the story out to her paper. She was unafraid to risk her life. And this courage almost got her killed in 1936, a story we will get to in a moment. She proved herself to be quite brave, during the war, as she was willing to expose herself to artillery bombardments and the constant rattle of killer machine guns.

"In 1933 she became the marquesa by marrying Marquis Alvarez de Cienfuegos, and, according to Catholic Church records, adopting a new name, Juana de la Santisima Trinidad. She also gained through marriage legal citizenship in Spain. Years later, this would prove her salvation.

"In the late thirties, she covered the vicious Spanish Civil War, pitting the entrenched Republican and democratic government against Francisco Franco's fascist forces, which were attempting to overthrow the existing nationalist regime. Franco's forces had slammed into the Iberian Peninsula from their Moroccan bases on July 18, 1936 to begin a drive to Madrid. The General's troops received military support from Nazi Germany and fascist Italy. Each country provided equipment, trainers, and financial assistance. The besieged government was supported mainly by the Soviet Union. In retrospect, we can now see that this was a preliminary episode leading to WWII. The overture to a larger war was being acted out in Spain, as Berlin, Rome, and Moscow tested their newest weapons and strategies.

"Jane Anderson, now middle-aged, jumped into the fray, covering the war from Franco's perspective. She amazed all with her ability to endure hardship and to keep up with the march. Her reports to the world publicized the atrocities of the anti-Franco Loyalist troops: defenseless prisoners brutally slaughtered, rapes, and the 'unspeakable excesses' against the church.' She, of course, did not mention the war crimes of Franco's forces.

"In September 1936, she was captured by Loyalist forces of the government and taken to Madrid to stand trial for espionage. The infamous 'Midnight Tribunal of Twelve' interrogated her for hours before declaring a guilty verdict. She was placed in a political prison to await her execution. In time, she was taken to Madrid's Plaza Torena, a cloistered courtyard that served as the location for firing squads. Here she was kept for many weeks. This experience, as noted by historians of the period, crippled her physically and emotionally as she witnessed brutality and torture, and was forced to exist on stale rice while being exposed to voracious rats, many of which bit her. The intervention of the State Department, however, saved her at the last minute from a firing squad. She was released on October 10, 1936 on the condition that she would leave Spain. One correspondent, who knew her, wrote about the Jane Anderson who survived the Loyalists."

She entered prison as one of the most beautiful women of Spain. When she came out she was haggard from scurvy and badly scarred by rat-bites. Her face was deeply lined. Her eyes carried a gleam that was near insanity and near terror, and that stayed with her for weeks.

"She also left prison and Spain with a deep hatred for Bolshevism and the international communist movement. At the opposite end of the spectrum, she fostered an emerging devotion for the fascists, whom she saw as the only real defense against Marxism. Lost to her were the liberal democracies, which in her mind, were without the political spine necessary to confront Stalin. In short, her treatment by the Loyalists drove her to the far right, to the fascists, and in time to the Nazis."

"There are times when I feel I have major gaps in my education," a stammering Ron said. "I don't know a darn thing about the Spanish Civil War."

"I guess I'm with you," Rachel said. "If they taught me about it in high school, I'm afraid it went into one ear and out the other. Sorry, Dad."

"I know just enough to get into trouble," Rita added. "So that leaves you, Mr. Samuels."

"A quick lecture my children."

The Spanish Civil War

In 1936 a liberal, progressive government took over Spain. The opposition, mainly Fascist sympathizers, were imprisoned. Military officers who engaged in political activities against the government were pensioned off. The regime tried to steer a middle course, but the government was criticized from the communist left and the fascist right. The communists wanted revolutionary change, a revolution. The ultraconservatives were against all reforms. Each side attacked the other, and the regime. On July 17, 1936, army regiments in Spanish Morocco revolted against the government. General Francisco Franco led the rebellious troops. He was against Bolshevism and was supported by Germany and Italy who sent thousands of troops to assist him, plus the latest tanks and planes. The people generally supported the government and were referred to as Loyalists. The whole business became a dress rehearsal for WWII. Unfortunately, both England and France, fearing bad relations with the dictators, Hitler and Mussolini, chose not to be involved by following a policy of nonintervention. They wouldn't send weapons to either side. Berlin and Rome followed, as noted before, a different tack. The democratic Loyalists only received assistance from Communist Russia. After three years of terrible fighting, which almost destroyed the country, Madrid fell to Franco in 1939. The Spanish republic was extinguished. Franco became caudillo (the leader) with absolute power.

"That's the abbreviated story, guys. If you want more facts and information, check out Ernest Hemingway's *For Whom the Bells Toll*. Rita, your turn."

"In 1938, Jane Anderson (the marquesa) did some broadcasting for the Franco government. Her work drew the attention of Radio Berlin. She was invited to join the USA Zone. She accepted the invitation. She was introduced to the radio audience as the *Georgia Peach* on April 14, 1941, as a world-famous Catholic lecturer, as one who had achieved martyrdom in Spain. She quickly adopted the usual Berlin line: 'Hitler was the great unifying agent of Germany.' She compared him to Moses, declaring that 'he would 'go forth from triumph to triumph, from strength to strength.' She saw him as reaching for the stars and said 'the Lord will prevail.'"

"Wasn't she tainting Hitler's Aryan philosophy by having him follow a Hebrew hero?" Rachel asked.

"What can I say, Rachel? I'm not sure she was playing with a full deck at this point. As an example, she said Hitler had made a commitment, both moral and financial, to Roman Catholicism and its teachings as he opposed and waged war against international communism. With reference to the German army, she said in the same vein:

I am proud to have been on the battlefield. I pay my tribute, as a servant of God, in the soldiers for they are the soldiers of the Cross.

"She even observed that 'the Archbishop in Germany wore the Iron Cross under his robes.' She also insisted that American troops had been stationed in Northern Ireland at Stalin's direction to crush the Catholic faith.' Her wanderings only get wilder." She attacked FDR and the American press, contending that the White House and the National Convention of Protestants, Catholics, and Jews had unfairly warned Americans against the 'contaminations contained in the broadcasts which I was privileged to offer the American people.' For her, the architects of this smear campaign was the President, 'who had chained the Christian forces in American to the godless hordes of Stalin.' She also stated that the Archbishop of Canterbury secretly prayed for a Soviet victory in the East. In her overheated prose, she said that 'Roosevelt has pulled a brass band out of his hip pocket, and a concentration camp from under the coattails of the brain trust...' She charged that Roosevelt plotted with Churchill:

... in the simultaneous declaration of war upon Japan... so the American people would go to war to save Stalin and the international banker which are one and the same

Eventually, her ravings went too far and backfired on her. On the evening of Mach 6, 1942, she made a major error in judgment during her broadcast. In an attempt to embitter American listeners against wartime rationing and food shortages, she hyped fine restaurants and cocktail bars in Germany where food was supposedly plentiful and inexpensive. She hoped this comparison would weaken American morale at home. She described her visit to a teashop."

Waitresses went from table to table with silver platters laden with sweets and pastries, and we were served with Turkish cakes with marzipan, of which I was very fond... My friend ordered great goblets of champagne... and he put in liberal shots of cognac to make it more lively. Sweets and cookies and champagne, not bad...

"Her broadcast was recorded and turned over to the US Office of War Information, which turned the tables on her. The broadcast was rebroadcasted, this time to the Third Reich in order to anger the average ration-conscious German. Though illegal, German shortwave radio listeners picked up the American broadcast with the desired effect. That was it for Anderson. Her editors were dismissed and she was taken off the air. Almost all records about the *Georgia Peach* were expunged. It was like she never existed."

"What happened to her?" Rachel asked, her curiosity peeked.

"Well, she wasn't executed. She was pushed into forced retirement until the Reich began to crack following D-Day. In late 1944, she was back on the air, this time saying:

The battle was between a new world order of social justice and a condemned civilization doomed to death through its own decadence' and all because 'America was in the hands of the Jews and Bolshevism.' As always, because of her prejudice, she confused which side was on the side of social justice.

"When the war ended," Ron asked, "what happened to her?"

"Aided by a Gestapo agent, she and her husband tried to reach Switzerland. They only got as far as Austria, where she was apprehended in Innsbruck on April 2, 1947. Rather than being placed in jail, she was placed under 'town arrest' in Salzburg. There the couple waited while the Franco regime orchestrated their release. On October 27, 1947, the Justice Department announced it was declining to prosecute Anderson, though she had been indicted along with Mildred and others in 1943. In the majestic language of the law, the indictment had charged the Atlanta native with 'knowingly, intentionally, feloniously, traitorously, and treasonably adhering to the enemies of the United States and giving to the said enemies aid and comfort.' And now the indictment was discharged."

"She was getting preferential treatment because she was married to a Spanish aristocrat?" Rachel asked in a heated voice.

"Damned unfair," Ron said. "Damned unfair."

"Essentially, the Justice Department said she had only had a short-lived involvement with the Nazi, and her broadcasts focused more on cultural aspects than outright propaganda. The exact wording was..."

It is true that she could be classified as a political commentator, although not a very effective one, but as she apparently stopped her broadcasting activities shortly after our entry into the war it does not appear worthwhile that further efforts be made to develop our case against her, notwithstanding the fact that she was indicted for treason in 1943.

"Whitewash," Ron cried out.

"Mildred's defense had a point here," Rita said. "Traitors were treated differently. But why?"

"Think about 1947," Samuels said. "In that year she and her husband were given new passports and invited to return to Spain. And the American government went along with it. So again, I ask why? In retrospect, we can only reach on conclusion. The Cold War was one. Franco was anti-Communist. The Truman Administration wanted allies in the struggle. Good relations with Madrid only cost two passports. In the end, the threat of Soviet Russia saved Anderson. She was released from custody and settle in Almohrin in postwar Spain. She lived there until just a few years ago. She died in Madrid in 1972.

"Jesus," Ron exclaimed. "She got away with it."

"She wasn't the only one," Rita explained. "Not by a long shot."

"You're kidding?" Rita asked. "Aren't you?"

Constance Drexel

"Constance Drexel," Rita said, "was born in Darmstadt, Germany, on November 28, 1894. Her father brought her to America a year later, and she gained American citizenship in Boston in 1898. Her father, Theodore, and mother, Zela, came from wealthy German families. They were not, however, related to the 'famous Drexel family' of Philadelphia and the Drexel and Company banking empire, or to Anthony Joseph Drexel, who founded Drexel University in the 'city of brotherhood,' no matter what later German propaganda suggested. She was educated both in the United States and Europe and was a graduate of the Sorbonne in Paris.

"When World War I broke out, she was one of the first American women to volunteer as a Red Cross nurse. She served in a French hospital at Domville in the summer of 1914. What she saw left a lasting impression on her."

To me, who had never seen blood and must now watch shot-torn peasant boys die in the twisted tortures of tetanus, dress the revolting, neglected wounds, feed living men in ghastly bandages concealing what had once been a face, it seemed as though no one could pay more than those poor, shattered wrecks of human beings had paid. And then, after a week or two, I lost the horror of it.

"Her career as a professional reporter began in 1915. Invited by Jane Addams to cover the International Woman's Congress at The Hague in April, Drexel sent cables to American papers. She also covered the Democratic Convention in 1916 and endorsed Woodrow Wilson for a second term in the White House. She argued to the convention that the Republican, Charles Evan Hughes, would never support the suffrage amendment. She attended the Paris Peace Conference and put her journalistic weight behind Paragraph 3 of Article 7 of the Covenant of the new League of Nations, which carried a women's equality clause. After that, she became the first female political correspondent on Capital Hill.

"By the mid-30's, she enjoyed a growing stature among the press corps. At the same time, she indicated a certain admiration for Nazi Germany. As to why a progressive Democrat would do this, the answer seems simple. Hitler had enacted many of the reforms she considered necessary. Germany provided a greater role for women in every aspect of the country's life. The aristocratic elite of Nazi Germany whom she considered parasitic was being eradicated. Welfare legislation for minors and social hygiene laws were being introduced. People were returning to work. The government was creating jobs. In all of this, she saw a more favorable example to what the New Deal was offering in America. In 1939, for reasons not fully known, Drexel left the US for Berlin. The German government paid for her ticket. Her only explanation for the sudden departure was the need to help her ill mother in Wiesbaden. As to why she later went to work for Radio Berlin, little is known.

"She made her first broadcast on in 1940. She was introduced as a 'famous American journalist' and member of a 'socially prominent and wealthy Philadelphia family. Her focus was on social and cultural affairs. After Pearl Harbor, she escaped internment by going to work for Radio Berlin. Again, there is no official explanation for this. Once the US was in the war, she confined herself almost exclusively to the cultural and pleasurable life of wartime Germany, the concerts and exhibitions, the abundance of food, clothing, and entertainment. Her intention, it seemed, was to contrast the stability of Germany with the 'shortages' in America. No matter, by all measures, she was considered a very poor propagandist. Words, according to her, were drafted and she merely mouthed them. Some, including William Shirer, considered her 'a forlorn person and a rather shabby journalist.' Even some of the Germans at Radio Berlin referred to her as a 'pest and crackpot.' According to Shirer, the Germans hired her 'principally because she was the only woman in town who would sell her American accent to them.' Drexel's own view of her work was a bit less critical. In 1942, when requesting an extension of her passport through Swiss authorities, she stated that,

... in speaking for the German radio, I am following my own ideas. I am not a speaker about political or military matters but reporting cultural activities such as activities in the theatre, music, and film.

She never saw herself as giving 'aid and comfort' to the enemy."

"The old question," Ron said, "what happened to her after the war?"

"I'm assuming she escaped the indictment," Rachel declared. "How did she do it?"

"On August 17, 1945, she was arrested in Vienna by American authorities. Foolishly she had revealed her identity to a reporter for the *Stars and Stripes*, the American military newspaper for the troops. This happened on a walk with the reporter to the Vienna City Hall. She was wearing an American flag lapel pin and claimed (or confessed) she had always been a 'loyal citizen, and had only broadcast on cultural questions.' At the time, she was 60-years of age.

"Ironically, she was returned to the United States after a year's detainment in Germany aboard the transport, *Ernie Pyle*, named after the legendary American journalist of the war. She arrived in New York City on October 2, 1946 and was quickly interned at Ellis Island. A board of inquiry determined that she had not forfeited her citizenship during her absence from the United States. In short, she could be indicted and tried as a traitor. That, however, would not happen."

"Here we go again," Ron said.

"How was her rabbit pulled out of a hat?" Rachel asked.

"Justice Department officials" professed no intention to prosecute her. According to them, their lawyers sent to Germany were 'unable to uncover evidence that would warrant prosecution.' Given this, treason charges against her were dropped. Supporting this view was a memo, dated June 14, 1946, from the Office of Strategic Services (OSS) indicating that Drexel was 'stranded in Germany and since she needed money she found a job with the American Propaganda Section of the

Reichrunfunk (Radio Berlin), but that her twice-weekly broadcasts dealt mainly with women, children, and the beauties of the German landscape. None of the broadcasts was political in nature.' The memo recommended taking no further action against her. Even though Walter Winchell, a very influential radio announcer, urged prosecution and a stiff sentence, charges were formally dropped on April 14, 1948. Constance Drexel was now a free woman. She would live out the rest of her life in Connecticut, where she died on August 28, 1956. She was 68-years old. She had been planning to move to Geneva, Switzerland where she hoped to reside in her remaining years."

"It can't be," Ron blurted out. "She gets off and Mildred is shafted."

"Cultural broadcasts, my backside," Rachel complained. "She did give comfort to the enemy."

"It does seem unfair, doesn't it, Mr. Samuels?"

"Rita, fairness is not a commodity equably handed out at birth. Only degrees of unfairness exist in these cases as determined by the facts and political considerations. What is a condemning proof to one may only be a mitigating fact to another, and always within the context of existing laws. Jane had the right citizenship. Mildred didn't. Constance Drexel stupidly (or smartly) got fired before she could do more damage to herself. In each case, the Justice Department reached a determination. Unfortunately, for Mildred the weight of broadcasting on a cumulative basis did not permit a way out. And even at that, a jury of her peers still only found her guilty of one indictment out of eight, and then only after protracted debate. Still, the question of judicial fairness shadows our research. Perhaps we'll know more after my wife gets home. We need to know about the indictment that proved to be Mildred's downfall. Until then, the *'deadly duo'* influence on Mildred continues to evade our full understanding, and any justification for imprisoning her at Alderson."

"As you say, Mr. Samuels, fairness always seems to be in short supply when it comes to traitors."

"Rita, such is the world."

CHAPTER 18
THE LANDING BEACHES

Home from Chicago

"You really covered a great deal while I was in Chicago."
"And so did you, Lynn."

Samuels and his wife were sitting outside in their patio on an unlikely warmish day in San Francisco, one calling for iced tea and Bermuda shorts, an almost outlandish thought in the land of creeping fog and Pacific Ocean breezes. Yet, here they were, reunited again after Lynn's long trip to Chicago to see Iva, the now pardoned Tokyo Rose.

There had been the usual welcome back questions offered by Samuels: "How was your flight? "Did you like Chicago?" "Was it worth it to see, Iva?" "Did you get the story?" Lynn followed with a mini inquisition of her own: "Did the blond down the street try to make dinner for you?" "Was it fun being a bachelor again, even for a few days?" "I assume you got some work done?" Mutually satisfying answers had been given, and then there had been an exchange of notebooks bulging with crimped notes, nicely typed reports, and a scattering of newspaper articles. For two days, they shared cups of Columbian coffee, microwave meals, and an emergency call to the Golden Flower Restaurant for a fast home delivery as they reviewed what each had learned about Axis Sally during the past few days.

"Ron and Rita did a first rate job. The *Unholy Trio* and the *Deadly Duo*, how aptly the names described Goebbels' radio gang, don't you think so, Robert?"

Indeed. Lynn."

"And what about my research? No questions?"

"Tons."

"Well?"

"Okay, I'll go first. No male modesty on my part. You prefaced your talk with Iva by first discussing Mildred's trial. More to the point, the jury's verdict. That struck me as taking the cart before the horse."

"Not in this case, Robert."

"An explanation, then."

"Simple. Sometimes the ending explains all that preceded the final curtain."

"On March 7, 1949, after a full day of deliberations, the jury in Mildred's treason trial was deadlocked. No decision had been reached. A tired group of seven men and five women were dined at government expense and then put to sleep in the Hotel Continental in Washington D.C. This followed weeks of testimony by POW's, wounded servicemen, and German collaborators, and, of course, the legal arguments of both sides to obtain a favorable outcome. All this was at great expense to the Justice Department, as well as the defense team.

The following day was no different for the jury. Ten indictment charges were considered, two were thrown out, and the other eight debated. Still, no decision was reached. Following lunch, the jury foreman, Henry G. Davis, requested twenty-two transcripts of Mildred's broadcasts, which had been recorded by the Federal Commuication Commission. They were provided. At 4:28 p.m. in the late afternoon the foreman announced that a verdict had been determined. Mildred was found guilty on indictment #10, and that charge alone. All the other indictments were thrown out. Succinctly, she was only found guilty of 'participating in the radio play, *Visions of Invasion*,' which was written by Max Otto Koischwitz, her 'man of destiny,' lover, and former teacher at Hunter College. Death in the waning days of the war had stripped him of his opportunity to face treason charges with the love of his life. Mildred alone would carry the weight of guilt for both of them. Upon hearing the verdict, she said, 'I wish those who judged me would be willing to risk their lives for America as I did.' What she meant by this has always been open to speculation.

"Two weeks later, Judge Edward M. Curran, passed sentence. Mildred would be fined $10,000 and be placed in jail from 10 to 30 years with parole eligibility after serving 10 years. She did not receive a life sentence because she had not actually written the radio play. Mildred's only response was to raise her chin and quickly walk out of the courtroom. Her sister, Edna Mae, who was in the audience, observed Mildred playing out the greatest drama in her life. Edna was quoted as saying, 'I don't think Ethel Barrymore could have done a better job of taking the verdict.'

"Reaction to the verdict and sentencing was immediate and very nearly unanimous. Some wanted her strung up. Others felt life in prison was too short. One survivor of D-Day and the advance across France summed up the passions of the day this way. 'She knew where you were located and she'd tell us to expect a visit and then they'd come over and bomb the hell out of us.' Men who had faced the worst of the war were not in a position to consider mitigating circumstances. Unfortunately, the anger spilled over on Edna Mae's family. There was open discrimination against her for supporting her sister, and, as some noted, 'quiet distain.' At the time, it did not appear, as discussed earlier, that Mildred fully appreciated the sacrifices in money and emotion made by her family on her behalf."

"Mildred really touched a nerve with this play."

"In spades, Robert. In spades…"

"I know a little about the play, too little."

"Sadly, I may know too much, way too much."

"The play was broadcast on May 11, 1944, less than a month before the D-Day landings on the beaches at Normandy. It would prove to be the most infamous radio broadcast of the war, *Vision of Invasion*. It was beamed to England, Canada, and the United States for the most part in an attempt to reach civilians and Allied troops alike.

"The play wasn't the usual propaganda stuff, slanted news, popular music, and outright distortions of the Allied failure to bomb Berlin into the next century. This radio play was something more, a wireless attempt to paralyze the home front, while straining the already taut nerves of troops preparing for the assault on Fortress Europe.

"In the play Mildred has the major role of Evelyn, an American mother, who has a nightmare, a premonition just before the Channel crossing. She dreams about her son, Alan, and his fiery death in waist high waters approaching the French coast. The play had a realistic sound track. Sound effects simulated the explosions of invading ships and landing crafts, the moans and cries of wounded men as they were raked by machine gun fire from fortified bunkers overlooking the bloody beaches. The play had the sense of a documentary about an event that had already taken place, which was already history and could not be reversed. And that, of course, was the horror for Evelyn, a mother symbolic of all future "Gold Star" mothers, who would lose a son on the beaches.

"The first scene set the pattern for the play. A commentator discusses the Dieppe Raid, which occurred two years earlier, and which is symbolic of what would happen again if the Allies were foolish enough to invade the continent. Dieppe was a port on the French coast.

British and Canadian troops had attacked with an ill-planned strategy. Over 5,000 men, mainly Canadian, had perished. It was, as the English say, a complete 'cock-up.' Now the disaster was being relived.

"A landing boat is described as it washes ashore with the whole crew burnt to death looking more like roasted geese than men. A small craft with about fifty dead men aboard, all killed before reaching land, lists silently in the offshore tides, a dismal cemetery not tied to the land. On shore, however, a big hay wagon is described traveling between the beaches and an improvised cemetery. It has been carrying the dead for two days, back and forth in an endless effort to clear the beaches.

"The radio play had little impact on Allied troops, who either didn't hear the broadcasts, or were so well trained that radio words could not dissuade them from their appointed task. But it did play harshly in homes across the British Isles and throughout the US and Canada. Though it was propaganda, there was an element of truth to the play. The Germans were waiting for the invasion. They were prepared. They would fight. That was beyond question. Thousands would die, perishing in the air, on the beaches, and at sea. This was inevitable. This is what disturbed the families of Allied troops. A chain of events had already been set in motion in London and Berlin. Frighteningly, in some respects, what was to take place had already occurred in the terrified minds of loved ones. Already, the 'We regret to inform you telegrams' had been printed."

"Jesus, Lynn, what the hell did they expect to accomplish with this play? Looking back, the whole effort seemed so futile."

"This is where things get sticky. There is considerable debate about the origins of the play and its purpose. And I guess that's why you sent me to Chicago, you sly fox. You wanted, no, you hoped Mildred had talked with Iva about it, right, Mr. Reporter?"

"The thought had occurred to me. They did spend time together playing cards and sharing meals, and I hope, jabbering."

"Chauvinist! Men discuss. Women jabber?"

"I stand corrected. A masculine miscue, not to be repeated."

"Apology accepted. Now, where was I?"

"The sentenced traitors were talking…"

"Your sensitive nose for a story was correct. The play did come up over cards. According to Iva's recollection, the following conversation took place."

"I was the star in the show, Iva. I played the mother, Evelyn. My boss and intimate companion, Max Otto, wrote the play, and Radio Berlin produced it after Goebbels approved it. I do think I gave the performance of a lifetime."

"If you say so."

"I do. I was choking with emotion. Tears streamed down my cheeks as I held the microphone and cried out:

Please, please, my son, I beg of you… your mother is on her knees begging you… please Alan, do not take part in this invasion — this trap. Please don't. I can't bear it.

"My voiced quivered. I certainly recall that I told Alan the invasion would be a slaughter, the worst slaughter in history."

"Mildred, how could you say those things?"

"It was in the script, Iva. I read what Max Otto wrote. I acted out what the Gestapo sanctioned, including my last lines:

Alan, the bells of Europe's bombed cathedrals are tolling your death knell. Please, while there's still time, please my precious son, lay down your arms… lay down your arms, and come home!

I couldn't decline the role."

"So you played it to the fullest?"

"An actress must act."

"I still don't understand the purpose of the play."

"Iva, Max and I knew there would be a slaughter on the beaches. We had traveled to the French coastline and seen the defenses facing the Channel. We could hope the expected invasion would be repulsed, but if it weren't, Germany would be doomed. We hoped the play would forestall the attack until the new 'magic weapons' were perfected at Peenemunde, the flying, unmanned missiles, the jet planes, weapons that would change the course of the war. We needed time. Germany needed time."

"Fine words, Mildred, but think of all the pain you caused in American homes. How could you be so insensitive? Was it because you had no children of your own? I mean, it's easier, isn't it, when your own children aren't involved?"

"Don't go self-righteous on me, Iva. You were no innocent babe in Tokyo."

"I never did anything like this. I never said anything against my country. Our country... I only read what was prepared for me."

"As did I. And look where it got us, Alderson. The military authorities arrested us. They didn't see it that way. The Feds didn't believe us, nor did two juries, nor the appeal courts. And, of course, that guy, Winchell. He wanted us hanging from a rope. If not the gallows, life imprisonment without parole, or deportation, you to Nippon, me to East Germany... No one understood the pressure and threats we were under. No one. Only us, a sorority of two."

"Still, the Nazis were beasts."

"We've been through this before, Iva. The Nips weren't Boy Scouts."

"But this play..."

"I was heartless because I had no children of my own? Let me tell you something about the origin of the *Vision of Invasion*. Then you can decide how awful I was. Okay?"

"Let's hear it."

"It all began with Max Otto. There's this myth that his personality overwhelmed me, influenced me to do anything he wanted as if I didn't have a mind of my own, that our love and his Svengali powers corrupted me because I saw him as 'my man of destiny,' a love I couldn't live without. I was called a 'stupid woman' by the prosecution for letting this man hypnotize me with his intellect, his stories of the beautiful mountains of Silesia, his courage to struggle against the Allies with words, and yes, the play, *Vision of Invasion*. It was claimed that we were depraved and sadistic because of this play. Otherwise, how could we, assumedly decent people, tell a mother about her son's death and then sadistically go into the details of his injuries? What could possibly be our excuse? Was it just sadistic joy? Was it just treason?

"There's always more to a story. I knew beyond any doubt that I had to do something to stop the impending carnage, which the invasion would bring. I didn't want to see my fellow Americans challenge the fortified beaches. I already felt Germany couldn't last another year. Berlin was doomed. The war was all but over. The pressure from the East was too great as Russian hordes drove westward, while day and night bombing raids destroyed German cities. It was over. The 'invasion' was not needed. The new super weapons were too late. The course of the war couldn't be changed.

"One night, one terrible night as the RAF bombers flew overhead and dropped their deadly arsenal, I curled up on the floor and waited out my fate. I closed my eyes, but I could see the planes, so many planes, and the bombs, each a dreadful reminder of my mortality, falling downward, downward toward me. I found myself praying that one would land on my residence, that I would be killed. Then the nightmare would be over, finally over, ended. The bombs fell, but I didn't die. For whatever reason I was spared. And then it hit me. I was inspired by a thought, which wonderfully, if not magically, was suddenly convulsing through my mind. A play. It would be the answer to everything. I could stop the killing on the beaches. Germany was dying but I could still save lives.

"I told Max Otto about my idea, a play, the mother, the son, the tormented beaches, all of it. At first, he was reluctant. Wasn't Hitler expecting the invasion? Wasn't he counting on it? Wasn't he hoping to destroy the Allied forces on the beaches and thus force his enemies to sue for peace? Without the invasion, none of this was possible. Was this not unlike Christ, who had to die if the soul of man were to be saved? I pushed hard over the next few days. Max Otto was a hard sell. I changed my tack. If nothing else, the play would postpone the invasion and give German V-1 and V-2 rockets a chance to win the war. Finally, after much persuasion, he went for it. My ruse worked. Max Otto wrote the play.

"After that, he worked day and night on the play. When I read it, I considered it a masterpiece, a true effort of his genius and my inspiration. It was realistic. It was convincing. It would be enough to turn back the invasion. It would, I prayed, be enough to cause thousands of young boys to vote for life, not death, and to turn back from those horrible beaches."

"Mildred, you're telling me the whole idea for the play was your inspiration?"

"Of course."

"You were the power behind the scene?"

"I inspired him."

"You did it to ward off an unneeded invasion?"

"Yes, I admit to that."

"To save a defeated Germany?"

"To save the lives of young men."

"You weren't influenced by Max Otto?"

"I didn't say that."

"What, then?"

"I was not a silly hen. We played off each other."

"That wasn't the way the jury saw it."

"They saw what the prosecution wanted them to see."

"But didn't a German actor testify against you?"

"You're thinking of Ulrich Haupt, a young actor who played Alan. Yes, he testified. He confirmed I had acted in the play, as had others. But he wasn't a really good witness for the prosecution. He was Jewish, at least his living mother was Jewish. Can you imagine that, a Jew playing an American GI in a play written by a German with an expatriate in the leading role? Haupt had been inducted into the Wehrmacht, but was assigned to the theatre. Though he didn't regard himself a Jew, he still lived under the constant threat of deportation to the East. When asked what would happen if he refused to play Alan, he stated the obvious, which also applied to me:

"My mother would have been sent to a concentration camp. My wife and three children would have been to concentration camps. I, too, would have been sent to a concentration camp."

"When asked if he might have been shot, he said, 'that would have been mild.' That would have been my fate, too. The prosecution never grasped that point. I lived in a world of absolute power where only the Nazis had it. My God, they would have killed Max Otto if he had not used his genius on their behalf. You, Iva, of all people should understand the constant dread we each experienced."

"You were innocent of exploiting American homes and fears?"

"I was trying to save those homes a terrible tragedy."

"What do you think, Lynn?"

"With Mildred, nothing is clear cut. She did the *Vision of Invasion* broadcast. But did she do it under duress? She promoted the play, but did she do it to harm the Allied cause? Did she really feel Germany was crumbling and the invasion was unwarranted?"

"And?"

"I don't know. Unfortunately, Max Otto died before he could testify. Would his testimony have backed up Mildred? We'll never know."

"What did Iva believe?"

"She equivocated. Mildred was responsible for her actions, but her actions were always against the backdrop of the Gestapo's presence. At the risk of her life, she didn't have the courage to defy the Reich. She also didn't want to see Max Otto pay for any defiance on her part."

"As you say, it gets complicated."

"I wonder, Robert, if it was worth it."

"What are you getting at?"

"The program didn't stop the invasion. Germany eventually fell. Max Otto died in a Berlin hospital. Mildred ended up in prison."

"There's that, Lynn."

"And the reviews were so awful. Many listeners were turned off by Mildred's hysterics, and what others called 'amateur night stuff.' Some thought the program was just a bore. The American press really killed her, claiming that her wild sobbing 'almost broke their eardrums,' while another reporter wanted her caught and jailed to prevent her from ever assaulting them again with mindless tripe. The prosecution, however, took a decidedly different view. The Justice Department wanted a conviction. With the loss of seven points of indictment, the JD accepted what legal morsel was left on the table. Mildred had called it the best performance of her life. The prosecution was willing to acknowledge this."

"No one else from the show went to jail?"

"No one, Robert."

"Strange justice."

"I hope I can sleep better tonight."

"What?"

"Each night, I can hear the first words and sounds of the play, 'menacing noises of ship's engines as the invasion fleet crossed the Channel and in the background Max Otto's voice asking, 'Why call it D-Day?' And then providing the answer: 'D stand for Doom and Disaster, for Defeat and Death; for Dunkirk and Dieppe.' I think Mildred and Max got to me."

"Lynn, I think she got to both of us."

CHAPTER 19

THE GERMAN PROFESSOR

<u>The Invitation</u>

"What do we have here?"

Robert Samuels checked the UPS mail folder carefully. He really wasn't concerned about a letter bomb, though in his journalistic career he had been the recipient of three invitations to the next world. Fortunately, alert postal inspectors at the paper had identified the lethal gifts and later traced them back to their senders. His would-be admirers now read the *Chronicle* in the State Pen. Of course, Samuels wasn't a trained inspector. He was merely cautious. He studied the package carefully, weighing it in his hands, gently feeling the contents (or trying to), and naturally, giving it a visual once over. The return address certainly caught his eye, M.G. Sisk, Columbus, Ohio. Ah, Mildred, he thought to himself, you're being coy returning to a name you hated in order to avoid bringing attention to a name others disliked. Fine. Sisk was okay with me. The "G" word would remain unsaid for the moment. "Now," Samuels said aloud, "What have you sent me, dear lady?"

Alone in his kitchen, Samuels carefully opened the mail folder. There was no "boom," only the beating of his heart and a sharp intake of his breath. He removed the contents, a stack of papers, each crowded with single-spaced typing except for the top sheet, which showed a delicate scroll as if each word had been carefully considered before written out in long hand. So far, so good, Samuels thought. No mini explosion, no germ-infested white powder. This day could turn out okay.

Samuels unclipped the top sheet and began to read.

Mr. Robert Samuels,

I must confess at the outset that I an unable to meet with you at this time. For a moment my reasons must remain confidential, as they are very personal. Please be assured that I have followed your series in the Chronicle with rapt attention, as you might expect. I must compliment you. You have been objective and fair-minded in your writing, and certainly sensitive to those issues that most concern me. You have weighed the facts and presented a balanced view from all that I can tell. Again, I'm most appreciative of your effort to tell my story, though I must admit, I was most hesitant at first to be in the public's eye again.

Initially, I did not approve of Edna Mae freelancing with my life when she first contacted you. She, of course means well, as she always has, but still I was upset. I had grown used to my anonymity. Working in a Catholic School and protected by a wall of nuns had ill-prepared me for a renewed public reappearance. Two publishing houses, and one major studio have already approached me for book and film rights. Fortunately, Mother Superior, who is very stout and astute, has run interference for me. All offers, of course, have been flatly turned down. Apparently some people want to see me in print or on the silver screen. I must admit it's flattering. In some ways I find it refreshing, and, yes, painful to relive the war years and the trial that followed, especially when I see what a deft hand you have in bringing Axis Sally into the light. But a film, I think not.

And, if anyone writes an authorized version of my life, it will only be you. You see, Mr. Samuels, I've come to trust you.

Now, I know you wanted to interview me about Max Otto, as you referred to him in your articles. In the absence of that interview, I have prepared an incomplete but, I hope, useful biographical sketch of Professor Koischwitz, whom I always called Max. It is fair to say that no one knew him better, and more intimately than I and, I trust, my observations and insights will prove useful to you. Feel free, of course, to research further any aspect of his life I touched upon. I understand a good reporter does that sort of thing. By mail, not by phone or in person, I will be available to assist you if necessary.

I do look forward to meeting you someday. I remain, Mildred G.

Samuels put down the cover letter. He sipped the last cold drops of coffee in his CAL mug, sat back in his chair, and considered what he had read. Mildred, he reflected, was testing him. Obviously, she was waiting to see how well he handled Max's story. If, by her standards, he did a good job, a personal interview had all but been promised. On the other hand... Well, Samuels concluded, there would be no other hand. He wanted the personal interview. Indeed, he needed it. The story of Axis Sally would be incomplete without it. But there was more. Though repulsed by Mildred's broadcasts at Radio Berlin, especially the anti-Semitic commentaries, he was also attracted to her for reasons he couldn't fully comprehend. She had tried to hard to make it "big" on the stage, to be someone of note, to share her love and life with another, to be secure from an impoverished life, and to simply find contentment. Perhaps that was what drew him to her. Wasn't what she wanted what we all want? And yet it had all gone so bad... The Nazi stage, intimacy with Max, a married man, and what monetary security she had at Radio

Berlin dearly paid for by a later Federal indictment for treason. She was certainly no golden-haired princess of righteousness, but nor was she a wicked witch of the dark side. Somewhere between these opposite poles was the Mildred who still eluded Samuels. He would not be content until he found her.

Two slices of crisp toast later, buttered and covered with strawberry jam, plus a coffee refill, and he was ready to learn about Max. What surprises, he wonderd, did Mildred have for him. It didn't take him long to find out. He picked up a pile of papers and began to read.

"I was not Max's lover when I attended Hunter College. Let's put that falsehood to bed. Yes, he was attractive, a charismatic Professor of German Literature on whom many of the co-eds had crushes, and in some cases, even intimacies. No matter what the rumors suggested I was not one of those heart-struck women. He was friendly and helpful during personal conferences, perhaps even a little flirtatious but nothing more. Of that I can assure you. Of course, it's true we met for coffee occasionally and he even visited me at my residence to discuss poetry and the arts. He was a man of great knowledge and I was flattered that he felt comfortable sharing ideas with me. He was tall, very pale, and all too slim for my taste. Regrettably, I was unaware that he had been diagnosed with inceptive tuberculosis at a young age. Eventually, he would die from the disease and heart failure in September 1944, He did not commit suicide as some claimed. I took many classes from him, as did others. He was a very popular teacher. Indeed, one year he was voted "teacher of the year" at Hunter. His classes were always full with a waiting list for the unlucky. I wasn't one of those. I always signed up early. I always sat in front. And I always came to class and on time, regardless of another shady rumor.

"I don't know how the story started. Perhaps some of my disenchanted colleagues at Radio Berlin gave life to it. I never knew for sure. The story concerned my first day at Hunter College in 1925. Supposedly, I overslept and was late to class, one given by Max. In my hurry to find a chair, I collided with a small table stacked high with pamphlets. I fell to the floor along with the pamphlets. All in all, I looked like a perfect fool. Things only got worse. As I sat down, a seam in my book bag split and the bag ruptured. My pen and pencil, plus a silver compact fell out and bounced along the floor, and then came the books, one after another, all slamming down at my feet. But that wasn't the end of it. As I tried to collect my worldly goods, my beaded necklace broke and the beads chased each other in every possible direction. Watching all this, the Professor said, 'This is college, not kindergarten.' He then pointed out that, as a 'true German' he insisted on order and punctuality."

Of course, this never happened. I was never late to class. I never acted like a foolish fop. Only one part of this salacious rumor was true. Max was a true German. He truly loved his country. And why not? His family had played an important role in the country's history. His great-grandfather had fought against Napoleon's legions. His grandfather took up arms in the Franco-Prussian War of 1870, which gave birth to a modern, united Germany. His own father served the Kaiser. All believed in and fought for the Reich. He loved his country with a depth that I have seldom seen in another human being. The soul and soil of Germany were precious to him. The intensity of his fondness for the mountains and rivers, and the deep valleys of Germany at times frightened me, while at other times I was envious. It was clear that he had a relationship to his country that I lacked about America. He knew he was a German. I simply knew I had American citizenship. There was, I believe, a psychic difference in our ties to our home country."

Samuels drained his coffee and thought out loud, "Perhaps that's a piece of the puzzle. Mildred was an American, but one without emotional ties to the country." He thought deeply on this observation. She never spoke fondly of Ohio, or New York City, or Boston. It was more as if she was passing through, as if she were watching a movie. But she never talked about the grandeur of the Rocky Mountains or the stark beauty of the western deserts. She was, it appears, unconnected to the land. She was rootless. True, she exploded when she heard about Pearl Harbor. But was the explosion about? Not the loss of lives and the pain and sadness that would visit American homes in the looming war… No, her anger was directed toward Japan for bringing the US into the conflict on the side of Britain. As for Max, it was true he became an American citizen in 1935, but his heart never left the Rhineland. He was always a German true to his country.

He continued to read.

"There have been accusations that Max was a Nazi sympathizer and that he influenced me with his belief in fascism. The same charge claimed that he nurtured sympathies for Hitler, even to the degree of subversion in the United States, that he was not only a professor, but a skilled operative of the Third Reich. I need to debunk some of this. Without question the Nazi Party under Hitler attracted Max. He saw in Hitler a resurgent Germany, what Max called the 'glorious wellsprings of Teutonic civilization.' At the same time, he saw western democracies as lifeless and corrupt, at the end of their ropes, countries in stagnation compared to the 'heroism of Siegfried and the genius of Wagner's operas.' At heart, he was a romantic and drawn to mysticism. In Hitler he found a kindred soul. Their hearts beat as one.

"As to being a spy, I never saw any evidence of that. True, his lectures espoused historical and philosophical tenets dear to him, and one could read a sympathetic view of fascism into his words. But, overtly undermining America, never in my presence. That wasn't Max's style. He tried to get his students to think for themselves. He didn't want them taken in by crass propaganda. He challenged the intellect. He wanted his students open to all ideas.

"Getting back to me he never tried to convert me to Nazism, either at Hunter or once I went to work at Radio Berlin. At the college, I passed my classes. In Berlin I survived another curriculum. If there were any philosophical connection between us, it was the teachings of Oswald Spengler. Max really did want me to understand Spengler's thesis."

Samuels got up from the kitchen table and walked out into the living room. He thought about another cup of coffee and then put off the idea. Even with decaf he was feeling too jumpy. He needed to calm down. He knew what was troubling him. Max, the guy was a muddle for Samuels. Was he an intellectual or rampant Nazi or some rather uneasy mix of the two? And he was dead. No way to interview him. Dependent on Mildred and what others had to say, as he was, was not always the best way to do research. He needed to change the subject. He would concentrate on Spengler, the German historian Max wanted Mildred to understand.

Samuels had studied Spengler in college and his theory that "civilizations underwent the same life progressions or stages as human beings." This view, first put forth in *The Decline of the West* published in 1918, stated that cultures rather than nations were the keys to history, and much like any organism they go through predictable stages because history was organic and cyclical, not linear with some sort of progression from lower to higher. For Spengler, the cyclical approach to history explained the "rise and fall of nations," really their civilizations, which were living things. For him, cultures passed through stages of birth, development, fulfillment, decay, and death creating, as they did an understandable "morphology of history." The linear view, from his perspective, saw history like rungs on a ladder, a sort of evolution upward from Egypt through the Greek and Roman periods, and then the Medieval period followed by the Renaissance, and now the modern period. Spengler considered this view nothing more than Western man's ego leading from an imperfect past to a more perfected form in the present.

Samuels recalled Spengler's trap. If the linear view were true, how could the tragedy of World War I be explained? Where was the perfection? With Western civilization collapsing around him, Spengler only saw a tragic vision of human history. He saw the demise of European culture in his world and in history.

Yet, Max had wanted Mildred to understand Spengler's thesis. Why? He would have to get back to Mildred's letter. Perhaps there was a clue there.

"I spent considerable time with the Professor discussing Spengler's ideas. I must admit I did neglect my assignments in order to read extensively about the dynamics of history. Of course, my grades suffered, but not my mind. Max enthralled me with his understanding of history. Slowly, I began to see and understand his vision. The Great Depression following the terrible war illustrated the decadence of Europe, and especially the democracies. They couldn't avoid war. They couldn't extricate themselves from the financial ruin of the 1930's. A cultural revival was necessary. The rationalistic and scientific tradition of the West had failed. A new gestalt was needed. In the romanticism and mysticism of Nazism was the answer to the looming twilight of European culture. I came to accept his view of history.

"After returning to Germany, Max went to work for Radio Berlin where he was put in charge of educational programs, including one he created that was called *"The College Hour."* He specifically designed it for college students in the US to hear over shortwave radio. In his first broadcast, June 27, 1940, he shared Spengler's views with his audience. He contended that war, if it came, was a product of 'inscrutable historical forces in Europe, which could not be escaped.' As he stated to his listeners:"

The establishment in Germany of an authoritarian government on the basis of leadership was the result of the slow and natural evolution, and the support of the masses.

"In other words, Nazism was a predictable outcome of history working itself out. He added a propagandistic side to this philosophical view. The United States should not presume to interfere with this movement of history. He tied this position to what he called the 'injured nation' argument, that Germany had been betrayed and humiliated at Versailles and that condition could not last. History was elastic in that sense. Germany needed redemption. Germany needed "living room." Germany needed a new history.

Admittedly, I was an impressionable young woman at Hunter, and Max was most persuasive. But it was never the case that Max intimidated me, or forced me to accept his beliefs. I could think for myself. This was most true when it came to the Jewish question.

Samuels put Mildred's letter down. He needed something to eat. Breakfast seemed like an eternity ago. He rummaged through the refrigerator and ended up parceling together a "Samuels special:" two thick slices of baloney, smeared with hot mustard and encased between two slices of Swiss cheese. On top of this, he added lettuce and thinly sliced sweet onions. The whole works was trapped by two slices of Jewish rye bread from *Brent's Deli*. It was the bread that did it. Monotheism and the "commandments" were certainly contributions to history, but as far as Samuels was concerned a slice of Jewish rye and a Kosher pickle, decadent as some might see them, symbolized the epitome of Hebraic civilization. For Samuels, history had a stomach. He eagerly bit into the past. Thirty minutes later, he was again reading Mildred's letter.

"Max has been accused of being anti-Jewish, an anti-Semitic. The same assertion had been made about me. To argue we never made negative statements about Jews would be foolish. We did. To argue we supported Hitler's 'final solution' would be equally foolish. One can dislike Jews without wishing their physical demise. Max never saw the concentration camps as an answer. He never saw the slaughter and extermination of a race as an answer. Nor did I. We didn't hate Jews. We disliked their influence and power, especially in banking and government, and, most prominently, in America, where they held President Roosevelt's ear. In the end, we merely wanted to expel Jews from Germany and any country under Nazi control. That is different than implying we favored the gas chamber. We did not.

"Max told me when he first felt the pangs of anti-Semitism. While at Hunter, he was told in 1930 that, popular as he was and published as he had been, he didn't have a chance of a full promotion. That is, gaining tenure as a full professor. The reason given was that his name sounded Jewish and that there was an unstated ceiling to limit the promotion of Jews on the faculty. I was never able to affirm this. But I do know Max was never granted the tenure he desired.

"As to Jews in Germany, Max tried to give an intellectual face to the excesses of the Third Reich. He saw the Jew as the 'outsider who's influence peaked during the Weimar Republic, but now they played a 'parasitic role' within the nation. For him, the Jewish age in Germany had come to an end. A new 'state religion' demanded their expulsion, not their elimination as a people. He acknowledged an anti-Semitic edge to the National Socialist movement. In the confrontation of mythic emotionalism of Nazism with Jewish intellectualism and rationalism, the Jew, a minority in Germany, would lose. They were, he argued 'denizens of a foreign land.' On this level, all non-Jews, including Max, exemplified some degree of anti-Semitism. Since I accepted Max's interpretation of events, I was also, to a degree, anti-Semitic.

"When Max talked about Jewish intellectuals such as Heine, Einstein, Freud, and Mendelssohn, he was forced by his convictions to arbitrarily create two designations of Germans. Though German citizens, the intellects noted were referred to as Jewish, not German-Jews. He could not deny their genius, but he could deny their national citizenship.

"He talked to me about the connections between international bolshevism and world Jewry. He felt they marched hand in hand. From all that I can recall, he downplayed this relationship while at Hunter until two things occurred. First, Germany prepared for a European war. Second, the US embarked upon war preparedness. By the mid-30's, he was convinced a Soviet-American alliance was in the offing and warned against it, sometimes not too subtly in his classes. He felt that an overwhelming majority of the Soviet government officials were Jews. He saw the same reflection in the numbers of Jews surrounding Roosevelt. By the early 40's, he now saw another threat, a cabal, both in Washington and London, where Jewish "big money-makers" were prepared to sacrifice millions of lives in defense of their precious capitalistic system. He considered this to be a tragedy on a global scale.

"So, was Max a bigot? And, by extension, was I? I would argue our anti-Semitism, if you wish to call it that, was not too different than what many Americans believed before the war. I would also point out that once we worked for Radio Berlin our broadcasts reflected, as they had to, the "party-line." Whatever our personal views about the "camps," we were in no position to challenge the prevailing view. To do so would have meant being fired, ostracized, or worse. It is easy, I must say, to judge others for their compliance, if not their lack of heroics, when the boot of the Gestapo was elsewhere. Things are never as simple as they seem.

Was Mildred right? Samuels thought. Would he have acted differently in the same circumstances? Would he have put his children and wife at risk? Would he have thrown away his heady position at Radio Berlin for Jews, who were already destined for a fate ordained by Hitler and his thugs, which he had no power to stop anyway? If he answered yes… Yes, I would have fought the regime. Mildred, of course, might easily turn the tables on him. Where were you, Mr. Samuels, when blacks were lynched in the South? Where were you when native-Americans were almost destroyed as a people? Where were you when Japanese-Americans were placed in internment camps? Where was your courage? She might have added, "Mr. Samuels, if you wish to stand on a higher moral ground, you better make sure you're not standing in a bog.

Enough, Samuels reflected. Enough. Time to get on with it. Okay, Mildred, what's next? Still more surprises?

"People often wondered why Max was attracted to me? I never wondered why. I knew. We loved each other. But, of course, love can be most complicated. Our love was. Max always needed a woman in his life, often more than one, and sometimes at the same time. Quite a guy… He enjoyed the co-eds at Hunter College. He flirted with women at Radio Berlin. Though married to a fine German woman, Max had numerous affairs. I wouldn't call him a womanizer. He simply had a need, whether physical or psychological, to have someone constantly in his life, to have someone close. Once I stayed in Germany and began broadcasting, I was that woman.

"It was an affair. I knew he was married. I met his wife and children. I dined in their home. I'm sure his wife was aware of the relationship. It was as if we all just accepted our fate. For my part, I needed a strong man in my life. Max was that man. I was cut off from the world after Pearl Harbor. My livelihood at Radio Berlin was somewhat dependent on Max's good will and influence. My life in Nazi Germany was precarious. Max was my savior. My hero. But this was secondary to my love for him.

"At my trial, people saw me as a hussy, a wanton woman who took advantage of an older man. They couldn't believe I loved and respected Max and that I always wanted to be with him. That nothing could separate us... That he was my man of destiny.

"Unfortunately, the judge at my trial never let me put into the record on incident that reflected my affection for Max. It was toward the end of the war after the Allied invasion of France.

"I was in Paris with Max covering the story of the invasion. Within a short time, we could hear the guns of the advancing Allied armies. Max was hastily recalled to Berlin. Before leaving, Max made arrangements with Werner Plack, who was a top administrator at Radio Berlin, to take me with him when he left Paris. He was, as things turned out, the wrong man to ask for assistance. We knew each other. We disliked each other. I was a celebrity. He was an administrator. Plack left Paris without me. I was stranded in the city. I had no transportation out. I called Berlin and asked for Max's help. I was told he had died, that he had committed suicide.

"I couldn't believe it. I wouldn't believe it. Max would never take his own life. Then, and surprisingly, I was told he died of natural causes at the Berlin-Spandau Hospital on August 31, 1944, and would be buried on September 4, 1944. Why the two stories? And what to believe? And lastly, what should I do?

"I considered staying in Paris and turning myself over to the Americans. I could also head for Berlin and be trapped by the advancing Russian armies. To travel west meant life. To travel east meant death. I chose to return to Berlin. I didn't try to save my own skin. I fled first to Holland where I bribed a train conductor with a can of coffee and headed back to Max. I arrived in time for his funeral. Only a woman in love would have done this.

"There were naturally other things, which brought us together. We each had a flair for the dramatic. I was an actress of some talent. He was a showman of some talent. Poetry was in our souls. Life was an expanding dream for us. We were living on the cusp of a new era. We were part of some grand adventure. Can you understand that? To be at the beginning; it was intoxicating.

"Beyond all this, we had each experienced career difficulties. The world had contrived to deny Max his rightful tenure as a full professor and very shortsighted producers had failed, as in my case, to recognize a true talent on the stage.

"To some extent, our relationship permitted us to comfort each other for failed and missed opportunities. If Max, as some have said, had a weakness for women, I fulfilled that need. We enjoyed each other's company. He was erudite and debonair. I had never known such a person. He wished to teach. I wished to learn. We were a perfect match of teacher and pupil, yet we were equals. And, if I may say so, our intimate moments brought two hearts together.

"Permit me to sum up my life with Max. He did not convince me to betray my country. I consciously stayed in Germany and hoped that my work at Radio Berlin would keep America out of the war. I chose my own fate. What I did was for love and my country."

Samuels put down Mildred's letter after reading her last words many times. They would stay with him until he finally met her. He had no doubt he would be mindful of them for a long time. Perhaps it would be best to say that the words would haunt him.

"It is possible to conclude, Mr. Samuels, that I am self-serving in my recollections or that time has altered my views of what actually took place. Being only human, it is quite possible. Wartime Germany and my trial, and incarceration afterwards certainly left emotional scars and painful memories. This I cannot deny. I will leave it to you, then, to sort out the whole affair. As for Max, I trust you will be kind to him in what you write. He died a long time ago with his country crashing down around him, a romantic overwhelmed by the passions of Nazism and too weak to fight the demons demanding his very soul. Perhaps that is his epitaph, and mine."

CHAPTER 20
THE OHIO VIXEN

Traveling to Ohio

"That's right, 'Edna Mae, "she's agreed to meet next week."
"Finally."
"Just a note in the mail, dated Columbus, Ohio."
"Anything about me, Mr. Samuels?"
"No."

Robert Samuels was in his office at the *Chronicle,* where he had just finished off two more articles in his series on Axis Sally. So far his work had proven popular with the public and it had even received critical acclaim from those in the business. There was quiet talk about a second Pulitzer. Anyway, just after he yelled, "copy boy," a stack of his daily mail arrived. Samuels was good about the mail. He liked reading the responses to his work, where sanity prevailed and the writer had something to say, whether favorable or not. So he always got right to it. He had learned long ago to do this, otherwise, the mail just built up, a pile equal to Everest if he didn't watch out. Five letters into the stack, he had found the letter from Mildred, and, upon reading it, saw an invitation to meet with her. Just a one liner: *Would he be available to meet next week?* No phone number, just a return address. He quickly fired off an affirmative response via special delivery mail. After that, he called Edna Mae.

"You're going?"
"Already booking with *United.*"
"Have you reached a final conclusion yet?"
"Leaning strongly toward?"
"The truth."
"Playing it close to the vest, Mr. Samuels?"
"Hedging my bets."
"I'll just have to keep reading the *Chronicle.*"
"Helps to pay the bills."
"Do give Mildred my best."
"I will. Keep good thoughts, Edna Mae."

The next call was to his wife.

"She's agreed, Lynn."
"Who has agreed?"
"Mildred."
"She'll see you?"
"Next week."
"I'll pack your overnight grip, Robert."
"I need to call, Rachel."
"Right."
"You call Rita and Ron."
"Done."
"Love you."
"Ditto, Robert."

Samuels then called his daughter at Freedom High School. The office secretary, always protective of Rachel's busy schedule and limited time, was reluctant to put him through. "Just leave a message," she had said. Of course, she changed her mind when she discovered Rachel's father was on the line.

"Hope this is good, Dad. I've got two angry parents here," she said softly.

"Their kid got an 'A-' instead of an 'A+'?"

"Not far off."

"Right."

"So what's happening? Did Axis Sally call you?"

"Again not far off."

"Tell me."

So Samuels did.

"Go for it, Dad."

"Next week."

"Cool."

"Very professional response."

"Isn't it?"

"Don't let the crazies eat you alive."

"Good advice for both of us."

"Love you, Rachel."

"Love you, too, Dad."

A few days later Lynn dropped Samuels off at SFX, but not before providing some wifely advice.

"Watch yourself, Robert."

"Meaning?"

"Don't fall even more under her spell."

"Me?"

"Your passion for this story borders on the obsessive."

"Just an enthusiastic reporter."

"Right."

"Lynn, say it."

"She's a survivor, Robert. She's turned seduction into an art form to survive her adventures. She's not a sly vixen."

"I'm an old reporter. I'm beyond temptation."

"Does she know that?"
"Subject never came up."
"It will, Robert, dear."
"You know this because…"
"I'm a woman."

What could Samuels say? No man had a reasonable answer to that declaration of gender wisdom. Discretion was necessary.

"I'll be on guard."
"Call me."
"Every night."

Three days and seven hours later United Flight 777 landed in Columbus, Ohio. Two long delays and three-milk run stops, accounted for the long flight. Meeting Samuels at the airport was the Mother Superior of the local Catholic school. She acknowledged him with a generous smile and a firm handshake. She had a no nonsense demeanor. After settling into her car, an antique Ford station wagon, a "woody," she got right down to business.

"Call me, Theresa."
"I'm Robert."
"No, you're Mr. Samuels, the reporter."
"You're the boss."
"I am."
"You have some ground rules for this meeting, Theresa?"
"How did you know."
"I'm a reporter."

At that Theresa laughed.

"I don't want Mildred hurt."
"Not my intention."

"She's been through a great deal."

"I know."

"Bringing up the past is difficult for her."

"Understandable."

"What do you hope to gain through this meeting?"

"An elusive piece of a puzzle I keep missing."

"I'm missing something here."

Samuels then explained Edna Mae's proposition, his research to date, and the stories he had submitted to the *Chronicle*. Theresa was aware of this.

"Full citizenship restored and personal redemption, Mr. Samuels, are they possible? Are you going to recommend a pardon?"

"Undecided."

"Why? You've already written five or six articles. I've read them all."

"There's a missing puzzle piece."

"Once you have it?"

"I'll decide."

"You could give Mildred false hopes."

"I'll explain to her what I told Edna Mae. No guarantees."

"She could still be hurt."

"Not by me, at least not intentionally."

"I'll pray for you, Mr. Samuels."

"I'm Jewish."

"I know."

Forty minutes later, Theresa dropped Samuels off at Mildred's apartment on the West Side of Columbus not far from the convent where Mildred taught. She left, saying two words, "Good luck."

Samuels knocked on the door of Mildred's first floor apartment. No answer. He knocked again, a little harder. The door finally opened.

Standing there was an attractive woman in her late 70's, wearing a long, black dress that clung tightly to her still athletic, dancer's body. Long whitish-silver hair fell gracefully to her shoulders. She stood with one hand on a hip, much like a movie star posing for a shoot. An inviting smile looked out at him. Samuels felt his heart miss a beat.

Before him stood Axis Sally.

At that moment, he hoped the Mother Superior would really put in a strong prayer for him. He knew he was going to need all the help he could get. In the back of his mind, he heard Lynn's charge, "vixen."

"Mr. Samuels, I presume."
"Indeed."
"Welcome."

CHAPTER 21
THE AWOL PILOT

Getting Acquainted

"What were you expecting, Mr. Samuels?"

Samuels was standing in the middle of Mildred's living room. Standing and staring, and flustered, and truth be told, feeling much like a shy high school boy on his first date.

"Perhaps you would like to sit down?"
"Yes, that would be nice."

Samuels sat down, careful to sit up straight and to maintain eye contact. Silly as it seemed, he felt as if he had floundered into a spider's web. Mildred sat down across from him, crossed her still attractive legs and smiled bewitchingly, or so thought Samuels.

"You're still staring, Mr. Samuels. Should I consider that a compliment?"
"You're not …"
"What you expected."
"I…"

"A retiring senior citizen wearing an oversized housecoat covered in pastel pictures of flowers?"

"I'm afraid so."

"No need to be afraid. I'm not the matronly type. Never have been, but, of course, you know that from your research. Nor do I especially like slippers and aprons. Meeting you in an old lady's attire had no appeal to me."

"I can see that."

"Can you? Then let me ask you, what do you think of the dress I'm wearing?"

"Most appealing. Perhaps attractive is a better descriptor."

"This is the dress I wore years ago at my trial, Mr. Samuels. It caused quite a stir. My defense attorney wanted me to wear something a little more conservative. He didn't want me to draw attention to myself. He didn't want me to look like 'Hitler's girlfriend.'"

"Wise counsel."

"Perhaps. As you can see, I didn't comply with his wishes. I was in the middle of a judicial and media frenzy. I dressed accordingly. So the flashbulbs popped and the news cameras twirled and I was back on stage, Axis Sally, the celebrity traitor."

"You speak with a touch of bitterness."

"A touch, yes, and why not. The Truman Administration, with elections coming up, wanted a show trial to demonstrate to the public how tough it could be on traitors."

"Harsh politics!"

"As you say, harsh. Dressing down wouldn't have helped my case. Axis Sally was in the limelight. I couldn't let her down."

"You speak of her in the third person."

"I do."

"As if she were someone else."

"Only my persistent shadow over the years."

"You kept the dress?"

"Mothballed it. Hadn't worn it for years. Had it cleaned when I decided to grant this interview."

"Why?"

"The interview?"

"No, the dress."

"I wanted you to see what all the fuss was about in the flesh."

In his mind Samuels could hear his wife's admonition. "Careful, Robert, she's a vixen. She's a survivor."

"Are you flirting with me, Mildred?" Samuels asked, not quite sure why he asked, or of the answer he expected or wanted.

"A little, an older woman's whim, nothing more. You've nothing to fear from me."

"Or from me, Mildred."

"That's why I agreed to meet. Would you care for some tea?"

"Please."

As Mildred made the tea, Samuels looked around. The apartment was small, almost Spartan, with a few framed pictures, really posters, by a Russian artist Samuels recognized, Marc Chagall. How surprising, thought Samuels, and how ironic. I wonder if she knows Chagall was a Jew. Of course, she must know. She taught art, didn't she? Along one wall were three books cases, each full of historical and biographical works, plus thick art books and slimmer ones on music and the theater. Whatever else, Samuels decided, Mildred was exceeding well read.

Returning with the tea and a dish of cookies, she sat down, saying, "Mr. Samuels, please. And don't worry about the cookies. They're sugar free."

"You know I'm a diabetic? How?"

"Yes, I know. As to how, that's my little secret. Okay?"

"Your sister?"

"You're prying."

"I am."

Samuels needed to change the subject. He did.

"I was noticing your art on the wall. All Chagall's."

"You know your art?"

"The *'Village'* is one of my favorites. You know, of course, he is Jewish?"

"Of course."

"And Russian."

"But not a Bolshevik."

"Great art is great art, Mr. Samuels. How's the herbal tea? One of my favorites."

"Very nice."

"And the cookies?"

"Also, very nice."

"Good, now let's get down to business. Why was this interview so necessary?"

"I need to give you a test, actually three."

"If I pass?"

"I will be close to meeting Edna Mae's hopes."

"Campaigning for a full pardon?"

"Like Iva's, yes."

"Redemption?"

"Yes, and, if the School Board agrees, naming a drama building after you."

"At Freedom High School where your daughter, Rachel, is the principal?"

"You are well informed."

"I always did my homework as a serious news broadcaster."

"It appears so. One precaution, Mildred, I can't guarantee the outcome of these tests. You know that, don't you?'

"I never expected you to."

"Sister Theresa is concerned about our meeting."

"She needn't be. I'm a tough, old gal. Don't worry."

"After reading what you wrote about Max, I believe that, Mildred."

"You handled his story with grace, Mr. Samuels. I thank you. Now what do you want to know? Something, I think, about my early family life, or my relationship to Mr. Sisk, my violent and hateful father? Or how I got along with my dentist-stepfather? You know, the Freudian thing."

"Unnecessary."

"Not into the unconsciousness?"

"Only what I can see and touch, and measured with objectivity."

"Am I what you can see and touch?"

"Objectively?"

"Reality, stark and clarified."

"A survivalist's mantra?"

"Indeed. Now back to my past. My college years perhaps, or my first years hustling theatre jobs in New York? They were, as I look back, quite interesting."

"No."

"My love life? Certainly, you would want to know more about the men in my life, wouldn't you?"

"I'm not a voyeur."

"Oh, come now Mr. Samuels, we are all voyeurs, indulging our hopes and dreams in the lives of others."

"You are a clever woman, Mildred."

"Not clever enough, it would seem. The subject of your interest continues to elude me."

"Then we should rectify that. Shall we start?"

Samuels took out a notebook from his overnight bag and opened it up to a completely blank page. Pen in hand he showed Mildred the empty pages. "I hope to fill up this notebook today."

"As you said, let's start."

"Three names, Mildred… Martin James Monti… Barbara Elliott… Warrant Officer Catherine Samaha… You recognize them, I'm sure?"

If it were possible for Axis Sally to be caught off guard, she was, but only for a moment.

"All names from my uneven past, which, it seems, you have unearthed. I have not thought of them for a long time, and I certainly had not expected to hear them today. If I say yes, do I pass you test?"

"Part I, yes."

"And the next part?"

"We talk."

"And how will I know if I pass this part?"

"I'll know, Mildred."

"Like Max, you seem to hold all the cards. Men always seem to have this advantage."

"Then let's start with an old foe."

"Who would that be, my inquisitive reporter?"

"Monti."

"Very good, Mr. Samuels. You passed my first test for you."

Monti

"I disliked the man from the first moment I met him. No, more to the point, I despised him."

"You know, Mildred, he was the only commissioned military officer sentenced as a radio traitor."

"I do. *Martin Wiethaup (aka Monti)* That was his radio name. Imagine, an American air force flier indicted for treason. He pleaded guilty in 1949 and was jailed until 1960 when he was released from his 25-year sentence. Had it been up to me, he would have stayed the whole time."

"Mildred, you really didn't like him."

"That's because I know all about him."

"On October 2, 1944 Martin went AWOL. He was in the American Army Air Force stationed in Karachi, Pakistan. He had been denied a transfer to Italy, where as he put it, 'the real fighting was taking place.'

His background was straightforward. He enlisted in 1943 to avoid being drafted. At the time, he was living in St. Louis. In the service, he qualified in the P-39 and P-38 Lightning light bombers, and was promoted to second lieutenant. However, his superiors found him to be undisciplined and difficult to work with. Believe me, I could have told them that. After going AWOL, he hitched a ride aboard a C-46 to Cairo, Egypt. From there he traveled by land to Tripoli on his way to Italy. Eventually, he made his way to Pomigliano Airfield, just north of Naples, where the 354th Air Service Squadron prepared newly arrived aircraft for assignments to line operations."

"The man got around."

"You have no idea. While at the airfield, two things happened. First, he requested a transfer again. Again, he was denied. Second, he saw a P-38 Lightning being worked on and requiring a test flight. Pretending to be the test pilot, he took off in the plane and headed northward to Milan. There he landed and surrendered to German authorities. They didn't know what to make of him. Was he a spy? Had he really deserted? In time they came to the conclusion that he was a voluntary defection. Now, unfortunately, another question emerged. What should they do with him? As for Monti, he was adamant that he wanted to join the Luftwaffe and fight the Russians on the Eastern Front. Can you believe that? He couldn't tell the difference between a Bolshevik and a slice of Russia rye bread. The Germans decided against this. Still, the question remained. How could they use him to their benefit? He was turned over to a military propaganda unit, where it was decided he should work at Radio Berlin broadcasting.

"Bringing him into contact with you?"

"Unfortunately, yes."

"I understand he refused to divulge any information about the Army Air Force, nor was he willing to speak ill of his home country."

"I've heard that?"

"You don't believe it, Mildred?"

"He was AWOL, wasn't he?"

"So you were forced to work with him?"

"Monti was given a microphone test and passed it. I don't know how he did it. The man was poorly educated, spoke questionable English, and couldn't put together a cogent thought, yet our radio manager, Heinrich Schafhausen, hired him. To this day, I believe there was pressure from his superiors to do this. I know that Heinrich found him to be 'immature and lacking in general education.' Still, he was hired as a commentator I must tell you I viewed him with great suspicion from the outset once I learned he was a former American pilot. I didn't know if he was a traitor or a spy. Either way, it might be bad for me. If he were a spy, he might testify against me after the war. I didn't want my actions misconstrued as treasonous at some later date. If he were a traitor, it would be documented that I worked with him. I knew I wasn't a traitor. I was a professional entertainer. I didn't want to be tarnished by his presence. I didn't want to be associated with him. After all, no one at Radio Berlin considered me a traitor."

"You were in a tough situation, Mildred. You were already thinking about the post-war period?"

"If Germany lost, yes."

"How could you know?"

"Easy. After the invasion of Normandy and your bloody B-17's' daily raid over German targets, blasting beautiful cities back into the stone age, leaving only rubble and death behind them. And Stalin's forces, always refusing to surrender Moscow, Stalingrad, and Leningrad, regardless of the human cost to keep them in the war. East and west enemies closing in on Germany... There was no good news. Only an impaired mind could not see the writing on the wall. It was all too clear to me. The war was lost."

"And getting back to Monti, you couldn't just refuse to work with him."

"That's exactly what I did. I walked out of the broadcast booth. I never said a word to him. I didn't want anything to do with him."

"Wasn't that a dangerous thing to do?"

"Exceedingly. But I didn't care at the moment. "I told Heinrich, 'either Monti is removed, or I go.' Obviously, I was being rather recalcitrant. And stupid. Heinrich didn't have the authority to remove Monti. I left his office shouting, "I have made my last broadcast,' and that was not a smart thing to say."

"You could be impetuous."

"I lived in the moment and, as you know, all too often I paid a price for my imprudence. Unfortunately, my feelings overtake my more sensible thoughts."

"What happened?"

"Things, Mr. Samuels, got completely out of control. I quickly received a message to meet with Kurt-Georg Kiesinger, the Foreign Office Liaison with the Propaganda Ministry. Kiesinger tried to persuade me to return to my duties. He tried to pacify my anger and fears. He pointed out the difficulties in my attitude and actions, and in my position as an American in Berlin without a passport. He was a fair-minded person. He was giving me a quiet warning. I refused to take it. I remained obstinate."

"Why? You knew your actions would cause trouble. Why would you put yourself at risk? It doesn't make sense."

"It was 1944. I was tired of living in fear. I was tired of being pushed around. And Max wasn't around to help me. It was silly, I know."

"They put pressure on you?"

"After I left his office, I tried to obtain my food rations for the week. I was denied. Horst Cleinow, the Manager of the Overseas Division of Radio Berlin, had ordered my ration card withheld until I returned to work. Even then, I didn't give in."

"Stubborn."

"Or foolhardy. The next day I received a letter summoning me to Gestapo Headquarters for an interview. I immediately called Dr. Anton Winkelnkemper and pleaded for help. He was Cleinow's superior. As had Kiesinger, he tried to get me to go back to work. Once more, I refused. I remember saying the following to him. 'If you can keep the Gestapo away from me, I will be grateful to you, and if you cannot,

I will take the consequences.' I went home wondering what my fate would be."

"You weren't worried about the Gestapo?"

"I was past worrying."

"But at your trial, didn't you state the opposite, that you were always fearful of the Gestapo?"

"Yes, that was my testimony."

"But?"

"Call it a lapse in judgment, or an exception to the unstated rule to stay clear of the Gestapo. Does it really matter?"

"Something about Monti got to you?"

"He was a traitor. I wasn't."

"And that's why you risked your life?"

"It was my life, was it not?"

"One question, then, Mildred. Did you fear for your life at Radio Berlin?"

"I always feared for my life with the Gestapo lurking about, especially when I acted irrationally as I also did when I heard about Pearl Harbor. At times, I could be my own worst enemy. Was that the test question?"

"Yes."

"Did I pass?"

"You did."

"Now what?"

"How did you get out of this fire?"

"The two gentlemen worked out something with the Gestapo. I never had the interview. I was persuaded to return to the work."

"Because?"

"They were releasing Monti."

"You got lucky."

"Monti had proven to be a total failure. He lacked even the basic skills as a radio commentator and analyst. He was a dull speaker. He exhausted his limited intellect immediately after welcoming his listeners. He was a lousy radio propagandist."

"Out he went?"

"And back in I came."

"Ending this story."

"Not quite, Mr. Samuels. I have a few test questions for you."

"Oh."

"What happened to dear Monti after his release?"

"He joined the Waffen SS. After Germany's surrender, he gave himself up to Allied Authorities in Italy. He was still wearing his SS uniform at the time."

"Bravo. Next question… What happened to his plane?"

"That's a tougher one, Mildred."

"You're giving up?"

"Remembering. The plane was stripped of its American markings. German efficiency. The underside was sprayed yellow for identification and German national insignias were placed on it. It was, I believe, assigned the code 'T9+MK.' It was then sent to a base where it was studied by German pilots. And here's the fantastic part. The plane survived the war. It was discovered in Austria in May 1945. After that, I'm not sure what happened to it… Probably ended up as scrap iron."

"Well done. I am impressed. Last question… What happened to Kurt-Georg Kiesinger?"

"Too easy. He got into politics after the war and in 1966, he became the Chancellor of West Germany."

"You are a clever man, Mr. Samuels."

"It appears, Mildred, we have each completed our first tests."

"It does, doesn't it? What comes next?"

CHAPTER 22
THE UNWANTED CHILD

A German Lunch

"Mildred, you didn't have to prepare lunch. The *Chronicle* did provide me with more than a meager entertainment allowance."

"No trouble at all. And where, dear Mr. Samuels, can you dine with authentic German chicken soup as they make it in Munich?"

"You've got me there."

Robert Samuels and Mildred were enjoying lunch before moving on to the next topic. Her Munich special soup was excellent, thick, hot, and full of large chunks of chicken and lots of vegetables, mainly peas and corn. She had also baked biscuits using an old German recipe. For dessert, she promised a Black Forest cake made with a sugar substitute so as to appease Samuels' apprehensions. Dark decaf coffee was also on tab.

Samuels found himself watching Mildred as she prepared lunch, moving much like a dancer, smoothly and gracefully from one task to another. He found it difficult to take his eyes off her, even if he had wanted to, and he didn't want to. There was an allure about her, an unstated aphrodisiac, more complex than overt sultriness, yet as powerful in its own way. Samuels found himself both unnerved by it, but also fascinated. Try as he may, he found himself increasingly caught up in its spell.

"You are an excellent cook, Mildred."

"When I put my mind to it, yes. During the war, one had to learn to cook with whatever was available. Of course, I was more fortunate than most. I had a generous ration card. Only the higher up Nazi officials did better."

"Did you buy on the black market?"

"Of course. Anyone who had plentiful Reich marks did. The under-the-counter-market prospered regardless of the harsh laws on the books. It was the same in France and Holland. Shortages and money always create an illegal market, don't you think so?"

"Even in prosperous times."

They ate quietly for a few minutes, enjoying the smells and taste of the hot soup and buttered biscuits. For a moment they were at peace with the world. Only quiet memories stirred of times past. Of course, it couldn't last. Samuels was here to get a story.

"Tell me about the 'unwanted child.'"

"You have probed my past."

"An investigative reporter has no choice."

"Nor does it appear that I do, painful as this will be for me. But it is a test, is it not?"

"With apologies, yes."

"Max always enjoyed this soup. It was his favorite. In fact, it was his mother's recipe, which he gave to me."

"You miss him?"

"Terribly. He was the cause of all my happiness and grief."

"But he was your '*man of destiny,*' was he not?"

"From the first moment I saw him at Hunter College. We were simply drawn together by a force we could not impede."

"Love at first sight?"

"Attraction."

"Which was renewed in Germany?"

Samuels wanted to move on to the topic at hand, the child nobody wanted. It was obvious, however, that Mildred needed to speak about Max. Long ago Samuels learned it was best to go with the flow. This he now did.

"Yes, our relationship reasserted itself. At the beginning of the war, I could have been exchanged with the other internees. I chose not to be exchanged. I wanted to be near Max. After D-Day, I could have stayed in Paris. I didn't. As you know, I hurried back to Berlin when I heard he had died. Rather an irrational thing to do. He was dead. I couldn't do anything about that. Why not just wait around for the Americans? A POW camp in France would be better than dealing with the Russians. But I couldn't do that. Once our relationship was renewed, I couldn't leave him, not even when he passed."

"Even though he lied to you about his marriage, and courted you at a time when his wife was pregnant with their fourth child""

"As you say, even though."

Mildred got up and cleared the table. It had been a good meal. Finishing up, Mildred said, "Mr. Samuels, you so remind me of Max. A favor, please."

"If I can."

Mildred didn't respond immediately. Rather, she went to a small cabinet in the living room on which there was an old black and white television. Opening up the cabinet, she brought out a record still in its sleeve. She blew a bit of dust off it before saying, "an old Tommy Dorsey record." Max and I used to dance to it. Would you care to dance with Axis Sally, just one dance to warm an old woman's heart?"

What could Samuels say? One dance, what could be the harm, he thought? Just one dance… The "unwanted child" could wait.

"Sure."

Mildred put the record on an almost ancient RCA phonograph and then carefully lowered the needle. Soon the swing music of Tommy Dorsey's strings enveloped the living room. Samuels walked over to her and Mildred flowed into his arms, closing her eyes, and resting her head on his shoulder. Usually stump-footed and graceless on the dance floor, Samuels found himself somehow drifting along to the music, comfortable with his feet and the woman in his arms. For a moment, he was sure Mildred was young again, sweeping through life and across continents in search of stardom and love, a dark-haired beauty seeking happiness in a troubled world. And for a moment, he knew, he was no longer Robert Samuels. He was Max, her lover and protector, the man who had stirred her intellect and rejoiced in their intimacies. He knew that, if he closed his eyes, even for a second, he might cross some invisible line of time and space, as he lost himself in Mildred's world. Admittedly, he wanted to. Only by doing this could he fully and finally comprehend the woman he was trying to know. And then, unable to resist the temptation, his eyes closed and the past closed in around him.

"Mr. Samuels." Mildred was quietly saying to him. "Mr. Samuels, the record has stopped."

Mildred was still in his arms, still draped closely to him. "I need to turn off the phonograph." She perched herself on her toes and gently kissed Samuels on the cheeks before saying, "Thank you for the dance." Undraping herself, Mildred moved away from Samuels, who reluctantly permitted her to turn off the ancient phonograph. Somehow he felt incomplete without Mildred in his arms. At that very moment he would have danced through the night embracing the history, if not the sensuality, flowing through Mildred. She sat down, adjusting her dress as she did so. Samuels, following suit, sat down across from her. He was at loss for words.

"That was a perfect moment, Mr. Samuels."

"It was."

"Now we must move on, don't you think? Another test…"

"I'm not sure I want to move on, as you say."

"Oh, my dear, Mr. Samuels, you must. Your infatuation must be with the past, not me."

"The distinction has disappeared."

"You must rediscover it if you are to help me. I do want a pardon before I rejoin Max. Only an objective, critical Robert Samuels can tell my story. The Robert Samuels I danced with cannot, at least not without great difficulty. You must try. Both our souls are at stake."

"Then tell me about Barbara Elliott."

"You have reached back far into my past."

"The story, Mildred."

"It all began when a slim, rather attractive woman, entered the newspaper offices of the *Evening Courier* in Camden, New Jersey. It was October 1928. She wanted to place an ad to find her missing husband, Charles, who had left her. She pointed out to the reporter taking her ad that she was pregnant, perhaps five months, and she was without resources. She had met Charles Elliott during a double date, fallen in love, and then agreed to a modern relationship. No marriage, just live together. Things went well for a time, and then he just walked out of their apartment and never came back. She told the reporter her name was Barbara Elliott and that she was staying at the Hotel Whitman.

"The next day the paper printed the ad, plus a human-interest story about a young woman in need. Her story was quickly picked-up by a Philadelphia newspaper. Other papers on the east coast followed suit.

After a few days, the story quieted down. No Charles Elliott appeared. Then a suicide note was found in the hotel, plus money to pay her bill. Essentially, the note said, she couldn't go on this way. The note was melodramatic, to the extreme. She wrote:

It is not humanly possible to continue any longer this bitter agony of bringing into this poor, deluded world another unwanted child.

She ended the note, saying:

It is the greatest maternal tenderness I can bestow upon my dear child that I end my life with his that he may not be numbered among the hosts of unwelcomed children.

"A day later, on October 19th, at around 7"30 a.m., Officer William Basier spotted a young woman on a bridge overlooking the Delaware River. The bridge, fifteen feet above the water, connected Camden to Philadelphia. The Officer saw the woman begin to climb up the side of the bridge. He quickly charged, grabbed her, and tried to restrain her from hurting herself. Reportedly, she yelled:

This is a free country and one ought to be able do what one wants. If I am not allowed to jump off this bridge, I'll jump off another.

"She was taken to police headquarters for her own protection. There she was questioned. She contended she was Barbara Elliott, a pregnant woman who worked as an interior decorator and had "influential friends" in Philadelphia. She also stated she had attended Ohio Wesleyan College. Taken before a judge, she said dramatically:

I refuse to bring an unwanted child into this world, and I was taking the easy way out.

"The judge decided to keep her in protective custody over the weekend. That night the story of her attempted suicide hit the headlines.

This led to a number of proposals for marriage from chivalrous men over the next few days."

"Barbara Elliott was in a pickle, Mildred."

"Very much so."

"You seem very intimate with the details," Samuels said with a smile. "Almost as if you knew Barbara Elliott."

"I did make her acquaintance," Mildred responded with a soft chuckle. "And once was enough."

"What happened next?"

"The story changed."

"Barbara Elliott was asked by a suspicious reporter the next day if she was aware of 'a 'moving picture producer known to be ready to release a film on marriage?' She denied any knowledge of such a producer. She said she was telling the truth. Then the world blew up in Barbara Elliott's face. A young man walked into the offices of the *Courier* on Monday announcing that he was Charles Elliott and that he wanted to see his wife. He was immediately brought to the police station, where he was strongly questioned. The interrogation revealed inconsistencies with his wife's story. The Chief of Detectives, John Golden, a suspicious man by nature, decided to reunite the couple. He wanted to measure their response to each other. The reunion was noted in the newspaper."

"One of happiness, I suspect," Samuels interjected.

"Absolutely."

"Barbara Elliot literally flung herself at 'the long lost husband,' and then she fainted. She did a fantastic Sarah Bernhardt. Once she revived, Golden told the couple that their story had too many holes in it, that it lacked 'verification.' He pointed out it was time to fess up."

"I assume they did."

"Charles did first. His real name was John Ramsey. He was a New York writer. After that it was Barbara Elliott's turn. She confessed to being an out-of-work actress named…"

"Mildred Gillars."

"You knew all along, Mr. Samuels."

"I did."

"And more?"

"Of course. You and Ramsey attended Ohio Wesleyan University and were in Theta Alpha Phi fraternity together. You were both impoverished actors. Then the two of you were offered major roles in a publicity conspiracy."

"My role, Mr. Samuels?"

"To play an abandoned mother-to-be. Ramsey would be the father."

"And paid by whom?"

"A movie producer who wanted to drum up business for his new film."

"Which was?"

"*The Unwelcomed Child.*"

"You know all."

"Hardly. Some gaps in the story exist."

"Then I will fill them in."

"We were offered $75.00 each for the job. We needed the money. We participated in the hoax. Of course, the police weren't too happy about the incident. They filed charges and we were brought before Judge Bernard Bertman, who promptly sentenced us to three months in jail for contempt of court. That's when I won my Oscar."

"Your greatest role to that point."

"Yes. With tears flowing, I apologized to the judge. I told him that financial desperation made me do it. I also pointed out, we had not received our $75.00, which had been promised. With a flair for the dramatic, I threw myself on the mercy of the court. The judge's response was as I'd hoped. He suspended our sentences. At that point I ran to the judge, yelling, 'You sweet thing!' Two police offers restrained me from giving the judge a big kiss. The surprised judge ordered us to leave town, but we didn't even have carfare to get back to New York. A few reporters were willing to pay the needed $12.75, pointing out that our acting almost put over the hoax, and that it was fun watching us in action. All in all, it was very exciting in some ways."

"But you did lie to the police."

"No, Mr. Samuels, it was acting. There is a distinction, however slight."

"With *'Visions of Invasion,'* was that also acting?"

"Perhaps my best role."

"When interviewing POW's as a Red Cross nurse?"

"Acting and impersonation are the opposite sides of the same piece of bread. And don't forget, my lapse from the complete truth provided their loved ones with information about them once I broadcasted."

"But the interviews bordered on a hoax."

"Mr. Samuels the entire war was a hoax. The Nazis promised the Germans peace and prosperity. The Communists made the same claim. And what did they give everyone? The worst war in human history! As for the winners, they made the same offer after first dividing up the world. All a hoax, all."

Samuels sensed he needed back off. He didn't want to push Mildred too far. He changed the subject slightly.

"Tell me about the production of the film."

"What a joke. We worked in an old dairy cow barn that reeked of manure, mildew, and sour milk cans. The barn was just outside of Camden and surrounded by tall, distasteful weeds. That was just great for the sinuses and lousy because of leg scratches. We worked 14-hour days, starting early and finishing late in order to capture the light. I was cast as a wanton woman somewhere between Mary Magdalene and Sadie Thompson of Hawaii fame. It was good training for my later indictment and appearance in court. I already knew my cues. In my scenes, I had a pillow under my dress and when I gave birth, nude baby dolls were used. For such a serious script, it was almost comical in its production. But somehow we did finish the movie. My last line in the film was, 'Take it away from me. I don't want it.'

"But it was never shown."

"The subject was taboo in 1928, too racy with an uncomfortable subject, children born unwanted by their parents. No theater would show the film."

"Mildred, perhaps we should rest for a while. I know I'm tired. And you must be."

"I'll get you a pillow and you can recline on the couch. I'll rest in my room. You are right. It is tiring going over the past. But one thing first, did I pass my second test?"

Samuels had hoped Mildred might put off this question, but there it was staring him in the face. He could try to nuance his answer. He could outright lie. But he could do neither with Mildred.

"I'm undecided. I think you know what the test was, right?"

"I'm no fool, Mr. Samuels. When am I acting as opposed to merely living out my life on the basis of what I truly believe? What part of my life is a script akin to Barbara Elliott's performance? Was all my life a matter of simply strutting on cue? That it, isn't?"

"It is."

"Then you must decide."

"I will."

"One thing, though, dear Mr. Samuels. When I was in your arms dancing, I was not acting. That was an unrehearsed moment I will always cherish."

CHAPTER 23

THE FLIGHT HOME

A German Dinner

"Mr. Samuels, time to awake."

Robert Samuels heard the voice, but he really didn't want to wake up. He was snug and comfortable on Mildred's couch under a warm quilt. And he wanted to continue the dream in which he danced with Mildred to the "swing" music of the 1940's, but this time without any concern for the varied issues related to Axis Sally. He was tired of all the traitor stuff. He was exhausted from the effort to prove Iva wasn't a traitor. He was equally weary of the effort to show that Mildred wasn't disloyal to America. He was just plain "out of gas" when it came to the "aid and comfort" bit in the Constitution. Happily, he would let someone else pick up the task. Maybe Ron... Or Rita... Why not? They were young. They had something to prove. It was time for this old man to retire from the inky world of the pressroom and self-imposed crusades. He just wanted another bowl of chicken soup and another Dorsey record. The whole world could just take a flying leap....

"Please, Mr. Samuels, do open your eyes."

"Oh, that insistent voice! Why not, thought Samuels? Okay, he would be back in the world of reality, wouldn't he? Was that really that bad? Did he really want to spend the rest of his life cocooned under a quilt? He decided he would take a peek. Squint tightly with one eye to see what the world had to offer. What he saw truly surprised him.

"Yes, it's me, Theresa, Mr. Samuels. Now no more pretending to be asleep. It's time for dinner."

"Mother Superior?"

"In the flesh," she responded in a flash."

"Why...?"

"All in good time. Now, up. You wouldn't want to upset a Mother Superior, would you?"

"Dinner," Samuels said as he roused himself from the couch, rubbing his eyes and letting his jaw chump on empty space, as his legs stretched and his body adapted to wakefulness.

"Mildred has been preparing some of her favorite German foods in your honor. Now bestir yourself. You certainly wouldn't want to disappoint her."

"How long have I been asleep?"

"Mildred, how long has your guest been out of circulation?"

"About four hours," came a familiar voice from the kitchen.

"No way."

"Unless the sun looks like a moon, yes."

"I apologize. I just wanted to close my eyes for a moment."

"The Good Lord provided sleep to nourish our bodies and to refresh our spirits. And in your case, our fine reporter, Mildred appears to have also worn you out dancing."

"Is nothing sacred?" Samuels asked half-smiling and a bit embarrassed.

"Mildred, I think your guest is turning a bit scarlet in the cheeks."

"Show him some mercy, Theresa, he's a long way from home," Mildred said as she walked into the living room still wearing her classy black dress, but now an apron clung to it, not an infatuated reporter.

"Ladies, I feel a little like Custer at the Little Big Horn."

"But, Mr. Samuels, we mean you no harm.," Theresa said. "And it's time to sit."

After washing his face and tidying up his appearance, Samuels went into the kitchen. It was apparent from what he saw that Mildred had worked hard to make a special dinner. On the table was a white linen table cloth and Mildred's best "old world" dishes," and bright, shiny silverware on top of linen napkins. A solitary candle was lit and next to each plate was a crystal glass for wine.

"Be seated, Mr. Samuels," Mildred beckoned, "at the head of the table, if you will. I'm still a bit traditional. It's nice to have a man at the head of the table., isn't that so Theresa?"

"Father Murray has no trouble with that tradition," she answered quickly with a wink. "No trouble at all."

"Mildred, you shouldn't have worked this hard."

"But I had too, Mr. Samuels. I'm still trying to influence your vote, if not with your dancing feet, perhaps with your stomach. Anyway, Theresa helped."

"I did the shopping. Mildred did the cooking."

"Conspiring?"

"Naturally."

Laughing, Samuels responded, "I can be tempted. What's for dinner?"

"Some of Max's favorites. I hope that doesn't put you off."

"Not in the least."

"For we have meatballs made with veal and cooked in a white sauce and flavored with lemon juice. This dish originated in Konigsberg. But it's found all over Germany today. Then we have boiled potatoes and green beans with a little sour cream and onions for extra taste. We also have a cucumber salad with a sugar/vinegar dressing. And for dessert we have quark pudding, a simple-fresh cheese dish, slightly sweetened."

"This is a banquet."

"Germans enjoy their food," Theresa said.

"And their wine," Mildred added. "For our dinner, Rhine Wine, light and tasty, and most enjoyable. Shall we pray, Theresa?"

Dear Lord, we, your humble servants, thank you for this food and we beseech you to give our guest, your son, the strength to pursue his quest and the courage to arrive at a just rendering of all that he learns about your dear daughter, Mildred. Your children are connected by the whims of history and the glory of your compassion and they are in need of your understanding and guidance. We ask this in your name. Amen.

"Amen," was said all around, and then the food was passed and wine poured, and eaten with joy. An hour later and two helpings devoured, plus more than his usual consumption of wine, Samuels felt prepared to take on the world again. Food really was, next to sleep, God's tonic for the weary.

"Wonderful food, Mildred."

"Thank you, Mr. Samuels."

"And an unusual prayer, Theresa."

"Oh?"

"Very interdenominational."

"Catholics can be pliable."

"Yes. It does seem that way. And conspiratorial?"

"When necessary. And along those lines, if I may, Mr. Samuels, how's Mildred doing with your 'tests.'"

"She told you?"

"She did. We have no secrets."

"Split decision so far to use a boxing metaphor."

"Meaning?"

"One point to her favor, and one in question.

"The last test will decide?"

"It will help, Theresa.

"Then it's time for her to bear this cross. Mildred?"

"I'll clear the dishes, clean up a bit, and we'll talk while enjoying dessert."

"You're sure?"

"Oh, yes. I want to get this cross off my back."

Ten minutes later Samuels asked a question. "Mildred, tell me about the Warrant Officer, Catherine Samaha?"

"You know about her?"

"Yes, a little."

"A quisling."

Catherine

"I was coming home. Under guard, I should add. The Truman Administration wanted me in the flesh. I had no vote in the matter. I said goodbye to Germany.

"Catherine Samaha was assigned by the military authorities in Berlin to guard and accompany me home in 1948 aboard a C-54 transport. I had been in jail almost every day for nearly 17-months, and now Washington wanted me back on home soil. During that whole time, I was never charged with any crime. No charges were made, and I was not provided with counsel. I was simply locked up except for the one short period, what the government called a 'Christmas Amnesty.' Believe me, I was ready to go home even if it was at the government's insistence. Catherine was from Ohio, a friendly person, and good listener, and, as it turned out, an agent of the FBI. Of course, at the time, I didn't know that everything we talked about, you know, girl to girl, would be shared with the authorities once we landed and she was debriefed. Eventually, what I said in casual conversation was used by the Justice Department at my trial."

"You felt betrayed?"

"What else, Mr. Samuels?"

"At the airport in Frankfort, I was met by a large number of reporters and flash photographers who wanted a glimpse of the notorious Axis Sally and a few quotes for their papers. I tried to oblige. The military provided me with a pair of black slacks, a nice jacket, wearable shoes, and, from some unknown person, a bouquet of red roses. I felt a bit like a celebrity, though a 47-year old one with silver hair. I posed for pictures. I must admit, I enjoyed my moment of notoriety, brief as it was.

"What I didn't fully appreciate at the time was how tired I was, even fragile, and how confused and disoriented my mind was after Max's death, barely escaping the Russians, hiding out from the Allied authorities, and my incarceration. Nor did I appreciate the fact that I was alone, isolated, grist for the judicial mill, which was about to grind me up. I had been assured that I was returning to America for interrogation only, not to be arrested. I really didn't expect to be kicked around by anyone, especially in my own country."

"Again, betrayed?"

"As you say…"

"Catherine, I can now see, played upon my ego. She complimented me on my dress and hair styling, and, of course, my alertness and poise with the reporters. False flattery, at its best, and I fell for it. We talked about any number of things before she turned the conversation to my work at Radio Berlin. And that's when I got into hot water, as they say.

"I told her that English was 'always my first love,' and that I always made it a point to not acquire a foreign accent for my show. I wanted my listeners to hear a real American gal broadcasting from Berlin. In response to her questioning about the show's preparation, I explained to Catherine the technical processes involved with 'film rolls' and magnetic recording cylinders. I explained how they could be used, erased, and used again. I wasn't sure if any of them had survived the war."

"Just innocent chit-chat."

"It seemed so."

"Then I made a terrible admission, one that legal counsel would never have permitted. Perhaps out of false bravado or ill-placed ego, I said I 'had free rein to travel to make my recordings,' and that I had latitude in what was recorded, since I had influence over the script. I never should have said those things, nor what followed. I boasted, foolishly, that I never used prepared scripts as a broadcaster for the USA Zone and that I could ad-lib my discretion. It was silly of me to say those things. They weren't completely true. I guess I was just trying to impress my guard. They were used in court to contradict my counsel's view that I just read what was placed before me, which was the truth. I didn't help my cause with the jury. I also really compounded things, pointing out to Catherine that I 'realized I was working against the American government during the war.' This gave the FBI the impression that I was an "employee of unquestioned loyalty to the Nazi cause.""

"Catherine was a bloody spy for the government," Theresa said, "playing a bloody game of entrapment with Mildred."

"What do you think, Mr. Samuels?"

"Mildred, you should have been more reticent, especially when you talked about Eva Braun."

"You know about that?"

"Yes. It came out in the trial. You never should have told the Warrant Officer about her. Your criticism of Braun's appearance and personality suggested jealousy on your part by the time the Justice attorneys got through with you. And, of course, you know what Walter Winchell did with it? He suggested you spent plenty of time with the highest Nazi officials and referred to you as 'Hitler's girlfriend.' He inflamed public opinion against you on his radio show and in the *New York Daily Mirror*. And he certainly took advantage of the *"Christmas amnesty."*

"That's the second time you've mentioned that," Theresa said. What's that all about?"

Christmas Amnesty

"After nine months of sitting in a military jail, I was released on December 23, 1946, for the Christmas holidays with one condition. I had to report to the military authorities every two weeks. At that point, no decision had been made by the Justice Department to prosecute me. The DOJ was still trying to determine if treason charges could be brought against me for '*electric acts*' such as radio broadcasting. No legal precedent had been set yet in the Robert Best case. The Justice Department approved of the temporary amnesty. The CIC went along with it."

"That was a good thing, wasn't it, Mildred, dear?"

"It was awful. I didn't know what to do? Where should I go? I had no friends in Frankfort. I had no money. I was really alone. Where was I to sleep? In Germany, at that time, as many as four or five people were sleeping in the same room, assuming that space was available. I was essentially an American refugee in post-war Germany. Eventually, I traveled some 50 miles to a small town called Dietz, where I found a room and received some food rations. I stayed there for about 23-days, I think."

"Then you returned to Frankfurt?" Theresa asked.

"To report in, yes. It was then that I was rearrested."

"But you didn't know what was happening in the US at the time?"

"I was completely in the dark, Mr. Samuels."

"What was going on?

"Rumors got out of hand, Theresa," Samuels said. "Very out of hand. Mildred?"

"Only later did I discover what was going on Mr. Samuels."

"In the US, the Christmas amnesty was interpreted to mean that Radio Berlin announcers, including myself, had been freed and had left the country. In my case, the idea got going that I was heading for Miami, Florida. That made the headlines, even though the Allied Military Government stated that I had 'reported on schedule.' The military also pointed out that they "produce me on an hour's notice if necessary." People across America wrote and phoned their representatives. What was going on, they wanted to know? The Christmas amnesty protest even reached the White House. Locked up in a tight presidential race, President Truman asked the Justice Department to get things under control. The President could not appear to look 'soft on traitors.'

"Things went from bad to worse on January 23, 1947. On that date, I checked in with the CIC as required. I also wanted to get a pass to go back to Dietz. Without warning, I was held for questions. There was no explanation. I was not told I was under arrest. I was not permitted to have a lawyer. I wasn't even given a change of clothes. I had been wearing the same stuff for nine months. I was confined. My world was a small cell and outside barbed wire."

"Things were closing in on you?"

"Reporters asked why I was being held? The military authorities focused on impromptu comments I had made during my release time. Once again, I talked when I should have remained silent. Whatever my motivation, I tried to warn America against the twin threats of Communism and Judaism, which threatened to undermine America. Adding to this, I said many GI's had sacrificed their lives for nothing, since both the Jews and Russia had won. In retrospect, I should have kept my thoughts to myself. The Justice Department took exception to what I had said, even if it was true. The DOJ saw my openness as an affront, 'a direct and public challenge to the Government.' The Attorney-General of the US, General Ramsey Clark, determined that I could not be set free again to 'spew the Nazi propaganda line,' or to try to reenter the US. Therefore, until a decision was made to either indict or free me, I would remain locked up under the military authorities."

Due Process

"That sums it up," Samuels said.

"Our government was out-of-control," Theresa added heatedly.

"No," Samuels responded, "the government was political and it was feeling the pressure of GI's, or the families of dead servicemen at a time when the war still touched nerves. Mildred, because of her statements, merely managed to get caught up in this mix of public anger and an upcoming election, all occurring against a backdrop of deteriorating relations with the Soviets. And guys like Winchell just took advantage of the situation."

"Still, the government treated Mildred awful."

"In a legal sense, yes, Theresa. She should have been given an attorney, no question about that. The charges, if any, should have been made known to her. Due process, as we generally understand it, was by-passed, but not forgotten. Mildred's attorney did raise this 'due process issue' during her trial, but to no avail."

"It seems like the government was out to get Mildred," Theresa said.

"Someone had to pay. The two women, Iva and Mildred had rubbed the American psyche wrong. Somehow the idea of women being traitors was unsettling. It was non-American. It ran against our notions of 'motherhood and apple pie.' Men, unfortunately, were expected to do despicable things, but not our women. They raised our sons. They weren't supposed to endanger them with propaganda. An invisible line had been crossed. Jane Anderson had wiggled off the Justice Department's hook. Constance Drexel had never even taken the bait. Whether a scapegoat or not, someone had to pay. Iva was the down payment for the Pacific conflict. Mildred was the payment for the European war."

"You make it sound so plausible, Mr. Samuels."

"Plausible and ugly since treason, when committed, doesn't respect gender lines. Both men and women are quite capable of treachery."

"Where does that leave me, Mr. Samuels?" Mildred asked. "How did I do on the third test?"

"Balancing all, I would say it's a tie. On the one hand, the military government acted highhandedy and did not provide you with legal counsel. That was a gross injustice. On the other hand, your statements to the reporters and the Warrant Officer, however motivated, compromised your later contentions in court. That was a self-inflicted wound.'

"When you weigh everything you know about Mildred to this point, how does it all add up, Mr. Samuels?"

How did it all add up, Samuels asked himself? There was evidence on the right hand, and conflicting information in the left hand. Complications and confusion… Still, what was at the end of all the questions?

"Tough call, Theresa. We know these things. Mildred, correct me if I make a mistake: One, you decided to stay in Germany rather than be exchanged for German civilians. Again, your motivations are not important here. Only the action… Two, you continued to work for Radio Berlin, even after Pearl Harbor. Even if Max influenced your decision, it was seen as your decision. Three, the 'criticism' of the President, even if shared by Americans who didn't like Roosevelt, carried a different weight coming from Radio Berlin during wartime. Four, statements about 'Jews,' regardless of their accuracy from your perspective, were inflammatory, especially in light of the holocaust. Five, the *Visions of Invasion* broadcast went beyond mere propaganda, the usual 'Germany is Right, America is Wrong,' prattle. Six, there was evidence you acted the part of a Red Cross worker, 'impersonating' one in order to get information from POW's. Seven, you made statements after the war that tended to 'incriminate' you, or at least compromise your legal position. Eight, American public opinion, spurred by rumors and the negative testimony of GI's, was completely against you."

"You've built a terrible case against me, Mr. Samuels."

"Not I, Mildred, only the historical record. But everything I enumerated must be set against one overwhelming fact. After Pearl

Harbor, you were an enemy alien without a passport in Germany and subject to the dangerous whims of the Gestapo. The hard question, then, is this: did the 'fear factor' outweigh everything else? In short, were all your actions motivated by the desire to simply stay out of the concentration camps?"

"And have you reached a conclusion?"

"Yes. The scales are almost equally balanced."

"In whose favor?"

"The jury in your first trial. I think they got it right. Of the ten original indictments, they threw out two to begin with, and then found you guilty of only one of the remaining eight. In the absence of the *'Visions of Invasion'* show, the jury would have set you free. I feel sure of that."

"What does all of this come down to, Mr. Samuels?"

"I need something to persuade me that the jury was wrong. I intend to go over all the appeal arguments looking for something to exonerate you, Mildred. On that you have my word. Truly, I want you to be free of this legacy of treason. But what I want and what I can provide may not be one and the same."

"Has your Jewish faith influenced your feelings, Mr. Samuels?" Theresa asked.

"Yes, from the beginning when Edna Mae came to see me. Obviously, it's not possible to completely deny what you feel and how you think. What you said on the radio, Mildred, tainted me, as well as other Jews of moderate means and no desire to support international communism. However, I have tried to keep my personal feelings chained up. I have tried to be objective. And I can assure you, others, who are perhaps more objective, will review your case before I reach a decision. But there are no guarantees this will all work out in your best interests, Mildred. I am cognizant of Theresa's concern that you not be hurt. That is my desire, too. I have come to like and care for you very much."

"And, Mr. Samuels, I've come to like you very much. No, it's more than that. I respect you. You are a decent man trying to do your very best on my behalf. I shouldn't expect more than that."

"I concur," Theresa added.

"Your vote of confidence touches me very much, more than words can convey. Before I leave for my hotel, I do have one request, Mildred."

"Which is?"

"Would you honor me with one more dance?"

"I would be delighted, but aren't you challenging temptation, Mr. Samuels?"

"Not in the least, Mildred. After all, with the Mother Superior here, we have a chaperone."

Arnold Reuben

Douglas Chandler,
NAZI Broadcaster

Elizabeth Gurley Flynn

Frederick W. Kalenbach,
NAZI Broadcaster

If the workers take a notion,
They can stop all speeding trains,
Every ship upon the ocean
They can tie with mighty chains.
Every wheel in the creation,
Every mine and every mill,
Fleets and armies of the nation,
Will at their command stand still.
— Joe Hill

Lyrics of Joe Hill

Best Available Image

Jane Anderson,, NAZI Propaganda

DON'T MOURN, ORGANIZE!

JOE HILL

Born 1879. Executed 1915.

Joe Hill

Rita Zucca - Itlian Axis Sally

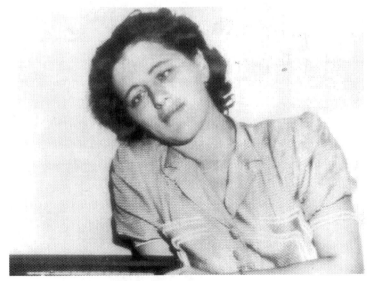

Rita Zucca - Itlian Axis Sally

Oswald Spangler

William Joyce, NAZI Broadcaster

Rita Zucca - The other Axis Sally

CHAPTER 24
THE WITNESSES

Family Questioning

"That's it, then. The whole story…"

"Dad, you had one heck of a trip."

"And with a vixen, Robert."

Robert Samuels was sitting at his desk in his study listening to his daughter and wife pepper him with questions about his recent visit to Columbus. No matter how many times he tried to close the subject, the ladies of his life kept coming up with another challenging question.

"Was she really that attractive, Dad?"

"For her age, Rachel, she was doing fine."

"How fine?" Lynn asked.

"Better than the average," Samuels said shyly.

"And she's a good dancer, too."

"Fair, Lynn, just fair."

"Was her voice really as sexy as the GI's thought?" Rachel asked.

"Well, she had a nice voice,"

"Sexy?"

"What's with these questions, guys. She's 77-years old. My goodness, she's a senior citizen."

"She cooked you two meals?"

"She prepared lunch, yes, Lynn."

"And a traditional German meal?"

"I already told you that."

"And you danced again after the dinner?"

"Right, Rachel."

"Wasn't that overdoing it, Robert?"

"Lynn, the Mother Superior thought it was good for Mildred's morale."

"Mildred, is it?"

"She preferred that to Sisk or Gillars."

"And why did her morale need boosting?" Rachel piped in with a big smile."

"Must have been my poor dancing."

"Dad!"

"I told you already... I left her in the lurch. I couldn't support her desire for a pardon. Not yet, anyway."

"When will you decide, Robert?"

"When I have all the facts."

"That's vague."

"That's responsible journalism."

"Did she ask about your family?"

"Back to that again, Lynn... No, she didn't ask."

"Did you volunteer that you're a married man?"

"That was perfectly obvious to her and Theresa."

"Theresa?"

"The Mother Superior, Lynn," Samuels said impatiently. "What we call a tough, mean officer in the Navy."

"She sounded rather sweet to me, Robert."

"Must have been my presence."

Samuels needed to get off this subject. Rachel and Lynn, he could see it now, were on the warpath. It would have been so much easier if Mildred had been a man. Then their comments would have been limited to one observation: "How was the weather?" But being with

Mildred that led to queries about Columbus' most famous femme fatale, at least as his wife and daughter saw it.

"My dear family. I've been home for two days. This inquisition must come to an end. I've told you everything. I've shared everything with Edna Mae, Rita, and Ron. I've written two stories for the *Chronicle*. Now I've got to read the report Professor Silverman prepared for me. Okay?"

"Ellen Silverman, over at CAL?"

"One and the same, Lynn."

"We took a class with her years ago."

"Right. *'Influences on the Supreme Court.'* Good class."

"Wasn't my final grade higher, Robert?"

"As if you didn't know. Mom got an 'A,' Rachel. I got an 'A-.' Mom has better handwriting and she writes faster, and she's got a better memory. And she knows how to spell. I think it's because she's left-handed."

"Not smarter?"

"Okay, left-handed and smarter. Now skedaddle, both of you."

"Skedaddle?"

"Out, Rachel."

Thankfully, Rachel and Lynn left the study. Maybe, Samuels reflected, maybe skedaddle did it. Much better than vamoose, or "out." But a lesson learned, he thought. Next time I visit a sexy wench, he promised himself, mums the word. This jealousy thing was tough on an old guy.

The Report

He turned to the report from Professor Silverman. It was written in neat handwriting, of which Samuels was most envious given his excuse for script. She wrote:

I look forward to our meeting next week. We'll go over Gillars vs. US (1950) and the relevant questions concerning her appeal. This case had always fascinated me, as have your articles in the Chronicle. As a preface to our meeting, I've summarized below the main problem confronting the prosecution as it went forward with the government's case in the 1947-48 period. That is, where were the two or more American witnesses who necessarily needed to testify at any future trial? At least two witnesses had to be located and questioned in order to meet the demands of the Constitution. I trust this information will be helpful. My best to your family. E. Silverman."

Okay, Samuels thought, I better get to the professor's report before the Savonarola-ladies come marching back to practice their inquisition skills.

The Report - Witnesses

The year 1947 proved to be a turning point in Mildred Gillars' life. The Army authorities in Berlin were prepared to release her, since the rather vague charges against her were open to questioning. The Army didn't want to hold her in jail indefinitely. This view was shared with the Assistant Attorney General, Lamar Caudle. The key to the problem was the lack of two witnesses, as required by the treason provision of the Constitution. Caudle needed two American soldiers, preferably POW's, who had actually seen Gillars committing treason on behalf of Hitler. How to find them was the question? By chance, Caudle shared his problem with Drew Pearson, the noted radio and newspaper columnist with a huge audience. Pearson found a way out of the government's predicament. He would broadcast an appeal to ex-GI's, who had been prisoners-of-war in German camps in the hope a few might have seen Axis Sally in action for the Reich. This proved to be a stroke of genius for the prosecution and the beginning of the end for Gillars. After a week two GI's answered the appeal, but they were unable to really help.

However, as often happens, they knew other POW's and one name led to another.

Caudle also went to Walter Winchell, this time telling him about the Army's willingness to drop the case. Winchell took to the radio and hyped his audience, particularly Gold Star mothers, enraging them against Gillars. Caudle then told the Army to hang on to the prisoner. Tongue in cheek, he told the military that Pearson and Winchell were on his side so keep Gillars locked up.

The big break came with Albert J. Lawlor of Stoney Brook, New York. He had been a POW in Stalag VII near the town of Furstenberg on the Oder between February 1943 and April 1945. He had actually seen Axis Sally. He stated:

A woman came to the camp with a man she called the Professor. This was around later 1943, or early 1944. They were there to make a propaganda broadcast. The woman called herself Midge or Madge. She spoke English well and said she had lived in the States. She said they were making records to broadcast to the US. I declined to participate.

That was witness #1. It was a start.

Shortly thereafter, a second POW surfaced. This was Robert Ehalt, a 36-year old, and a former Army Ranger who had been held in Stalag IIB. He had refused to let his men be interviewed by a woman, again calling herself Midge. She wanted the guys to make recordings. She wanted them to say, 'we were being treated well and had plenty to eat.' The men refused to do this. In response, the woman grew angry, saying we were a 'bunch of ungrateful people.' This woman, Midge, spoke perfect English and said she had once lived in NY's Greenwich Village. She seemed particularly interested in the 1st Ranger Battalion, since she had followed our group through the campaigns from North Africa to Sicily and Italy. Once more, he stated, there was a man with her, whom she referred to as the Professor.

Witness #2 was now on record.

Another POW, Gilbert Lee Hansford of Cincinnati, who was a veteran of the 29th Infantry Division, came forward. He had lost a leg in the Normandy fighting and was placed in a hospital in Paris by the Germans. This was in August 1944. According to Hansford, who was heavily sedated at the time, "she (Gillars) walked up with two German officers," and stated that "she was working with the International Red Cross." She told the group of us that she was 'here to make recordings so your folks will know you are still alive.'

Hansford and his men spoke into a microphone. They recorded messages for broadcast to their families at home. It was later determined by American technicians that propaganda had been inserted between the messages of the GI's. One of the insertions, when made known to the jury, proved devastating to Gillars. In the insertion, she said:

It's a disgrace to the American public that they don't wake to the fact of what Franklin D. Roosevelt is doing to the Gentiles of your country and my country.

Still another POW in the camp with Hansford was John Lynsky, who was so injured that he could only stand with two crutches when Gillars visited him. He recalled that she wore a "little Red Cross pin,' and identified herself as a Red Cross worker. As had many others, he refused to cooperate. He didn't make a recording.

Some of the most damaging testimony came from 36-year old Michael Evanick, a paratrooper from New York. He had been captured on D-Day after parachuting behind German lines in Normandy. He identified Gillars as the woman who interviewed him in a German POW camp near Paris on July 15, 1944. Evanick stated he recognized Axis Sally's voice, since he had listened to her broadcasts in North Africa, Sicily, and Italy. He told Gillars this. According to his testimony, she said, 'I guess you know me as Axis Sally?' Gillars gave him a drink of cognac and a cigarette and told him to make himself comfortable in a chair. She sent for a microphone and began the interview with him. She asked him if he was feeling better that he was out of the fighting? He replied, "I feel 100 percent better in the front lines where I get enough to eat." She was very angry at this response. She lost her composure and kicked over the microphone. After regaining her poise, she asked him what we did in the camp. He said the men "sunbathe." She wanted to know more. I said we "just sit in the sun, burning ourselves to death, because we are hungry and are watching American planes come over and bomb every five minutes." She was not very happy with my response.

Eugene McCarthy, a 28-year old from Chicago also came forward. He has been in Stalag IIB in Germany. His testimony contained a surprise story about a carton of cigarettes. He stated he and others were alone with Gillars for at least an hour. He described Gillars as nervous and chain-smoking. Calling herself Midge, she attempted to make small talk with the men. She asked them for an American cigarette, and then another. About that time a carton of American cigarettes was passed into the room. He didn't know who did this. We passed the carton to her. She took the carton and thanked us generously. Then she opened the carton. It was full of horse manure. Midge or Gillars exploded. She said we were the worst bunch of American prisoners she had ever run into." She said, 'We would regret this.'

McCarthy pointed out in his testimony that he had spent 15-months in a POW camp, and he saw one buddy shot each month by the guards, a total of 18 while he was a prisoner. Because of this, he had no sympathy for Gillars. For him, she had sold out her country. From his perspective, horse manure was too good.

The POW witnesses responding to Pearson's pleas and Winchell's angry commentary provided the 'eyewitness' testimony to give the Justice Department a "reasonable chance of conviction."' Ultimately and unfortunately for Gillars, these POW's and their testimony provided a backdrop against which the famous "indictment #10" was seen and judged to be treason.

In the case of these witnesses, I might add, the past had truly come back to haunt Gillars. The government had met the first test of the Constitution. There were two witnesses. The chief prosecutor, John M. Kelley would build upon the testimony of the POW's to emphasize again and again one theme: "She (Gillars) thought she was on the winning side, and all she cared about was her own selfish fame" in broadcasting for the Nazi regime, which she did so in a 'sadistic manner.' Prosecutor Kelley was out for blood."

Samuels considered what he had read. There it was again, the disconnect between the wartime actions and perceptions of Mildred and the woman he knew, who worked with children in a Catholic School and made authentic German meals for a hungry reporter. He wondered aloud, "which woman did I dance with to swing music in Columbus?"

CHAPTER 25

THE APPEAL

One on One

"Mr. Samuels., so good to see you again."

"Likewise, Dr. Silverman."

"You had no trouble finding my office, I hope?"

"No problem. The undergrads were glad to help me move through all this new construction."

"A temporary mess until Hobbs Hall is renovated. Then I can get my old office back. I feel like a fish out of water sharing space with ecologists and environmentalists. I always have this terrible feeling I'm congesting and polluting."

"I'm surprised you haven't been pegged for one of their never-ending suits against something on behalf of mankind."

"Oh, but I have."

"And?"

"I might just help out the Sierra Club."

"Good outfit."

Robert Samuels had gotten up early Tuesday morning, showered, shaved, and then shoved off once he had downed his corn flakes and sliced bananas in a bath of 1% milk. With one cup of coffee in his trusty unbreakable, drip-proof car cup he was gone. He wanted to squeeze onto the Oakland-Bay Bridge just after the impossibly early mad car rush caused by the daily conjunction of the Bay Shore freeway along the peninsula and the Mission Street entries in the city. He just did. He loved the ride over the Bay with its views of great cruise ships, naval vessels, and freighters from all over the world. And the East Bay and Berkeley, and CAL… After passing Treasure Island, the Bridge slid smoothly downward in a long graceful grade to the land of working folks in Oakland, and, adjacent to the docks and industry of the East Bay, the center of student protest, demonstrations, and, believe it or not, an unparalleled education at the University of California. Samuels loved the sight of the campus, especially the campanile, which stood out very much like the Washington Monument in D.C, beckoning scholars from all over the globe to participate in the never-ending quest for truth. And, of course, that's why he was on campus and in Dr. Silverman's temporary digs. He was on his own quest.

"Well, where should we start, Mr. Samuels?"

"I'll leave that to you. You're the doctor."

"Still trying to tickle the funny bone of humanity?"

"Alas, yes. Doesn't get any easier these days."

"Well, keep trying, the world needs to laugh more."

"About Axis Sally, I'm not sure."

"Our topic, but one thing, please, I'm Ellen. Okay?"

"Fine. And I'm…"

"Mr. Samuels, right?"

Samuels nodded. People just refused to call him Robert, except for his spouse. Perhaps it was because he was a reporter. It was always Mr. Samuels unless he was at the *Chronicle*. There he was Mr. P, (aka. Mr. Samuels). Such was the life of a Pulitzer Prize winner.

Treason Defined Again

Interrupting his thoughts, Professor Silverman said, "Lets start with a little review of treason. You know, of course, that the Constitution spells it out quite well. Treason against the United States 'shall consist only in levying War against them, or adhering to their Enemies, giving them aid and comfort.' That's it except for the provision concerning two witnesses providing testimony in open court. It's hard to believe, but it wasn't until 1945 that the Supreme Court reviewed a treason conviction (*Chandler v. United States*)."

"My ignorance never fails to impress me, Ellen."

"Certainly, you know the name."

"Only slightly."

"Well, then..."

"Douglas Chandler, an ugly American, an anti-Semite, and a supporter of fascism, a man who called himself Paul Revere in his Radio Berlin broadcasts. The Feds nailed him after the war. He lost his case to stay free. When his later appeal was denied, he lost his citizenship and went to jail, having been indicted on ten points and found guilty on each and every one (1947). After spending 16-years in jail, his sentence was commuted by President John F. Kennedy on condition he would immediately leave the United States. He was released from the federal penitentiary at Lewisburg, Pennsylvania on August 9, 1963. He flew to Germany to be with his daughter. I think he's still alive.

"The Chandler case and others dealing with traitors established that 'for a prosecutor to take an aid and comfort indictment to a jury he must prove four elements beyond a reasonable doubt:

(1) an overt act.
(2) two witnesses testifying.
(3) an intent to betray the United states.
(4) the act provided aid and comfort to the enemy"

"If I recall, the difficulty is with the fourth point."

"Mr. Samuels, right on. The first three are overt and objectively proven. In treason cases, the Court determined that 'the minimum function that an overt act must perform in a reasonable prosecution is that it shows sufficient action by the accused, in its setting, 'to sustain a finding that the accused actually gave aid and comfort to the enemy.' This definition of treason provided a prerequisite in order to prove 'aid and comfort.' As you can see *Chandler v. United* States was an important case with heavy influence on and for Axis Sally *(Gillars v. United States, 1950)."*

"Precedents were set with the Chandler case?"

"Indeed. For example, an overt act, viewed in isolation and apart from its setting, might be interpreted as not providing 'aid and comfort' to the enemy. But within a certain setting, the same overt act may take on incriminating significance. Chandler, by participating in preparing broadcast scripts after first discussing them with Nazi officials, broadcasted knowing full well that the mission of Radio Berlin was to further the enemy's mission in wartime by transmitting to the US propaganda designed to reduce American morale. The sum total of his participation provided the setting, not just one overt act. The same rationale would be used by the Court in the Gillars case."

"To coin a German word, the *'gestalt'* counts."

"True. One other point bearing on traitor cases… The 'levying war' notation in the Constitution is generally misunderstood. Most people think it means treason can only occur when the US is at war. One can be convicted of treason in the absence of a formal declaration of war, whether troops are in the field or not. The formal declaration by Congress is not required. Treason can occur in relative peacetime. This position of the Court had implications for Gillars' broadcasting prior to Pearl Harbor."

"I think I understand," Samuels said a little reluctantly, "and I should have taken more law classes."

"You're doing fine. Let's move on to the indictment against Gillars, which was reviewed by a Court of Appeal. It's, I'm afraid, somewhat technical. I'll read it to you slowly."

The Indictment

"The indictment alleged:

That appellant was a citizen of and owed allegiance to the United States, that within the German Reich, after December 11, 1941, up to and including May 8, 1945, in violation of her duty of allegiance she knowingly and intentionally adhered to the enemies of the United States, to wit the Government of the German Reich, its agents, instrumentalities, representatives and subjects with which the United States was at war, and gave to said enemies aid and comfort within the United States and elsewhere, by participating in the psychological warfare of the German Government against the United States.

This participation is alleged to have consisted of radio broadcasts and the making of phonographic recordings with the intent that they would be used in broadcasts to the United States and to American Expeditionary Forces in French North Africa, Italy, France, and England.

The indictment charges the commission of ten overt acts, each of which is described, and, finally that following commission of the offense the District of Columbia was the first Federal Judicial District into which appellant was brought."

"In other words," Samuels said, "she committed treason while broadcasting during the war for Radio Berlin."

"Basically, yes."

"You have a copy for me?"

"Yes. And also information about indictment #10, which the jury found applicable to treason, and which the Court of Appeals upheld."

That on a day between January 1, 1944 and June 6,1944, the exact date being to the Grand Jurors unknown, said defendant, at Berlin, Germany, did speak into a microphone in a recording studio of the German Radio Broadcasting Company, and thereby did participate in a phonographic recording and caused to be phonographically recorded a radio drama entitled "Vision of Invasion," said defendant then and there well knowing that said recorded radio drama was to be subsequently broadcast by the German Radio broadcasting Company to the United and to its citizens and soldiers at home and abroad as an element of German propaganda and an instrument of psychological warfare.

"That's a mouthful, Ellen. In layman's language she recorded a dramatic show, which was aired to the US by Radio Berlin."

"The law profession gets paid by the word, Mr. Samuels."

"No wonder attorneys are doing well."

At that, they both laughed, though with a bitter edge to their levity. Words reflect and symbolize actions, which can and are judged on the basis of law, mores, and traditions. In a Mildred's case, she had affronted all these elements with her actions at Radio Berlin.

The Defense

"Gillars' defense team, Mr. Samuels, was led by James J. Laughlin, who provided a decent, logical argument on her behalf as follows.

1. Gillars was an American citizen during the time of the alleged treason.

2. As a citizen, her constitutional rights were violated by her arrest and three-year internment.

3. The oath of allegiance that Gillars signed after Pearl Harbor was a legal renunciation of her US citizenship in accordance with the 1940 Nationality Act.

4. If the jury believed she was an American citizen at the time of the broadcasts, then the Federal government didn't treat her as one and violated her constitutional rights, including:

    . habeas corpus
    . unlawful search and seizure
    . self-incrimination
    . due process

5. If, on the other hand, the jury believed she had renounced her citizenship after December 7, 1941, then her arrest and incarceration were illegitimate, and she should be acquitted, since she wasn't a US citizen at the time she broadcasted *'Visions of Invasion.'*

"His arguments certainly seemed clear enough."

"As we'll see later, the Court of Appeals had a rational rebuttal for each and every one of his assertions. Logic, if you will, existed on both sides of the courtroom, leaving Gillars caught in the middle."

"Where, unfortunately, she had placed herself."

"There is that. Laughlin, however, tried to extricate her. He passionately pointed out that treason must be something more than the spoken word:

Things have come to a pretty pass if a person cannot make an anti-Semitic speech without being charged with treason. Being against President Roosevelt could not be treason. There are two schools of thought about President Roosevelt. One holds he was a patriot and martyr. The other holds that he was the greatest rogue in all history, the greatest fraud, and the greatest impostor that ever lived.' Of course, this, passion, as we saw earlier, runs into the question of context. What you say in the middle of a presidential election is one thing. What you broadcast during wartime is quite another.

"It would seem so."

"Still seeking some sort of legal edge, Laughlin even brought to the Court's attention the great influence that Max Otto Koischwitz had on Gillars as her former teacher at Hunter College, as her supervisor at Radio Berlin, and as her lover with whom she lived. In short, this man had Svengali-like influence over her, which caused her to make the broadcasts in question. Naturally, this position ran counter to the notion of free will and personal responsibility for one's actions."

"As my wife likes to say, we all have free will and absolutely no choice about it."

"Smart lady. She did get an 'A' as I recall in my course on '*Influences on the Supreme Court.*'"

"She did. I got an 'A-.'"

"Well, don't fret, Mr. Samuels. You're doing 'A+' work now."

"Me fret? Never."

"Good. Let's review another defense raised by Laughlin, what might be called the 'fear factor.' He pointed out that his client was never in a position to refuse her employer, which in truth was the Reich, supported by the Gestapo in a terrifying police state. Multiple witnesses, who were colleagues at Radio Berlin, testified to situations where they were directly threatened with exile to a concentration camp. Laughlin pushed hard, explaining to the Court that this danger always and continuously applied to Gillars. Daily survival, he contended, depended on '*collaboration.*'"

"The Court of Appeals had a response to this, too."

"Absolutely. And we'll get to that in time."

"It's hard for me to see how the presence of fear could be denied by the Court."

"The Court didn't, as you put it, deny the presence of fear. It just saw it in another context."

"The law seems to be very flexible in measuring human behavior."

"That's why we have legal representation."

"And the more expensive that representation, Ellen, the better our chances before our peers?"

"Too often, yes."

"Tough system."

"It's the one we have. Now, before I forget, Laughlin did put forth still another argument on behalf of Gillars, the so-called 'loyalty' defense. He insisted that his client had remained loyal to the United States during the war, even though she hated President Roosevelt. He insisted that she never betrayed her country. He, by way of example, illustrated how she visited POW camps to interview soldiers and then asked shortwave listeners to inform the families of POW's about their safety. More than that, she refused to work with a real traitor, the AWOL flier, Martin James Monti. Surely, this was proof of her loyalty, he pointed out."

"Good arguments, but each could have an 'on the one hand, she did this because, and on the other hand, what she did was because...' I suppose even a third hand might enter the picture."

"Using your metaphor, Mr. Samuels, while justice is supposed to be blind, there are, when lawyers are involved, many hands involved in the interpretation of the facts as they apply to law. Without question, Laughlin provided what defense was possible. I'm convinced no one could have done better."

"He had a tough case?"

"The toughest. Still, Laughlin persisted. He wrapped up his defense, saying that his client was 'trapped in Hitler's Germany without a valid passport and relied on the good graces of her German hosts.' As he said, 'she had no passport, no money. She had to remain where she was.' He emphasized that she was a loyal but misunderstood American trapped in an impossible situation.' He pointed out in conclusion that his client had done noting to hurt the United States, that she loved her country. Again, every argument he made was open to differing interpretations."

"I'm beginning to see that."

"It's the role of legal representation to put his client in the best possible light. Laughlin did so. In doing this, he didn't sanction Gillars' actions at Radio Berlin. He didn't condone what she had done. He merely defended her on the basis of 'due process' provided for by her constitutional rights. No client can ask for more."

"As you say, Laughlin did his job."

"Leaving the Court, Mr. Samuels, to sort things out. And when you think about it, the jury did a remarkable job. It didn't roll over for the government. It made the prosecutors work hard. The jury found Gillars innocent with respect to seven of the eight surviving indictments. It fussed and debated indictment #10 for a full day before reaching a verdict of guilt. That was not an easy task at a time when the public wanted the blood of traitors. Gillars was, I think, fortunate to truly have a jury of her peers who did struggle with the facts, the applicable law, and the need to grasp that elusive commodity called justice. In an imperfect world, they did pretty well."

"Ellen, I've been looking for the appropriate words to end my series on Axis Sally. I think you just provided them."

"Don't forget to put me in the footnotes. You know how it is, publish or perish at CAL."

"I'd be delighted."

"How about a break, lunch at the faculty dining room, and then we'll hammer at Gillars' appeal, which was denied?"

"I always follow the advice of counsel. Let's eat."

CHAPTER 26
THE KEY QUESTIONS

Chicken Pot Pie

"That wasn't a bad lunch."

"The faculty cafeteria, Ellen, was much better than what I remember of the Student Union's offerings."

"They didn't serve Pacific salmon in your day, Mr. Samuels?"

"Fish sticks."

"Nor Napa's best?"

"Grape punch."

"Fresh Romaine lettuce?"

"Cole slaw."

"My goodness, how did you survive?"

"McDonalds."

"The gastronomical savior of CAL's students."

"We felt more like indentured servants to the Regents."

"Well, there is that. But you did enjoy your chicken pot pie?"

"My favorite meal."

"Really?"

"Without question. If I were lost in the Gobi desert, or in the frozen wastes of Greenland, or, let us say, in the humid swamps of Brazil, all I would want is a case of chicken pot pies and a microwave."

"You would need a very long extension cord."

"Ellen, for those chunks of chicken and scatterings of peas and corn, all mixed in a tasty gravy, it would be worth it to hire bearers to carry the cord."

Robert Samuels and Dr. Ellen Silverman were back in her office following their short respite in the faculty cafeteria. Now it was time to get into the legal nitty-gritty of Mildred's appeal.

"Several matters were raised by the appellant as grounds for reversal, Mr. Samuels. Let's discuss the key ones in Gillars' appeal.

The Question - The Sufficiency and Weight of the Evidence?

"The appellant (Gillars) asserted that the verdict was contrary to the evidence presented to the jury and to the weight of that evidence."

"In layman terms, Ellen."

"Since the original Justice Department indictment referred to ten overt acts of treason, and since two were immediately withdrawn by the prosecution, and since seven of the remaining eight overt acts were found wanting, thereby acquitting Gillars of any intention to betray her country, it was not consistent for the jury to find her guilty for only one overt act, #10 dealing with the '*Vision of Invasion*' radio show."

"In other words, it didn't make sense for a guilty verdict on the basis of only one overt act if she was acquitted on the other seven."

"From the appellant's perspective, yes."

"So what happened, Ellen?"

"The Court pointed out that consistency in the verdict is not necessary. Each count, you see, is a separate indictment and is regarded as such. The weight of one indictment can and did provide sufficient evidence to support a guilty verdict."

"It seems unfair that one count should have greater weight than the other seven."

"What you're forgetting, Mr. Samuels, is what composed that weight."

"Illuminate, please."

"The jury was aware of the following facts as they related to the appellant in this case. She:

(1) Was an employee of the German Broadcasting Company, which was run by the German government under the supervision of Dr. Joseph Goebbels, who provided the daily propaganda focus adhered to by all broadcasters.

(2) Read scripts that focused on anti-Communist, anti-Semitic, and anti-Roosevelt themes.

(3) Made broadcast recordings on phonographic discs.

(5) Was the highest paid performer on the Overseas Service with a salary double that of her immediate superior.

(6) Produced the largest number of broadcasts compared to her colleagues, particularly other American broadcasters.

(7) Impersonated International Red Cross officials in order to record messages from POW's.

(8) Admitted to starring in the dramatic play, *'Visions of Invasion.'*

(9) Attempted to impact the invasion of Europe with her broadcasts.

(10) Went into hiding under an assumed name to elude capture by United States forces after the fall of Berlin.

"That's a lot of weight, Ellen."

"Sufficient for the Court to uphold the jury's verdict. The Court summed up its position, stating, there 'was no inconsistency between the jury's conviction on overt Act No. 10 and acquittal on others. They (the jury) might reasonably have distinguished between the nature of *Vision of Invasion* and other recordings."'

"Okay, round one goes to the prosecution. What's next?"

Question – Whether the Indictment Stated an Offense?

"The appellant contended that treason is not committed by words because, by their nature all utterances are an exercise of freedom of thought, and this presupposes that such freedom cannot be prohibited by condemning the expression of thought by words. Got it, Mr. Samuels?"

"In basic terms, Ellen, expression of thought or opinion about the Government or criticism of it is not treason."

"You got it."

"To use the power of government to stop political expression would be an oppressive use of power, since such power could be used to destroy political enemies by accusing them of a crime; that is, by way of an example, speaking critically of those in high office."

"Mr. Samuels, you may earn a law degree before the day is out."

"Perhaps a small degree."

"The defense also claimed that the First Amendment bars expanding our definition of treason to include "the mere expression of views, opinions, or criticism."

"Seems like James Laughlin presented a strong argument for the defense."

"He did, but not strong enough. The Court held that "words may be an integral part of the commission of a crime if the elements which constitute treason are present; that is, if there is adherence to and the giving of aid and comfort to the enemy by an overt act."

"Elements, Ellen?"

"Again, from the perspective of the Court, treason is not committed by mere expressions of opinion or criticism, but words spoken as part of a 'program of propaganda warfare in the course of employment by the enemy in its conduct of war against the United States, to which the accused owes allegiance,' may be an integral part of the crime.'"

"In other words, if I think but don't say certain things, I'm safe. If I say the same things in a letter-to-the-editor, I'm okay. But if I repeat the same ideas and words before a microphone in Berlin during WWII, I'm possibly committing treason. That about it?"

"Pretty good, Mr. Samuels. The evidence suggested to the jury that words, understood in a certain way, might be considered treasonable acts. Therefore, the First Amendment does not protect one from accountability. The amendment in question 'protects the free expression of thought and belief as a part of the liberty of the individual as a human personality. But there is more to this. Words may constitute treasonable acts in the furtherance of a program of an enemy to which the speaker adheres and to which he gives aid with intent to betray his own country. Words are not rid of criminal character merely because they are words.' Okay?"

"Be careful what you say during wartime," Samuels replied, "especially when you're an enemy alien living in Germany and working at Radio Berlin?"

"Another strike out for the defense."

"The defense needs to hit harder, Ellen. Pop-ups in the infield won't win this game."

"Well, there are more innings to go."

Questions – Did the Political Nature of Treason Entitle the Appellant to Asylum in Germany? And did the Court have Jurisdiction over the Appellant?

"These two challenging questions were raised by the defense with the hope they would have merit before the Court. What's your reading, Ellen?"

"The appellant was arguing that she was entitled to asylum in Germany based upon the Extradition Treaty between the United States and Germany (1930). This treaty provided for 'the surrender on requisition of a person charged with or convicted of certain crimes committed within the territorial jurisdiction of one of the signatories and found within the territory of the other.' The treaty was understood to apply only to fugitives who have fled the country where the crime was committed. In this case *'crimes'* did not include treason, therefore Gillars was entitled, she thought, to asylum in Germany. The Court, of course, took a different position, arguing that the 'State can voluntarily offer asylum, if it wishes.

"Since post-war Germany was under an Allied Military Government, the occupational Army need not offer asylum, especially where the crime was high treason. The existing treaty was made with a civilian government, not an Army of Occupation. Therefore, the treaty did not apply. Right, Ellen?"

"You're catching on."

"You're a good teacher."

"Buttering me up?"

"Stating a fact."

"Okay, Mr. Samuels, now, as to the question of jurisdiction. The appeal judges held that the Court had 'jurisdiction to try the appellant notwithstanding that she was brought against her will into the District of Columbia from Germany. The defense countered that the Army had been used in Germany as a *'posse comitatus,'* to arrest Gillars in Berlin and that this was unconstitutional. Laughlin pointed out that it was not lawful for the Army to do this, executing civilian laws, 'except in such cases and under such circumstances as such employment of said force may be expressly authorized by the Constitution or by act of Congress.' Continuing, he reminded the Court that violation of these provisions was a misdemeanor' with fines and imprisonment available as punishment."

"I've heard of a posse, but not this one, Ellen."

"The notion of a *'posse comitatus'* grew out of the post-Civil War period in the former Confederate states. The idea was to keep the US Army out of the picture when it came to enforcing local civilian laws; that is, 'to put an end to the use of federal troops to police state elections' in the reconstructed former Confederate states. The Congress intended to 'preclude the Army from assisting local law enforcement officers in carrying out their duties.' Of course, the Court didn't accept Laughlin's view."

"Let me guess," Samuels said. Since Germany was a defeated nation, she was under the military occupation of the United States and other Allied countries. In the absence of an elected civilian government in Germany at the time of Gillars' arrest, the American Army of Occupation was the legal government and could not be construed to be a *'posse comitatus.'* The Army was the law enforcement agency in the aftermath of the war. How am I doing?"

"You nailed it, Mr. Samuels, "right on the head. I'll just add this… The right to arrest is a part of the right to govern. The Army of Occupation was authorized to arrest the appellant, because the military had jurisdiction over the appellant."

"Another judicial fastball for a strike."

"Ready for the next pitch?"

"Probably not, if the strike zone continues to widen."

Question – Was Self-Incrimination Involved?

"The defense, Mr. Samuels, took the position that the use of recordings made at Radio Berlin by the prosecution amounted to self-incrimination on the part of Gillars, and that this amounted to a violation of the Fifth Amendment that 'no person 'shall be compelled in any criminal case to be a witness against himself.' In short, the recordings should not have been used in the courtroom."

"I can already see what the Court of Appeals would do with this one, Ellen."

"Let's hear it, then."

"Simply this, Gillars wasn't forced to incriminate herself. She already had by making the recordings that only replicated what she had eventually broadcasted."

"Not bad. As the Court said it, 'there was no compulsion upon the accused in the introduction of this evidence. She was not forced to provide the incriminating recordings. The evidence consisted of phonographic reproductions of statements previously made by her. She had no part in their use at the trial except that they were a record of what she had said and done. In sum, the past had caught up to Gillars. The recordings in question were used and heard over the airwaves. Anyone could hear them. They were in the public domain. There was, therefore, no constitutional provision prohibiting the jury from hearing the contents of the recordings if they were relevant to the case."

"And they were relevant."

"Exactly, Mr. Samuels."

"Another strike?"

"Afraid so."

Question – Were the Records Introduced in Evidence Obtained in Violation of the Appellant's Constitutional Rights?

"Okay, Ellen, I can handle this one."

"Shoot."

"The evidence was not obtained in violation of Gillars' rights."

"And you reached this position because?"

"Because she always strikes out."

"True, but that's not an answer to support what the Court eventually ruled."

"Time for you to enlighten me."

"This question turns on the idea of constitutional protections against 'unreasonable searches and seizures' noted in the Fourth Amendment. In Gillars' case, there was no violation. The Court pinned Laughlin's ears on this one by merely replaying the history involved in obtaining the recordings."

A special agent of the United States Counter Intelligence Corps (CIC) was authorized to locate Gillars. He (1) located her former residence; (2) questioned the tenants; (3) learned about property stored in a nearby building possibly belonging to Gillars; (4) went with the superintendent of the other building to the basement thereof; (5) the superintendent opened the door to the basement; (6) the agent found manuscripts and recordings in the basement; (7) obtaining these materials was consented to by the superintendent who had custody over them; and (8) no objection was made, and no force was used to obtain the materials.

"One fastball for a strike after another, Ellen."

"According to the court records, Gillars testified that she 'did not know if these records were her own property.' This being the case, it was difficult for the Appeals Court to 'perceive any prejudice in their admission since there was in evidence recordings of the identical programs obtained through independent sources in a manner not subject to the appellant's objection.' In other words, Mr. Samuels, the FCC had already recorded the recordings, and the agency was not subject to objection by the appellant under the Fourth Amendment."

"Another big 'K' for Gillars. God, why do I have the feeling she's batting against Bob Feller and Robin Roberts?"

"In a way she is, Mr. Samuels. The Court of Appeals is the 'big leagues,' isn't it?"

Question – Did the Appellant Act Under Threat, Compulsion, and in Fear of Her Life?

"This sounds like an easy for Gillers," Samuels said with confidence. There's no question that fear pervaded Radio Berlin, at least as far as the American broadcasters were concerned. I don't see how the Court could rule against her on this one. Certainly, the Court was not oblivious to the presence of the Gestapo and the ongoing threat of being sent to a concentration camp."

"Correct. No one disputed the presence of a threatening environment at Radio Berlin. But that wasn't the real question. Gillars complained that she was 'precluded from proving that she was under threat, compulsion and in fear of her life in participating in the recordings.' Her argument rested upon the exclusion of certain testimony of witnesses regarding the fear under which they all performed similar work.'"

"I don't understand. How could the Court void such testimony?"

"It all depends on who is threatened."

"Ellen, isn't a threat a threat?"

"Yes and no."

"Any possible distinction eludes me."

"The Court, Mr. Samuels, ruled that testimony 'of threats to persons other than the accused was immaterial and irrelevant.' Threats to others were one thing. Threats to Gillars were something else again. She needed witnesses who would testify that they had seen her threatened to the degree that her life was in jeopardy. She couldn't produce such witnesses. The best any witness could do was to say that Gillars told him that she was threatened. At no time did the Court argue that there were not threatening conditions at Radio Berlin. That was never the issue. It was one thing to be threatened. It was another thing to have a witness testify to the truthfulness of your claim."

"To me, it sounds like legalistic splitting of hairs," Samuels replied.

"Be that as it may, Mr. Samuels, the Court was unable to discover any competent evidence, which was excluded, that the appellant worked under threat or compulsion, including any threat to be sent to a concentration camp. The Court understood that the appellant believed that 'active opposition would have meant death.' But, as the Court pointed out, she was 'not charged with having refused to engage in active opposition.' Those were the hairs the Court split."

"Technically, the Court maybe right. But in the real world of the Gestapo, I believe, Ellen, that Gillars was threatened, which doesn't mean she didn't want to cooperate. With the ever-present threat of concentration camps hovering around her neck, she chose to survive. While I don't like what she broadcasted, I fully understand why she grasped the microphone."

"As you say, there's the law and there's the real world."

Question – May Treason be Committed by a Citizen of the United States While Residing in the Territory of an Enemy?

"This is a tricky one, Mr. Samuels. The appellant believes that the crime of treason under the laws of the United States 'does not have extra-territorial scope,' suggesting that 'treason is not committed by an America citizen who resides in an enemy country.' The Court rebutted this argument, stating that the 'Constitution does not forbid the application of the criminal laws of the United States to acts committed by its citizens abroad.' Further, the Court indicated that the Constitution speaks to 'giving aid and comfort within the United States or elsewhere.' An overt act of treason, therefore, may be committed both inside the country and outside — that is, elsewhere. Extra-territorial application of our treason laws is legal."

"Living in Germany didn't prohibit treason charges against Gillars?"

"Correct. Ordinarily, a criminal statute is used to protect the domestic order and not to reach across national boundaries to 'take hold of persons within the jurisdiction of another nation.'"

"But…"

"But treason was directed against the very nation (America) and by 'its very nature consists of conduct which might ordinarily be exerted from without in aid of the enemy.' The act of treason naturally attaches itself to the enemy wherever the enemy is located. Therefore, the range of extra-territoriality is expanded. Gillars broadcasted from Germany. The reach of our treason provisions reached across time and space to find her, judge her, and convict her."

"Another shot across the bow, Ellen"

"Another metaphor… Okay by me. But one other point concerning Gillars' actions… The appellant tried to argue that living in a foreign country placed an individual under some obligations of local allegiance. When you live in Canada, you follow Canadian laws. Understandable. Also, by living in a foreign country, you must by the nature of things engage in trafficking with its citizens and government, or with the enemy in time of war. Given this, the appellant contended that 'doubt should be resolved against extra-territorial application' of the treason provision of the Constitution.' In popular lingo, the long arm of the law should not stretch to Berlin."

"I'm sure the Court had an answer to this claim."

"Indeed. The Court did not dispute that a 'citizen in enemy country owes temporary allegiance to the alien government,' and that the citizen must obey its laws and may not plot or act against it. But local allegiance did not require or compel the appellant to 'assist Germany in the conduct of its war against the United States.' The Court summarized its view as such.

This defendant, while residing in the German Reich, owed qualified allegiance to it. She was obligated to obey its laws and she was equally amendable to punishment with citizens of that country if she did not do so. At the same time, the defendant, while residing in Germany during the period stated in the indictment, owed to her Government, that is, the United States Government, full, complete, and true allegiance.

"These guys are tough to beat," Samuels said, now resigned to the inevitable. "Every defense proposal would seemingly be knocked down. I'm ready for one more legal calamity. Got one?"

"A most curious one, Mr. Samuels."

Question – Whether the Appellant Owed Allegiance to the United States?

"It's getting late, Mr. Samuels."

"You teach a night class, don't you?"

"*Contemporary American Legal History*; I think you would enjoy the course."

"I'm sure I would. I feel as if I've already had two seminars today."

"Hopefully, the *Chronicle* will give me a discount rate as my seminar fee."

"I'll work on it, Ellen. So what's left to go over?"

"The whole question of allegiance, which I usually spend two hours on with my pre-law students. We'll deal with the topic in less than thirty minutes. Ready?"

"Probably not, but go for it."

"Right. An essential element of a crime of treason is that the accused must be 'shown to owe allegiance to the United States.' If you're a citizen, the government can bring an indictment of treason. In Gillars' case, she was a native born citizen, who retained her citizenship when Japan attacked the US and throughout the war. Gillars' counsel stipulated that, "she is now and always has been a citizen of the United States of America. She has always maintained this position throughout her trial and this appeal, even though 'her passport was taken from her while she was in Germany.' Okay, so far, Mr. Samuels?"

"Right with you with one exception, the passport business."

The defense maintained two things at once. First, Gillars was always a citizen. Second, Gillars did not owe allegiance to the US because her passport had been 'unqualifiedly revoked by an authorized consular agent of the United States. Taken together, the twin position suggested citizenship on the one hand, but not outright allegiance on the other. Confusing?"

"Yep."

"Excellent legal response. The Court ruled that the 'evidence did not indicate revocation,' only that the passport was retained when she went for a renewal. She was given a receipt for the passport and never returned to the office. Now here's the sticky part... 'Revocation does not cause a loss of citizenship or dissolve the obligation of allegiance arising from citizenship. A passport is some, though not conclusive, evidence of citizenship. Revocation of the passport does not deprive an American of citizenship.' Keep that in mind, Mr. Samuels."

"With both hands... But how does the *oath of allegiance* she took in Germany factor in with all this?"

"Good question. The defense believes that allegiance to the US was mitigated by what happened after Pearl Harbor, when Gillars signed an oath or affirmation of allegiance to Germany. This interpretation of law equates this act with the dissolution of her citizenship and allegiance to the US. In other words, she had expatriated herself and should be acquitted on that account."

"Seems like a good argument, but since she lost her appeal, I'll assume the Court disagreed on this point, too."

"You assumed correctly. The Nationality Act of 1940 stated that a 'person shall lose his nationality by taking an oath or affirmation or other formal declaration of allegiance to a foreign state.' Such an act is done in 'due form and/or with solemnity.' Now what did Gillars affirm? After her blowup and criticism of Japan and Hitler following Pearl Harbor, and after being threatened by an interview with the Gestapo, she was advised by her immediate superiors to sign something indicating her loyalty to the Reich. She consulted Dr. Karlson, a close friend, and the man she wanted to marry, as to what she should do. According to Gillars, he 'sat down at a typewriter and wrote in German something to the effect that, she swore her allegiance to Germany.' She signed the document Mildred Gillars and submitted it to Mr. Schmidt-Hanson as you know. That got her off the hook with the Gestapo and eventually put herself on one with our Justice Department."

"Because?"

"Again, the Court disputed the appellant's claims. There was no indication that the paper, which she said she signed was 'intended as a renunciation of citizenship.' Moreover, there was no testimony whatever that 'it was sworn to before anyone authorized to administer an oath or indeed before anyone at all.' Finally, the 'exact content' of what was written is uncertain. No original document or copy was available to the Court."

"Axis Sally was cooked."

"That's another way of putting it. The Court found her legal position unsupportable and summed up its position relative to the question of allegiance and whatever oath Gillars signed as follows:

A natural and inherent right of our people, indispensable to the enjoyment of the rights of life, liberty, and the pursuit of happiness, "Expatriation is the voluntary renunciation of one's citizenship, a voluntary act done with intent to renounce or forswear allegiance to the country of one's birth. In order then to be relieved of the duty of allegiance imposed by American citizenship, one must do some voluntary act of renunciation or abandonment of American nationality and allegiance, according to law."

"In the Court's opinion, Mr. Samuels, Gillars did not do these things."

"She was like a fly trapped in a legal morass. No matter which way she went, there was a legal impediment to tie her to treason."

"It's like that sometimes."

"Still, even with all that we've discussed, she was only found guilty on the basis of one indictment."

"Amazing, isn't it, Mr. Samuels.

"I've got a lot to think about, Ellen.

"I'll look forward to your next article. I kept all of them and, if you will give me permission, I'd like to pull them together for a class I've been thinking about."

"A class…"

"*The Media and the Law* and I would like you to co-teach the course with me. What do you think?"

"Well, I already teach one course at San Francisco State, but I am flattered that you have me in mind."

"Now you can teach on both sides of the Bridge."

"I'll really consider it."

"Good. Now I have one last question for you. Of all the things we discussed, what one point or lesson will always stay with you?"

There is one lesson," Samuels said with a tight smile, "which any future traitor should learn."

"What's that?"

"Go to law school first before committing treason."

CHAPTER 27

THE FINAL JURY

<u>Consultation</u>

"Robert, we're all here," his wife said quietly. "Won't you leave never-never land and join us?"

"Mom, Dad's got that faraway look again on his face."

"Zoning on this day of all days, Rachel."

"Do you believe this?" Rita asked, raising her voice. "He invites us over and then hops a mental streetcar to wherever he goes."

"How does he do that?" Ron asked.

The truth was Robert Samuels was zoning. While his body sat comfortably on the soft couch in his living room, his mind was a migrant, strolling elsewhere in the recesses of his thoughts, where he could hang out with himself far beyond the reach of others. He enjoyed his occasional travels to this indeterminate locale, which was marked on no map and only an "X-spot" in his escapist mind. Alone on his special island of ideas and feelings, he could walk along a sandy beach and watch the waters of humanity lap at his feet, as he tried to figure things out. And he had some things to figure out. What was he to do about Mildred? The time had come to share with her his conclusions. And what about Edna Mae? He owed her an explanation, too. What would he write for the *Chronicle* in the last of his series on Axis Sally?

But those questions, he knew, had already been settled. He had written his scripts for the phone calls. He knew what he would say concerning a pardon. It was just a matter of picking up the phone. Already, he had written the final article for the *Chronicle*. He could see the words even before his old Underwood felt them. The last article was already history.

But now he had to deal with his family and youthful colleagues. They would want to know, too. And, why...? They would be insistent. Samuels knew it was time to return. The calls had to be made. His mute Underwood awaited his prancing fingers. The story of Axis Sally had finally come to an end.

"Hi, everyone."

"The sphinx awakes."

"How long have I been out, Lynn?"

"Not long. Perhaps one or two presidential elections."

"That long?"

"If they keep records for zoning, Dad, you're in the Guiness Book."

"Remember us?" Rita asked, pointing a accusing finger at herself and then Ron. Your journalistic buddies?"

"How do you do that?" Ron asked, still fascinated by Samuels' ability to depart for places unknown, almost at will.

"Magic," Samuels said.

"Well then, it's time to share a few tricks with us, Robert. As you asked, we've assembled."

He had, Samuels remembered, requested the meeting. They deserved to know. Still, he could fence and tease a bit with them.

"You've read all my notes concerning my visit to Dr. Silverman?"

"Of course," Rita said flatly, "Your scribbling and her well typed summaries of the case."

"And you've read my latest articles for the *Chronicle*?"

"The latest, but not the last," Ron added.

"You've finished it, Robert?"

"It's in here," Samuels said, nodding to a large business-size envelope. Wrote it earlier. I thought I'd take it over to the paper later."

"Do we get an early peek?" Rachel asked imploringly. "We are family, right Mom?"

"Unless we don't get to peek."

"And professional colleagues, too," Rita added.

"And you want to avoid expensive faculty parking lot tickets," Ron joked with a deadpan face.

"Okay, guys. I get the picture."

"So?" Lynn questioned. "Where's the beef?"

"I think it's. *'Show me the beef,'* Mrs. Samuels," Ron said, a little amused with the image of a hamburger somehow symbolizing the story of a traitor to the Nazi cause. But, then again, he reminded himself with an invisible laugh, Hamburg was a German city.

"You'll get your peek," Samuels said, "but first you must earn it."

"Is this some kind of game, Dad?"

"It could be characterized as such."

"Isn't that sort of silly?" Rita questioned.

"I think you'll find it quite serious."

"Is this something you dreamed up while zoning?" Ron asked.

"Let's just say the idea matured recently."

"What are the rules, Robert?"

"Rules? More like guidelines. All of you know everything I know. I haven't kept anything from you. So here's the deal. Edna Mae wants her half-sister, Mildred, pardoned, exonerated and redeemed in the eyes of the public. And then she wants the new drama building at Freedom High named after Mildred."

"Old news," Rita said interrupting.

True, but given that, Rita, if you were writing the last article in my series for the *Chronicle* about Axis Sally, what would you say?"

"I'd…"

"Yes?"

"That's the test?" Rachel asked.

"If you wish to humor an old man."

"Then I'll go first," Ron said.

Ron's View

"No pardon. That's where I'm coming from. Regardless of her motivation, and whatever her true feelings, she filled the airwaves with spiteful anti-Semitic crap at a time when Jews were being deported in crowded trains to death camps. She was a Jew baiter, holding a whole group guilty for the economic ills of the whole world and the political leanings of Communists everywhere. True, she didn't publicly sanction the "final solution," nor did she personally separate children from their parents at Dachau, but she didn't speak out against it either, particularly once the war was over. She was always concerned with her own skin, not the flesh that was turned into soap and lampshades by those psychopaths in Berlin."

"No compassion for her?"

"None, Mr. Samuels. She complained about being penniless and hungry after the war, but she didn't shed one tear for the millions who didn't survive. She was a self-absorbed Jew hater. Pardon her? Not me! She can take her self-indulgent memories to the grave for all I care. Jail time was too good for her."

"Ron, too harsh, too harsh," Rachel said, surprised by Ron's vehemence.

"I agree with Rachel," Rita said quickly. There was more to her than just her anti-Semitic views.

"Rita," Ron replied, "you're a good Catholic, compassionate and caring. I respect that, but I'm a Jew. In Germany, you could hide within the Christian family. I couldn't. I was the one who would be carted off, not you."

"Still, Ron, we don't know for sure that she really agreed with the Nazi solution to the Jewish question," Lynn said, measuring her words carefully.

"Does it really matter? If the Gestapo came to this house, Mrs. Samuels who would they point a bloody finger at? Your husband! Me! Of course; each of us is tainted with Jewish parents. At that moment would you care how strongly Gillars supported the regime with her slimy stuff over the airwaves? Would you?"

"I need to think about that, Ron."

"Fair enough. My problem is that I've thought about it."

"Dad, don't you have anything to say?"

"I'm a listener for a while, if you don't mind."

"We talk, you listen?"

"Rachel, I already know what I think. If I share my conclusions with you at this point, I'll influence, even contaminate your views. No, it's best that I stay out of this for a while. Rita, your turn… Okay?"

Rita's View

"I can't deny what Mildred Gillars broadcasted. I certainly don't agree with what she said about, Jews and President Roosevelt. And I find her interviews with GI's unacceptable, especially when she impersonated International Red Cross personnel. Keep that in mind, please. While many things influenced her actions, I want to focus on one, her failure to find love and a lasting, positive relationship with someone."

"Her fate boils down to romance, Rita?"

"A factor to be considered, Mr. Samuels. Let's review… Her biological father was an alcoholic and a violent man. Her stepfather wasn't violent, but he was an alcoholic, too. And reading between the lines, it appears he made unwarranted advances on his beautiful, stepdaughter. Why else would Mildred's mother send her to a Catholic school away from home for a while? At Ohio Wesleyan College, she had a youthful, collegiate romance with Calvin Elliott, but it flamed out. She called off a proposal for marriage and moved. He couldn't. A few years later, he committed suicide. We know she was intrigued and impressed by Dr. Koischwitz when she attended Hunter College. We don't know how far the relationship went. Did she have intimacies with him? She denies it, at least at Hunter. But is she telling the truth? He's dead and she's not talking. And then there was the influence of Charles Newcomb, her Professor of Oratory at Ohio Wesleyan. He's the man who encouraged her to pursue a career in acting. What was her relationship with him? Again, was she having an affair with him? We don't know. We do know that when she moved to Cleveland, he followed her. After Hunter, there was her affair with Bernard Metz, the young, Jewish diplomat in the service of the British government. They were a couple in New York. When he was posted elsewhere, she followed him to North Africa and, I think, not only to see the picturesque views of Algiers. But, again this relation floundered for reasons we can only speculate about.

"On to Germany. There she met Dr. Paul Karlson, whom she apparently was in love with and wanted to marry. We know nothing about this relationship except that he wouldn't leave Germany if they married. She would have to stay in Germany if they wed. Then, what happens? Pearl Harbor! And afterwards, Karlson was eventually conscripted into the Army and forced to serve on the Eastern Front, where he apparently died in the wastelands of Russia. Once more, she's alone. Into the vacuum steps her former Professor, Max Otto, and now she begins an affair with him, even though he's a married man with three daughters and a fourth child on the way. Whatever else, I do think she loved the Max Otto, or needed to love him in order to survive in wartime Berlin."

"Her life seems like grist for a tabloid, Rita."

"Rachel, the woman needed a man in her life. That is beyond question."

"To protect her?"

"And others. Recall Max Otto's admission that the Gestapo might kill him if she wouldn't go to work as a radio commentator. That, of course, appealed to her ego. Her need to be admired and needed was always a strong factor in her life. Without doubt, dear Max played on her needs. She reciprocated. Either way, she never left him, and by returning from Paris to Berlin for his funeral, placed herself at risk from the onrushing Russians. He was, I believe, as she said, *'her man of destiny.'* Unfortunately, the relationships in her life with men were questionable and unsatisfying from my perspective, but they did provide the karma that brought her to our attention as Axis Sally."

"You pity her?" Ron asked harshly.

"No. She made the decisions she made. I'm just trying to understand what role the men in her life played, which influenced those decisions."

"Romance and propaganda... Not my cup of tea," Ron quickly replied. "If anything, I see her as a woman using men, manipulating them to get what she wanted."

"Well," said Rachel, are you speaking as an objective journalist, or a Jewish male, who can't show any compassion for a woman trapped in a world of depression and war, that little picnic we call the 1930's and 40's."

"Perhaps I can add a word," Lynn said before Ron could fire back. "Rita touched on a salient point. Mildred needed men in her life. We can't dispute that. It was her tragedy that marriage and family after college didn't come her way. Her Bohemian lifestyle made that difficult. There was a spirit in her that pushed her away from matrimony and I think I know what it was."

"Mom, tell us."

"It's really pretty simple. She saw what happened in her mother's two marriages. That set the scene for Mildred. Marriage was suspect. Men were suspect. One had to be careful about each. Lasting commitments could be dangerous. That's it. Mrs. Samuels' pop psychology."

"And speaking as your spouse, well stated. Let's move on, if you will, people. Rachel, the floor, as they say, is yours."

Rachel's Views

"I think Gillars was driven by some insatiable need to be somebody. I guess it started when she was a near child prodigy, at least in her mother's eyes. She could read at an early age, memorize lines, and pushed by her artistic mother, played the piano, sang, and danced. In high school she appeared in a number of plays and received generally good reviews for her performances. This was also true at Ohio Wesleyan where she continued to find herself on the stage. Again, she had good reviews in a play called *'Mrs. Dane's Defense.'* After college she went to New York, where she tried to find a place on the legitimate stage. Her only success, as far as I can tell, was in a play called *'My Girl.'* It was a comedy and a major success. It ran for 291 performances, no small feat in 1923-24. Though she was successful in this play, she quit, telling the director, she needed more serious parts if she were to get any where in her acting career. She found life on her own after leaving the show most difficult, living on very little, nearly starving, and always in fear of being evicted from her shoddy apartment. Then, of course, came the Barbara Elliott role. She was convincing as the pregnant, unmarried woman, who lied to reporters and the police to promote a movie. She lied skillfully or acted beautifully, two trademarks of her life from that point on, wrapped up, I think, in self-deception about her encore at Radio Berlin.

"With the coming of the Great Depression, she had learned some life lessons, chief of which was that she wanted more than a hand-to-mouth existence She wanted, indeed craved, celebrity status. She wanted her true talents recognized. She was ambitious and strong-willed and when given a chance to star at Radio Berlin, she took it. Whatever her political leanings, a personal need to be successful professionally was the prime motivating force behind her actions. She was predisposed to be Axis Sally. It was a role in search of a star. Max Otto was the right man in the right place to offer her the opportunity. It was her chance for stardom. She took it. The fact that it might prove temporary in a world at war was not for her a consideration or concern for her. However transitory Mildred' stay at Radio Berlin would be, she had made it and would enjoy every minute of it. And even with the end of the war and her arrest, she had one more performance to give during her trial, where once more she was on stage. So there we have it, a woman who wanted success and achieved it, but at a great price as it turned out."

"You're saying, Rachel, that ambition trumped love and politics in driving her behavior?"

"Not exclusively, Rita. But along with everything else, it was a powerful motivating force. It can't be excluded."

"I guess you can be an anti-Semite and still be in love while looking for your next stage role," Ron said. "But as far as I'm concerned, what's important is what the end results were. Broken romantic relationships are just that, broken and limited, and usually no more than two people get hurt unless kids are involved. A stage show closing down throws a lot of people out of work, but it's not the end of the world. But hateful propaganda can influence millions by justifying the worst human behavior — what we've come to call *'crimes against humanity.'* Don't misconstrue what I'm saying. I don't hold her responsible for the work of the Gestapo. I hold her responsible for not coming home to help her country destroy the Nazi Regime. Whatever her personal needs, romantically or professionally, they paled by comparison to the need for victory over the bastards in Berlin. I'm afraid that's my bottom line."

"Rachel, you've focused on an aspect of her behavior, as has Rita, but ladies, you haven't said what you would do. You may not agree with Ron's view, but he has one. No pardon for Mildred Gillars. What's your position, Rachel?"

"I'd like to abstain."

"No can do... You're on the jury. Pardon Gillars? Maintain the status quo? Which will it be?"

"Let Rita go first."

"If Rita agrees."

"Okay with me. How about a partial pardon."

"Not possible, Rita. Pardons aren't an apple pie. You really can't slice them up easily. Pretty much, it's a full pardon or nothing. So what will it be?"

"It's difficult."

"It is. Just ask yourself one question. In the final analysis, did she commit treason? She either did or she didn't."

"She did it under duress."

"Perhaps."

"She had no choice."

"Maybe."

"She didn't have a passport."

"So what?"

"She was trapped?"

"You're begging the question, Rita."

"And you're pushing."

"I am."

"No pardon," Rachel cried out, interrupting the push and shove match between Rita and her father. "No pardon."

"Well, Rita?" Samuels asked.

"Okay, she committed treason."

"Difficult decision, Rita. Imagine how it must have been for the jury."

"I don't want to."

"Well, who's left?"

"As if you didn't know," Lynn said.

Lynn's View

"I'll be brief. I'm a mother. I could forgive Mildred Gillars for almost anything, but not helping to write and direct *'Visions of Invasion'* in addition to starring in the radio play. If I had been a mother at that time with a son or husband in the invasion force, I didn't need to be reminded of what the beaches would be like. I didn't need to hear the screaming, crying, and desperate pleas of wounded men. I didn't need to hear the roar of planes and cannons, and the spitting of machine guns, and the explosions. I knew what was going to take place. I knew what had happened in North Africa, Sicily, and Italy. I saw the newsreels. I read the newspapers. I knew what was happening in the Pacific at Guadalcanal and on the other island beaches. I didn't need to have it thrown in my face by Gillars.

"I saw the mailman pause for the longest time across the street before walking up to the front door. I heard the cries of my neighbor and a few weeks later I saw the Gold Star flag in her window. I didn't need Axis Sally to remind me of what might happen to my loved ones. I don 't care why she did it. It doesn't matter. She did it. She rubbed salt in the wound. She played unfairly. She didn't ask the Germans to lay down their arms. She didn't cry out for a truce. So what does it all come down to? The jury got it right. She went too far with *'Visions of Invasion.'* She went too far."

No one spoke. What was there to say? It had been a painful review of history. It had also been personal, a kind of catharsis dredging to the surface those thoughts and feelings, which are sometimes best left in the depths of our unconsciousness. In a way, all of them had gone through something akin to what the jury must have experienced. And how much more difficult it must have been for them, as the war was still a recent and painful memory. The bitterness of the struggle against Nazi Germany was still in the air when they convened behind closed doors to decide the fate of an accused traitor. They didn't have the luxury of more than 30-years separating them from the conflict. Still, they had done their job long ago. Samuels was immensely proud of that jury. He was also equally proud of his little group. One way or another, they had worked it out. Gillars would not be pardoned.

"Samuels' Verdict

"Dad, we haven't heard from you."

"I have a confession."

"You rigged this game," Rita asked.

"In a way, yes. I fibbed earlier when I said I'd call Edna Mae and others after our meeting. I fudged."

"Fibbed and fudged… What are you saying, Dad?"

I made the calls earlier today."

"Before we indulged your little game?" Rita asked a bit put out.

"I'm afraid so."

"Was that fair?" Ron asked.

"Prudent."

"Meaning?" Lynn asked.

"You might have convinced me otherwise."

"You called the Mother Superior?"

"Yes, Lynn."

"And Ida Mae?" Rachel asked.

"My first call."

"And?"

"They understood. My last call was to Mildred."

"And?" asked Rachel.

"I gave her the news."

"Which was what?" Lynn asked very impatiently.

"It's all in here," Samuels said, holding up the envelope containing his last story in the series about Axis Sally. "We must all bear the consequences of our actions."

"Mildred accepted that, Robert?"

"She did."

"And?"

"Axis Sally will not be pardoned."